Flowers on Main

Also by New York Times *bestselling author*

SHERRYL
WOODS

WELCOME TO SERENITY*
SEAVIEW INN
MENDING FENCES
FEELS LIKE FAMILY*
A SLICE OF HEAVEN*
STEALING HOME*
WAKING UP IN CHARLESTON
FLIRTING WITH DISASTER
THE BACKUP PLAN
DESTINY UNLEASHED
FLAMINGO DINER
ALONG CAME TROUBLE**
ASK ANYONE**
ABOUT THAT MAN**
ANGEL MINE
AFTER TEX
THE INN AT EAGLE POINT***
FLOWERS ON MAIN***

*The Sweet Magnolias
**Trinity Harbor
***Chesapeake Shores

SHERRYL WOODS

Flowers on Main

Doubleday Large Print
Home Library Edition

MIRA

This Large Print Edition, prepared especially for Doubleday Large Print Home Library, contains the complete, unabridged text of the original Publisher's Edition.

MIRA

ISBN-13: 978-1-60751-854-9

FLOWERS ON MAIN

Printed in U.S.A.

Dear Friends,

Welcome back to Chesapeake Shores and the tightly knit, if far-flung, O'Brien family. If you read *The Inn at Eagle Point,* you know it's going to take a lot to get these folks back together, and there's nothing I like more than trying to reunite a dysfunctional family.

This time you'll get to know Bree, the middle sister, whose career as a playwright at a regional theater in Chicago started so brightly. Now, though, she's returned to Chesapeake Shores, her heart in tatters and her spirit wounded. But being back home among family and friends isn't as serene as she'd been hoping, because in order to build a future, she needs to confront her past.

I'm sure every woman would like to have a past as sexy, headstrong and amazing as landscaper Jake Collins, but few of us would like to deal with the kind of complications that have torn him and Bree apart.

And, as if their struggles to find their way back to each other aren't complicated enough, Bree's mother, Megan, and her father, Mick O'Brien, are busy sorting out their own very contentious relationship under the watchful eye of everyone in the family and in Chesapeake Shores.

I hope you enjoy meeting more of the residents of this wonderful seaside community. Enjoy this visit, and plan to come back again. The welcome mat is always out.

Sherryl Woods

1

Bree O'Brien sank her fingers into the rich, dark soil and lifted up a handful so she could breathe in the scent of it. This was real, not like the shallow world in which she'd been struggling to make a name for herself for the past six years. Gardening was something she understood. Plants could be coaxed along with water and fertilizer and loving attention in ways that a theater production could not. A vase of flowers, artfully arranged, had only to please the recipient, not an entire audience, each of them a critic in one way or another.

She'd been relieved when her sister Abby had called her about the opening of the Inn at Eagle Point, now owned by their sister Jess. It had given her the perfect excuse to flee Chicago, where her last play had been savaged by the critics and closed a mere week after it had opened. In six years she'd had one regional theater triumph and two box-office and critical disasters.

Some playwrights might be thrilled to have just one big success, even far, far off Broadway, but Bree had always wanted more. She'd expected to be up there with Neil Simon, Noel Coward . . . heck, even Arthur Miller. Of course, that had been after her first success, when she was way too full of herself. She'd thought herself capable of Simon's comedic timing, Coward's wit and Miller's complex dramatic skill. There'd even been a few critics who'd shared that opinion.

That had made it all the more humbling when the second play had received only lukewarm praise and a shortened one-month run. The third had been skewered by those very same critics who'd sung her praises earlier. Her first play was suddenly being called a fluke. More than one suggested she was washed up at the age of twenty-seven.

She'd been relieved that no one in the family had been in Chicago for the play's opening to witness her downfall or to see the reviews that had followed. She wouldn't have been able to bear watching them struggle to be supportive. It was awful enough that everyone at the theater had been a part of the most humiliating moment of her career. None of the actors had even been able to look her in the eye as the director—her *lover,* for goodness' sake—had read review after scathing review at the opening-night party before finally crumpling up the papers and tossing them in the trash.

One of these days, she supposed she'd muster up enough confidence to sit down in front of her computer and try again, but for now she was happy to be back in Chesapeake Shores, in familiar surroundings, with her family fussing over her just because they loved her and not because they knew her life was in shambles. She'd needed girl time with her sisters, a rousing game of tag football and nonstop teasing with her brother Connor and his buddies, and a chance to hug her nieces—Abby's twin daughters.

She'd needed to be back home even more than she'd realized, back in her old room where the only writing she'd ever done was in her diary or stories and plays written for her own satisfaction and no one else's eyes.

What she'd also needed, but hadn't admitted to a soul, was distance between herself and acclaimed playwright and director Martin Demming, a mentor for a time, a lover even longer. Lately, though, the relationship hadn't been working. Maybe she was already raw and overly sensitive after those vicious reviews, but it seemed to her he'd taken an almost gloating satisfaction in her failure. She hadn't been prepared for that.

So, here she was, three weeks after the opening of Jess's inn, kneeling in her grandmother's garden, yanking out weeds and letting the warmth of the sun soak into her bare and protectively sunscreened shoulders. For the first time in months, the tension that knotted there had finally eased. She felt . . . She searched for the right word, then realized it was *content.* She felt content with herself, even with her life, despite the current upheaval. She couldn't recall the last time she'd felt that way.

Oblivious for now to all the warnings about sun damage and Marty's constant and annoying admonitions about ruining her pale-as-Irish-cream complexion, she turned her face up to the sun and felt it ease the headache that came whenever she thought about the life she'd left behind.

Even as the thought surfaced, her hands stilled and she gasped slightly. *Had* she left it behind? All of it? Chicago? The theater? The writing? Marty? Had she really left it forever? Could she uproot herself from the world that had meant everything just a few short months ago? Was that what she was doing here, on her knees in the dirt, days after she was supposed to return to the life she'd always dreamed of? Was she giving up? Hiding out? Or merely licking her wounds before going back into the battle zone once again?

And that's what it was, Bree realized, a battle zone, with way too many potential enemies—the producer, the director, the actors, the critics and the public, all of whom had their own views on what her work was or ought to be. Some days everything came together in an amazing collaboration. At other times, it was a highly charged emotional war with all of her carefully crafted words, scenes and motivations picked apart by those who thought they knew best.

She sat back and heaved a sigh. Oh, how she wished she had an answer to any of those questions.

"You've pulled up three of my summer phlox," Gram said, a clucking note of disapproval in her voice as she interrupted Bree's dark thoughts. "Do you want to tell me what's on your mind before you ruin the perennial garden I've spent years cultivating?"

Bree looked from her grandmother—hands on hips, petite and feisty in her straw gardening hat, sneakers and bright-pink cropped pants and matching blouse—to the tall, dark purple phlox already wilting amid the weeds she'd tossed aside to her left. At the sight of the flowers, she groaned. "I got the roots. I'll put them back in the ground with some extra water and fertilizer. They'll be okay, Gram."

Gram gave her a penetrating look that suggested she knew exactly what was going on with Bree, but was waiting for her to bring up the subject.

"Can you say the same for yourself?" Gram asked. "Will you be okay?"

Bree deliberately looked away and turned her attention to replanting the phlox. "I have a lot on my mind," she murmured, afraid that she would confirm Gram's suspicions if she said more. Of everyone in the family, only her grandmother seemed to truly understand her, to see inside her heart even when Bree was silent. To her father and even to her outgoing siblings, she was mostly an enigma.

"Your distraction's plain enough," Gram agreed. "What you need is to share some of it, make the burden a wee bit lighter. If you don't want to tell me whatever's on your mind, go over to the inn and have lunch with Jess or call Abby. She'd be happy to take you to lunch in Baltimore, I'm sure. She can show off that new office of hers. You can have a nice heart-to-heart chat."

"Jess has her hands full. She doesn't have time to listen to me moan and groan. The same with Abby. Now that she and Trace are engaged and she's commuting to Baltimore practically every day, she has little enough time for herself and the twins without wasting it on me."

"Nonsense! Either one of them would make the time, because they're your sisters," Gram said impatiently. "With the O'Briens, family comes first. We stick together no matter what. Didn't I teach you that years ago?"

She'd certainly tried, Bree recalled. It had been a hard lesson to learn after their mother had taken off for New York, fed up with their father's endless round of business trips and his neglect of their family. Gram had been the glue that held the rest of them together. She'd been the one who'd tried to nudge them into making peace with Megan on her visits home, encouraged them to keep an open mind toward their mother. Not that any of them had. They were young and unforgiving, and the complexities of their parents' relationship had eluded them.

Lately, Bree had noticed that her father

was making more of an effort to connect with all of them. Mick had shelved an entire project in California to be home for the opening of the inn, though he'd taken off again soon afterward. Even their mother had come back for Jess's big day, which had created its own problems, but Bree had to admit it had been nice to have everyone—at least everyone except her brother Kevin around for a few days. Kevin's tour in Iraq had kept him from being home for the festivities.

Those few days had reminded Bree of the kind of family harmony they'd had years ago, before Mick's acclaim as an urban architect and developer had taken him all over the world. It was exactly that kind of camaraderie that Bree had needed most when she'd left Chicago.

She could have told any family member about what had happened, and they would have done anything necessary to try to bolster her spirits. She knew that. She also knew she wasn't quite ready for the pity none of them would be able to hide or the sound, pragmatic suggestions Mick or Abby might have offered.

It would be better, she thought, to suck

it up, make her own decisions and then get on with her life, not wallow in self-pity or dump all of her problems on her sisters, Gram or anyone else. What she needed, as always, was the peace and quiet to find her own way.

"Maybe I'll call Jess or Abby later," Bree hedged eventually. "Why don't I go inside and fix us some lunch. We can eat out here or even on the beach." She was suddenly overcome by a wave of nostalgia. "Remember when you used to make picnics for us when we were kids? We'd spread a blanket on the sand and spend the whole afternoon along the shore."

Gram regarded her with amusement. "Do I need to remind you that you were the first one to complain about the sand getting in your food and the sun being too hot?"

Bree laughed. "I guess I'd forgotten that part. Okay, we can eat on the porch. There's no sand on the porch, and there *is* a lovely breeze."

"Actually, I can't today," Gram said, a note of apology in her voice. "I have a meeting at the church." She studied Bree worriedly, then added, “But I can cancel if you’d rather I stay here so we can talk some more.”

Bree wasn’t ready to bare her soul. “No, go. I’ll be fine. Maybe I’ll walk into town, do a little shopping and then have lunch at the café.”

Gram nodded. “If you decide to do that, give my best to Sally and bring home one of those raspberry croissants of hers. I’ll have it for breakfast tomorrow.”

Bree feigned shock. “You’re actually going to eat someone else’s baking? Or are you trying to figure out her recipe so you can make them yourself?”

“When someone has a knack for something, I’m perfectly content to leave them to it. Sally’s croissants melt in your mouth. Why try to improve on that?”

“I think I’ll tell her you said that,” Bree teased. “It’ll please her to know that the greatest baker in Chesapeake Shores admires her croissants.”

Gram drew herself up indignantly. “It’s nothing I haven’t told her myself, young lady. I’m not beyond giving credit where it’s due. Now go along with you. Try to come back with a smile on your face. It troubles me to see you looking so lost."

Bree knew that Gram was attuned to her moods, but she hadn't expected her to hit on such an apt description. She was lost. Having one person who could read her and was always willing to lend an ear, offer advice or whatever else she needed brought unexpected tears to her eyes. If she wasn't careful, she'd start bawling right here and now, and Gram would stay put and pry the whole pitiful story out of her.

Instead, she forced a smile. "I'm just sorting through a few things. It's nothing for you to worry about."

The words were as much for herself as for her grandmother. It would be too easy to let herself wallow in that feeling of love and acceptance, to wrap herself in it and forget all about her dreams. Chesapeake Shores would be the perfect safe haven.

Then again, maybe it was time to take a really hard look at those dreams and see if they still fit, after all. Bree had the O'Brien streak of stubbornness in spades, but maybe there was no shame in letting go for once. Moving on. Making new dreams.

If only she had even a vague idea of what those new dreams might be.

Mick O'Brien stood on a street corner in New York City with his cell phone in hand, trying to work up the courage to make a call to a woman he'd known most of his adult life. Megan was his ex-wife, for heaven's sake! Dialing her number shouldn't be harder than facing down an entire planning and zoning commission dead set on vetoing one of his developments. Yet he'd done that numerous times without batting an eye, while just the prospect of making this call had his palms sweating.

Losing his nerve, Mick snapped the phone shut for the third time and turned on his heel. He wound up in a coffee shop somewhere on the Upper East Side of the city, just blocks from Megan's apartment, cursing his own cowardice or maybe the decision that had brought him to New York in the first place, after all these years.

Seeing Megan again at the opening of Jess's inn had unleashed something inside him. He'd suddenly remembered the way it had felt to love her, how he'd always felt ten feet tall when she'd looked at him. All the years of burning anger and resentment over their breakup had disappeared in the space of a heartbeat when he'd seen her walking toward him on the beach, her figure as lithe as a girl's, her auburn hair whipping in the wind.

They'd even shared a few rare moments of real harmony, when he'd included her in the gift he'd given Jess to celebrate the inn's opening. When he'd told their youngest daughter that the outrageously expensive stove she'd wanted was a present from him and her mother, the icy tension between them had thawed a few degrees. Bridging the distance between mother and daughter had brought him the kind of satisfaction he hadn't felt in years. At least until he'd received a check in the mail from Megan for her half. *That* had annoyed the dickens out of him.

Although he and Megan had seen each other only a few times in Chesapeake Shores, it had been enough to convince Mick of the cost of clinging to his own stupid pride. Years ago that stubborn pride had kicked in and kept him from begging Megan to stay. Now, sensing that they might have another chance, he wasn't going to let anything stand in the way of his reaching out.

Except maybe fear, he thought with chagrin as he sipped his coffee and stared at the cell phone lying on the scarred, Formica-topped table in this noisy, busy neighborhood eatery.

Maybe it would be easier if he just showed up on her doorstep. Megan was too much of a lady to slam the door in his face, while she might find it a whole lot easier to hang up on him.

He was so busy contemplating his strategy that he jumped like some scared teenager when the cell phone rang.

"Yes, hello," he muttered, embarrassed even though the person on the other end of the line couldn't possibly know how idiotic he felt.

"Have you seen her yet?" his mother demanded.

Mick frowned. How was it that Nell O'Brien always knew what he was up to, even when he'd been very careful to keep this trip to New York a secret from everyone in his family? He'd seen no point in stirring up speculation—or a storm of objections, for that matter—when he had no idea how things between him and Megan were likely to go.

He'd detoured to New York on his way back from business meetings in Seattle and Minneapolis, thinking that if he made a damn fool of himself, no one would have to know about it. Now here was his mother, with that second sight of hers, guessing exactly what he was planning.

"I don't know what you're talking about," he said defensively, hoping Nell had simply taken a lucky guess.

"You're in New York to see Megan, aren't you?" she declared with conviction.

"What gave you that idea?" Even as he spoke, he could imagine her rolling her eyes at his response. She'd never liked wasting time stating the obvious.

"Your office said you flew to New York this morning after you finished up your meetings in Minnesota. Since you haven't set foot in that city since the day Megan moved up there, and since you've been mooning around here ever since she left after the opening at the inn, I put two and two together."

"Well, your math skills are lousy," he claimed. "I haven't seen her."

She laughed at that. "That can only mean you've chickened out now that you're there. You're probably sitting in some bar trying to work up the courage to see her."

"I'm not in a damn bar," he muttered. Saints protect him from a mother who'd always been able to read him like a book. "And I have not chickened out. Did you track me down just to hassle me, or was there something else on your mind?"

"I had something else on my mind, but now I'm thinking we should be talking about whether you have any idea what you're doing. You and Megan have been divorced for years. She left because you neglected her and this family and didn't change your ways when she called you on it. You know I love you, but I don't see how any of that has changed. You still spend more time away than you do with your family."

"In case you haven't noticed, my family has pretty much scattered."

"And in case you haven't noticed, one

by one they seem to be turning up again," she retorted. "Yet you're still running from one job to the next."

"Maybe I'm ready to slow down," he said, testing the idea on himself as much as her.

"Retire? You?" she asked, her tone incredulous. "I don't believe that for a minute."

"I didn't mention retirement," he retorted irritably. "I said I might be ready to slow down."

"Maybe? Might? Seems to me you ought to be sure about a thing like that before you go getting that woman's hopes up, then turn right around and dash them again."

Much to his dismay, he conceded to himself that she had a point. Not that he intended to admit it aloud. "Look, I have things to do. Just tell me why you called."

Apparently she realized that his patience had worn thin, because she actually answered the question, rather than launching a full-scale lecture or asking more questions of her own.

"I called because I'm worried about Bree," she told him.

"Bree?" he asked, startled. "What's wrong with her?"

"Men!" Nell muttered, her tone disparaging. "Mick, she's your daughter. Didn't you notice how quiet she's been ever since she got here? For that matter, haven't you wondered what she's still doing here?"

"Bree's always been quiet," he said, genuinely puzzled by his mother's observation. She'd always been happiest locked away in her room with a pad of paper or a book. Of all of his children, she was the one he'd understood the least. She'd never had the outgoing nature of her siblings. Nor had she suffered from the usual teenage highs and lows—or if she had, she'd channeled that into the writing she hid from everyone in the family.

"This is different," his mother insisted. "And she hasn't said a single word about going back to Chicago. Something's happened, Mick, I just know it. I tried to talk to her earlier, but she told me she was fine."

"Then maybe she is."

"She is *not* fine. You need to stop worrying about the past and get back home to deal with your daughter. She needs you."

"No," he said at once. "If Bree needs anyone, it's you. You've always understood her better than I have. Come on, Ma, you know I'm right. If you can't get her to open up, then there's not a chance in hell I'll be able to."

"Well, this time I think maybe she needs all of us."

He frowned at Nell's somber tone. "Ma, what exactly do you think happened to her? If that jerk did something . . ." He let his voice trail off. He'd never liked Martin Demming. He was too old for Bree for one thing, and an arrogant son of a gun for another. Mick had heard a few too many condescending remarks directed at Bree. It had taken every ounce of restraint he possessed not to tell the man off the last time Mick had been to Chicago. Only a plaintive look from Bree had kept him silent. It had made his heart ache to see his sensitive daughter listen to that demeaning nonsense without fighting back.

Nell interrupted his thoughts. "I don't know if this has anything to do with Martin Demming or if it's about her work. That's my point. We need to find out what has her so upset. When are you coming home?"

"That depends," he said, still thinking about his mission to see Megan again.

"Oh, for heaven's sake," she said impatiently. "Either call Megan the minute we hang up or get on a plane and come home. You're needed here."

"I'll be there first thing tomorrow," he promised.

Heck, if things went well, maybe he'd even convince Megan to come back to Chesapeake Shores for another visit. If Bree really was in some sort of trouble, having her mother around certainly couldn't hurt. In fact, it might be just what she needed.

He sighed even as the manipulative thought occurred to him. Who was he kidding? He was the one who needed Megan at home again. Always had. If a crisis with their middle daughter gave him the perfect excuse to get her there, he wasn't too proud to take advantage of it. There'd be plenty of time to regret his tactics later . . . but only if they didn't work.

The back booth at Sally's all but had a Reserved sign sitting on it. Every day, right at noon, Jake Collins, Mack Franklin and

Will Lincoln sat in that booth and ordered the day's special. Today it was ham and cheese on a croissant with potato salad, Jake noted as he glanced at the chalkboard behind the counter on his way to the booth. When he got there, he stopped short. He wasn't sure which shocked him more, that it was already occupied or that the person whose face was buried in the menu was Bree O'Brien.

It took less than a heartbeat for him to note that her bare shoulders were pink from the sun, that she wore the turquoise sundress that had always been a favorite of his, that she looked exhausted.

Before any of that could really sink in, he wheeled around and bumped straight into Mack, then brushed past him without stopping.

"Where are you going?" Mack demanded.

"Let's go to Brady's for lunch," Jake said in a clipped, urgent undertone as he paused just long enough to give Mack a hard look that begged him to stop asking questions.

Mack stared at him blankly, obviously not picking up on Jake's signal. "Why?"

"Because I'm in the mood for a crab-cake sandwich and a beer," Jake said impatiently, weaving past three women blocking the aisle.

He didn't wait to see if Mack followed but headed right back out onto the street, where he stopped and sucked in a deep breath. Damn, that woman should not be able to get to him like this, not after six years. And she'd done it without even once looking him in the eye or opening her mouth. It was pitiful. *He* was pitiful. Why should it matter to him that she looked as if she hadn't slept in a week?

"Would you mind telling me why you're both out here?" Will asked when he came upon them standing on the sidewalk in the blazing late-July heat. His crisply ironed sport shirt was wilting and he'd tugged off his tie. He was clearly anxious to get inside in air-conditioning.

"I have no idea," Mack responded with a shrug. "Jake's apparently developed a sudden craving for a crab cake."

When Jake met Will's gaze, he saw the knowing amusement in his friend's eyes. That was the problem with hanging out with the same bunch of guys since elementary school. None of them had one damn secret from the others. Will, with his Ph.D. in psychology, was capable of guessing the source of Jake's suddenly skittish mood.

Will sighed. "I was wondering when he was going to find out that Bree's in town."

Mack looked momentarily surprised, then nodded. "Just now apparently."

"It took longer than I expected," Will said.

Jake stared at them. "You knew Bree was here and didn't warn me?"

"I'd heard," Will admitted.

"Me, too," Mack said, looking chagrined. "We figured she'd be gone before the two of you crossed paths."

"How'd she look?" Will asked, his gaze on Mack rather than Jake.

Mack shrugged. "Jake was blocking my view."

"Well, it's probably better that Jake finally got a glimpse of her," Will said thoughtfully. "It was bound to happen sooner or later."

"Absolutely. Her family's here," Mack added. "It's not like she'd stay away forever."

"Would you two stop talking as if I'm not here," Jake grumbled. "This isn't about Bree O'Brien. I just decided I'm in the mood for a crab-cake sandwich. That's it."

"Last time I checked, Sally made a halfway-decent crab-cake sandwich," Will remarked, calling him on the blatant lie.

"Hardly anyplace around here that doesn't," Mack agreed.

Jake tired of their amusement at his expense. "Oh, give it a rest," he grumbled. "If you want to eat here, we'll eat here. I just thought it would be good to try someplace different. We're in a rut."

"And you realized that not five minutes ago?" Will inquired skeptically. "We've been in the same rut for five years."

"Six," Jake muttered. "It's been six years."

The three of them had started eating lunch together every day right after Bree had left Chesapeake Shores. It had been Will and Mack's halfhearted attempt to boost Jake's spirits, even though they weren't a hundred percent certain what had happened between Jake and Bree. The couple had broken up, that much

Jake's friends knew, and also that Jake was hurting. That was all that had mattered.

His buddies had rallied around him, being supportive in the only way guys knew how, by hanging out with him and trying to keep him distracted, and by not mentioning the source of his discontent unless he brought her up first. Which he hadn't. Today was one of the few times in all these years that Bree's name had even crossed his lips.

Good friends that they were and happily single, Will and Mack had also dragged Jake out regularly for happy hour and tried to interest him in other women. More often than not, they were the ones who met someone attractive and left with her, while Jake went home alone to his empty bed and dark thoughts. He'd gotten used to the pattern and to the loneliness. It was pitiful, all right, but it was the life he had.

And it beat the pain he'd felt when Bree had left. He wasn't going through anything like that again, even if he wound up living like a hermit for the rest of his days, which his sister, Connie, told him regularly he was in grave danger of doing.

"Maybe it's a good sign," Will speculated, his expression thoughtful. "Him wanting to shake things up finally."

"Could be," Mack agreed.

The two men exchanged a look, then turned toward Mack's SUV, which was parked closer than Will's fancy foreign sports car or Jake's bright green Shores Nursery and Landscaping truck.

"We'll go to Brady's," Mack said, throwing a commiserating arm across his shoulders. "And then we'll beat some sense into you."

2

Bree heard what sounded like a collective sigh being released and looked up to find herself the object of a roomful of staring customers and to see Sally regarding her with an oddly disapproving expression.

"What's going on?" Bree asked.

"You didn't see him?" Sally asked.

"See who?"

"Jake."

Bree felt as if someone had slugged her in the stomach. "Jake was here?"

"For about two seconds. Took one look at you and flew right back out the door. Took two more of my best customers with him."

"Oh, God, I had no idea. I thought . . ." Her voice trailed off. She had no idea what she'd thought. For six years she'd tried not to let a single thought about Jake creep into her head. When it did, usually when her defenses were down and she felt most vulnerable, it left her feeling raw and guilty, even though she'd done nothing wrong. As soon as that thought crossed her mind, she winced at the lie. If she were being totally honest, she'd done plenty wrong.

Glancing up at Sally and trying to gather her composure, Bree said, "I . . . I . . ." She couldn't seem to think straight. The order she'd planned had flown right out of her head with Sally's mention of Jake. "Can I have another minute, please? Whatever I get, I'll make it takeout so I won't tie up the booth. I just need to sit here for a couple of minutes, okay?"

Sally nodded, her expression more sympathetic. "I'll be back."

As soon as Sally was gone, rather than glancing at the menu again as she'd promised, Bree's thoughts spun right back to Jake and the tragic way their relationship had eventually fallen apart.

Sure, what had happened was just one

of those things. Losing a baby—one she'd told no one except Jake that she was carrying—should have drawn them closer. Most couples pulled together after a tragedy like that.

Instead, Bree had taken it as a sign that they weren't meant to be. She'd seized on the miscarriage as an excuse to flee to Chicago and go after the future that had seemed so elusive just a few days earlier.

Jake's reaction had been exactly the opposite. Ecstatic about the unexpected pregnancy, he had been talking about a wedding, a family and the future with such high hopes and excitement. As much as she'd loved him and hoped for that same future eventually, rather than sharing his joy, she'd felt miserable and, far worse, trapped.

And then, almost before she'd had time to grapple with the idea that she was pregnant, the baby was gone and, God help her, she'd felt free. She'd taken off for Chicago and the job awaiting her there without a backward glance, leaving Jake alone to mourn not only the loss of their child, but of her and all the dreams he'd spun.

Oh, they'd gone through the pretense of

staying in touch at first, even occasionally talking about the future, but it had quickly been clear to Bree that the relationship was over. She'd struggled for weeks trying to think of the kindest way to say that to Jake.

In the end, he'd figured it out for himself after surprising her in Chicago one weekend and discovering her sequestered in her tiny apartment with Marty. There'd been nothing going on, but obviously Jake had felt the chemistry between her and the famed playwright. Ironically he'd known before she had admitted it to herself that she was falling in love with the charming, charismatic older man.

That's what they'd fought about, the excuse he'd used for breaking up. And once again, despite the quick and painful stab of guilt she'd experienced, all Bree had felt was relief that she hadn't been the one to end things. She'd even convinced herself that allowing Jake to be the one to break up was her final gift to him. For a woman who prided herself on being insightful about human nature, somehow she'd been delusional about that. What she'd been was cowardly.

She had treated him so badly. She could admit that now. Jake was a wonderful, sexy, amazing guy, and maybe they could have made things work, but she'd felt relieved that she hadn't had to find out. She'd known deep down that she would have come to resent him if she hadn't had a chance to find out what she was made of as a playwright. She'd needed that chance to work with a respected regional theater, to be mentored by someone like Martin Demming. It was all she'd dreamed about from the first time she'd seen a play onstage and put her own words and characters down on paper.

Sally returned, cutting into her thoughts. "Have you decided yet?"

"The special's fine," Bree said, though she had no idea what it was. Her appetite had fled anyway, so it hardly mattered.

Sally made a note of it, then hesitated. "Look, maybe I shouldn't say anything, because I have no idea what happened between you and Jake, but you should know that he, Will and Mack come in here every day at noon and sit in this booth. They're regulars."

The words were innocuous, but the

tone was heavy with implications. It amounted to a warning from the usually diplomatic Sally.

"And you don't want me chasing them away," Bree concluded. "I understand. I'll do my best to stay out of their way. I'll probably be leaving town soon anyway."

But even as she said the words, knots of tension formed in her shoulders again. That ought to tell her something, she thought. She crawled out of the booth, aware that other customers were staring, friends of Jake's no doubt, people who probably hated her as much as he did. She went to wait for her order by the register, paid Sally and fled.

She took the meal to a picnic table in the park along the waterfront. While osprey and even the occasional eagle swooped high above her, she picked at the sandwich, then scattered the bread for the waiting seagulls.

Now what? she wondered. The debate over whether to stay or go was raging inside her, turning her stomach queasy.

Staying, which she'd only recently begun to consider, was rife with problems. It wasn't as if this were Chicago, where she and Jake would never cross paths. Here in Chesapeake Shores they were bound to. How could she come back and disrupt his life after what she'd done to him? Obviously he still hated her, if he'd fled the café without even acknowledging her. Worse, she couldn't really blame him. What she'd done was cruel.

When she thought about all that, the guilt was overwhelming. How could she possibly stay here, especially when it was clear that Jake wasn't the only one judging her? She'd squirmed under all those accusing eyes in the café, felt the sting of Sally's disapproval. Chances were not one of them knew even half of what had happened, but they'd chosen sides anyway. Jake's side. After all, he was the one who'd been left behind. She might be an O'Brien, with all that implied in this town, but she'd left. She was no longer one of them.

Then, again, how could she allow what had happened so long ago to keep her from finding peace for herself? Over the past three weeks she'd increasingly come to believe that she belonged right here. She hadn't figured out what she wanted to do with herself, much less any of the details, but when she thought of staying, she felt a kind of serenity that had eluded her for some time now.

"I want to come home for good. I want to live in Chesapeake Shores," she said aloud, while the waiting seagulls regarded her solemnly, hoping for more scraps. The words sounded right, convincing. Surprising.

Like her sister Abby and her brothers, Bree had been only too eager to leave behind the town that had absorbed so much of her father's time, then skyrocketed his career as an architect, developer and urban planner in a way that had taken him away from them. Now, it seemed, she was ready to come home. The decision, barely made, felt right.

Except for its impact on Jake. If she decided to stay, first she had to find some way to coexist with the man whose heart she'd broken. Unfortunately, based on today's reception, it seemed unlikely he'd make that easy for her.

"Maybe it shouldn't be easy," she murmured as the seagulls watched her quizzically and a couple of weekday tourists regarded her curiously.

She smiled wryly. She must present quite a sight, with no makeup, the sea breeze whipping strands of her hair out of the clasp meant to hold it atop her head and talking to herself. If she were a character in one of her own plays, there would be quite a story behind this scene.

In fact, there *was* quite a story behind it. What she couldn't quite predict for the real-life version was whether it would turn out to have a happy ending or wind up a tragedy.

The crab-cake sandwich was sitting heavily in Jake's stomach. One beer had turned into two before he'd cut himself off and returned to work. He planned to lock himself in his office at the nursery and spend the afternoon catching up on paperwork. As much as he hated that side of the landscaping business, at least it required concentration, which meant his mind wouldn't be wandering to thoughts of Bree the way it had all during lunch, despite Will and Mack's best attempts to talk about anything and everything else.

They'd exhausted Orioles baseball, the upcoming football season with the Ravens, politics and even the usually lively recitation of Mack's dating exploits. The latter, unfortunately, had cut a little too close to the unspoken topic of Bree, so Jake had cited a busy afternoon schedule and cut the meal short.

En route to his desk, he kicked his trash can across the office, then threw a stack of seed catalogs on the floor. It was when a chair hit the wall that his sister came flying into the room.

"What on earth has gotten into you?" Connie demanded, ducking behind the door when an empty soda can came flying in her direction.

"If you have an ounce of sense, you'll get the hell out of here," Jake growled, turning his back on her to stare out the window at rows of shrubs and trees currently being examined by an elderly couple at the behest of one of his best salesmen. He recognized the Whitcombs. He'd been working for them since his days of cutting grass as a teenager. They'd been asking lately about crepe myrtles to fill in their landscaping. The trees that flowered in late summer came in an increasing range of colors now. Molly Whitcomb had her heart set on a dark purple one, while Walter liked the more traditional pink. Jake wondered idly who was winning the battle.

He heard his office door click shut and turned around expecting to find himself alone, but his sister was calmly sitting on the chair opposite his desk, her expression patient.

"So, you don't have an ounce of sense?" he asked, amused despite his sour mood.

"That's what I hear," she said. "I certainly don't run from trouble, the way you apparently do."

Jake bristled. "What the hell does that mean?"

"You and Bree—just about face-to-face at Sally's, and you turn around and take off. Sound familiar?"

He scowled at her. "How did you hear about that?"

She rolled her eyes. "Oh, please, did you honestly think that news wouldn't be all over town within five minutes? That's the joy of cell phones, little brother. The local grapevine works at lightning speed these days."

"More's the pity."

"So, do you want to talk about it?"

"No."

She shrugged. "What else is new? You haven't wanted to talk about Bree for six years. Now, personally, I think you'd get her out of your system a whole lot faster if you'd rant and rave and tell the universe exactly what you think about her."

"Bree is out of my system," he insisted. And what he thought of her wasn't fit for saying aloud. "I broke up with her, remember?"

Connie gave him a sympathetic look, the kind that made him want to break things.

"You may have said the words, Jake, but she broke your heart long before that. Don't even try to deny it. I was here. I saw what it did to you when she left for Chicago. And something tells me there was a whole lot more to the story than you've ever admitted."

"I do not want to discuss this," he reminded her fiercely. "I mean it, Connie. The subject of Bree is off-limits. If you bring up her name again, I'll fire you."

"No, you won't," she said serenely. "But I'll drop it for now. Or at least I will after you've answered one question for me. What are you going to do if she's back here to stay?"

"Bree's a hotshot playwright in Chicago. She's not staying, so it's not going to be an issue." *Please God, let me be right about that.*

"I'm just asking, what if—"

Jake cut her off. "Drop it, Connie. I mean it."

She sighed. "Consider it dropped, for now anyway. Are you coming for dinner tonight?"

Ever since her divorce five years ago, he usually had dinner with Connie and his seventeen-year-old niece two or three times a week. A good deal for him, Jake acknowledged, because his sister's cooking was a whole lot better than his. So was their company most of the time. It seemed best to steer clear tonight, though, with the whole conversation about Bree still a little too fresh. If Connie could pester the daylights out of him, his niece was worse. Jenny Louise thought his love life "sucked," and considered it her own personal mission to point that out to him on a regular basis. If she'd caught wind of the incident at Sally's, he'd never hear the end of it.

"No," he told Connie flatly.

"I'm fixing your favorite—meat loaf and mashed potatoes and fresh green beans."

Jake almost regretted turning her down. Not only was the meal his all-time favorite, but nobody made it better than his sister. She used their mom's old meat-loaf recipe, complete with mushroom gravy. Unfortunately, he knew in this instance, it also came with a scoop of sisterly advice and a side of meddling from Jenny Louise.

"No, thanks," he said.

Connie studied him for what seemed like an eternity, then nodded. "Okay, then, I'll save you some and bring it in tomorrow," she said at last. "You can have it for dinner tomorrow night."

"I won't turn that down." He walked around the desk and dropped a kiss on her forehead. "Thanks, sis."

"I could bring enough for two," she said, her expression innocent. "You know, in case you wanted to have someone over."

Jake frowned. "I'm not talking *about* Bree, I'm not talking *to* Bree, so I'm sure as hell not inviting her over for dinner."

A satisfied grin spread across Connie's face. "Did I say a single word about Bree?" she inquired, then answered her own question. "I did not. The fact that you immediately leaped to that conclusion speaks volumes not only about your obsession with her, but the absence of any other woman in your life."

On that note, she sashayed out the door, apparently very pleased with herself. Jake would have thrown something after her, but he figured she'd just take that as more proof that she was right.

Which she was, damn it all to hell.

There was a big, noisy deli on the corner a few blocks down the street from Megan's condo. She made it a point to stop there on her way home from work whenever the prospect of the silence in her apartment didn't appeal to her. With Abby and the twins now living in Chesapeake Shores instead of just a few dozen blocks away here in New York, she was at loose ends more often than she liked.

She was almost to the deli's door when she glanced through the window and spotted Mick sitting at a table sipping coffee. Shock stopped her in her tracks. Her heart flipped over in her chest, just the way it had the first time she'd met him more than thirty-five years ago. How was it possible to still feel that rush of emotion after all these years, especially with a bitter divorce and fifteen years of separation behind them?

When she'd felt a little twinge of affection—okay, more than a twinge and more than affection—a few weeks ago, she'd blamed it on being back in Chesapeake Shores surrounded by family, if only for a few days. Of course she'd felt a little sentimental. Today, right here in New York where she'd made a new life for herself, the rush of emotion caught her completely off guard. It was also a whole lot more worrisome. She'd never tried to deny that she still loved Mick. But she also knew it was folly to consider going back to him. No matter what Abby believed, Megan knew he hadn't changed, not enough anyway.

As she debated with herself whether to go or stay, he glanced up and caught sight of her. A smile broke across his face and in that instant, she was lost. No one had ever looked at her the way Mick did, as if the sun rose and set with her.

She gave him a little wave, then went inside. Drawing in a deep, calming breath, she prepared herself to face him without losing control of her emotions or the situation. She was a smart, accomplished woman. It ought to be easy enough.

Ever the gentleman, Mick stood as she approached. His kiss grazed her cheek, but then he pulled back, looking as embarrassed as a schoolboy caught stealing a kiss in the cloakroom.

"Sorry," he murmured as he slid into the booth opposite her.

She regarded him with amusement. "It's okay, Mick. There's nothing inappropriate about giving your ex-wife an innocent peck on the cheek. Now tell me, of all the delis in New York, what brings you to the one in my neighborhood?"

He gestured toward the cell phone in the middle of the table. "I was going to call you. I thought maybe we could grab dinner, if you don't have plans."

So he had come to see her, she thought, not sure whether she was pleased by that or more terrified than ever.

When she still hadn't responded after a couple of minutes of silence, he regarded her with an impatient expression. "Do you have plans?"

She shook her head, determined not to make it easy for him or maybe struggling to decide if spending more time with him was wise.

He obviously had some idea of what she was up to because he frowned. "Then will you have dinner with me?" he inquired with exaggerated patience.

Since she'd planned to eat right here anyway, she finally nodded. "Sure, we can grab a bite here."

He glanced around the deli with its rush of customers and clattering silverware, with its legion of abrasive waitresses and waiters. "Here? I was thinking someplace, you know, a little classier than this."

"I eat here a lot," she said. "The food's good. Besides, we're already here."

The last place she wanted to be with her ex-husband was some cozy, romantic restaurant with expensive wine, an even pricier menu and candlelight. That was the kind of place a man took a woman he was courting. Casual was good, safer. She could pretend this was nothing more than a chance meeting of two longtime acquaintances.

Acquaintances who happened to share five children, she amended wryly.

Mick shrugged eventually. "Whatever you want." He beckoned for a waiter, an older man who beamed at Megan.

"Your Monday usual, Ms. O'Brien?" he asked with the familiarity she'd come to expect from the staff. "Iced tea, the corned-beef brisket and parsley potatoes?"

"Sounds perfect, Joe. How's your wife?"

"Back to her old self," he said. "Thanks for asking."

"And Mary? Did she get her grade on her exam?"

The man's smile spread. "An A plus," he told her proudly.

Megan turned to Mick, who was listening to the exchange with obvious surprise. "Joe's granddaughter is studying to be a doctor at Columbia."

"Congratulations!" Mick said. "That's quite an accomplishment."

"She's the smartest one in the family," Joe said. "Now, tell me what I can get for you."

Mick didn't bother with the menu. "I'll

have whatever she's having and more coffee."

Joe nodded and left.

"That man did not say two words to me when he took my order earlier," Mick said. "You had him chattering like a magpie."

She laughed. "I come here a lot. Joe treats me like family."

"So even in a city the size of New York, you've created a small-town atmosphere for yourself," he said.

"I had to work at it," she admitted. "At first I was too intimidated to talk to anyone except the people I worked with and then Abby once she moved here. Then I discovered that if you ask a few questions, show an interest in people, they behave exactly the way they would in Chesapeake Shores."

Joe returned and set another cup of coffee in front of Mick and gave her a tall glass of iced tea, then discreetly vanished with a wink, suggesting he'd have a lot of questions for her tomorrow about the man sitting across from her now. For years now, he'd clucked over her lack of a social life like a protective father.

Because she wanted a few answers for

herself and not just to be prepared for Joe's interrogation, she looked Mick in the eye. "You never did tell me what you're doing in New York. Do you have business here?"

He shook his head, looking surprisingly uneasy for a man of his accomplishments and confidence. "I had business in Seattle last week, then in Minneapolis. I decided to take a little side trip on the way home."

"You never liked New York," she said. It was one of the reasons she'd chosen it after the divorce. She'd wanted to be someplace where they'd shared no memories and where it was unlikely Mick would be popping up too frequently.

"Still don't," he admitted. "But you're here."

She swallowed hard at the glint in his eye. The simple comment held a world of meaning. "Mick, don't."

His gaze held hers. "Don't what? Don't be honest with you?"

"Don't say things like that. You and me, we had our chance. It's best to leave it like that."

His expression remained solemn. "I don't think I can do that."

"Of course you can. We haven't crossed paths in years, not even when I came home to see the kids when they were younger. There's no reason for that to change."

Again, he looked directly into her eyes, the gaze bold, disconcerting. "I think there is. The sparks are still there, Meggie. Just because I was a damn fool doesn't mean they've gone away."

She reached for a packet of sweetener, not because she wanted it but because she needed something to do with her hands. When she started to tear it open, it flew from her grasp, spreading powdery sweetener everywhere. She would have cleaned it up, but Mick covered her hand.

"Don't," he said. "Leave it." Again, he beckoned for Joe, who was there in an instant with a damp cloth and a questioning look.

She forced a smile for him. "Thanks. I'm all thumbs tonight."

"Don't worry about it," Joe said. He glanced at another waiter heading their way. "Here come your meals. You'll let me know if you need anything."

"Thanks," Mick told him. When Joe and the other waiter had left, Mick pushed the plate aside and turned in her direction. "Does it really bother you, me being here?"

She thought about the question, *really* thought about it. "It's not that exactly. I mean, you're on my turf, so it should be easy, but you keep saying things that throw me off kilter. I don't know what you want."

"Another chance," Mick said simply. Before she could even close her gaping mouth, much less respond, he added, "Not right this second, but soon. A little at a time, you know? Maybe dinner here, like this. Then another visit to Chesapeake Shores. Or maybe you'd like to come with me to Seattle. We can play it by ear, do what feels right."

"I don't know, Mick," she said, fighting temptation. "I've adapted to living on my own. I have a life here. Yours is . . ." She hesitated, then shrugged. "Yours is wherever you happen to be working at the moment. That didn't work for us before. Why take a chance on hurting each other again?"

He held her gaze, his expression earnest. "It's taken me fifteen long years, Meggie, to figure out everything I did wrong when we were married. Don't let all that soul-searching go to waste."

She smiled at the idea of Mick soul-searching. He was the kind of man who seized the moment, who went through life on bluster and gut instinct. "Soul-searching, huh?"

He grinned then. "Swear to God."

The appeal of that grin reminded her of the way it had been between them when they first met, with Mick persuading her to do a thousand little things that went against her better judgment. Thank heaven most of the risks had been to her heart, because he could probably have talked her into skydiving with that charming way of his and she'd have wound up breaking every bone in her body. Then, again, a broken heart took longer to heal.

She tried her brisket but had no appetite left. Like Mick, she pushed the plate aside, knowing she'd hear about that from Joe later. The only thing he clucked over more than her social life was her habit of merely picking at her food.

"How about this?" she said eventually. "Maybe we can see each other from time to time, the way you said, but let's not call it a second chance or starting over or anything like that. We'll just be two old friends getting together, enjoying the moment."

He sat back, his expression a bit smug, clearly counting her response as a victory. "You can call it whatever you want," he agreed. "Now, how about coming home with me tomorrow? Ma says there's a problem with Bree. She thinks we might need to rally the troops."

Megan saw right through him. Give the man an inch and he took not just a mile, but the entire interstate between New York and Chesapeake Shores. "I'm not going home with you," she said flatly.

"Not even if your daughter needs you?" he asked, not even attempting to mask his disappointment.

"Let's just say I'll need confirmation on that from someone other than you," she retorted.

"You don't trust me?"

She laughed at his indignation. "Not from here to the corner."

He shrugged, looking sheepish. "It was worth a try," he said. "And Ma really is worried about Bree."

"Then she or Bree can call me and fill me in," she said, not relenting. "Though Bree has never been in the habit of confiding in me."

"I think that's part of the problem," Mick said, his expression thoughtful. "Bree's not in the habit of confiding in anyone."

She frowned at his tone and his surprising insight. "You're really concerned, aren't you?"

He nodded. "I've learned to listen to Ma. When she says something's wrong, it usually is."

"Then call me and fill me in once you have a better idea of what the problem is. If Bree really does need me, then of course I'll come."

"I'll tell her you said that," he promised. "Now, I'd better head for the airport and see if I can still get a flight yet tonight."

The sharp stab of disappointment she felt at the meal being cut short was a warning. She might think she had control of the situation, but that was far, far from the truth. Once Mick O'Brien got an idea in his head, he was all but impossible to ignore or dissuade. Especially for a woman who still had a soft spot in her heart for him.

3

Jake was very glad the job he was on required hard, backbreaking labor. He hadn't slept a wink the night before, thanks to that near miss with Bree. He'd worried that Connie could be right, that Bree might be staying in Chesapeake Shores. Then he'd worried even more that she might leave again. Nobody could ever suggest that his life was ruled by logic, he thought dryly.

He trimmed back another boxwood in a bedraggled hedge so his equipment could get a better grip to yank it from the ground. His broad, tanned shoulders were slick with sweat and the bandanna tied around his forehead was damp. He was wearing a pair of cutoff jeans and work boots. Sunglasses, covered by protective goggles, shaded his eyes as he worked with the power saw to cut a few more branches. The noise was deafening. As the last branch snapped off, he turned off the saw. But even as silence fell, it seemed as if the air still vibrated. He whipped off his goggles and turned to find Bree standing a few feet away, her expression uncertain. She looked cool as a cucumber in another of those sundresses she favored, this one a pale green.

He was tired. He was dirty. And he was in no mood for this, whatever it was that had brought her here. If things had been different between them, he might have admired her audacity in tracking him down.

"Hello, Jake."

"I'm busy," he said, snapping the goggles back into place and turning on the saw.

He'd wait her out. Cut off every damn branch, every tiny twig if he had to. He was not having this conversation with her. He was never speaking to her again. He'd made that decision when he'd found her all cozy and friendly with Martin Demming years ago. That had been the last straw, the deathblow to his hope that they might still salvage their relationship. The mere fact that she'd come home and was standing right here, apparently intent on butting into his life, didn't change any of that.

He kept on cutting, ignoring her, until he'd left the base of the very last bush barely sticking out of the ground. When he was through, pleased with himself for not caving in to his desire to drink in the sight of her, he looked up and found her still standing right there. Her patience had always been a stark contrast to his rush through life, but today he found it more annoying than ever.

"Go away, Bree."

"Not until we've talked," she said, her chin jutting up stubbornly.

He whirled around and scowled at her. "Now? You want to talk right now? Where the hell was that eagerness to have a conversation six years ago? You didn't seem inclined to say two words to me back then. You just took off. Half the time you wouldn't even answer my calls, so I had to come to Chicago. And what did I find when I got there? You and Demming sharing a bottle of wine."

"Having a glass of wine with a friend is hardly a crime," she said mildly.

He retreated from the accusation and tried to make himself clearer. "The wine wasn't the problem and we both know it. It was the way he was looking at you." He shook his head. "No, it was the way you were looking at him. *That* was the real problem. Anybody with twenty-twenty eyesight could tell you were infatuated with him. We'd been apart how long by then? Three months, as I recall."

There was a flash of guilt in her eyes that told him he hadn't mistaken anything that night. He'd gotten what was going on between them exactly right. And even now, dammit, it still mattered. It continued to hurt that she'd been able to forget about him, about the baby they'd lost and the plans they'd made. Worse, she'd done it so quickly, so easily, as if nothing between them had ever mattered.

"I'm sorry, Jake."

"Yeah, well, so am I. You'll have to excuse me if I don't want to rehash things at this late date."

He tried to stare her down. It would have worked at one time, but today she held her ground. He sighed. If she was intent on having her say about something, it would be easier in the long run to let her get on with it. After all, he didn't have to listen. He could tune her out, think about . . . His imagination failed him. He couldn't think of anything that would be compelling enough to keep his attention diverted from the words coming out of Bree's mouth.

"Okay, two minutes," he snapped. "What do you want?"

"I'm thinking of staying in Chesapeake Shores," she began.

He tried not to let her words cut right through him, but they did. Just one more decision that had come too late to matter, one more way she could rip out his heart on a daily basis.

"Well, bully for you," he said, because she was clearly waiting for a response.

She did wince then, but she didn't back down. "I wanted to know if that would be okay with you, if we could at least try to get along."

"We can stay the hell out of each other's way," he said. "That's the best I can promise. Take it or leave it. Go or stay. It makes no difference to me." The lie tripped off his tongue convincingly, he thought. At least he hoped it did. He would not let her see that she still got to him. It was one thing for Mack and Will and his own sister to see right through him, but not Bree. That would be too pathetic.

There was a quick flash of hurt in her eyes, but then she nodded slowly. "Okay, then," she said softly, a quiver in her voice that told him she was near tears. He steeled himself against it. So what if he hurt her? It was nothing to the pain she'd caused him.

She turned on her heel and walked away, giving him a perfect view of her excellent backside. Just staring after her stirred him in ways it shouldn't. What was wrong with him? Was he a total jerk? A glutton for punishment? Because he knew with every fiber of his being that given a chance, he would take her to bed. Not into his heart again. Never that. But sex? Oh, yeah.

After her uncomfortable—okay, *awful*—confrontation with Jake, Bree sat in an Adirondack chair on the front porch, her feet propped up on a post, a notebook in her lap. She was making a list, something that was more like Abby than her. She had to get a handle on what she could do if she stayed here, because if she didn't have a solid plan in mind, it would be too easy to drift back to the life she knew in Chicago, lousy as it was. So far she hadn't written down one single thing, maybe because she couldn't stop thinking about Jake and the way he'd looked at her.

Had she hurt him again for no good reason? If she couldn't come up with a plan, then she couldn't stay, and that whole ugly scene would have been for nothing. Hearing the anger and disdain in his voice had dredged up the way she'd felt on the night he'd walked out of her apartment and out of her life. She'd known then, just as she had today, that she deserved every bitter word. Why she'd expected anything different was beyond her. Had she honestly expected him to welcome her home with his familiar crooked smile and a solid, reassuring hug? The idea was ludicrous. Men didn't just forgive and forget. Most of them wanted to get even. If that was his goal, to hurt her as she'd hurt him, he was well on his way.

A hint of forgiveness would have been nice, she admitted to herself with a sigh. Jake had been more than the man she'd loved six years ago. He'd been her best friend. He'd been the one she would have talked to about this crossroad in her life. Now they couldn't even exchange a civil word.

When her cell phone rang, she answered eagerly. Any distraction was better than this sudden rootlessness she was feeling.

"Bree, thank goodness," Jess said, sounding frantic. "Can you get over to the inn right now?"

"Sure. What's going on?"

"I have a wedding here in three hours. The florist who's supposed to be doing the flowers is in the hospital. He didn't have a backup, so the wholesaler just dumped boxes and boxes of flowers on my doorstep. I have no idea what to do with them."

"Give me ten minutes," Bree said at once. "Do you have vases, wire, ribbons, anything for making arrangements?"

"I have vases. That's it."

"Are the bouquets made, at least?"

"Not that I can see."

"Okay, make it a half hour. I'll pick up some supplies on the way. Is there any way you can call the bride's mother or a bridesmaid and find out what they had in mind without starting a panic?"

"I'll try. The matron of honor is actually upstairs. Lauren's a lot calmer and more practical than Mrs. Hilliard. I'll ask her to meet us in a half hour."

"Perfect."

Rather than risking a wasted trip to Ethel's Emporium for supplies they might not have, Bree raided her grandmother's greenhouse and sewing room. She arrived at the inn with ribbon in a variety of colors, some scraps of lace and everything else she thought she might need.

She found Jess and Lauren Jackson, who'd been in Abby's class at school, waiting for her, surrounded by open boxes of long-stemmed white roses, white snapdragons, white orchids and white lilacs. There was one box filled with trailing ivy.

"Hey, Lauren," she said, looking over what they had to work with. "Any idea what the bride had in mind?"

"Simple. Her bouquet was going to be white orchids and lilacs. There are three attendants, and we're supposed to have a single white rose with some long white ribbons." She glanced at Jess. "I think there are supposed to be stands with vases of roses and snapdragons up by the minister, and then small arrangements on the tables. It's not a huge wedding, just family and a few friends, so there are only four tables, maybe. Is that right?"

Jess nodded. "She said something about the ivy going across the table from the centerpieces."

"Okay, then. I think that gives me enough to work with. Are the groom and best man and ushers supposed to have flowers for their lapels?"

Jess and Lauren regarded her blankly.

"I have no idea," Lauren admitted. "I'll call Tom, that's the groom, and ask him." She took out her cell phone and dialed. When he answered, she explained the situation and asked about the flowers, then shook her head for Bree's benefit. She lowered her voice. "There is no need to panic, Tom. I swear it. Someone's here right now, and we have it all under control.

Whatever you do, do not say anything about this to Diana. She'll freak out. Bye."

She stuck her phone back in her pocket. "Everything set here?" she asked Bree. "Do you need me to stay and help?"

"No. I can take it from here. I'll do the bouquets first, if you want to send someone down in an hour to get them. If they're not right, we'll have time for adjustments."

"You're a lifesaver, Bree. I'll make sure Diana knows about this." She grinned. "After the ceremony, anyway."

When Lauren and Jess were gone, Bree took stock of the flowers and went to work. The bouquets were easy enough, thanks to the bride's desire for simplicity. She held them up for Jess's approval when she came back from checking on things in the kitchen to make sure the food for the reception was on track.

"What do you think?" she asked her sister.

"Classy and elegant," Jess said at once. "I'm in awe of you."

"Let's see how you feel when I'm through with the tough stuff."

As she finished each centerpiece, she carried it into the dining room where four tables were set with white linens, sparkling crystal, white candles, sterling-silver place settings and silver-edged china. She set the low arrangement of flowers in the center, then pulled strands of ivy between some of the place settings. She studied it, decided it didn't look quite right and went back to gather some of the extra rose petals to scatter across the table with the ivy. She stood back again and concluded it didn't look half-bad.

Jess came in as she was placing the last arrangement. "Oh, my," she said, her voice filled with delight. "Bree, they're beautiful. A professional couldn't have done better. I swear if you weren't off making a name for yourself as a playwright, I'd insist you do this for a living."

Bree regarded her with surprise. "Really?"

"You've always had a knack with flowers, but what you've done here today, especially under pressure, it's amazing. Much better than what I've seen from the florist that people around here usually use. The Hilliards are going to be ecstatic. You really did save the day. I'll see to it that they pay you accordingly."

"I don't need to be paid," Bree said. "This was an emergency. I did it as a favor to you. Besides, it was fun. I've always loved doing stuff like this."

"You do work like this, you get paid," Jess insisted. "And I'm taking pictures of these arrangements, too."

Bree regarded her blankly. "Why?"

"Who knows, maybe one of these days you'll get sick of Chicago and decide you want to take up floral design," she said jokingly. "These will be the first pictures for your portfolio. I'm starting one for the inn, so I can show clients other events we've held here."

Bree gave her a hard hug. "You are a very smart woman, sister of mine. Bring the pictures by the house later, so we can show them to Gram. She'll be thrilled to see that some of those flower-arranging lessons she gave me have paid off."

On the way home, Bree thought about the sense of satisfaction she'd gotten from what should have been a few incredibly stressful hours. She was halfway back to the house when an idea began to take shape. She made a U-turn and drove into town.

She rode slowly along Main Street, then pulled into a space in front of the only empty storefront downtown. It was two doors away from Sally's, which could be a drawback in terms of the potential for crossing paths with Jake, but that also meant that everyone in town would know about a new shop within days of its opening. Most people in town had breakfast or lunch at Sally's at least once a week, if only on Sundays after church. As she sat there, the vague idea in her head evolved into an actual plan.

She'd been in the space many times over the years when it had been a dress shop. She could imagine its possibilities for what she had in mind. She pictured the window filled with baskets of flowers, maybe even stands filled with colorful, ready-to-go bouquets on the sidewalk out front when the weather wasn't too hot to wilt them. She could even envision the sign painted in the window in ornate gold script entwined with a few decorative flowers: FLOWERS ON MAIN, and beneath that, in a much smaller font, *Proprietor Bree O'Brien.* She could see it all as clearly as if it had been in the back of her mind for years, just waiting for an incident like today's to lead her here.

In some ways she was as plodding and careful as Abby, but in others she was as impulsive as Jess. She went with her gut more often than not, and this felt right. Maybe if she hadn't been going over her options for days now, if the decision to stay here hadn't already been made, she would have waited, taken some time to examine this from every angle. As it was, she felt certain that this was something that could work, something she'd be good at, something she'd enjoy.

Before she could talk herself out of it, she reached for her cell phone and called the number of the management company listed on the discreet sign in the lower corner of the window. It was a number she should have known by heart, since her uncle had started the management company and one of her cousins was running it these days.

When Susie answered, Bree almost faltered. Should her cousin know about this before anyone else in the family? The answer was tricky since there were still some hard feelings among the various branches of the O'Brien family that went back to the construction of Chesapeake Shores. She waved off her doubts.

"Susie, it's me, your cousin Bree."

"Well, hey there. I'd heard you were in town when Jess opened the inn, but I didn't catch much more than a glimpse of you at the party."

Bree laughed. "Big bashes like that give me hives. I put in an appearance for family solidarity and all that, then hid out in the kitchen helping the chef."

"I thought you'd be back in Chicago by now."

"I decided to stick around. That's why I'm calling, in fact. I'm interested in leasing the space that's available on Main Street."

"Really?" Susie said, not even trying to hide her shock. "I thought you were doing so well with your plays."

"I was doing well enough," Bree hedged. "But I want to do something different. How about I come by now and sign the paperwork?"

"It's a two-year lease," Susie reminded her. "We don't like instability downtown."

"I'm not crazy about instability myself," Bree said. "Two years is fine."

"Do you mind if I ask what kind of business you're planning to open?"

"A flower shop," Bree said, her voice brimming with excitement. "Flowers on Main."

"You even have a name for it?"

Bree laughed. "And that's about *all* I have at the moment. And a lease, if you'll wait for me to get over to the office."

"I'll wait," Susie promised. "I want to hear all about why you've decided to come back home."

Mostly so she could report it to the rest of the family, Bree was certain. Still, word would get around soon enough. She just had to make sure that Gram, Mick, Abby and Jess heard about it from her before anyone else went running to them with the news.

And by the time she talked to her family, she was going to have a whole lot more than a lease and some vague idea that she could reinvent herself as a florist. Otherwise they'd start worrying about her the same way they fretted about Jess, convinced that she'd jumped into something without thinking it through.

Which, of course, was exactly what she

was doing. But for the first time in months, she actually felt a stirring of excitement deep inside, a resurgence of self-confidence. Maybe her destiny had been to work with flowers all along. Or perhaps this was just a stopgap measure until she got her feet back under her. Either way it felt right for now.

"You're going to do what?" Marty demanded, his tone incredulous when Bree worked up the courage to call and tell him she wasn't coming back to Chicago. "Surely you're not serious. What can possibly have possessed you to even consider giving up the theater to open a flower shop? Are you having some kind of breakdown?"

His scathing tone stiffened her resolve. That a man who'd claimed to love her could even ask such a question in that tone was proof that she'd made the right decision. Chicago was not the place for her, and he was most definitely not the right man.

"Thank you," she said wryly.

"For what?" he asked, clearly confused.

"For making it clear that I'm doing the right thing."

"What are you talking about? I certainly said no such thing."

"No, you said I must be having some kind of a breakdown."

"Well, aren't you? No one in their right mind would give up the opportunity you've had here to stay in that little hick town playing with posies."

"I think I'm more suited to 'playing with posies,' as you put it, than to being demeaned at every turn by you."

"When have I ever demeaned you?" he demanded, sounding genuinely shocked by the accusation. "All I've ever done was to support your work and offer constructive criticism."

"Potato, potahto," she said.

"What the hell does that mean?"

"Your version of constructive criticism is to tear me down until I'm no longer convinced I can write a coherent thought or a well-drawn character. Oh, I'll admit, in the beginning I was so in awe of you that I took every word as a pearl of wisdom, but I see now that in taking your criticism to heart, in molding my stories to win your approval, I was losing myself. The voice that I brought to my first play faltered in the second one and disappeared completely by the third."

"You're blaming me because your third play was a disaster?" he asked, incredulous.

"No, absolutely not," she said swiftly. "I blame myself, because I listened to you. Don't get me wrong, Marty. You taught me a lot in the beginning. You're an amazing playwright. But I can't be a carbon copy of you. I needed to be myself, and somewhere along the way I forgot that."

He was silent for so long, she thought maybe he was too furious with her to speak. But then he said, "Maybe that's true."

She was so stunned by the admission, she didn't have a response.

He went on in that same thoughtful tone. "Now that you understand that, though, this is exactly the wrong time to turn tail and run. You need to come back here and get back to work. I'll still help you, if you want it, or I'll leave you alone." He turned on the familiar charm. "You're good, Bree. Those last reviews aside, you can't lose sight of that. Besides, I miss you. I need you back here with me."

That almost swayed her. Marty never

admitted needing anyone. Then she remembered how quixotic his moods could be. He might need her today, but by tomorrow his ego would kick in, and he'd need no one, least of all her. Besides, if she was leaving Chicago at least in part because their relationship had turned toxic, then she could hardly go back because of some faint hope that it could change. She couldn't allow him to charm her into forgetting how things between them had deteriorated.

No, she decided firmly. She needed to stay right here in Chesapeake Shores, at least for now. She needed to tackle something new, get a fresh start. The thing about writing was that it could be done anytime, anywhere. If inspiration struck, she had her computer and she had her contacts in the theater. Staying here didn't mean she'd never write another play, just that if she did, it would be hers from act one scene one right on through to the closing curtain.

"It's too late, Marty. I'm not coming back, at least not for the foreseeable future."

"I'll come there. I'll change your mind."

"Please don't even try." It might feed her ego a bit to have him come, but more worrisome was the possibility that she would succumb to his persuasion. She knew all too well how skilled he was when he wanted something. "If you care about me, even a little, you'll let me make this change. Accept it and wish me well."

"A few months," he said with obvious reluctance. "You'll be going stir-crazy and you'll call me begging to come back."

"Maybe I will," she agreed.

"I can't promise you it won't be too late," he warned.

"I can live with that."

"Bree, my darling, you're making such a terrible mistake," he said.

"It's mine to make."

"And there's nothing—" He cut himself off with a heavy sigh. "No, I am familiar with your streak of Irish stubbornness. I can't change your mind now, can I?"

"No."

"Will you come if I send a ticket when the next play opens?"

"It's yours, isn't it?" she said, remembering how thrilled the theater had been to get the play for its pre-Broadway run. Rehearsals had just begun when she'd left town.

"The first in five years. I want you here.

You were my inspiration, my muse, when I was writing it, after all."

The flattery was deliberate, she knew. She was also aware he'd probably said something similar to other women. Marty was like that, scattering little hints about his gratitude far and wide, so that everyone thought they owned a share of his success.

"I'll think about it," she promised. In a few weeks, perhaps she could go back for a visit without feeling like a failure. She'd made friends there, people other than Marty she would miss. It would be a chance to catch up.

By then, too, she'd have her business up and running. She'd have her fresh start, an exciting new beginning. Marty's seductive charm wouldn't be a match for that.

"I'll be in touch, then," he said to her.

Only after they'd hung up did she realize that not once in the entire conversation had she sensed even the slightest hint of surprise on Marty's part that she was closing the door on their relationship. Unlike Jake, whose passions still ran high over their breakup after six long years, Marty had let her go with barely a whimper of regret. For all of his claim to miss her and need her, she didn't doubt for an instant that he would move on by the end of the week, if he hadn't already. He was the kind of man who couldn't survive for long without the adulation of a woman.

For the first time since she'd fallen, awe-struck, into his orbit, she actually felt a little sorry for him. She didn't miss the irony that it was seeing Jake again, hearing the anger in his voice and seeing the heat in his eyes, that showed her just how deep real love was supposed to run.

And despite many good memories, just how shallow her relationship with Marty had truly been.

4

Bree glanced around the kitchen table where her father, Gram, Jess and even Abby were seated. It was such a rarity to have them all here at the same time these days—especially Mick—that she regarded them with suspicion.

"This is a surprise," she said carefully. "Jess, why aren't you at the inn?"

"Gram wanted to have a family dinner," Jess replied casually, though she didn't meet Bree's gaze, which pretty much contradicted her attempt at innocence.

Bree turned to her older sister. "If that's

so, where are the twins, Abby? Where's Trace? He's practically family now."

"Busy," Abby said tersely. Her cheeks turned a guilty shade of pink, which immediately told Bree she was right to be suspicious. Her family was up to no good, and it had something to do with her.

"Besides, the girls are always exhausted after a day on the beach," Abby added a little too quickly. She had a telling habit of going on too long when she was nervous, which was exactly what she was doing now. "And you know how hard it is for the grown-ups to talk seriously when Carrie and Caitlyn are chattering nonstop."

"And just why would the grown-ups need to talk about something serious?" Bree inquired, turning her attention to Gram.

Gram deliberately ignored the question and passed a bowl mounded high with mashed potatoes. "Mick, carve the chicken," she ordered. "We'll talk after we've eaten."

"About what?" Bree persisted. "Does everyone at this table know what this is about except me?"

Mick reached over and gave her hand a squeeze. "It's nothing for you to fret about, girl. Everyone here is family. We all care about you."

Bree stared at him long enough for the words to really register, then shoved back her chair to stand. She was trembling so badly her knees wobbled, so she clung to the edge of the old oak table. Even if she hadn't been a private person who kept her problems to herself, she would have been deeply offended by what was happening.

"Then this isn't a pleasant family dinner at all, is it?" she said, scowling at everyone there. "It's some kind of weird O'Brien intervention. Well, I don't want any part of it. I don't need your questions or your sympathy."

She ran from the room and made it all the way out the front door before she allowed the tears gathering in her eyes to fall. She brushed at them impatiently so she could see well enough to make her way down the steps and across the lawn. She was at the edge of the grass and at the top of the steps down to the beach before Abby caught up with her.

"Bree, wait!" her big sister pleaded. "I'm so sorry we ambushed you. I think we all agreed to it for Gram as much as for you. You have her worried."

"I'm old enough to figure things out for myself," Bree said with a sniff, accepting a tissue that Abby handed her. Maybe because Abby was the mother of twins, she always seemed to have some in her pockets, while Bree never did.

"Of course you are," Abby said, accompanying her down to the beach.

There was still plenty of light to see clearly, though shadows were starting to fall. In an hour or so the sun would drop below the horizon behind them, setting the water on fire before it went. For now, though, the sky was mostly puffs of white and bits of mauve against the blue-gray of twilight.

Bree dug her feet into the cool sand at the water's edge, allowing the gentle waves to wash over them. She sucked in a deep breath of sea air and waited for the calming effect to kick in. This wasn't Abby's fault. It wasn't Gram's, either. Or even Mick's or Jess's. If anyone's, it was hers, for expecting to keep her turmoil to herself, to find her own way without anyone's help or interference. She should have known that sooner or later it would come to this.

"Want to hear the biggest irony of all?" she asked Abby.

"What's that?"

"I figured everything out today, made a decision about what I'm doing next. An hour ago I could hardly wait to share that news with everyone. I was so excited." She sighed. "And then I walked into the kitchen and there you all were, ready to pounce."

Abby nudged her in the ribs. "Don't be so dramatic, Ms. Playwright. Nobody was going to pounce."

"Ha," Bree scoffed. She hesitated, then added, "You got the rest of that wrong, too. I'm not a playwright anymore."

Abby's step faltered, but she kept her expression neutral. Bree had to give her credit for that. She'd make a fine actress if she ever decided to change careers. Then, again, maybe that's what made her an outstanding stockbroker, the ability to maintain a calm facade when the market was falling apart around her.

"What happened?" Abby asked eventually.

"It wasn't working for me anymore," Bree said simply. "Not the work, not Chicago, not my relationship with Marty. I think when

I came home for the opening at the inn, I already knew I wouldn't be going back. It just took me a few weeks to sort through everything and figure out what was going to come next. I knew the only way to keep all of you from worrying would be to have a concrete plan."

Abby stared at her, her expression stricken. "But Bree, writing plays is all you've ever wanted to do," she protested. "You can't give that up just because you've hit a rough patch or because your relationship with Marty isn't working. Take some time, get your feet back under you if that's what you need, but don't give up your career just like that. You have money in the bank, thanks to the trust fund Dad set up for each of us. You can take all the time you need to write your next play. You don't have to do that in Chicago or go back to Marty. Do it here, if you want."

"I can't. I don't have any confidence in myself right now. Maybe I will in a few weeks or a few months. If so, then I'll certainly start writing again. But in the meantime, I need to focus on something completely new. I need a challenge that will be fun at the same time."

"Such as?" Abby asked, her skepticism plain that such an option existed or that Bree would be happy doing anything other than writing.

"Did Jess mention that I was at the inn earlier?" Bree asked.

Abby shook her head, looking confused by the apparent change in topic. "I got to dinner just before you did. I'd barely sat down when you showed up."

"Well, I was there. She called me because the florist had sent flowers for a wedding, but no one to arrange them. She was in a real bind."

Abby looked even more confused. "And she called you? Why?"

Bree frowned at the suggestion that working with flowers was somehow beyond her. "Who do you think worked side by side with Gram all these years to make the arrangements for our house? She taught me everything she knows. She used to say I was a natural."

"All I remember is you yanking flowers and weeds indiscriminately out of her garden and getting yelled at a lot," Abby said lightly.

"Which was why she decided to teach

me the difference and to appreciate everything in her garden," Bree explained patiently. "Anyway, apparently I saved the day for the bride and groom's big ceremony and reception," she said, then faced her sister. "And you know what? I loved every minute of it. Despite the stress and having almost no time to pull it off, it was the most fun I'd had in ages."

"Okay," Abby said, her tone still cautious. "So, now what?"

"I've rented a space downtown, and I'm opening up a flower shop, Flowers on Main," Bree announced, then laughed. "Can you imagine? I'm going to have my own business, and I get to work with flowers all the time."

"No, I can't imagine," Abby said, in a way that told Bree she disapproved. "Why would you make a decision like this without talking it over with any of us? Good grief, Bree, you can't have thought about it for more than an hour or two."

Bree scowled at her. "I thought about it long enough," she said flatly. "And it was my decision to make. You said yourself, not five minutes ago, that I have the start-up money."

"Bree, sweetie," Abby began with exaggerated patience. "I know you love flowers, and you're obviously looking to make a big change in your life, but this is retail. You can't hide out in the backroom all day. You're going to have to put yourself out there, be friendly to everyone who comes in, no matter how idiotic their request might be. Are you sure you can do that?"

It spoke volumes that Abby thought her social skills were wanting—in fact, it was downright insulting—but Bree could hardly deny it. "It will be good for me to learn to be more outgoing," she insisted.

"And what about business? Do you know anything at all about running a business of any kind, much less a flower shop?"

Bree was getting annoyed with all the doubting questions. "I know as much as Jess did when she bought the inn," she said heatedly. "And what I don't know, I can learn. I'll read books, visit other shops and ask questions. I'm not a complete moron."

"Of course you're not," Abby said, backing off at once. "I'm just saying this will be a huge change for you. You've always valued your privacy."

"After what happened tonight, can you blame me?" Bree snapped. "Put you, Gram, Mick and Jess in a room and it's like a force of nature. I don't stand a chance. I'm almost glad I didn't tell everyone. If they're all going to react like you, I don't want to hear it. I won't let any of you tear me down. I've had enough of that to last ten lifetimes."

With that, she took off running along the edge of the bay. This time, though, Abby didn't follow.

Mick looked up from his pie when Abby walked back into the kitchen alone. "Where's your sister?"

"On the beach," Abby said. "She's mad at me, at all of us, for that matter."

"Oh dear, this is my fault," Gram said, looking stricken. "It's exactly what I'd hoped to avoid. I should never have asked you all over here tonight. I should have been more persistent myself, gotten to the bottom of things."

"You were only trying to be supportive," Jess said, reaching for her grandmother's frail hand.

"That's right, Ma," Mick told her. "Don't

blame yourself for caring." He turned back to Abby. "Do you have any idea what's going on with Bree?"

"I do, but I'm thinking it might be best if you convince her to tell you. If I blab, it'll just be one more thing she can hold against me."

Mick didn't have the kind of patience it might take to wheedle the information out of Bree, but he knew Abby was right. She wouldn't appreciate her big sister filling them all in. He pushed aside his plate, stood up, then leaned down to kiss Nell on the forehead. "Stop worrying, Ma. I'll get to the bottom of this. I promise." He glanced at his daughters. "Finish your dinner. I'll sit outside until Bree gets back."

On the porch, he settled back to wait, lighting the pipe that he only rarely smoked these days. The scent of the tobacco still carried him back to the days when his father would take him along to a pub on one of their trips to Ireland to visit distant relatives. In those noisy, crowded neighborhood pubs, before Ireland's laws changed, thick smoke filled the air, which usually made him cough, but he could always pick out the slightly sweet scent of his father's pipe. Tonight he found the aroma oddly comforting.

"Dad, you know perfectly well you shouldn't be smoking, not even a pipe," Bree said as she climbed the steps and settled into the rocking chair next to his. "You only do it when you're upset or trying to recapture old memories. Which is it to-night?"

He gave her a wry look. "Do you really need to ask?"

"If you're waiting for me to apologize for running off, I won't," she said.

"I'm not expecting you to. I would like it, though, if you'd tell me what's going on. I'm your father. I'd like to fix things, if I can."

She laughed at that. "When have you ever been around to fix things?" she asked, then regarded him apologetically. "Sorry, that's not fair. You were here when we were little, but this isn't a scraped knee that needs a bandage and a kiss."

Mick felt a sharp stab of guilt at the ac-curacy of her assessment. He felt awkward and out of his element, but he'd resolved not long ago to try to fix things not just with

Megan but with his entire family. He'd made strides with Abby and Jess, though there was still a long way to go. Now was as good a time as any to start with Bree.

He puffed on his pipe, then met her gaze. "Fair enough," he told her. "But I'd like to make up for all the times I wasn't around, put the two of us on a new footing. At the very least I can listen. I'll offer advice, if you want to hear it. You can always ignore it if you don't like it. That would fit the family pattern. O'Briens seem to be genetically predisposed to carving out their own path in the world, regardless of the wisdom of those who've gone before. I respect that."

He waited for a response. She seemed to be weighing his offer, perhaps trying to decide if she could trust his promise to respect her decision.

Maybe because he'd never been a patient man or maybe because he needed her to see that he had some insight that she might not be crediting him with, he finally cut into the silence.

"You've left Demming, haven't you?"

Her eyes widened. "How did you know that? Did Abby tell you?"

"Abby refused to say a word after she came back from the beach. And it wasn't so much that I knew anything. I suppose I was just hoping that was the case."

She frowned at his statement. "You didn't like him?"

"Hated him, as a matter of fact."

She looked startled. "But you never said a word."

"You're a grown woman. Some mistakes are yours to make."

"And you thought Marty was a mistake," she said, still sounding just a little stunned. "Why?"

"He was condescending to you," he said simply. "No man has a right to talk to anyone the way he spoke to you. The only thing I found more offensive was that you took it as long as you did."

She sucked in a breath at the gentle scolding. "I admired him," she admitted in a small, humiliated voice that made Mick want to draw her into his arms and tell her she was worth a thousand Martin Demmings. "And he wasn't always like that. He taught me so much, Dad. He really did. And when he wanted to be charming, no one could possibly resist, least of all me. I suppose I craved the kind of attention he lavished on me at the beginning."

"And now you've seen him for what he is," he told her. "Good for you."

She smiled then, and she was his little girl again, basking in his praise. Seeing the way her eyes lit up, he had to ask himself what the hell he'd been thinking by staying away so much that any of his kids had lost confidence in themselves. There wasn't a one of them—even Jess with her ADD—who wasn't smart and strong and talented, each in their own unique way.

Unfortunately, Megan had taken off and he'd lost himself in work. He'd left it to his mother to teach the kids to value themselves. He knew without a doubt Nell O'Brien had done that in every way she knew how, but obviously it hadn't been enough for Bree to counter being all but abandoned by both her parents during those critical early teen years. She'd been easy prey for a man like Demming.

"So, is it just breaking up with Demming that has you so miserable?" he asked.

"I'm not miserable," she immediately said with a lightning-quick flash of heat.

"Okay, you're the expert when it comes

to words. You tell me the right one to describe your mood."

She considered the question, her expression thoughtful. "Lost," she said eventually. "Gram said that a few days ago and she got it exactly right."

"Why would a woman who's making a name for herself in the career she chose be feeling lost?" he asked, trying to make sense of it.

"Because the name I'm making isn't that great anymore," she admitted.

"You got rave reviews for that first play of yours," Mick reminded her. "There was even talk about taking it to New York."

"And then the second play didn't do so well, and the third one bombed," she said, her voice empty of emotion.

"Then you'll write a fourth," he said confidently. "Better than the first one."

Bree shook her head. "Not now. My heart's just not in it. I need to start over, try something new." Her gaze met his. "Which is why I rented a space on Main Street and plan to open a flower shop in it."

Mick couldn't have been more stunned or dismayed if she'd announced an intention to take up pole dancing. Not that there was anything at all wrong with owning a flower shop—or pole dancing, for that matter, if one was so inclined—but Bree's talents lay elsewhere. So did her heart, no matter how wounded she was feeling at the moment.

He knew, though, that he had to tread carefully. After all, he'd promised to limit his advice and to accept her decisions.

"Are you sure you want to make such a drastic change?"

She nodded, her expression eager. "I really do." She must have seen the skeptical look he hadn't been able to hide, because she added, "I know what you're thinking, but I can keep my laptop in the back room, write whenever I have some free time."

"Bree, honey, I know those Main Street leases are for two years. That's a long time to be tied down."

"I prefer to think of it as having some stability in my life," she countered.

"Flowers," he said, then shook his head. "You're sure you'll be happy fiddling with a bunch of posies?"

"Marty asked the exact same thing," she said, giving him a pointed look that made him cringe. "And the answer is that I think so. There's only one way to find out for certain."

"Okay, then," he said, concluding she needed support and practical thinking, not criticism, right now. "How much of your trust-fund money are you putting into this? I don't want to see you lose that nest egg."

She frowned at that. "Thanks for the vote of confidence, Dad."

"I didn't mean it that way."

"Yes, you did," she said. "And it's okay. It just makes me want to work harder to prove you wrong. Besides, I thought you always said that you put the money into those funds so we'd be able to buy a house or start a business when the time came. That's all I'm doing."

"Then I don't have a leg to stand on, do I?" he said, relenting. "You'll tell me what I can do to help. I'll come down there with you tomorrow, if you want me to. I can help you figure out any construction you'll need, custom cabinets for supplies, a front desk, an island workspace in back. Whatever you want, that'll be my gift to you."

"The trust fund was more than enough," she objected.

"I bought that fancy stove for Jess. A few cabinets and storage nooks and crannies is the least I can do for you. Or would you rather have me buy you one of those big coolers that they keep the flowers in?"

She hesitated, then asked, "Would you build the cabinets yourself?"

He recognized what she was really asking. Would he be right there, spending time with her, making himself a part of this crazy new project of hers?

"I have crews that are better at this than I am," he told her. Her immediate expression of dismay told him he'd been right about what she really wanted, so he quickly added, "But if you don't mind that things might be less than perfect, I suppose I can still find my way around with a few tools and some wood."

She jumped up and threw her arms around him, the way she had when she was little and he'd just come home from a business trip. "I want you to do it," she said, giving him an exuberant kiss on the cheek. "Then I'll be able to tell everyone who comes in that the interior was handbuilt by the famed architect Mick O'Brien. If you're involved, it's going to be amazing,

I just know it. Heck, one of these days my shop could qualify to be put on the National Register of Historic Places."

"More like a few hundred years," he retorted. "And that's assuming someone doesn't come along after the two of us are dead and tear them out so they can sell hot dogs."

She laughed at that, her entire demeanor suddenly carefree. Mick didn't kid himself that it would be that easy to wipe away all the hits she'd taken in Chicago, but if opening a flower shop could put that kind of sparkle in her eyes even for a little while, he was not going to be the one to question it.

Jake, Will and Mack were having lunch at Sally's when he noticed his friends exchanging meaningful looks, which could only mean they had something to say about Bree and they weren't sure how he was going to react.

He set down his BLT and frowned at them. "Just say it," he ordered. "What have you heard about Bree that you think I haven't?"

"She's staying in town," Will said, his expression sympathetic. "Sorry, pal. I know that's going to be tough on you."

Jake shrugged as if it were of no importance. "Yeah, she mentioned something about that when I talked to her."

"You talked to her?" Mack said incredulously. "You had an actual conversation with Bree O'Brien, the woman of your dreams, the woman you've never gotten out of your head?"

"And you never said a word to us?" Will added, radiating indignation. "Didn't you think it was worth a mention, at least?"

"Not really."

"When did this happen?" Mack asked.

"What did she say?" Will wanted to know.

"And what did you say to her?" Mack asked.

Jake shook his head. "You two sound like a couple of amateur reporters for the local weekly. It was no big deal." Which, of course, was the biggest whopper he'd ever uttered as an adult.

"Do you believe him?" Will asked Mack.

"Not for one second. He's either delusional or putting on a show for our benefit."

"I thought Will was the shrink," Jake said irritably to Mack. "Now you're one, too?"

"I'm as intuitive as the next guy," Mack responded.

"Which means not at all," Jake snapped back. "Can we drop this?"

"Since you and Bree are so chummy again all of a sudden, do you know what she's planning to do?" Will asked Jake.

"She mentioned she might stick around. That was the sum total of the conversation. Believe me, I had no interest in having a long heart-to-heart with her." Sleeping with her, now that interested him, but he was pretty sure this was the worst possible time to mention that.

"I might know something," Mack admitted. "I was with Susie the other night."

Jake and Will both stared at him with shock.

"You and Susie O'Brien? Since when?" Will demanded.

"It wasn't a big deal," Mack said, though the faint reddening of his ears said otherwise. "I ran into her. We had a couple of drinks."

"Well, well, well," Jake began, amused. "And you two thought I was holding out.

Last time I checked, Susie O'Brien had told you hell would freeze over before she ever accepted a date with the likes of you."

"Which is why this wasn't a date," Mack explained patiently. "It was a couple of drinks. Not a date."

"Who paid?" Will asked.

"I did," Mack said. "What kind of man do you think I am?"

Jake lifted a brow at that, but Will was grinning.

"Sounds like a date to me," Will said. He glanced at Jake. "You?"

"I'd call it a date," Jake concurred, so happy to have the attention shifted to another of the O'Brien women he would have called it anything anyone wanted him to just to prolong the conversation.

Mack glared at both of them. "Do you want to hear what I found out about Bree or not?"

"Not," Jake said at once.

"Don't listen to him," Will commanded. "Talk. He needs to know what's going on, whether he'll admit that or not."

"Bree rented the empty space two doors down from here. For two years."

Jake swallowed hard and tried not to let his immediate sense of panic show. Two years? A lease? This couldn't be good. He'd reconciled himself to running into her for a few more weeks, maybe even a couple of months, but he'd convinced himself she'd go running back to Chicago and her boyfriend there sooner or later. He'd banked on sooner. Later was bad. Very, very bad. Two years was an eternity of keeping his defenses up.

He bolted from the booth. "I need to get back to work," he declared, throwing a handful of bills on the table. "I'll catch you guys later."

"Well, he took that news well," Will said loudly as Jake was fleeing.

Mack's voice carried even more clearly. "No big deal, wasn't that what he said?" He laughed. "I told you the man was delusional."

Jake sighed. He wasn't delusional. He was in more trouble than he'd been in for six long years, and the only way he could think to get out of it was to get a redheaded vixen out of town before she drove him out of what was left of his ever-loving mind.

5

Megan found herself worrying about Bree for several days after Mick left. It was par for the course that after not getting his way about luring her back to Chesapeake Shores, he'd forgotten all about the fact that he'd used their daughter's problems as bait. She supposed he'd call again or turn up in New York whenever it suited him, oblivious to his lack of consideration in not checking in to reassure her about Bree. Or maybe he'd assumed she would call, if she cared. It would be just like him to wait her out as some kind of perverse test.

Annoyed no matter which tactic he was employing, she picked up the phone and dialed the once-familiar number at the house in Maryland. Nell answered on the first ring. Megan could envision her in the kitchen, her morning cup of tea and a freshly baked scone in front of her.

Oh, how she'd missed those scones and their morning chats when she'd fled to New York. Before that, when Nell had been living in her own small cottage designed by Mick, she'd walked over nearly every day with freshly baked scones for the two of them to share while they talked about anything and everything.

Nell had been far more than a mother-in-law. She'd been a friend, though the one topic that had been off-limits was Megan's frustration with Mick's increasingly long absences. Nell would have understood, but Megan hadn't felt it fair to drag her into the middle of their problems.

Instead, she'd wound up leaving Nell to care for her children. It had never been her intention, but she couldn't help noting the irony in it.

"Megan!" Nell said, sounding vaguely

wary, but definitely not surprised. "How are you?"

"Doing well, and you?"

"Never better. I imagine you called to speak to . . ." Her voice trailed off.

Megan chuckled at her confusion. "It is a puzzle, isn't it?" she replied. "It's not as though I've stayed in touch with anyone there in any sort of predictable way."

"The truth is, at first I assumed you'd called to speak to Abby, but of course you'd call her on her cell or at the new house or at her office. Is it Mick you're calling for?"

"Actually, I wanted to talk to you," Megan said, deciding to take advantage of the opportunity that had presented itself. She wanted to make amends to this woman who'd always been so kind to her. The overture was long overdue. "We didn't get much time alone when I was there for the opening of the inn. You were unhappy I'd come, weren't you?"

"At first," Nell admitted in her typically blunt way. "But the visit went smoothly enough. I saw you were making an effort."

"I was. I wanted it to be a first step with

my children and with you. I know you were furious with me when I divorced Mick and left town."

"Not furious," Nell claimed. "Disappointed, and it was about the children, not me or even my son. I knew as well as anyone why you felt you needed to leave Mick. It saddened me that it had to come to that, but I couldn't blame you."

"Have I ever told you how grateful I am that the children had you?"

"They should have had their mother," Nell said fiercely.

Though the remark stung, Megan agreed with her. "Yes, they should have. And I wanted them here, you do know that, don't you?" she said, a pleading note in her voice. Nell O'Brien had mattered to her, and she'd always regretted losing that connection along with the rest of her family, to say nothing of losing the older woman's approval.

"Seemed to me it was a halfhearted effort at best," Nell said, not conceding an inch.

"I can't deny it looked that way. Somehow I let Mick convince me they were better off with the two of you," Megan explained. "I didn't fight him and I should have. Once I was settled here, I should have fought tooth and nail for joint custody at the very least. I know that now, but my visits there were such disasters, no matter how often I came or how hard I tried, it seemed best to let them stay where they were happy."

"Children don't always know what we're thinking. They only understand our actions," Nell reminded her.

"Believe me, I know that. And the message I sent to all of them was that I didn't care, when that was the furthest thing from the truth."

Now that the door had been opened, Megan poured out all the things she'd felt back then. "I loved them so much I couldn't bring myself to rip them from the life they'd known. I thought visits to me in New York would help make them feel part of my life here, but they were all so angry, none of them wanted to come and, when I insisted, they were sullen. Mick was so sure they'd come around if we gave them time. Instead, it allowed their wounds to fester. They ended up hating me."

The explanation—too little and much

too late—was received in silence. "Spilt milk," Nell said eventually. "You and Abby have found a way back to each other. You'll do the same with the rest of them."

"I hope so. And that's the other reason I was calling. Mick told me there's something going on with Bree. Do you know anything about that?"

"A bit, but she just walked into the kitchen. Why don't I let you speak to her." Nell's next words were muffled, but then she said, "You take care of yourself, Megan love. And come back soon for another visit. You're welcome here anytime."

Megan's eyes filled with tears at the sincerity she heard in those words. "You have no idea how much it means to me to have you say that. I miss you, Nell. I really do."

"Then you'll pay us a visit soon. Now, here's Bree."

There was a pause and then Bree came on the line, her voice cool and clipped. "Hello, Mother."

"How are you?" Megan asked, treading carefully. If she plunged right in with too many questions, she knew how quickly Bree was likely to end the call. There'd been too many other conversations over the years that hadn't lasted past the pleasantries.

"Fine," Bree said, her tone unyielding.

"Are you enjoying your time in Chesapeake Shores?"

"Sure. It feels good to be home."

"How much longer do you think you'll be there?"

"Actually I'm home for good," Bree said. "Look, Mother, I'm really busy, so unless there's something specific on your mind, I need to go."

Bree's calm announcement that she was staying in Chesapeake Shores stirred a hundred questions, none of which her daughter was likely to answer in a hurried phone call.

"I'll let you go then," Megan said reluctantly, then added, "Bree, if you're not going back to Chicago right away, you could come to New York for a visit." She warmed to the idea. "We could see some plays together. I know how much the theater means to you. It would be fun."

"Sorry, I don't have the time right now," Bree said, slamming the door on the idea. "Goodbye, Mother."

She cut off the call before Megan could

attempt to persuade her to make the trip or even to say goodbye. The abrupt and unsatisfying conversation wasn't really unexpected, just disappointing.

It did accomplish one thing, though. Despite the fact that she was hardly an expert on Bree's moods these days, even she could tell there was something wrong, and it was more than a lack of desire to chat with her mother. So, Mick and Nell had been right to be worried. She was, as well. Maybe time and her actions had stripped her of the right to her anxiety, but it was there just the same.

Her first priority when she arrived at her job at the gallery where she'd been working for the past fifteen years was to arrange for some time off. Once again, she'd be making a trip to Chesapeake Shores. Since the visit for the opening of Jess's inn had broken the ice for these recent drop-ins, the prospect didn't scare the living daylights out of her the way that one had.

The prospect of seeing Mick, however, did send a shiver down her spine. Fear? Anticipation? It was getting harder and harder to tell.

* * *

Bree carefully replaced the receiver after speaking to her mother and would have walked right out of the kitchen if Gram hadn't ordered her to sit.

"I've poured you a cup of tea, and there are fresh orange-cranberry scones on the stove," Gram said as she gestured toward a seat at the table.

Bree hesitated, wanting to bolt, but mostly wanting to avoid a discussion about her mother. "I really need to get over to the shop. There are a million plans that have to be made." After doing just a few days of research, she was already starting to feel a little overwhelmed by how much she didn't know.

"Your plans can wait a few extra minutes," Gram said. "I know I won't be able to talk you into the kind of breakfast you should have, but you can stay long enough to share a cup of tea and some conversation with me."

"I don't mind the tea," Bree replied. "It's the conversation I'd rather not have."

"Now, that's a fine thing to be saying to your grandmother," Gram said, lapsing into an Irish lilt that came mostly from being raised in a home with two parents who'd come over straight from Dublin. Gram herself had grown up right here in Maryland.

"Sorry," Bree apologized. "I just don't want to talk about Mother."

"You were rude to her just now," Gram chided.

"I don't know how else to be with her. She left us years ago. Am I supposed to forget that?"

"Of course not, but you seem to have forgotten that she tried repeatedly to get you to New York, either to stay or for a visit. You refused and your father allowed you to get away with that." Gram gave her a penetrating look. "You know, of all of you children, you're the one I would have thought would jump at the chance to go to New York. Isn't that the ideal place for an aspiring playwright to be? Yet, when the time came, you went off to Chicago. You settled for regional theater, rather than taking your mother up on her offer to let you stay with her while you studied with some of the country's best playwrights. Did you hate her more than you wanted your dream?"

Bree hesitated before answering. She'd

never hated her mother, not really. She'd been as angry as the rest of them, but the truth was, Megan's absence had caused hardly more than a blip in Bree's life. Whatever pain she'd felt had been channeled into her writing. It was one of those life experiences a good writer could weave into a story.

"I had an offer to study in Chicago," she said eventually, defending her decision to take the internship with Marty. "Something concrete."

"So it was safety you were after?" Gram asked, her tone skeptical. "And New York would have been a risk?"

"Something like that," Bree said. Risks were something the rest of the family craved. She preferred predictability.

"Okay, then," Gram said. "Let me ask you one last thing, and then I'll let the subject drop. Was the real risk that you wouldn't be able to make it in New York? Or that you'd get close to Megan and find your heart broken again?" Her gaze met Bree's and held. "Or were you really afraid you'd finally have to let go of all that anger that had been bottled up inside for so many years?"

Tears stung her eyes. Her grandmother knew her so well. Better than anyone else. Even now she didn't wait for Bree's answer.

"You can deny the anger all you like, but keep in mind that anger can become its own driving force," Nell told her. "It's not healthy, child. You have to let it go, or it will eat you alive and ruin your life. What Megan did all those years ago was wrong. You can decide it's unforgivable and go right on hating her, or you can reach out and accept the olive branch she's been offering. I think you'll be happier in the long run if that's what you do, but it's your decision. Just make sure you understand the consequences—not for her, but for you—before you drive her out of your life forever."

Bree frowned at the advice. "Why should I make it easy for her?" she asked bitterly.

"You don't have to," Gram said mildly. "But I can see which way the wind is blowing around here. I think she and your father are making peace. She's become a part of Abby's life already, and she's reached out to Jess, you and Connor now. If you reject her out of spite, you could wake one day and find yourself on the outside." She touched Bree's hand. "I don't want that for you. For all your stubborn O'Brien independence, I think you need family, perhaps even more than the rest of us."

Bree didn't want to admit Gram might be right. She certainly didn't want to confess how disturbing she found the prospect of everyone else reuniting and leaving her behind.

"I'll think about what you said," she promised eventually. Standing, she bent over and kissed Gram on the cheek. "Love you."

Gram's hand found hers and squeezed. "And I you. Never, ever forget that."

Bree left the kitchen with a lot on her mind, troubling thoughts she didn't especially want to deal with. Thankfully, though, she had a long, long list of things to do. Maybe that would drive all those dark thoughts right out of her mind.

"No, no, no," Bree muttered a few hours later as she hung up the phone. Why hadn't she made this one call before she'd gone off and signed a lease to open a flower shop? It wasn't like she could back out now. There were too many people—okay, Abby mostly—awaiting her failure for that to be an option.

"What's the problem?" Jess asked, regarding her with concern.

Bree had set up a temporary office at the inn, while the painters and Mick were working on the shop. As much as she'd wanted to spend the extra time with her father, the noise level made it impossible to make all the phone calls that needed to be made. She could have made them at home, but this was better. It gave her a few hours a day with Jess, and she'd discovered she liked having someone around with whom she could discuss ideas for the business. Jess had learned a lot about starting something new, had made more than her share of mistakes along the way. She wouldn't judge Bree for making a few, as well.

"This day just keeps getting better and better," she muttered. "First I had to deal with Mom."

Jess's eyes widened. "You talked to Mother?"

Bree nodded. "She called the house."

"For you or Dad?"

Bree hesitated. "Me, I think. At least Gram handed the phone to me the second I walked into the kitchen." Thinking about what Gram had said earlier, she frowned at her sister. "Do you really think she and Dad could patch things up?"

"If you'd asked me that a few months ago, I'd have said hell would freeze over first, but after seeing them together the night of the opening party here, I honestly don't know. Anything's possible."

"How do you feel about that?" Bree asked her.

Jess hesitated, her expression thoughtful. "Weird, I guess."

"Me, too," Bree admitted.

Jess gave a dramatic shudder. "Let's not talk about Mom and Dad getting back together. Who was that on the phone just now and what did they say to upset you?"

"I've just discovered that there is one major flower wholesaler close enough to supply the store," she reported to her sister, not even trying to mask her dismay. This was an unexpected and very unwelcome wrinkle.

"So what?" Jess asked. "As long as

they're good, you'll be fine. Are you worried that the prices will be higher because it's virtually a monopoly or something?"

"I'm worried because that wholesaler is Jake Collins," she snapped. "Why didn't you tell me he now owns Shores Nursery and Landscaping?"

Jess blinked at her tone. "Hey, don't jump on me. I thought you knew. He's worked there forever, even when you were going out."

"There's a huge difference between him working there and owning the place. And as I recall, they didn't operate as a wholesaler back then. Now he's apparently one of the biggest growers around here, too. What's he doing, taking over the flower world, acre by acre?"

Jess shrugged. "I don't see why any of that matters. It's been years since you two split up. You're both adults. This is business. Surely you can be civilized."

Bree wasn't so sure of that. Their last encounter had been anything but civilized. She'd expected a little anger, but not the heat radiating off Jake in waves that could have roasted marshmallows.

"It will be awkward," she said finally in

what was the most massive understatement she'd ever uttered.

"Then don't deal with him," Jess suggested, still unconcerned. "As big as the business is now, he probably has plenty of people working for him. Deal with one of them. He's usually out on jobs anyway. I see him all over the place." She grinned. "He looks really, really fine, by the way."

Bree knew, though she had no intention of acknowledging just how fine she thought he looked. This situation was disastrous enough as it was. If Jess or anyone else in the family thought there was so much as an ember of that relationship that wasn't stone cold, they might try to fan it back to life.

"I can't avoid him. It seems I have to deal directly with *Mr. Collins* if I want to open an account. *Mr. Collins* makes those arrangements. *Mr. Collins* decides if Shores Nursery can accommodate another wholesale customer. If not, she's sure *Mr. Collins* would be happy to recommend an alternative, although there's no other grower or supplier half as good within a fifty-mile radius. I wanted to reach through the phone and strangle her perky little neck."

Jess stared at her. "Okay, Bree, what's

really going on here? Is this just about some kind of old news between you and Jake?"

Bree regarded her blankly. "Of course, what else could it be?"

"I'm not sure, but to tell you the truth, for a second there, you sounded a little jealous."

"Jealous? That's ridiculous." She frowned. "It's just that this woman sounded so, I don't know, adoring. It made me a little crazy."

"I'll say," Jess confirmed. "What I don't get is why. I thought you were the one who dumped him."

"It wasn't exactly like that," Bree said.

Interest sparked in Jess's eyes. "Then what was it like?"

Bree sighed. "Never mind. You said it. It's old news. I'll figure out some way to deal with Jake to get the flowers I need."

Of course, that assumed that if she ever succeeded in getting past his obviously protective gatekeeper, *Mr. Collins* would even give her the time of day.

Jake crumpled up the fifth message he'd had from Bree in two days and tossed it in the trash can. He scowled when he realized that Connie had caught him doing it. She marched into his office, a lecture clearly on the tip of her tongue.

"Don't start with me," he warned.

"You need to call her back," she told him in her oh-so-patient mother-hen voice.

"I don't have to do anything," he said grimly.

"Now, there's the mature reaction I'd expect from someone your age," she commented. "Let me rephrase. You need to call her back if you expect me keep working here, brother dear. I'm getting tired of trying to fend Bree off, much less pretending that I don't know perfectly well who she is and why you're avoiding her. If she ever recognizes my voice, she's going to start asking a whole bunch of questions I don't want to answer. You don't pay me enough to run interference between you and Bree."

"I'm paying you enough to get your daughter through college, which is more than anyone else would," he retorted. "She starts next year, if I recall correctly. How's that tuition money adding up? Can you afford to walk out on me?"

She gave him a sour look. "Sometimes

it is very hard for me to understand why Mom always liked you best. You are not a nice man."

"But I am a very good brother," he teased. Because of that, she knew he would never, ever fire her, despite his constant threats. And she wouldn't quit for the same reason. Connie's ex-husband paid decent alimony and child support, but Jake considered it his responsibility to see that she and Jenny had whatever else they needed.

"You're an annoyance," she retorted.

"But you love me, anyway," he said. His expression sobered. "Please, keep Bree away from me. Consider it your personal mission."

"Assistants aren't allowed personal missions," she retorted.

"But sisters are."

"Jake, you're the one who made the rule about not taking on any new wholesale customers unless you personally approve it. You said we only have so much stock available and you don't want to get overextended and wind up disappointing a good customer. Do I not have that right?"

His expression brightened. "That's it.

Call her back and tell her we've talked. You can explain that unfortunately, due to huge demand, we're not taking on anyone else right now."

"But the florist in Myrtle Creek just closed," she reminded him. "Jensen's was one of our bigger accounts. If Bree's done her homework, she's going to know that."

"What makes you think she's done her homework?" he asked wearily. "Last time I checked, she was writing plays, not running any kind of business."

"And last time I checked, she was the smartest woman you've ever known. She's certainly smart enough to ask around about the best suppliers in the region. I'll bet that's exactly how she got our name. Ted Jensen probably recommended us when he decided to retire after his heart attack."

Okay, that was possible, but not insurmountable. "If she brings that up, tell her we'd only kept supplying Ted because he'd been a customer for years."

Connie rolled her eyes. "That ought to go over well. How on earth will it look if we refuse to supply a new business right here in Chesapeake Shores, a business owned by an O'Brien, no less? You'll never hear the end of it. The chamber of commerce will be all over you. And if you think there was talk when you and Bree broke up, it'll be nothing compared to the speculation that would stir up."

They were still debating the point when the door to the outer office snapped open and Bree strode through and straight into his office. She was wearing shorts that made her legs look endless and a halter top that made his mouth water. Strands of curly auburn hair had sprung free of the knot on her head and with the sunlight behind her, it looked as if she was on fire. The color was high in her cheeks, as well. She was not a happy woman. Jake braced himself to deal with all that heat and sexiness and walk away unscathed.

"If the mountain won't come . . ." Her voice trailed off as she spotted his sister.

"Connie, hi," she said. Unmistakable relief spread across her face as something else apparently registered. "Oh my gosh, you're the one I've been talking to on the phone all this time. I'm so sorry. I should have recognized your voice. Why didn't you say something?"

Connie grinned. “Frankly, I was just as glad you didn’t. I really didn’t want to get caught between you and this hardhead over here. Now you two can battle this out between yourselves. I’m going home to cook dinner.” She gave her brother a smug look. “Shall I make a plate of humble pie for you? Or will you be making other plans for dinner?” She glanced pointedly at Bree when she said it.

“I already have dinner plans,” he retorted. As of two minutes ago, he planned to drink it.

6

"You've been avoiding me," Bree accused, sitting across from Jake, her shorts hiking up. She hadn't worn such a revealing outfit deliberately, but judging from the rapt gaze on Jake's face, she was glad she had. At this point she was willing to take advantage of any edge she had. Maybe that didn't speak well of her as a woman, but she was desperate. After a week, it had become clear that Jake was even less anxious to deal with her than she was with him. Both of them had to find a way to suck it up and figure out a way to conduct business.

"Have not," he muttered. "I've been busy."

"Well, you don't appear to be busy right this second," she said cheerfully. "So let's make this deal now and I'll get out of your hair. Unless you drive the delivery truck, you'll never have to deal directly with me again."

His jaw hardened. "There's not going to be any deal, Bree. Not between us."

She leveled a look directly into his eyes. "This is business, Jake. I'm not asking you to go out with me or to trust me or to have any kind of personal contact beyond whatever it takes to get this agreement on paper. It's simple. I'm opening a flower shop. You sell flowers. It's pretty cut-and-dried."

"Nothing with us was ever simple or cut-and-dried," he said, walking slowly around his desk to perch on the edge. Their knees were almost touching, hers bare, his clad in faded denim. "It's bound to get complicated faster than the ink will dry on our agreement."

She swallowed hard, but managed to keep her voice steady. "How so?"

He leaned forward, oh so slowly, until her pulse fluttered wildly at the nearness of his mouth. It hovered over hers. Their breath intermingled. Suddenly she wanted his lips on hers with an urgency that took her by surprise. Memories of a hundred other kisses—deep, tantalizing, soul-stirring kisses—swarmed in her head and left her dizzy. What had made her think for a single second that this kind of sizzle could be doused by simple determination?

As if he sensed her turmoil, he drew back, his expression smug. “See what I mean?”

Oh yeah, this definitely had *complication* written all over it. But she couldn’t let that stand in her way. She wouldn’t. Flowers on Main was going to be her fresh start. She’d do whatever it took to make it a success.

Jake had obviously made a success of his business. She’d been astonished by the size of the nursery, a little awed by everything she’d heard when she’d asked around about the best flower supplier in the region. Seeing it today with its greenhouse, outdoor displays of flats and flats of colorful plants, rows of flowering shrubs and trees, had been an eye-opener. This wasn’t the tiny Shores Nursery of old. Jake had expanded it beyond her wildest expectations. Given what he'd accomplished, surely he could understand why her new business mattered just as much to her.

"I need these flowers, Jake," she said simply.

"Get them from someone else. There are other growers."

"Everyone says you're the best. And you're the closest."

"I'm also unavailable."

"Are you speaking personally now, or professionally?"

He frowned at her flip attempt at humor. "Both, just to keep the record straight."

"That kiss that almost happened said otherwise."

"It didn't happen, did it?"

"All that proves is that you've got great willpower. I'm duly impressed. In fact, a man with that much willpower surely won't be tempted to ravish me just because I get a few posies from him every few days, so there's really no reason not to deal with me, is there?"

"How about I don't want to? Do you have an argument for that?"

"Because you're scared," she accused.

"Of you? Don't be ridiculous."

"Prove it."

His eyes widened. "You're making this a challenge?"

"Why not?" she asked with a careless shrug. "Let's see if you've got what it takes to stay away from me, Jake. Make this deal. Deliver the flowers personally. And keep your hands to yourself. That will suit me just fine. I can prove I only care about business, and you can prove you're over me. Sounds like a win-win to me."

She saw him struggle with himself. He clearly wanted to show her that she no longer meant anything to him, that he was well and truly done with her. But he also knew he didn't stand a chance of making good on it. Whatever there'd once been between them, it was still there. The air was practically humming with it.

And, based on the obvious inner struggle he was waging, it apparently still had the power to rip his heart out for a second time. No wonder he wanted to stay as far away from her as humanly possible. She could hardly blame him. She was more than a little shaken at the moment herself. She was supposed to be mourning the end of her relationship with Marty, not stirring up old feelings with Jake.

"Okay," he said at last. He moved behind the desk, shoved a few stacks of catalogs and papers aside, shuffled through another one and then handed her a form. "Fill out this credit application. Drop it off with Connie in the morning. I'll waive the payable on delivery clause that's standard for new customers for the first year. We'll bill you every thirty days."

"Don't do me any favors," she said.

"I'm not. I know your credit will check out. That's all I care about. When are you opening?"

He was all business now, which should have made her ecstatic, but she couldn't help being a little bit annoyed. She had to force herself to match his cool tone. "The first Saturday in September, in time for the Labor Day–weekend crowds."

"I'll see that you get your first delivery before nine o'clock that Friday morning. I'll need to know what you want on the Monday before, earlier if there's something that has to come from another grower. Connie will see that you have a list each week of what's available. If you need deliveries more than once a week, we'll adjust the schedule. Or you can come by here to get what you need to fill in."

"Thank you."

"Like you said, it's business. Don't read anything into it. Close the door on your way out."

She frowned at the dismissal, but she knew better than to try to prolong the encounter. She'd gotten what she came for.

And then some.

Jake cursed when his hand actually shook as he reached for his phone after Bree was finally out of his office. He'd been dead serious earlier when he'd decided to drink his dinner, but he wanted company. A man who could still be rattled by an ex-lover six years after the breakup was pitiful enough without turning into a solitary drinker.

If he'd ever been the type to gravitate toward willing female companionship of the kind that didn't ask questions or make demands, tonight would have been the night to seek out such a woman. Unfortunately, he'd never seen the value in simply hooking up. He'd always wanted more.

He'd wanted what he'd had with Bree. Or what he'd thought he had, anyway.

That left him with Will and Mack. And when Mack turned out to be busy, it left him with Will.

"Ground rules," he said tersely when they met in the bar at Brady's. "No questions. No trying to psychoanalyze my mood. We are here to drink. Okay?"

Will gave him a knowing look. "You must have had one hell of a meeting with Bree today."

Jake scowled at him. "No questions. Didn't I make that clear?"

Will grinned. "You did. And if Ms. Davis, our English teacher, were here, she'd explain to you that the sentence I just uttered was a statement, not a question. Bree O'Brien is the only person I know who can put you into this kind of mood."

Jake downed half his beer. "Okay, wise guy, I know I told you not to try to psychoanalyze my mood. I was very clear about that."

"But this is so much fun," Will retorted. "Your love life is much more interesting than watching the Orioles blow another lead, which they're doing, by the way." He gestured toward the TV above the bar, his expression mournful. “How can they do that night after night?”

“Because they’re having a lousy season,” Jake said, warming to the safe topic. “The pitching sucks. The bullpen’s worse.”

“Can’t argue with you there,” Will agreed just as Mack joined them.

Jake stared at him. “I thought you had a date.”

“It wasn’t a date,” Mack said, his expression sour.

“Which means he was out with Susie O’Brien again,” Will said.

Mack scowled at the assessment, but Jake chuckled. “Don’t mind him. Will thinks he has a deep understanding of our sad love lives. Of course, that raises the question of why he doesn’t have a love life of his own to worry about.”

“I had a date just last night,” Will said indignantly. “A real one, not like whatever’s going on between you two and the women you maybe are and maybe aren’t dating.”

Mack’s expression brightened. “Do tell,” he said. “Give us a shining example by which we can live our lives.”

Will frowned. “Mock me if you will, but

this could be the one. This was our fourth date in two weeks."

Jake and Mack exchanged a look. Will rarely went out with the same woman more than twice. Either he got bored or they got tired of having him analyze them. In one instance, when he'd gone out for two months with the same woman, he'd belatedly realized she'd actually been using him for free counseling. He'd sworn off dating for months after that.

Just as Mack was about to speak, Will stopped him. "Don't worry. This isn't another Jasmine. In fact, Laura's a psychologist, too. She has a practice in Annapolis. She just bought a weekend place here."

"And this is the first we've heard about her?" Jake chided. "Are we not your best friends? Aren't you supposed to run something this serious past us?"

"No," Will said succinctly. "You're my best friends, but you don't have veto power over the women in my life."

"I'll remind you of that next time you try to exercise your veto power over the women in mine," Mack grumbled.

"I'd never veto Susie," Will told him.

"I'm not dating Susie," Mack repeated.

Jake nudged Will in the ribs. “Protesting too much, wouldn’t you say?”

“I would,” Will agreed, clinking his beer bottle to Jake’s.

Mack looked as if he might want to crack his beer bottle over one of their heads, but instead, he took a long drink, then regarded Jake innocently.

“So why are we here? Does this have something to do with Bree?”

“I’m guessing yes,” Will said. “Jake’s not talking, though.”

“Because there’s nothing to say,” Jake insisted.

Because they’d each ruled out further discussion of the women in their lives, they fell silent. Sipping their beers, they turned their attention to the game just in time to see the relief pitcher walk in the other team’s winning run.

“Orioles suck,” Mack said.

Will nodded.

“You got that right,” Jake said, then sighed. It pretty well described the way his whole day had gone.

The smell of freshly cut wood filled the air inside what would soon be Flowers on

Main. Bree stood back and admired the stainless steel–topped island that would be her primary work space in the backroom. It had nooks and crannies and drawers for storing vases, boxes, ribbons, wire, florist tape and anything else she might need to create spectacular arrangements.

"What do you think?" Mick asked, standing beside her. "Is it what you had in mind?"

She turned and threw her arms around him. "It's perfect, Dad. Thank you so much. I can't believe you were able to create that from the scribbles I gave you."

He laughed. "Believe me, it wasn't the scribbles. It was the way you described what you needed for it to be functional. Running over to Ted Jensen's place one morning helped, too. I figured after all the years he's been in business, he'd know what you'd need."

"Since he's closing down, I probably should have bought his furnishings instead of having you go to all this trouble," Bree said.

"Absolutely not," Mick countered. "You're starting out fresh. Everything should be top-notch. I did make an offer on his coolers, though. Told him I'd need to run that by you, but they're in good condition and it'll save you some start-up money."

Bree bristled that he'd done such a thing without asking her, then realized she was being silly. He'd left the final decision to her, after all. If Mick had made a contact that could save her money, she needed to consider it. "I'll go and take a look later today," she promised.

"Okay, then, let's take another look at this floor plan," Mick said. "I want you to show me again where you think the front counter ought to be."

They started into the front room just as the door opened and Megan stepped inside. Bree wasn't sure which of them was more shocked, her or her father.

"Megan!" Mick said, his face lighting up. "I wasn't expecting you. Bree, honey, did you know your mother was coming?"

"No," she said tersely, watching as Mick crossed the room and pressed a kiss to her mother's cheek.

"How could I stay away when I heard about your new business, Bree?" Megan said, giving Mick a pointed look that Bree couldn't quite interpret.

"Well, I'd stay and show you around," Bree said, "but as you can tell, there's not much to see and I have to drive over to Myrtle Creek."

She was almost out the door, when she realized Megan was on her heels.

"Why don't I ride along with you," Megan said, her expression suggesting she wasn't about to take no for an answer.

Bree gritted her teeth. "Up to you," she said and went to her car. "Are you sure you wouldn't rather get settled after your trip down from New York? You'll be staying at the inn again, right?"

"I'm thinking about staying at the house, but I need to discuss that with your father first," her mother replied. "You don't have any objections, do you?"

Bree shrugged. "It's not my house."

"It is your home," her mother corrected. "And your opinion does count with me."

"Then I think you should stay at the inn, assuming Jess has a room available. It's been very busy. I'll call her and check." She pulled her cell phone out of her pocket, flipped it open and dialed.

She ignored the hurt in her mother's

eyes as she waited for her sister to pick up. “Hey, Jess, this is Bree. You’ll never guess who’s here.”

“Mom,” Jess said. “Abby called me about an hour ago and told me she was coming.”

“Do you have a room available at the inn? I can bring her by right now.”

“Sorry. We’re fully booked. I told Abby the same thing. She said Mom could stay with her and the girls.”

“Perfect,” Bree said eagerly. “I’ll tell her. I can run her over there.”

“Not now. Trace is in New York for a few days, so Mom won’t be able to get in until Abby gets home from work.”

Which meant Bree would be stuck with her for the rest of the afternoon. “Wait, doesn’t Gram have a spare key to Abby’s?”

“Of course,” Jess said. “I don’t know why Abby didn’t think of that.”

“I’ll run by the house and pick it up. Bye, Jess.”

When she disconnected the call, she saw her mother regarding her with a bland expression.

“Have you palmed me off on Abby now?” she inquired lightly as Bree whipped her car out of the parking space.

"It's not like that," Bree said, but of course it was *exactly* like that and they both knew it. "I'm sorry if it sounded that way, Mom. It just seemed to make sense for you to stay there."

Because she felt guilty, she turned toward Myrtle Creek rather than going straight to Gram's. It wouldn't kill her to be polite to her mother for an hour or so.

"Since Abby's made peace with me and the rest of you haven't, that's what you mean, isn't it?" Megan said. She met Bree's gaze. "Did you know your father came to see me in New York a couple weeks ago?"

Bree swallowed hard and shook her head. "I had no idea."

"He wanted me to come back with him then."

"Why?" Bree blurted. Was Gram right? Were the two of them getting back together? Bree didn't even want to consider the possibility. Unlike her younger siblings, she'd never longed for a reconciliation.

"He wanted me to come here because of you," her mother said.

"Me, but I didn't . . ." Her voice trailed off.

"You didn't want me here," Megan finished for her. "I can see that. Your father seemed to think you might need me, whether you want me around or not. After we spoke the other day, I sensed the same thing."

"Mom, it's a little late for you to pop up and want to have heart-to-heart chats with your daughters. We all grew up without you. Gram did a good job filling in for you."

"I know that. Believe me, no one is more grateful than I am that she was here. And I don't expect any of you to bare your souls to me, but I am older and perhaps a bit wiser. I'm also a good listener, if you need to talk. Most important of all, I love you and I'd never judge you. You can tell me anything."

Bree gave her a bewildered look. "What do you think there is to tell?"

"Was there a man who sent you fleeing from Chicago?" Megan asked, her tone gentle. "Someone who broke your heart?"

"There was a man in my life there, but he's not the reason I left."

Her mother regarded her calmly, her expression patient.

"At least not the whole reason," Bree

amended. “And I really do not want to talk about Marty or Chicago. I have a whole new life stretched out in front of me. That’s what I’m focusing on.”

“And I applaud you for that. Sometimes, though, the past has a way of catching up to you.”

“Tell me about it,” Bree murmured, thinking not of Martin Demming, but of Jake.

A light sparked in Megan’s eyes. “Now, there’s definitely a story behind those words.”

“Mom, let it go, please. I don’t need or want your motherly concern. I don’t need advice. I’m handling everything.”

“If you say so,” Megan said quietly. “But I have to wonder.”

“Why? Why can’t you just believe me and drop this?”

“Because we’re halfway to Baltimore when I was almost a hundred percent certain you said your appointment was in Myrtle Creek.”

Bree glanced at the signs as she whizzed past and realized her mother was exactly right. She’d missed her exit twenty miles back.

“You could have mentioned that sooner,”

she grumbled as she turned the car around at the next opportunity.

"I thought perhaps you'd decided to take me straight to Abby's office so you could dump me on her doorstep."

"That's not amusing, Mother."

Megan grinned at her. "I wasn't trying to be amusing, just to prove that I know you better than you think I do. Don't tell me that thought didn't cross your mind."

"So you think driving halfway to Baltimore was some sort of Freudian slip?"

"Or perhaps an unwitting admission that you were more interested in what I had to say than you wanted to admit."

"That's pretty convoluted reasoning," Bree accused, then grinned back at her mother. "It sounds like the kind of logic one of my characters would love."

"Then you are still writing?" Megan asked.

Bree's smile faltered. "Not at the moment, but I'll get back to it."

"It would be a real shame if you didn't. You're very good."

"How do you know? Did Abby send the reviews?"

"She did, but that's not how I know. I was there."

Bree blinked at that. "There? As in the theater?"

"For every play," her mother confirmed.

"Even the bomb?"

"Don't you dare call it that," Megan said indignantly. "The characters and theme in that play were right on the money. Since being in New York, I've seen a lot of good theater productions, so I think I know one when I see it."

Stunned by her mother's assessment and suddenly anxious to hear more, Bree pulled into the parking lot of a strip mall that had a coffee shop at one end. "I'd like a soda. How about you?"

"I'd love a cup of coffee," Megan said.

"And peach pie?" Bree asked, suddenly remembering it was her mother's favorite.

Megan's expression brightened. "You remembered that?"

"How could I forget? It was the one thing Gram baked that we had to fight you to get our share. You were always trying to come up with excuses to send us away from the table without dessert."

Her mother immediately looked guilty. "You knew what I was doing?"

"Of course. We all did. Sometimes we deliberately misbehaved to help you out."

Inside the coffee shop, when they had their drinks and their pie, Bree lifted her gaze. "Tell me why you thought the problems with the last play weren't my fault."

Her mother's expression turned thoughtful. "For me, what makes a good play—a good drama, that is—are the characters. Are they people an audience can relate to? Is the story solid? I liked the people you wrote about. I cared what happened to them."

"Then what went wrong? Why did the critics hate it?"

"Okay, maybe I'm being completely biased here, but I think it had to do with the performances, and since I'd seen many of those same actors in your other plays and they were good, then it seems to me it must have been the director who steered them wrong."

Bree sat back in astonishment at her mother's insight. Marty didn't always direct. He'd filled in at the eleventh hour on her third play because the director they'd hired had a last-minute conflict. At the time she'd wondered if his directing style wasn't a little heavy-handed, but she'd still been too much of a novice and too much in awe of him to question his decisions. When he'd reworked dialogue, removing every last speck of subtlety, she'd argued, but eventually given in to his expertise. If the seasoned actors in the cast weren't balking, how could she?

Listening to her mother pick apart the production with the eye of someone who understood drama, who could somehow separate the words spoken from the actor's performance and the director's staging, was an eye-opener.

"You really saw what I wrote, despite what happened on that stage," Bree said, amazed. "Why couldn't anyone else see that?"

"For one thing, it's the critic's job to assess what's actually on the stage, not what it could have been if things had been done differently. For another, I know your heart. And it's in everything you write. I'd love to see that play done again by someone who truly understands the characters."

"What about the second play?" Bree asked, genuinely wanting to know.

Megan's brow wrinkled. "My least favorite, actually."

Rather than being upset, Bree merely wanted an explanation. "Why?"

"I felt as if you were rushed writing it. The characters never felt completely real to me."

"You're right. I was blocked at first, and then, with a deadline staring me in the face, I did rush. Marty said it was fine, but I never believed that. I was surprised it did as well as it did."

She lifted her gaze to her mother's. "I wish I'd known you were there. Why didn't you tell me?"

"I didn't want to make you nervous or upset you. Those were your nights. It was enough just to share in them. I was so proud of you I could hardly stand it, though. I wanted to leap up and shout that you were my daughter, especially during the encores on that first play when they brought you up onstage."

"My knees were knocking," Bree admitted.

Megan squeezed her hand. "I could tell, but you looked amazing. I'd never seen you look so confident and happy." Her expression turned somber. "How did you lose that confidence, Bree? What happened?"

She was about to blame it on the reception given to the last two plays, but she knew better. For reasons she didn't entirely understand, Marty had started to undermine her at every turn, but she didn't want to dwell on that right now.

Changing the subject, she asked, "Did the family know you were there at the first play? That's the only one they were all able to get to."

"No. As I said, it was your night. I didn't want to be a distraction. I flew back to New York right after the play ended."

"I wish I'd known," Bree said.

"You wish that *now,*" Megan said insightfully. "You wouldn't have felt that way then or even a couple of hours ago. And that's okay. We're making progress, you and me. At least I hope we are."

"Maybe we are," Bree conceded.

Megan met her gaze. "This reconciliation business won't be easy or smooth.

We may fight. We may fall down. The important thing is that we both keep trying. Can you do that?"

Bree gave the question the thought it deserved, then nodded. "I want to."

"Then we will, because I want that more than anything, too."

"Maybe you should stay at the house after all."

To her surprise, Megan shook her head. "No, I think going to Abby's will be for the best. We're going to need some space at first. So will your father and I."

"Do you think the two of you will . . ."

"Reconcile?" Megan supplied. "It's much too soon to tell. To be honest, that will be a whole lot trickier than mending fences with you and your brothers and sisters. I don't want to push it by staying at the house."

"Are you just trying to prove to me how wise you are?"

"Either that or I'm admitting that I've missed Carrie and Caitlyn like crazy and can't wait to spend some time with them."

"I think I'll go with the whole wisdom thing," Bree said. "Otherwise, I'd have to admit that I'm halfway jealous of a couple of five-year-olds."

Megan reached for her hand. “You don’t have to be. There’s always been room in my heart for all of you.”

For the first time in fifteen long years, Bree actually believed that.

7

With a spring in his step, Mick walked into the kitchen at home at the end of the day and looked around for some sign of his ex-wife. He'd been anticipating this moment ever since she'd appeared at Bree's shop, wondering how it would feel to find her waiting here the way she'd always been before he'd gone and ruined their marriage. Unfortunately, she was nowhere in sight. There was only his mother wearing a scowl on her face.

"Where's Megan?" he asked Nell.

"Haven't seen her," his mother said as she set dishes on the table with a vaguely disgruntled thump. "Though I did hear through the grapevine that she's in town."

Mick nodded, ignoring the testy tone in her voice. "She turned up at the shop earlier, then she and Bree went off together. Given the way Bree greeted her, I figured Megan would be back here long before now, most likely alone."

"Well, I haven't seen them. Maybe they're over at the inn. Will she be staying there the way she did last time?"

Mick shrugged. "Beats me. As soon as I've had a shower, I'll take a walk over there and check things out. Is there time before dinner?"

"Since nobody's bothered checking in with me, I suppose we'll have dinner whenever anyone turns up," Nell said, clearly miffed. "You might as well take your time."

Mick realized that ignoring his mother's mood wasn't accomplishing anything. She evidently had something on her mind. He studied her intently for a moment, then asked, "Is there a problem, Ma?"

"Problem? No problem other than the way people come and go around here without the slightest bit of consideration."

He frowned. "Is this about Megan showing up unexpectedly?"

"No, it's about all of you. I spend my afternoons these days trying to decide what to cook and once I've decided that, then I have to take a guess about how many people I might be feeding. I thought I raised the whole lot of you better than that."

Mick finally grasped the problem. She was feeling unappreciated and taken for granted. He couldn't say he blamed her.

"You did raise us to be more considerate," he assured her. "And you're right, we've all been taking you for granted. I'm sorry. It won't happen again. I'll see to it."

"You?" she said incredulously. "You're no better than your children."

"Again, sorry," he said. It still amazed him how this diminutive woman could reduce him to feeling like a six-year-old with a few scolding words.

Just then the screen door burst open and was allowed to slam closed as Carrie and Caitlyn came running into the kitchen. "Where's Grandma Megan?" Carrie demanded.

"That seems to be the question of the hour," Nell replied tartly as Abby followed her daughters into the kitchen. "Are the three of you staying for dinner? Was I supposed to know that?"

Mick grinned as Abby tried to decide how to respond to Gram's obviously sour mood.

Eventually Abby put her arms around Gram and gave her a hug. "You don't have to feed us. We just came by to pick Mom up and take her over to our place."

"Well, you wasted a trip," Gram told her. "She's not here and I haven't seen her, so you might as well take a seat. We're having potato soup and pot roast."

Abby gave Mick a quizzical look. He shrugged.

"Gram, why don't you pour yourself a cup of tea and relax," Abby suggested. "I can take over in here. Just tell me what's left to do."

"The soup's on the stove and the pot roast is in the oven," Nell replied. "There's nothing left to do except wait to see who shows up."

Mick saw the moment when understanding dawned for Abby. She sent the twins outside to play, then made sure her grandmother sat down with her tea.

"Gram, I'm sorry if we've been treating your kitchen like a restaurant where we think we can pop in anytime," she apologized.

"I told her we were all going to start being more considerate," Mick said.

"Absolutely," Abby replied.

Nell's cheeks turned an embarrassed shade of pink. "I'm sorry for making such a fuss." She put her hand atop Abby's. "You know you're welcome here anytime, all of you. I love having those girls of yours underfoot. I've missed them since you moved into the new house with Trace."

"I'll make sure you see them more often," Abby promised. "But I'll schedule the visits ahead of time."

Mick hadn't thought it possible, but his mother looked even guiltier and more embarrassed.

"Ma, is something else the matter?"

"To tell you the truth, I feel like an old fool, complaining about everyone popping in here. This is your home. You have every right to come here whenever you please."

Suddenly, in a rare moment of insight, it dawned on Mick what was really upsetting her and it had little to do with tonight's dinner or who might unexpectedly pop in for the meal. "You're worrying about Megan coming back here and taking over, aren't you?"

She didn't deny it. "No home can withstand having two women thinking they're in charge," she said. "If you and Megan reconcile, then she has every right to expect to run things around here her way. And I still have my cottage. I can go back there."

Struck by the real dismay in her voice, Mick sat down next to her. "Ma, Megan and I are a long way from reconciling. And if that time does come, you'd never be displaced around here. Surely, you know that. It's your home as much as it is mine. If you want to go back to your cottage, that's your decision, but please don't do it because you think you won't be welcome here."

"Gram, you belong here," Abby agreed. "This will always be your home."

"But Megan will have her own ideas," she argued.

Mick didn't want to make light of her fears, but there was one thing he knew about his ex-wife that had apparently escaped Nell. “Ma, Megan has about as much interest in running a household as I do. Trust me, she’ll be more than happy to let you stay in charge of this place, if that’s what you want to do.” He gave her a pointed look. “But you’re getting way ahead of yourself. Not even I can see that far into the future yet and you know what an optimist I tend to be when I set my mind to something.”

He realized Abby was staring at him.

“You’re courting Mom? I mean, I know you’ve been seeing her, but it’s getting serious?”

He felt his face turn red. “I wouldn’t call it courting her, exactly. I popped in to see her in New York a couple of weeks ago. We had dinner. We didn’t smash dishes over each other’s head. That’s the most positive thing I can say about the evening.”

Abby’s expression turned thoughtful. “And now she’s here for an unexpected visit. Interesting. Where is she now?”

“She’s with Bree,” Mick said. “I thought they’d be back by now. Call your sister and see if they stopped by the inn.”

Abby reached for the phone just as Jess appeared . . . alone.

"Well, they're obviously not at the inn with Jess," Mick said.

"Mom and Bree?" Jess asked. "They're missing?"

"They're not missing," Mick said. "They're just not back from Myrtle Creek. Why don't the two of you help Gram set the table. Stay for dinner. I'll run up and grab a quick shower."

Abby gave him a knowing look. "So you'll look all spiffy when Mom gets here?"

"So I won't smell like sawdust and sweat," Mick retorted.

For a moment he stood there watching two of his girls as they pitched in to help his mother get a meal on the table. It reminded him of all the family meals they'd shared through the years . . . and all the ones he'd missed. The bickering, the chatter, the laughter, it was all so familiar. Why hadn't he appreciated it enough when he'd had it? How could he have let business keep him away so often when moments like this were the only thing that truly mattered?

At first he'd deluded himself that chasing jobs all over the country was something he was doing for his family, providing them with everything they could possibly need. Then, when Megan had made it clear that she cared more about him than money, he still hadn't gotten the message. He'd bristled at what he'd viewed as an ultimatum, his pride had kicked in and he'd let her slip away.

After that, the house had felt empty, despite five children underfoot, so he'd stayed away to avoid that awful sense of loneliness. He wasn't sure which was worse, feeling abandoned or the accompanying guilt because he'd known that the divorce was his fault since he hadn't tried to work out a compromise. All he'd cared about was that it was easier to bear losing Megan when he was far away and swamped with work. Having his mother there looking after the kids had eased his conscience.

He was still thinking about all that as he showered and dressed in crisply pressed pants and a clean dress shirt with the sleeves rolled up. He patted on aftershave, then grimaced at his reflection in the mirror. Abby was going to have a field day when she caught a whiff of that scent. Oh well, he supposed he could take a little good-natured teasing from his oldest daughter. It was more important to make a good impression on Megan.

To his dismay, she still wasn't there when he returned to the kitchen. Everyone else was seated at the table, evidently waiting for him. Caitlyn and Carrie bounced impatiently in their chairs.

"Grandpa Mick, we didn't think you'd ever get here," Carrie told him.

"We're really, really hungry," Caitlyn added. "We *love* Gram's pot roast."

"Sorry, angels. You all could have started without me." He put his napkin in his lap, then frowned when he realized there were no extra place settings. "Bree and Megan still not back?"

"Bree called. They decided to stop at Brady's for dinner," Abby said, watching him intently for any hint of a reaction.

"Good for them," he said. "They can use the time together. I'm hoping it will be good for Bree to have her mother here to confide in."

"Nice try, Dad, but I can tell you're disappointed," Abby said.

"Now, why would I be disappointed

about that? Didn't I go to New York to convince Megan that Bree needed her?"

Now it was Jess regarding him with an odd look, the same look Abby had had on her face earlier. "You went to New York?"

"And it had little enough to do with Bree," Gram commented, giving him a pitying look.

"Of course it was about Bree," he insisted.

"Really?" his mother said. "And after the visit, you stayed in touch with her to make sure she'd know what was going on with your daughter?"

He flushed at that. "Well, no."

"Because you were miffed that your ploy hadn't worked and Megan didn't rush right down here with you," Nell guessed.

"Ma, you don't know what you're talking about," he grumbled. "Megan's here now, isn't she?"

"Because she called and talked to Bree for herself and realized how serious things were."

"She's here for Bree," he said tightly. "That's all I ever wanted."

"Which doesn't explain the dress shirt and the aftershave," Abby teased.

"Maybe I have plans for after dinner," he said.

"With Mom?" Jess asked, studying him curiously. "Am I the only one who's not sure what's going on with you two?"

"Oh, I think we can all agree on what Dad wants," Abby said. "Mom's the wild card."

Mick frowned at her. "Would you give it a rest?" He made a show of looking at his watch. "I'm running late. You'll have to excuse me."

All three women stared at him.

"You're leaving in the middle of dinner?" Nell asked. "You've barely touched your food."

"Sorry. I'm afraid I have to go," he said, dropping a kiss on her cheek.

"Can we come with you?" Carrie asked.

"Yes, can we?" Caitlyn added. "Please."

Since he had no idea where he was going, Mick saw no reason they couldn't come along. He'd take them downtown and buy them ice cream. They could play on the swings for a while. At least it would get him away from the house. And if he returned them directly to Abby's, it was possible Megan would be there by then.

"If your mother approves," he said, glancing at Abby. "You okay with that?"

"Sure," she said, her expression filled with amusement. "Don't keep them out too late."

"I'll have them at your place by eight-thirty."

His daughter's grin spread. "Sounds like a plan. I imagine Mom will be there by then."

He feigned surprise. "Did she mention what time she and Bree would be arriving?"

"She didn't, but knowing Bree, it will be an early evening."

"Well, then, catching a glimpse of your mother would surely be a lovely end to the day," he said as if he hadn't calculated carefully to make sure of it. He held out a hand for each of the twins. "Let's go, girls. I can hear ice cream calling my name."

"Grandpa Mick, ice cream can't talk," Caitlyn said seriously.

He feigned surprise. "You sure about that?"

She nodded, her expression serious.

"Then it must be the hot-fudge sauce I hear," he claimed.

"Grandpa Mick, you're silly," Carrie said with a giggle.

He winked at Abby. "So they tell me, little one. So they tell me."

It probably was a little silly for a man in his fifties to be as giddy as a teenager at the prospect of seeing his ex-wife again before the night was over.

Bree was stunned that she'd spent the entire afternoon and most of the evening with her mother. More surprising was that she'd enjoyed it. After the rocky start there had been very little tension between them, primarily due to Megan's admission that she'd made three trips to Chicago to see Bree's plays. Bree still couldn't get over the fact that her mother had cared enough to do that. It had gone a long way to filling the empty spot in her heart, a hole she would have sworn to anyone else didn't exist.

When she pulled up in front of Abby's, she was almost sorry that the day was ending.

"I had fun today," she told Megan.

"Me, too."

"I wish you'd reconsider and stay at the house."

"This is better," Megan assured her.

"Do you know how long you're going to be in town?"

"Just through the weekend," Megan told her. "I'd like to stop by the shop tomorrow, though, if it's okay. I'd love to take a real look around and hear what you have planned."

Bree nodded. "I'll be there in the morning."

"I'll see you then."

As Megan stepped from the car, two small bodies hurled themselves at her.

"Grandma Megan, we've been waiting and waiting for you," Carrie exclaimed.

Megan laughed. "You have? Well, I've been waiting and waiting to see you."

"Grandpa Mick's here," Caitlyn said excitedly. "He's been waiting and waiting, too."

Bree saw the surprising spark in her mother's eyes. "You probably shouldn't keep him waiting, Mom. I'll see you tomorrow."

Megan suddenly slapped a hand to her brow. "What was I thinking? I have a rental car. It's still down by your shop and my luggage is in the trunk. It never even crossed my mind."

"Give me your keys," Bree said. "I'll get the luggage and someone can drop you off at the shop in the morning. The car will be fine there overnight."

"I should go with you," Megan began, only to be interrupted by a chorus of protests from the twins.

"Stay here, Mom. It'll take me ten minutes to run over there, fifteen tops."

"Are you sure you don't mind?"

"Of course not."

As she drove back into town, Bree thought about how much had changed in a single afternoon. Before today she would have objected to going out of her way for her mother. In fact, she would have felt she didn't owe her even the tiniest act of kindness. Now she was simply glad that her mother was here for a few days.

For a few hours she'd been reminded of the times when she was little when Megan had arranged special outings just for the two of them. She'd done that with each of the kids, taking Bree to the library or bookstore, Abby for walks on the beach. She took Connor to Baltimore Orioles games, even though she claimed not to understand the first thing about them. She'd even covered her antipathy toward worms to take Kevin out fishing in their old rowboat. Bree hesitated for a minute, trying to recall what Megan had done with Jess, then realized that there'd probably been very few special outings with her younger sister. Jess had been only seven at the time of the divorce.

As she pulled into the parking spot next to her mother's rental car—the only car left on the block in front of the shop at this hour—she glanced up and realized that the sign painter had apparently come while she was over in Myrtle Creek. FLOWERS ON MAIN had been painted on the front window and adorned with bright blossoms. Her name, in dark blue edged with gold, appeared in a lower corner of the glass.

"Oh, my," she murmured, tears springing to her eyes. It was exactly the way she'd envisioned it. Suddenly the whole thing felt real. It was all taking shape. In a few more weeks she'd be open for business and her life would be heading along a whole new, surprising path.

Main Street at night had a charming, old-fashioned feel to it. Tourists wandered along, window-shopping at a leisurely pace, ice cream or snow cones in hand. Every shop was unique, every lighted window filled with enticing gifts, souvenirs, colorful gourmet-kitchen gadgets. Now she would be adding her own contribution—a brilliant display of flowers each and every day. She could hardly wait to put her own stamp on this town her father had envisioned and then built from scratch.

"It looks good."

Jake's voice startled her so badly, she accidently hit the horn, which shattered the quiet of the evening. She stared up at him accusingly. "You nearly scared me to death. Where did you come from?"

"I just finished grabbing a burger at Sally's and saw you sitting here. I thought maybe something was wrong."

"Why would anything be wrong?"

"Because most people don't park on Main Street at this hour and sit staring at a building," he said reasonably.

"I came to get my mother's luggage out of the trunk of her rental," she said, gesturing toward the car next to hers.

Jake's brows shot up. "Megan's in town?"

She nodded.

"And you're okay with that?"

"It was a little dicey earlier today, but actually it's turning out to be okay."

"What brought her to town? I know she was here for the opening of the inn, but I didn't think she'd turn out to be a regular visitor, not after the way all of you practically shunned her when she came back after the divorce."

Bree gave him a wry look. "Well, you could have knocked me over with a feather, too. It seems she was worried about me."

Jake leaned against the side of the car and gestured toward the shop. "You mean because of this?"

She wasn't surprised that he understood that much. She supposed a lot of people were trying to figure out why she'd leave a supposedly successful career in Chicago to come back to Chesapeake Shores and open a flower shop.

She nodded. "Because of this."

"What'd you tell her?"

"That I wanted a fresh start."

"This seems like an odd choice for that," he said. "Don't people usually go someplace new to start over, instead of returning to the scene of some really bad memories?"

She looked up and met his gaze. "Not all my memories of this place are bad," she said. "And the ones that are . . ." She shrugged. "You've been able to put them behind you. Why can't I?"

His gaze held hers. "They're not behind me, Bree. Not by a long shot. And now that you're back, they're pretty much in my face every single day."

With that he shoved away from the car. "See you around."

The pain in his voice cut through her. "Jake?"

He paused, but he didn't turn around.

"I'm sorry."

He hesitated for what seemed like forever, then said, "Yeah. Me, too."

Bree watched him go, her heart aching. Maybe coming home had been a really lousy idea, after all. Then she glanced back at the window of her store and a smile crept across her face. No, she thought with a renewed sense of commitment. This was right. She was counting on it being right.

And somehow, one of these days, she'd find a way to make it up to Jake for all the pain she'd caused him. She just wished she had even the vaguest idea how she could possibly accomplish that.

Crossing the lawn clutching her granddaughters' hands, Megan saw Mick stand. He'd always been polite that way, but now she sensed a barely restrained eagerness in him, as if he was having to stop himself from coming down to meet her.

"Grandma Megan's here," Carrie announced unnecessarily.

"I see that," Mick said, smiling.

"She's gonna stay with us," Caitlyn added.

"Is that so?" Mick's gaze held hers, a question in his eyes.

"I thought it would be best," she said, responding to that unspoken question. "Bree needs some space right now."

He nodded in understanding. "Where'd she run off to?"

"I sent her after my luggage. I stupidly forgot that it was still in the rental car."

"I could have gone."

"She said she didn't mind."

"Come on, Grandma Megan," Carrie urged. "You gotta come see our rooms. Trace says we're big girls, so we each have our own now."

Megan shot an apologetic look toward Mick. "Well, aren't you lucky," she told Carrie. "Show me."

She followed the girls inside and left Mick on the porch. Only after she was inside, did she realize that she'd been practically holding her breath. How could he make her so nervous after all these years? They'd been married for nearly two decades, for heaven's sake. They had five children. There was nothing he didn't know about her or she him.

Except how to stay married, she reminded herself. They'd certainly gotten that all wrong.

When Abby found them in Caitlyn's room a few minutes later, she gave her a commiserating look. "Careful, Mom, or they'll insist on showing you every book on their shelves and every toy in their new toy boxes. I'm afraid Trace is spoiling them rotten."

"And I love seeing it all," Megan told her.

"But they need to get to bed. Why don't you join Dad on the porch," she said, sending Megan a conspiratorial wink. "I think he's poured a glass of wine for you. And I convinced Trace that he needed to come inside and leave you two alone."

Flustered that Abby seemed to understand that something was on the brink of happening between her and Mick, Megan tried to come up with an excuse to get out of going outside. None came to mind, especially when her luggage wasn't here. Without that, she couldn't even claim that she wanted to head straight to bed.

"Fine. I'll do that," she said, though she lingered over her good-nights to the girls.

"You're stalling, Mom," Abby accused, her eyes filled with amusement. "Does the idea of sitting on the porch in the dark with Dad scare you for some reason?"

"Of course not," she said at once.

Abby followed her into the hall and squeezed her hand. "It shouldn't, you know. You both want the same thing."

"Are you so sure about that? Has he actually said something?"

"Enough," Abby said. "Just take your time and let things happen naturally."

"I thought I was the one who's supposed to be giving advice on love," Megan grumbled. "Isn't that a mother's job?"

"But you're the one being courted," Abby told her with a grin. "I'm engaged. My future's all set."

Megan smiled at her. "I couldn't be happier for you. I hope you know that."

"I do."

"And we should start talking about your wedding."

"Tomorrow," Abby said emphatically, steering her toward the steps.

Megan relented and walked downstairs. She took a deep breath before she finally walked out onto the porch.

"There you are," Mick said, relief in his voice. "I thought maybe you'd gone to bed."

"I might have," she admitted, "but Bree's not back yet with my luggage."

There was just enough moonlight to see that Mick frowned at her words.

"You afraid of spending a little time with me, Meggie?"

"I don't know how to answer that," she confessed.

"It should be easy enough," he said with a familiar trace of impatience. "Either you are or you aren't."

Her temper stirred. "That's the trouble with you, Mick O'Brien. Everything's always black and white. Haven't you figured out by now that life's filled with gray areas?"

"So that's another of my failings?" he retorted. "Are we going through the whole list?"

She scowled at his tone. Things were disintegrating quickly, but she couldn't help the retort that sprang to her lips. "Maybe we should."

He sat back then, sighing. "Ah, Meggie, let's not do this. I'm sorry."

"In New York, you told me you'd done a lot of soul-searching," she said, an accusing note in her voice. "It doesn't seem like it."

"I have a dark soul. Sometimes it's difficult to see in all the corners."

She laughed then. "How can you still make me laugh, even when you've made me furious?"

"I wouldn't be able to make you furious if you didn't care just a little bit," he said.

"I've never denied caring, Mick. It's all the rest that comes with it that I couldn't do anymore—the neglect, the absences, the lack of consideration."

"You're the second person tonight to accuse me of being inconsiderate," he said.

"Did you hear either one of us?"

"It's hard not to hear such a thing when it's coming from two of the women I care most about in the world."

She smiled at that. Nell had always been able to bring him down a peg or two in ways Megan hadn't. "So, what was Nell upset about?"

"It started out to be about no one telling her if they were coming for dinner and wound up being about you."

"Me? What did I do?"

"It's what you might do that's troubling her. She thinks if you and I should happen to find our way back to each other, she'd be in the way."

"I hope you told her that would never happen!"

Mick frowned at the heat in her voice. "Displacing Ma or the reconciliation?"

"Either," she said at once. As his frown deepened, she reached for his hand. "I'd never try to displace Nell. She has more right to that home than I do."

"And the reconciliation?"

She lifted her gaze to his. "That remains to be seen," she said softly, liking the way his eyes lit up at her words, the way his fingers closed around hers.

"At least you're keeping an open mind," he murmured, seemingly satisfied. "That's probably more than I deserve."

Because she couldn't resist, she said, "It is, but it seems I have a soft spot for a man with a quick wit and the gift of blarney."

"Then fair warning," he said. "I intend to use both to win you back."

Megan tore her gaze away. It troubled her knowing just how easily he might be able to do that. Hadn't she learned one single lesson from being married to this man for all those years? His love was a magnificent thing, but that only made the neglect and disappointments that much harder to bear.

Flustered, she stood up. "I'm tired. I'm going to bed."

"Your bag's inside the door," he told her. "Bree dropped it by while you were upstairs with the girls."

"I told you I was waiting for it to get here," she said, scowling at him. "Yet you didn't think to mention that before."

"I wasn't ready to let you go," he said simply. "Good night, Meggie. Sleep well."

As she went inside, letting the screen door slap shut behind her, something told her she was unlikely to sleep a wink. Images of a stubborn, contrary Irishman were likely to fill her head. She really did need to hurry back to New York before he also managed to steal her heart.

8

Bree felt as if she'd fallen down a rabbit hole and wound up at the Chesapeake Shores—or maybe in the O'Brien version of the—Madhatter's Tea Party. Everything felt a bit topsy-turvy in her world.

When she'd arrived at her shop first thing this morning, she'd found her father already at work, though judging from his mood, he wasn't happy about being here . . . or maybe he wasn't happy in general.

Before she could grapple with getting to the bottom of his mood, her mother had walked in. Her father had immediately scurried off, muttering something about needing more wood, which was odd, since there was a whole pile of lumber in the back of his truck. Her mother had stared after him, her expression stunned. She'd toured the shop, murmured a few vague words of approval, then claimed she had places to be. She hadn't bothered to come up with specifics on her way out.

Bree stood in the doorway, staring after her, then frowned when her father almost instantly reappeared.

"Okay, Dad, what happened between you and Mom last night?" she demanded, following him inside. "And where's the wood you ran out of here to get?"

Mick flushed brick red. "I don't know what you're talking about," he muttered, turning on the circular saw so she couldn't be heard over the noise.

Regarding him with a defiant look, Bree switched the power tool right back off. "You can't avoid me that easily. I asked you a question. In fact, I asked you two questions. I'd like answers to both."

He scowled at her. "You'll have to remind me."

It took a great deal of restraint not to

roll her eyes at his deliberate evasiveness. "Let's start with the easy one. Where's the wood you claimed you needed?"

"In the truck," he said at once, clearly happy with himself for having a ready answer.

"That wood was already in the truck. You didn't leave here to buy more and you didn't bring any inside, which begs the question of why you came up with such a ridiculous excuse to avoid Mom."

"What are you this morning, the lumber police?" he grumbled.

She grinned despite herself. "Actually I think I'm doing okay at this investigating stuff. Now I'm asking again, for the third time in case you've lost count, what happened between you and Mom? Something must have for you to go flying out of here the second she arrived."

"Did you ask her why she was avoiding me?"

Bree stared at him blankly. "Avoiding you? She came here knowing you'd be here."

"But she barely even glanced my way."

"Because you took off before she could even say hello," Bree retorted impatiently.

"Tell me what's going on. Did the two of you have a fight?"

"No fight," he said tersely, starting to reach for the switch to start the saw.

Bree put her hand over the switch. "Talk."

He shook his head as if he couldn't quite figure her out. "You know I'd expect this kind of inquisition from Abby. She's always had this idea that Megan and I would eventually get back together, but you never seemed to care one way or another. Why are you suddenly so interested in the dynamics of my relationship with your mother?"

"Because you're both acting weird. I'd discuss it with her, but she bolted, so I'm left with you." She tapped her foot impatiently. "I'm still waiting for that answer."

Mick looked as if he wanted to argue or maybe take off for the second time that morning, but she fixed him with an unrelenting gaze. He finally shrugged. "I made a damn fool of myself, if you must know."

Now, *that* was a shock. Bree stared at him in bewilderment. "How?"

"I told her I wanted her back, and she couldn't get away from me fast enough."

Bree tried to wrap her head around all the information in that sentence. “You proposed?”

“No, I didn’t propose,” he snapped as if that wasn’t even a remotely logical conclusion. “I just made my intentions clear.”

“And Mom did what?”

“She went to bed.”

“Alone, I assume,” Bree said.

Mick scowled at her. “Of course alone, not that it would be any of your business if it had been otherwise.”

“Now let me get this straight,” she said slowly, trying to unravel the whole convoluted mess. “Mom didn’t swoon into your arms the second you uttered what wasn’t a proposal but some kind of declaration, so now you’re mad at her?”

“I’m not mad. I just feel like a fool. I got ahead of myself, something I’d sworn I wasn’t going to do.” He ran his hand through his hair. “I’m too damn old to do this. I don’t know the rules anymore.”

Bree couldn’t help it. She laughed, which earned such a scowl that she promptly sobered. “I don’t think there are rules, Dad. If there were, more of us would get it right just by following them.”

He must have heard something in her voice she hadn't even been aware of, because he immediately looked contrite. "I'm sorry. I shouldn't be going on and on about this with you. You have your own relationship issues to work through."

"No issues," she assured him. "The thing with Marty is over, kaput, ended, no longer important."

Mick looked skeptical. "Really? Then why was he calling you this morning?"

Bree was as puzzled by that as her father was. "He called here?"

"Actually he called your cell. You'd left it on the counter yesterday. I thought about letting it go to voice mail. In fact, I did just that the first five times he called. By the sixth time, I couldn't take another second of listening to that ridiculous ringtone you have, so I answered it."

"You didn't yell at him, did you? There's really no point in it at this stage."

"It would have served him right if I had, but no. Any yelling that gets done will have to come from you. The message is there on the counter, along with however many he left on your voice mail. He wants you to call him back." He held up his hand. "Let me correct that. He *expects* you to call him back."

Bree picked up the slip of paper, balled it up and tossed it in the trash bin across the room. Mick grinned when she made the shot.

"Good place for it," he commented happily.

"Now let's get back to you and Mom," she said.

"Let's don't. In fact, let's make a pact. I'll stay the hell out of your love life, if you'll ignore mine."

She hesitated, then shrugged. After all, she was hardly an expert. "I can do that. From what I can tell, you don't have one anyway."

"Neither do you," he retorted, then chuckled. "Now, aren't we a sorry pair, each of us gloating about the other one being all alone?"

Bree kissed his cheek. "I'm not gloating, Dad. I swear it."

"Well, if Marty's your only choice, then I *am* gloating," he replied.

She wondered what he'd have to say if she told him that Marty wasn't the one he needed to worry about. The man who had her all twisted up inside was the one she'd let slip away six years ago. Something told her if she confessed that to her father, he'd know all about the kind of regret she was feeling. Hadn't he done the same thing with her mother—let her get away?

Jake was walking out of Sally's with Will and Mack when Bree exited her shop a couple doors away. She started to turn in their direction, then made a swift U-turn and headed in the opposite direction without so much as a wave to acknowledge them.

Will and Mack stared after her, then turned slowly to Jake.

"I thought you said you were going to supply flowers for her business," Mack said.

"I am," Jake replied tersely, unable to keep himself from staring after her. She was wearing that turquoise sundress again, the one that showed off her shoulders. The skirt had swirled, then caught in the breeze when she'd turned, showing off more of her shapely legs than she'd probably intended.

"I assumed that meant you'd reached

some kind of détente," Will said, snapping his attention back from the sight of her departing back.

"We have," Jake snapped.

"Didn't look that way just now," Will observed. "Or was it part of your agreement that you'd avoid each other in public? Are you trying to keep the grapevine in check, because I have to tell you that moments like that one will do the exact opposite."

"Do you know how little I care about what people in this town have to say?" Jake asked. "In fact, if the two of you didn't repeat everything like a couple of little old ladies, I'd never know a damn thing."

Will blinked at the attack. "Did I happen to strike a nerve, pal?"

"I'd say yes," Mack chimed in, clearly enjoying the exchange.

"Who asked you?" Jake grumbled. "I need to get to work. I have to finish Mrs. Finch's landscape work today. Her lilac bushes are starting to overrun the property. And she's going to stand over me and watch every branch I clip to make sure I don't ruin them. That's about as much of a hassle as I can take in one afternoon."

"A convenient excuse," Will murmured.

"Very convenient," Mack added.

Jake replied with a suggestion that according to most reports was anatomically impossible. Walking away from the two of them, he climbed into his truck, pulled out into traffic and made a right turn from Main Street onto Shore Road. No sooner had he turned the corner than his cell phone rang.

"Mrs. Finch's house is the other way," Will informed him cheerfully. "Or were you hoping to catch up with Bree by going that way?"

Jake disconnected the call without responding. It didn't help his mood that not two seconds later, he spotted Bree sitting outside at one of the sidewalk cafés that had opened over the past couple of years. In addition to the dress that practically begged for a man's attention, she'd added sunglasses that seemed to cover half her face and a wide-brimmed straw hat meant to keep her fair complexion from freckling. She looked mysterious and sexy. His pulse scrambled at the sight of her and his foot hit the brakes, causing the blare of several horns behind him.

Muttering a curse at his own stupidity,

he wheeled into the first available parking space and walked back to the Panini Bistro, which specialized in grilled sandwiches and salads. Standing over her, he clutched the back of a chair with a white-knuckled grip and tried to figure out what to say to explain his presence. When nothing rational came to him, he settled for an attack.

"This has to stop!" he said, drawing her attention away from the book in which she seemed totally absorbed.

She regarded him with surprise. "Jake!"

"I mean it, Bree, this has to stop."

She removed her sunglasses and returned his gaze evenly, though her expression was justifiably bewildered. "Am I supposed to know what you're talking about?"

He wasn't even sure *he* knew what he was talking about. He just knew that being blindsided by his intense reaction each time he caught a glimpse of her was beginning to get to him. Since he didn't want to admit to that, he took a different tack.

"Just now, you deliberately walked away when you saw me with Will and Mack."

"Okay," she said slowly, clearly not comprehending. "I thought you wanted us to avoid each other."

"I do. I did." He shook his head. "It's not working. It stirs up questions, at least from those two, questions for which I have no answers."

She studied him quizzically. "Such as?"

"How we can work together, if we can't even pass each other on the street without it being awkward?"

"And you thought it was awkward back there, when I deliberately tried to stay out of your way?"

"Of course it was."

"Jake, you're going to have to make up your mind," she said with exaggerated patience. "I'm willing to do anything and everything I can to keep from making your life difficult, but you have to tell me the rules."

"There are no damn rules," he muttered, feeling like even more of an idiot. "It's a free world. You can come and go anyplace you want to."

"Except where you are," she guessed. "Can you fax over your schedule every morning? Or have Connie do it, though she might have several uncomfortable questions for you if you decide to go that route."

He bristled at the suggestion. "Don't be ridiculous. And don't even think about involving my sister in our situation. This is between you and me, no one else."

He wasn't a hundred percent sure what possessed him then, but the next thing he knew, he'd hauled her up out of her chair, slanted his mouth over hers and kissed her. That kiss held every pent-up emotion, every bit of longing, every trace of anger he'd stored up for six long years.

After her first startled gasp, she slowly slid her arms around him and melted into his embrace, her mouth soft and sweet under his. The ease with which the attraction sparked into an inferno infuriated him. He pushed her away roughly, then turned on his heel.

He'd made it down the sidewalk, past half a dozen startled and fascinated diners, when she called after him.

"Jake?"

He turned to find her hat askew, her cheeks pink and her lipstick smudged. It took every ounce of self-respect he'd ever possessed to keep from going right back to her for more.

"Yes?" he said tightly.

"I'm confused," she said, her gaze locked with his.

"Yeah, well, join the damn club," he said. This time when he walked away, he didn't look back.

"What the heck happened to you?" Mick asked when Bree made it back to the shop after her encounter with Jake.

Distracted, she gave him a puzzled look. "Nothing. Why?"

"Let's just say if you'd just come in from a date, I'd be out trying to track down the guy who left you looking like that."

Embarrassed, she pulled a compact out of her purse and took a quick look at her mussed hair, flushed cheeks and lips that looked as if they'd recently been plundered. Which they had been. She wasn't sure whether to hate Jake for that . . . or for stopping way too soon.

"It was windy," she claimed to her father. "My hat blew off, so my hair's a tangled mess."

"Uh-huh," he said, his skepticism plain.

"Did that vicious old wind take your lipstick off, too."

"No, that was my lunch," she said. "Lipsticks just don't stay on through a meal these days."

"If you say so."

"Look, I need to head over to the inn," she told him. "I've got a lot of paperwork to do this afternoon. Are you going to be okay here?"

He gave her an amused look. "I built a town," he reminded her. "I think I can get this counter finished without your presence."

"I just meant . . ." She had no idea what she meant. She hadn't had a single coherent thought since her encounter with Jake, even though she'd sat in the bistro for a solid half hour after he'd left, trying to collect her thoughts. She'd eaten her sandwich without it even registering. She was still just as dazed.

"I'll see you at home later," she told Mick eventually.

"One last thing before you go," her father said, touching her cheek. "Whatever happened put a sparkle in your eyes for the first time since you got back to town.

It's good to see. You might want to consider repeating it."

Bree nodded, because she had no idea how else to respond to that. "See you later," she said on her way out the door.

So, Jake had left her with a sparkle in her eyes, a decided hum in her bloodstream and more questions than answers. Now she had some idea why he'd been annoyed by all those unanswerable questions Will and Mack had thrown his way. She was a little bit exasperated herself at the moment.

And more than a little scared, because the one thing this afternoon had confirmed was that whatever passion there had once been between her and Jake, it was stronger than ever, even if he wasn't one bit happy about it.

Jake was exhausted and emotionally drained by the time he got back to the nursery after six o'clock. The only good thing about finishing up his day this late was that his sister wouldn't be around to cross-examine him about whatever she'd heard via the grapevine this afternoon. Given his performance with Bree on Shore

Road, he imagined she'd heard quite a lot.

He passed through the sales area, greeted the employees on duty, took a quick mental survey of the plants on hand, then headed for his office. He intended to spend ten minutes glancing through messages and checking his calendar for any new landscaping jobs Connie had lined up, then he was going straight home to a shower and a cold beer.

Instead, he opened the door and found his niece sprawled across the sofa in his office with some punk kid half on top of her. Jake tried to remind himself that he'd been a hormone-driven teenager himself at one time, but it was hard to think through the haze of red fury spreading through him.

Jake grabbed the boy by the back of his shirt and set him on his feet. Jenny jumped up, trying frantically to button her blouse.

"I thought you were gone for the day," she said, trying to back toward the door, a look of utter panic on her face.

"Because that would make this so much better?" Jake queried.

The boy, one he didn't recognize, stared

at him belligerently. "I'm out of here," he said, trying to saunter past Jake.

"Sit!" Jake bellowed. "Both of you."

Jenny reached for the boy's hand and tried to pull him down beside her on the sofa.

"Not there," Jake said. "Over here. In chairs." He moved the two chairs so there was a reassuring amount of distance between them, then waited until both teens were seated. His niece looked as if she was about to die of embarrassment. The boy looked marginally less belligerent now.

"Okay, is one of you going to tell me what you thought you were doing here?" He shot his most intimidating look toward the squirming young man. "Let's start with you."

"Coming here was my idea, Uncle Jake," Jenny said in a voice barely above a whisper.

He gave her a quelling look. "I'll get to you." He turned again to the young man. "What's your name?"

"Dillon," he said in a voice with a telltale quaver in it. "Dillon Johnson."

"Okay, Dillon Johnson, start talking."

"We, um, we wanted to be alone, you

know what I mean? My house always has a bunch of kids around. I have three younger sisters." He gave Jake a pleading look. "You gotta know what that's like."

"Sorry," Jake said. "Only one older sister, so I'm not feeling much sympathy. Keep going."

Dillon blanched at his tone. "Okay, well, Jenny's mom was home from work. And neither one of us has a car, so Jenny said we could come here. To be alone. Nothing was going to happen, I swear it."

"Nothing? Really? I walked in and you had my niece's blouse halfway off. That's already way past nothing."

"It . . . I . . ."

Jake gave him a hard look. "Good. We're agreed that you'd crossed a line."

The boy nodded, his expression finally meek.

"And now we're going to agree that nothing like this will ever happen again. Not here. Not in your house. Not at my niece's house and definitely not in the backseat of anyone's car. Is that right? You and I have an understanding?"

The boy blinked rapidly. "Yes, sir."

"Then you can go now," he said more gently. "Do you have a way to get home?"

Dillon nodded. "We rode our bikes over here." He scrambled for the door, cast one last apologetic look in Jenny's direction, then took off.

"How could you?" Jenny asked him, close to tears. "He's the first real boyfriend I've ever had and you've ruined it."

"If he really cares about you, I won't have ruined anything. He'll abide by the rules."

"But everyone hangs out and . . ." She blushed furiously. "You know."

"I do know, sweetie, and I also know exactly where that can lead." In fact, he knew it with the kind of bitter regret that only someone who'd paid such a high price could ever understand. "I know you and your mom have talked about this."

"Well, duh. Of course we have."

"Then I don't need to spell out the possible consequences, do I?"

"We weren't going to do *that,*" she insisted.

The naive statement told him all he needed to know about how important it was that he get through to her before something life-altering happened.

"But what you were doing leads to *that,*" he said. "Sometimes before you know it."

He ran a hand through his hair, trying to think of the best way to approach this. Jenny watched him expectantly. He was not prepared to be having this kind of conversation with a kid, especially not his sweet, innocent niece. It seemed like only yesterday when all Jenny Louise cared about were her dolls and getting a piggyback ride on his shoulders.

Suddenly he stood up. "Let's get out of here."

She stared at him suspiciously. "Where are we going? Are you gonna tell Mom about this?"

"Yes," he said firmly. "But first you and I are going out for pizza."

Her expression brightened at once. "Really?"

He ruffled her hair. "Really, and we are going to have ourselves a very long talk about boys."

She frowned at that. "Do we have to?"

"Based on recent evidence, I think so."

"But I told you, Mom and I have already talked about all that."

"But apparently it didn't sink in," he said meaningfully. "Besides, she doesn't have a guy's perspective. I do. Believe me, sweetie, guys look at stuff like this a whole different way than girls do."

She gave him an impudent look as he was putting her bike into the bed of his truck. "Does that mean you're going to tell me what you were thinking when you planted a big ol' kiss on that woman at the bistro today?"

Jake reddened. "How'd you hear about that?"

"My friend Molly left school at lunchtime and she saw you. She said it was pretty hot."

Jake's stomach clenched. "Please tell me that wasn't what gave you the idea to use my office for a rendezvous with your pal Dillon."

"Well, it did make me think maybe you'd understand, that you wouldn't get all uptight the way Mom would." She gave him a rueful look. "I guess I was wrong."

"I guess you were."

And he, heaven help him, now had one more regret to add to the list he'd been compiling ever since he and Bree had locked lips. That had definitely been a bad move. A very bad move.

Unfortunately, it was one he knew without a doubt he was doomed to repeat. He just hoped next time he wouldn't have to explain it to his impressionable seventeen-year-old niece.

9

When Jake reached his sister to explain that he and Jenny Louise would be stopping for pizza, she sounded frantic.

"She's with you?" Connie asked, clearly bewildered. "Why? How'd that happen? I've been calling everywhere looking for her. She didn't leave me a note, nothing. This isn't like her, Jake. I've been terrified that something happened, that she got in a car with one of her friends, even though she knows that's not allowed, and they had an accident. I was about to start calling hospitals."

"Stop worrying, sis," he said, casting a

scowl toward his niece. “I’ll explain everything when I bring her home. I just wanted you to know she’s with me and that she’s fine. Believe me, one of the things we’ll be discussing is not taking off without leaving a note. It won’t happen again.”

“Jake, she’s not your responsibility. Besides, I have dinner ready here,” Connie protested. “Just bring her home. I’ll set a place for you. There’s plenty of food.”

“I think maybe both of you need a cooling-off period. Trust me, Jenny and I have some things we need to get straight before you see her.”

“What things? Jake Collins, is my daughter in some kind of trouble? If she is, you’d better tell me right now. I won’t have you hiding things from me.”

“We’ll fill you in later, I promise,” he said. “We’ll be there in an hour.”

Connie didn’t sound one bit happy about the delay, but she finally relented. “One hour, and then I’m coming to the pizza shop after you. Neither of you will be happy about the scene I’m likely to make, either.”

She’d do it, too. Jake knew that. “We’ll be there.”

He disconnected the call and saw Jenny biting on her lower lip. She looked scared when she turned to him. “Is she mad at me?”

“For not checking in to let her know where you were? Yeah, she’s mad. What were you thinking? Couldn’t you at least have left her a note?”

“And said what?” she said more spiritedly. “That I was going to your office with my boyfriend? That would have gone over big.” She gave him a knowing look. “Or should I have lied and said I was having dinner at Molly’s house?”

“How about not going to my office with your boyfriend in the first place?” he suggested. “That’s definitely my first choice.”

“It won’t happen again,” she swore. “I promise.”

“Damn straight it won’t,” he muttered. He pulled into a parking space near the shop that sold pizza by the slice to beachgoers during the day. In the evening, it catered mostly to the town’s teens and local families.

For the next forty-five minutes he tried to give Jenny a crash course on the thought process of a teenage boy. When he'd finished, she stared at him incredulously.

"But what you're really saying is that they don't think at all, except with their . . ." She blushed furiously. "You know."

"Exactly," he said.

She regarded him wistfully. "Then it wasn't really about me at all? What happened back in your office? That was just Dillon's hormones looking to hook up with anybody?"

He tucked a finger under her chin and forced her to look at him. "I'm not saying that Dillon doesn't like you. I'm not saying he doesn't respect you. I'm just saying that when it comes to sex, for a guy his age that pretty much drives all the other thoughts right out of his head. That means it's up to you to look out for yourself. You need to have enough respect for yourself to know where to draw the line and make sure whoever you're dating knows that, too. There's such an amazing future ahead of you, Jenny Louise. You're going to college in another year. You can be anything you want to be. Don't blow that because some boy gets you into a situation you don't know how to control."

"Because I could wind up pregnant," she said, echoing what he and, no doubt, her mother had told her.

"Yes, even with just about every precaution in the world, you could wind up pregnant," he said from experience. He and Bree had practiced what they'd thought was safe sex. They certainly hadn't planned the pregnancy that had changed their lives, and they'd been a whole lot older than Jenny. They were still dealing with the fallout. He didn't want any of that for his niece.

He looked into Jenny's troubled eyes. "Am I making sense to you?"

She nodded.

"Good. Now, let's get home before your mom comes in here and we both wind up getting a lecture or worse."

"What could be worse?" Jenny asked.

"A really, really embarrassing scene."

"Been there, done that," his niece admitted with a sigh. "Let's definitely get home before that happens."

Jake drove to his sister's house and pulled into the driveway. When he opened his door to get out, Jenny didn't move. A glance revealed tears tracking down her cheeks.

"I really, really don't want Mom to know what I did," she whispered. "Please, Uncle Jake. She's going to be so disappointed in me, not just because of Dillon, but because I broke into your office. She'll say it's a violation of your trust and it was."

"You didn't break in," he corrected. "You have a key."

"Yeah, like that's going to matter to her," she said. "If I swear never, ever to do anything like this again, could you just not tell her?"

He hesitated. He saw the misery written all over her face, but he understood that his sister had every right to know about something this serious.

"I'll tell you what," he said at last. "I won't tell her."

Jenny's expression brightened. "Really?" she said incredulously. "Thank you, thank you, thank you."

He held up a hand. "Don't thank me yet. I won't tell her, because I'm going to let you do it."

Her expression faltered. "You want me to tell her? Everything?"

He nodded. "Everything."

"Are you gonna be there?"

"I am, just to make sure you don't leave anything out."

"Gee, thanks for the vote of confidence," she said sarcastically.

"Trust has to be earned, sweet pea. You made a pretty big dent in mine this afternoon, but owning up to your mistake to your mom would be a big step in regaining it."

"If you say so," she mumbled unhappily.

"I say so," he told her. "Now, let's go inside and get this over with."

Jenny trailed after him at a pace a turtle could have outrun, but she did follow. They found Connie sitting at the kitchen table, half her attention focused on the rerun of a TV sitcom, the other half directed toward the clock on the wall as they entered.

"You made it with a minute to spare," she said as Jake grabbed a bottle of beer and a soda from the fridge and sat down opposite her. He handed the soda to Jenny to give her something to do with her hands.

Connie focused on her daughter. "Where were you this afternoon?"

"Gee, get straight to the point, why don't you?" Jenny sniped, then winced. "Sorry." She glanced in Jake's direction and he nodded encouragingly.

"At the nursery," she confessed softly.

Connie frowned. "When? I didn't see you."

"I waited until you left, then I went to Uncle Jake's office." She swallowed hard. "With Dillon."

Connie stared at her blankly. "But why would you . . . ?" Her voice trailed off as she glanced at Jake. "No."

Jake nodded again.

Connie was a petite woman, but when she drew herself up into full mother-hen mode, she was formidable. "Jennifer Louise, please tell me you and Dillon did not break into Jake's office to make out."

"Mom, that is so old-fashioned. Nobody 'makes out' anymore."

Connie gave her a wry look. "They may not call it that, but I guarantee you they still do it. The more important issue here is whether that's what you and Dillon were doing in your uncle's office."

With obvious reluctance, Jenny bobbed

her head once, her expression filled with embarrassment and misery.

Again, Connie turned to him. “And you caught them?”

“Oh, yeah,” he said. “But it hadn’t gone very far, which is why Jenny and I have been having a nice long chat about boys tonight. We’ve agreed that nothing like this will ever happen again, at least until she’s thirty or married, whichever comes first.”

Jenny’s lips quirked into a smile. “I definitely did not agree to *that,*” she said.

“Oh, my mistake,” Jake said. “It was forty.”

Connie looked from him to her daughter and back again. “This is not a joking matter.”

“No,” he agreed, sobering at once. “And Jenny understands that, don’t you?”

She nodded enthusiastically. “I do, Mom. I really do.”

“Well, the opportunities are going to be few and far between for at least the next month,” his sister said, her hard gaze locked on her daughter. “No e-mails, no texting, no leaving the house except to go to school.”

Jenny looked shocked, but then she

made the huge mistake of turning belligerent. "Who's going to enforce that?" she demanded.

"I am," Connie said evenly. "I will take you to school in the morning. I will pick you up after school. You can sit with me at the nursery until I get off. In fact, since you violated your uncle's trust, instead of just sitting there, you can work for him."

That sparked a tiny bit of interest in Jenny's expression. "What will I get paid?"

"Nothing," Connie responded, then held out her hand. "Turn over your cell phone now."

"But—"

"Do you really want to argue with me right now?" Connie demanded.

Jenny took the cell phone out of her purse and dropped it on the kitchen table. She glared at Jake. "Boy, this went well. Thanks."

And then she bolted from the kitchen.

Connie sighed heavily. "I don't believe this. She was hooking up in your office? Honestly?" She put her head down on her arms. "I'm not sure I'll make it till she's an adult."

Jake laid a hand over hers. "Yes, you

will. And she'll get there without doing anything really stupid that could ruin her life. I really believe that. She's smart, sis. And I think I gave her a real eye-opener today about how boys think. Hopefully it will be enough to make her think twice, maybe even a half-dozen times before she ever lets another one put his hands on her."

"How far . . . ?"

"Not that far," he reassured her. "They still had their clothes on." He saw no point in mentioning the state of Jenny's blouse. "You okay?"

She lifted her head and met his gaze. "Do you really think you got through to her?"

"I do," he said confidently, then grinned. "But it wouldn't hurt to keep a very close eye on her for the next, say, ten years."

His sister laughed, just as he'd hoped she would. "I'll settle for getting her out of high school and through college."

"Let's concentrate on high school for now," he said. "No matter what we might prefer, the college thing might be a little unrealistic."

"You were the one who wanted to protect her for the next ten years," she reminded him.

He shrugged. "Hey, I was always the dreamer in the family." He stood up and dropped a kiss on her forehead. "She's going to be just fine. So are you."

She gave him a grateful look. "Thank you for caring what happens to her, to us."

"Always," he promised.

At least it had kept his mind off Bree and that kiss for several hours now. And, even more amazing, his sister hadn't brought it up, either. That kind of distraction was worth just about any kind of aggravation.

Bree was finally able to work in the little nook that was going to be her office in the shop. The construction had been completed, the coolers installed and Mick had almost finished painting everything in a rich dark blue with white accents. She had to stick her head outside every now and then to get away from the paint fumes, but she was getting more and more excited as her opening day approached. Tomorrow the bulk of her supplies were due to arrive and the paint would be dry enough that she'd be able to unpack them and slip them into their designated nooks and crannies.

Just as she sat back, a smile on her lips as she contemplated the way everything was coming together, the front door opened and her sisters sailed in. She recognized the expressions on their faces, too. They were on a mission.

"It's two weeks until your opening," Jess announced as if it might have escaped her attention.

"I know that," Bree responded.

"Well, what are you going to do?" Abby asked. "I haven't heard any plans."

"I'm going to hang an Open sign on the door and wait for the customers to flock in," she said, knowing that the comment would drive Abby the organizer nuts.

She grinned when Abby regarded her with shock. Even Jess looked a little shaken.

"You have to advertise at least," Jess said. "Starting now."

"And there should be some kind of an event," Abby chimed in. "Something to draw attention to the business."

"I doubt there's a soul in town who doesn't know about this shop and when it's opening," Bree countered. "Most of them have been snooping around in here since Dad started working on the place. I'm pretty sure the grapevine has worked more effectively than any advertising ever could. Why spend the money?"

"Because we're O'Briens," Jess said. "People expect some kind of big splashy event from us."

"I'm not throwing a party for the entire town. That made sense for the inn. It doesn't for a flower shop. For one thing, only so many people can even fit in here."

Abby's expression turned thoughtful. "Okay, you have a point," she said. "Then we'll make it an open house for the whole day. That should spread out the crowd. And we could serve—"

Again, Bree held up her hand. "Not serving food. This isn't a restaurant."

"Champagne, at least," Jess said wistfully.

"And have everyone falling-down drunk? I don't think so."

"One glass of champagne isn't going to have people crashing into the gutter," Abby said. "If you really object to it, how about punch instead? That can be festive. We could set up the counter with a really pretty fountain with pink punch splashing down. I think there's a whole set of antique punch cups at the house. It could be beautiful."

"And how am I supposed to conduct business if there's punch splashing all over the counter?"

"Your first day isn't about conducting business," Jess said. "It's about getting people excited about your shop."

"She's right," Abby said.

"So I shouldn't expect to sell flowers that day?" Bree asked dubiously. "What am I supposed to do with the flowers I was planning to order? It won't look like much of a flower shop if they're not on display and in the cooler."

"Another good point," Jess said.

Bree gave her a wry look. "I'm delighted you all think I have at least a slim idea of what I'm doing."

"You're looking at this all wrong," Abby said. "This is public relations. The punch, the flowers, all of it, that's selling the business you're going to have. It's the launch party, the spin, the sizzle. You'll get down to the nitty-gritty of selling flowers later."

Bree remained skeptical. "I'm not sure

I should blow off the biggest day of a holiday weekend."

"Friday," Jess said at once. "We'll have the party on Friday afternoon and evening. Then you can open your doors officially on Saturday morning and you'll have a line down the block."

"I suppose that could work," Bree admitted.

"When is your first order of flowers being delivered?" Abby asked.

"I told Jake Friday morning."

"Make it Thursday. That will give us all day Thursday and Friday morning to turn this place into a showcase. You'll have your open house Friday afternoon, say, from four o'clock to eight, so people coming into town for the Labor Day weekend will hear the music and stop by to see what's going on."

Bree stared at her. "Music? Aren't you getting a little carried away?"

"Absolutely not. I convinced Dad that the town should move the concert right up here to the green that night, instead of having the band play in the gazebo by the water. He's already spoken to the mayor. That's just one of the advantages of having a dad who wields a lot of influence around here. Things tend to happen just the way we want them to. So, the concert is a done deal. And they'll start at six, instead of eight, which will be just perfect, don't you think so?"

"Perfect," Bree said, her head spinning. She focused on her older sister, her suspicions aroused. "So, did the two of you have this all worked out before you even walked in the door just now? Was this whole discussion just your way of coaxing me to go along with what you already had planned?"

Jess was the one who looked guilty. Abby merely shrugged. "You tend to like to think things are your own idea."

"But none of this was my idea," Bree said.

"But you're excited about it now, aren't you?" Abby said confidently. "How could you not be? It's going to be fabulous."

"Bulldozers," Bree muttered under her breath.

"What was that?" Abby inquired, her lips twitching.

"I said you're a couple of bulldozers."

Jess grinned. "Yes, but we love you, so you'll forgive us."

"And be duly grateful when your business is a smash hit," Abby added.

"How much is this little event of yours going to cost me?" Bree asked.

"Not a thing," Abby said. "It's our gift to you, Jess's and mine. Mom's chipping in, too. She told me she wanted to do something special for the occasion. She'll be down that weekend. I'll make sure she knows she needs to get here Thursday so she can help us get everything set up."

Bree's eyes stung with tears. "I can't let you pay for this. Jess is still trying to get the inn on its feet and—"

"Of course you can," Jess interrupted. "Heck, Abby invested a fortune in the inn for me and bought rugs on top of it. We can at least throw a party for you."

Bree swiped at her tears and tried to smile. "In that case, let's talk about that champagne and those hors d'oeuvres again."

Abby gave her a hug. "Not to worry. It's all on order already."

"You were that confident I'd cave?"

"Hey, you're an O'Brien," Abby said. "If there's one thing we love, it's a good party."

Except for me, Bree thought, but kept it to herself. They were so excited by their plans, it almost didn't matter that they'd swept her along against her will. She was the O'Brien who'd always sat alone at the top of the steps looking on, never one of the revelers.

What the heck, she told herself bracingly. Maybe it was time that changed. After all, this was meant to be a fresh start. She might as well go for broke.

Jake happened to be in his office when he heard Connie on the phone with Bree. She was saying something about moving up the date for the first flower delivery and a party, jotting the dates on her desk calendar. He could have waited until she got off the phone to find out what was going on, but curiosity got the better of him. Even though he knew he'd hear about it later, he held out his hand.

"Let me speak to her," he said.

Connie stared at him, incredulous. "Really?"

"Just give me the phone," he ordered. "And go do something."

"What?"

"Anything. Water the plants in the greenhouse or whatever else will get you out of here."

Her eyes sparkled with amusement. "Interesting. You want privacy to have a business conversation with one of our clients. Some people might wonder how Bree rates that special attention."

He merely scowled at her until she got up and left the office. When he put the phone up to his ear, he heard Bree asking, "Connie, what's going on? Connie!"

"It's me," he said.

"Jake," she said, her voice filled with surprise and maybe a touch of dismay. "Where'd Connie go?"

"I sent her on an errand."

"I see."

"So, what do you need? I heard Connie say something about a delivery-date change and a party."

Bree explained that her sisters had talked her into holding an open house. "So I'll need the flowers here on Thursday instead of Friday."

He considered making things difficult for her by claiming that he couldn't make a delivery on a different day on such short notice, but what would be the point of making her beg, when they both knew he'd do it.

"Is it a problem?" she asked when he remained silent. "Connie didn't seem to think it would be."

"You'll have your flowers," he responded tersely.

"Will it still be okay to get the order form to you on Monday or will you need it sooner?"

"The sooner you get it in, the better your chances for getting everything you want," he told her. "In fact, if you can have it ready today, I can stop by and pick it up before I meet Will and Mack at Sally's."

"Really? You'll come here?"

"It's not as if it would take me out of my way," he said, annoyed that she seemed to be making some kind of a big deal out of it. "Sally's is practically next door."

"Of course. I'll have it ready for you by eleven-thirty. You meet them at noon, right?"

"Have you been keeping tabs on me?" For some ridiculous reason, the idea pleased him.

"No, of course not," she said at once.

"Sally mentioned that when she warned me to stay away around noon, so I wouldn't chase the three of you off."

"Oh, right," he said, deflated. "I'll see you later, then."

"Yeah, see you later. If for any reason I have to go out, I'll put the order form in an envelope and tape it to the door."

Irritated that he'd put himself in the position to cross paths with her, only to have her suggest she might not be around after all, he snapped, "You'll have to be there."

"Why?"

"So we can go over the order," he said reasonably, relieved that he actually did have a logical excuse. "I've been doing this a long time. I might have a better idea of the quantities you'll need than you do. You don't want to spend a fortune on flowers that'll wilt before you can sell them, do you?"

"Right, fine," she said, sounding testy herself now. "Then I'll make it a point to be here. And Jake, do me a favor, okay?"

He hesitated, then asked, "What?"

"Try to be in a better mood when you get here. If you're going to get all surly and impossible every time we have to deal with each other, I might have to look for another wholesaler, after all."

Before he could summon up a response to that, he heard her phone click off. In turn, he slammed his back into its cradle.

"Blasted woman!" he muttered.

Connie immediately poked her head into his office, which suggested she hadn't gone nearly as far away as he'd ordered her to.

"Something wrong?" she inquired, her expression innocent.

"Not a damn thing," he said, stalking past her and straight out the door, which he slammed behind him.

He was pretty sure he could hear her hoot of laughter all the way to his truck. Now there were two women on his bad side. And sadly, he couldn't think of a single way to avoid dealing with either one of them.

10

Bree was so flustered by the prospect of seeing Jake that she almost called Jess or her father to come over to the shop to run interference. To be honest, she didn't trust herself alone with him. There was no telling what impulse might suddenly hit her. And after what had happened the other day at the sidewalk café, his mood was clearly unpredictable, as well.

She hadn't seen him since that totally unexpected, totally mind-blowing kiss. Though she hadn't been able to get it out of her mind, she still had absolutely no idea why it had happened or what it meant.

Judging from his tone on the phone, which was cautious one minute and exasperated the next, he was probably as confused as she was. It also seemed entirely likely that he was regretting it. She wished she did. Instead, the whole incident was burned into her brain and her libido was screaming for more.

Since this meeting was inevitable and she had to learn how to deal with Jake without coming unglued, she dug the current order form Connie had faxed over earlier out of her desk and tried to focus on that. Jake had been right, it was a little intimidating trying to decide what to order and the right quantities.

As she glanced over the page, she wanted every flower listed, but her artistic instinct cautioned her against going overboard. The shop needed to look simple, classy and elegant. It would help, too, if it didn't have the overpowering floral scent of a funeral parlor. She also liked the idea of surprising combinations, rare or exotic blooms with something as common as gerbera daisies, for instance.

Afraid that she'd change her mind half a dozen times, she made several copies of the form, then marked her first choices on one and guessed at the quantities. She mixed colors that would blend well together in arrangements, flowers that could be mixed in bright, less expensive bouquets. It helped when she sat back and envisioned the sort of arrangements she wanted to have on display for the party. Pale, splashy hydrangeas with dark greenery and stems of pink and white roses in a glass vase, for instance. Or maybe a tall, cobalt-blue vase filled with sunflowers.

She sketched her ideas out on a pad of paper and completely lost track of time. When the front door opened promptly at eleven-thirty, she looked up in surprise to find Jake there, standing hesitantly just inside the door, a scowl on his face.

"Still in a bad mood, I see," she said, her own tone deliberately cheerful.

He blinked at the accusation, then managed a forced smile. It wasn't the easy, crooked smile she'd once loved, but at least he made an effort. And smile or no smile, she instantly responded to the sight of him, her blood humming with anticipation.

"It looks good in here," he said eventually, after tearing his gaze away from her to survey the shop. "Your dad did a great job."

"He did," she agreed. "I'm thinking of having a plaque installed in his honor. It'll give me bragging rights to have an interior designed and executed personally by a famed architect."

"Not a bad publicity ploy," he said as if she'd been serious. "I'll bet the Internet has a listing of everything he's ever touched. Followers of that kind of stuff travel all over to see designs by the great names in that field."

She grinned at him. "I was actually joking," she said. "I'm not interested in having my shop be nothing more than a tourist destination, and I think Dad's happy enough with the town on his résumé. The inside of my flower shop wouldn't add much." She waved her order form at him. "I've been working on this and I've made a lot of notes, but you were right. I really could use your advice."

He nodded, grabbed the chair opposite her desk, dragged it around and squeezed in next to her. The action put them thigh to thigh in the tight quarters. Jake gave her an impudent grin that practically dared her to complain. When she bit back a comment, he nodded, evidently pretty pleased with himself.

"Let's see what you have here." Before looking at the form, he glanced at the sketches scattered over the top of the desk. His eyes lit up with surprise. "I'm in and out of a lot of shops in the area, so I know what's being sold. These are good, Bree. Really good."

She met his gaze, pleased by the praise. "You really think so?"

"I wouldn't have said it if I didn't. We're way past the point of uttering little white lies to be polite."

"Yes, I suppose we are," she said, though she couldn't honestly say where that left them. Most of the time she felt as if they were complete strangers.

Not now, though, not with his leg touching hers, his heat radiating right through her, reminding her what it felt like to be surrounded by all that raw, passionate masculinity. Now it was all she could do to catch her breath and maintain some sort of facade of calm.

"Bree?"

"Yes, what?" she said, aware that she'd missed something.

Jake regarded her quizzically. "Everything okay?"

"My mind wandered, that's all."

He gave her a knowing look. "Yeah, I have that problem myself sometimes."

"What were you asking?"

He gestured toward the order form. "I jotted down a few things on here. See what you think."

She barely skimmed his notes, then nodded. She really needed to get him out of here before she made a complete fool of herself and threw herself at him. "Looks perfect," she said.

"Okay then. We'll go with this. And when everything arrives here next week, if you decide you need anything else, I'll work with you to make sure you have it."

"I thought you didn't intend to set foot near this place," she said, raising the subject that she'd tried to bring up on the phone earlier. "I figured today was some kind of rare exception."

He shrugged. "The way I recall it, you dared me to come around and keep my hands to myself."

She swore under her breath. She'd forgotten that. "Sure. Right. And the kiss the other day? What was that?"

"It didn't happen on these premises," he said. "Just one of those in-the-moment impulses."

She had to fight the urge to chuckle at the way he was spinning the rules to suit himself. She nodded sagely. "That makes perfect sense, I'm sure. At least to you."

He stood up abruptly. "Lunchtime. I need to get to Sally's."

Disappointed by the sudden absence of heat and contact, she merely nodded. "Of course."

He stood there for what seemed like an eternity, as if he was debating with himself. Finally he muttered something that sounded like, "What the hell," then bent down and brushed his lips across hers. When he stood up, he was grinning.

"No hands," he said with a wink.

And then, while she was still open-mouthed with astonishment, he left, tucking the order form into the back pocket of his faded, butt-hugging jeans as he went. Naturally the gesture kept her eyes glued to his backside as he walked away. She picked up one of her sketches and fanned herself, but the breeze that it generated was no match for the fire raging through her veins.

Outside Bree's shop, Jake nearly knocked Mack over in his rush to escape.

"Well, well, well," Mack murmured, his eyes lighting with amusement. "Look who just got caught fraternizing with the enemy."

"I wasn't fraternizing with anyone," Jake claimed, hoping to hell there was none of Bree's lipstick on his mouth to contradict the claim. "And Bree's not the enemy. She's a client. I was picking up an order." He pulled the paper out of his back pocket and waved it under Mack's nose. "See? Proof."

"Interesting that you feel the need to prove anything to me," Mack said. "What's that Shakespeare quote about protesting too much?"

Ignoring the comment, Jake pushed past Mack and went into Sally's. "Let's order," he said as soon as he was seated in their regular booth. "I'm starved."

Mack's amusement only seemed to deepen. "Yeah, a close encounter of the feminine kind usually stirs up my appetite, too."

Jake seized the opening. "How is Susie these days?"

Mack frowned. "Would you stop asking about Susie, please? We're not dating. How many times do I have to tell you that?"

"Until you can make me believe it," Jake responded cheerfully. He paused as if giving the matter great consideration, then shook his head. "Nope. So far, not quite believing it."

Will slid into the booth. "Are we talking about Mack and Susie? I spotted them walking along Shore Road the other night at midnight."

Mack flushed brick red. "Her car broke down. She called me for a ride."

Will blinked at the response. "So you were what? Walking her home after she'd asked for a ride?"

Mack sighed heavily. "I was downtown. I didn't have my car, so yes, I walked over to where her car was stalled out. I tried to get it started. When nothing worked, I walked her home. What was I supposed to do, leave her stranded or let her walk alone at that hour?"

Jake nodded with exaggerated understanding. "You behaved like a perfect Southern gentleman," he concurred. "I am curious about one thing, though. Why would Susie call you instead of, oh, maybe anyone in her very large family?"

Mack looked up with relief when Sally appeared at their table, order pad in hand and her expression harried.

"Okay, guys, what's it going to be today?"

"Cheeseburger, fries and a soda," Jake said, eager to get back to teasing Mack.

"Same for me," Will said.

Mack, however, studied the menu with the deliberation of someone who'd never seen it before. "I'll have . . ." His voice trailed off.

Will grinned. "Don't keep us in suspense, man. What are you ordering?"

"I'd like to know that, too," Sally said, regarding him with impatience. "The place is mobbed, in case you haven't noticed. If you expect to eat before one o'clock, I need to get the order in."

"Burger, fries and iced tea," Mack said

with obvious reluctance. Then he scowled at Jake and Will. "With a side of peace and quiet."

"You'll need to go elsewhere for that," Jake told him.

Mack gave him a knowing look. "I know why you're harassing me. You don't want me telling Will where you were right before lunch."

"Where?" Will asked, his eyes filled with curiosity.

"The flower shop," Mack confided in an exaggerated whisper.

"Oh, boy," Will said, his fascinated gaze now on Jake. "What was that about?"

Jake gave both of them a sour look and stood up. "Hey, Sally, make my order to go. I suddenly remembered I have somewhere I need to be."

Both men laughed.

"Where?" Mack asked.

"Pretty much anyplace but here," he told them, then headed for the counter, where Sally managed to produce his take-out order in record time.

"Thin skin," Mack commented loudly enough for him to overhear.

"Pot calling the kettle black," Will retorted. "Now, let's get back to you and Susie."

Mack's groan followed Jake all the way out onto Main Street.

Every outfit from Megan's closet was scattered across her bed. She stared at the mess and shook her head. She'd packed for overseas travel with less anxiety. For some reason the upcoming four-day trip back to Chesapeake Shores had her in a complete tizzy.

Okay, she knew the reason: Mick. Like some teenager facing a first date with the guy of her dreams, she wanted to impress him. No, she wanted to knock his socks off, make him rue the day he'd ever let her get away.

Of course, the last time she'd been down there, when he'd openly admitted his intention to win her back, it had scared her to death. And now she wanted what? To have him whip out an engagement ring because he was breathless at the sight of her? She'd probably pass out on the spot.

When her phone rang, she seized it, eager for anything that would distract her from this utter insanity.

"Hey, Meggie," Mick said, his low voice sending heat spiraling right through her.

She swallowed hard. Maybe this wasn't the best distraction, after all. She was having a hard time thinking straight.

"Meggie?"

"Hi. I wasn't expecting to hear from you," she said with forced cheer. "Everything okay?"

"Everything's great down here. Bree's right on track for her big opening. I don't know if what she's doing is the right decision for her in the long term, but she has a sparkle in her eyes these days. I can't argue with anything that could put that there."

"I agree. She sounded really excited when I spoke to her yesterday. This may not be the best solution for her future, but clearly it's what she needs right now."

"When are you getting here?"

She glanced at the piles of scattered clothes and wondered if she'd ever make any headway with packing. "I'm taking an early shuttle on Thursday morning."

"Why don't I pick you up at the airport," he suggested. "There's no reason for you to waste money on a rental car when I have extra cars just sitting in the garage."

"You'd let me drive one of your classic cars?" she asked, stunned.

He laughed. "Not a chance. You can drive my car. I'll drive the Mustang convertible. It'll make me feel like a kid again. If you play your cards right, I'll take you for a spin in it, but that's as close as you'll get to being behind the wheel."

"I have driven it, you know," she said, deliberately taunting him. She knew how he felt about those precious cars of his.

"When?" he asked, sounding genuinely shocked.

"Every time you made me furious by leaving town."

"Megan O'Brien, you drove my classic cars?" he blustered. "Do you have any idea what these things are worth? How much the insurance is?"

"I believe you mentioned it a time or two." More like a hundred, especially when Connor or Kevin pleaded for permission to drive one of them. She doubted he knew about their excursions in the cars and she wasn't about to fill him in at this late date.

"So you did it just to spite me?" Mick asked now.

"Something like that."

He fell silent. "I suppose I should thank my lucky stars you never crashed one."

"Yes, you probably should, given my mood when I was behind the wheel. You have no idea how tempted I was to at least put the Mustang back in the garage with a couple of good-size dings in the fender."

"Do you have any other diabolical tendencies I missed while we were married?"

She chuckled at his suddenly wary tone. "Perhaps one or two, but I think I'll keep you guessing about what they might be. Still want to pick me up at the airport?"

"Of course I do. Seems like I'm going to need to keep a real close eye on you. Then, again, I was planning to do that anyway."

The edge she'd felt she had vanished in the blink of an eye. When the man said something like that, how was she supposed to resist?

"Meggie?"

"Yes."

"I'm looking forward to this weekend."

"Me, too."

"You gonna be my date for the party?"

"I assumed the whole family would be going together," she said, hedging.

"Probably will," he agreed. "But I want it clear that you'll be there with me, even if you and I are the only ones who know that."

"You could always resort to a branding iron," she commented dryly.

"I'm not claiming you as my property," he chided. "I'm asking you to be my date, a partner, the way we used to be."

"Oh, Mick," she whispered, her voice filled with nostalgia and regret. "We stopped being partners a long time ago, way before the marriage ended. You made decisions unilaterally that affected all of us. When I questioned anything, you told me everything you were doing was for the good of the family. If I disagreed, you told me I didn't have any faith in you."

Mick sighed. "I can't deny any of that, but I do remember how good it was when we were a team," he said. "I want that back, Meggie. I miss it."

"I'm not sure it's possible to recapture the past."

"Then we'll make ourselves a new set of

rules, put our relationship on a whole new footing. What do you think?"

"I think that optimistic streak of yours is in overdrive," she responded.

"You used to think that was a good thing," he reminded her.

"It was," she said. "It is. I want to feel what you feel, Mick. I really do. I'm just not there yet. Losing you, long before the divorce, that took a toll."

"Then we'll take all the time you need," he said, giving in, but clearly not giving up. "See you on Thursday. You tell that pilot to fly safe or he'll have to answer to me."

She laughed at that. "He'll have to answer to me first."

"Bye, Meggie."

"Good night, Mick."

Long after he'd hung up, she sat clutching the phone and wondering how she was going to resist all that charm of his. She hadn't been able to do it over thirty years ago. It was unlikely her resistance had improved with age.

Mick walked onto the porch after his conversation with Megan and found his mother already out there, rocking the way she did when she was worried. He sat down next to her.

"What's on your mind, Ma?"

"Megan," she said, slowing the rocker long enough to direct a hard look his way. "Do you have any idea what you're doing, Mick?"

"Of course I do."

"Tell me what happens once you've won her back."

"First of all, winning her back isn't a sure thing," he began.

She waved off the comment. "Don't put on a show of modesty for my benefit. We both know you usually get whatever you set your mind to. Failure's never been an option for you. Do you recall how many people told you this town couldn't be built the way you envisioned it? You never once lost faith in your vision."

"I appreciate the vote of confidence," he said, "but Megan's changed. She's not the sweet, docile woman I married."

"She never was sweet or docile," Nell corrected. "She just loved you so much that she tried to do things your way. For a time that worked because you adored her and tried to meet her halfway. There was balance in the relationship."

"And then I let work consume me," Mick said. "I've heard it before, Ma, and I can hardly deny it." It was the second time in less than a half hour that he'd had to admit as much. He directed a look her way. "I know none of you believe me when I say I'm changing, but think about this. How much time have I been spending at home recently?"

"More than usual," she conceded.

"I walked away from one job," he told her. "Two more offers came my way just this past week and I turned both of those down. There are half a dozen projects in various stages of construction right now all over the country and I've assigned people to oversee each of those. That doesn't mean I won't fly in to take an important meeting or have a look around. After all, my name's associated with these developments, but I'm pulling back from the day-to-day operation of the company."

"How long is that going to last?" Nell asked, her skepticism plain. "One crisis and you could be gone for weeks. I'm not saying that's unreasonable, but it will pretty much shatter the illusion that you've changed."

"Megan and I were married long enough that she can understand the difference between a crisis and a lifestyle," he claimed, though he was sure of no such thing. Crises had a way of coming up back to back. The next thing he knew, the new pattern could look pretty much the same as the old. He could tell from Nell's dubious expression that she knew that as well as he did.

Mick knew there was only one surefire solution. He'd have to retire, turn the company over to the men he'd hired and trained, then trust them to manage it as he would have. Retirement might have been easier if any of his children had been interested in the business, but they weren't. To his regret, they'd all made that plain. Kevin and Connor, the most likely choices, could barely tell a hammer from a saw. As for putting anyone else in charge, he just didn't know if he was ready to do that or even capable of keeping his nose out of the business he'd started.

"I'm too young to retire," he said glumly. "I'd go completely stir-crazy."

Nell's lips twitched. "More than likely," she agreed. "You're a man with a lot of energy and drive."

"Then what do you suggest?"

"It's not up to me," she said, suddenly all innocence.

"But you have an opinion, I'm sure." To his knowledge, she'd never been without one, not on any topic related to their family, anyway.

"First, this is something for you to be discussing with Megan. Put all your cards on the table, tell her how you're feeling about her and the business, and work it through together. It's important to make her part of deciding the best solution."

He nodded. "No problem."

"Okay, then. Second, I think you should turn your energies toward something you can do right around here. Maybe not in Chesapeake Shores, but close by."

He could tell from the glint in her eyes that she'd given this some thought. "Such as?"

"Habitat for Humanity," she said at once, her expression alive with excitement. "Let's face it, you've accumulated enough money to last for two lifetimes. All of your children are provided for. You don't need the income. Put all of that energy and expertise to work as a volunteer, helping to build homes for folks who desperately need them. You could live right here at home. You'd have control of your schedule. And you'd be doing something good."

She gave him a sly look. "A man who'd do something selfless like that might be the kind of man his ex-wife could trust."

She was suggesting he walk away from his company, walk away from the acclaim that had gone along with it. But what she was offering instead had definite allure. Mick had done precious little for others during his lifetime beyond writing checks to charities. He'd certainly been generous about that, but not with his time. And hadn't he learned from his experience with Megan and his children that time was the more valuable gift?

He reached over and squeezed his mother's hand, noticing how much more frail she was these days. A part of him wanted to do something like this just because she'd suggested it, just because it so clearly mattered to her, but there was a lot to consider.

"Well," she prodded impatiently. "What do you think?"

"I think it's an intriguing idea," he admitted.

Her expression immediately brightened. "You'll consider it, then?"

He nodded slowly. "I'll make some calls, explore the possibilities."

"I have a list of people you should start with," she said, reaching in her pocket and extracting something that looked like one of her grocery lists, filled with names and phone numbers in her tidy handwriting.

"Of course you do," he said with a laugh. "Ma, do you have any idea what a treasure you are?"

She looked a little flustered by the question, but pleased. "When you look at me like that, I do," she said.

"I hope I've made you proud."

"Ninety-nine percent of the time, you have," she said with her usual blunt candor. "But we'll get that up to a hundred percent yet. For one thing, you need to start making peace with your brothers. It's way past time to let go of all the hard feelings that split the three of you apart when you were building this town. Those differences don't justify keeping either Jeff or Thomas at arm's length, especially after so much time has passed. They're family, Mick. Seeing them out of duty when I demand it isn't the same as acting like brothers."

He knew she was right, but he wasn't the only one holding on to an old grudge. His brothers bore their share of blame for the rift. "Let's just focus on this plan of yours with Habitat for Humanity for now," he said tightly.

"Pulling this family back together with you at the middle of it is even more important," she corrected. "Helping all these other folks at the same time would be a wonderful bonus."

Though he was only partially convinced that this was something he wanted to do, when she said things like that, she made it all but impossible for him to say no.

"I'll make these calls," he told her. "For now that's all I can promise."

She beamed at him. "And for now, that's enough."

But they both knew she wouldn't let him alone until he'd considered the idea from every angle. In the end, there was every likelihood she'd get her way, even when it came to reconciling with his brothers. After all, despite all his reservations, Mick knew one reconciliation could lead to another. Making peace with Tom and Jeff, showing he could be the bigger man and make the first overture, might very well pave the way to starting over with Megan.

And that mattered more to him than any grudges from the past, any fancy communities he might build or any accolades he might win.

11

Jake had made his delivery to Flowers on Main just five minutes earlier, leaving Bree surrounded by what seemed like a mountain of flowers. She stood in awe amid the buckets of hydrangea stems in their brilliant blues, soft pinks and creamy white, plus tall yellow sunflowers, long-stemmed roses and fragrant tea roses, daisies in shades from yellow and orange to red and pink, impressive and fragrant stargazer lilies, sprays of tiny orchids and delicate freesia. Surrounded by all that color, she breathed in deeply, then promptly sneezed loudly enough to bring Abby out of the back room.

"Now, that's not a good sign," her sister said, her eyes alive with mischief. "Please tell me after all this, you're not allergic to flowers."

"Let's hope not," Bree said.

"What's next?" Abby asked. "Shall we get all of these flowers into the coolers? Do you want some in the back room so you can start arranging them?"

For a moment, Bree simply took it all in, overwhelmed by the task that lay ahead. It made that wedding she'd pulled together at the last minute seem like child's play. What on earth had given her the idea she could handle all this?

Abby came up behind her and gave her a hug. "Hey, it's going to be great," she said as if she'd read Bree's mind. "We have a list of what needs to be done."

"You have a list," Bree said, "because you're organized. It never even occurred to me to make a list."

"Because you're the creative genius behind the business," Abby reassured her. "All the nuts and bolts of running your shop will fall into place."

Bree gave her a wry look. "You weren't this generous with your praise when Jess was messing up," she reminded Abby.

"Because Jess isn't you. She's scattered because of the attention deficit disorder. I had to take a hard line with her to keep her focused. For a bit it seemed she'd forgotten all those techniques that had helped her to get through school and then college. *You* just need a little gentle nudging. This place is going to be amazing. Even if you never did a thing with these flowers, people would love walking in here. It smells fabulous and the colors are stunning."

"Whatever you say," Bree said skeptically. "So what's first on your list?"

Despite Abby's claim that everything could stay exactly where it was and be fine, naturally her big sister had not only a list but had set priorities.

"Getting all these flowers out of the middle of the floor so you can work," Abby said briskly. She opened a cooler door, then went to pick up the bucket of sunflowers. "Tallest in the back so you can spot them?"

"Makes sense to me," Bree said, picking up the long-stemmed red roses and the bucket of pink roses, as well. She handed them to Abby, who remained just inside the cooler door. They worked in assembly-line fashion until all the flowers were out of the main room.

Abby looked at the colorful array visible through the cooler's glass door. "The flowers really are beautiful, Bree."

Bree laughed. "Maybe so, but I think things will sell better if I actually put together some arrangements and bouquets for display."

"Then I'll leave you to that and I'll get to work on decorating the counter with Gram's Irish-linen tablecloth and installing the fountain for the punch. Dad's bringing by a table for the hors d'oeuvres later."

Alone at her workstation, Bree's hands shook as she reached for the cobalt-blue vase she intended for an arrangement of splashy sunflowers. The minute she had the flowers in hand and began to work, though, her nervous stomach calmed and she worked quickly and confidently. The end result of all those years of learning flower arranging from Gram's instinctive talent for it was a simple, decorative and summery display that would brighten any seaside cottage.

"That looks fantastic!" Abby said when Bree carried it into the showroom.

Bree gave her a suspicious look. "Are you going to rave about everything just to build my confidence?"

"Absolutely not," Abby insisted. "You know me. I'm blunt to a fault. Now tell me, what's the price on that arrangement?"

Bree blinked at the question, did a quick calculation of the cost of the vase, the flowers and raffia bow and came up with a figure.

"Not enough," Abby said. "People would pay twice that in New York."

"We're not in New York," Bree argued.

"Then split the difference," Abby suggested. "I guarantee you didn't figure your time into that original price. It's worth something."

"I don't want people to suffer from sticker shock," Bree said worriedly.

"But if you price things too low and have to raise the prices in a month to cover all your costs, it'll be that much worse. Make sure they know this is going to be a classy shop and that they'll get what they pay for. You can always do another beautiful arrangement that's less expensive for people who don't have that kind of money."

Before Bree could respond, her cell phone rang. She grabbed it without checking the caller ID, then regretted it the second she heard Marty's voice.

"Have you come to your senses yet?" he asked without preamble.

"I don't have time to talk, Marty," she said, immediately put on the defensive. "My open house is tomorrow, the grand opening on Saturday."

"Then you're actually going through with this nonsense?" His incredulity and the biting sarcasm in his tone were offensive. When he sounded like that it made it doubly difficult to recall why she'd fallen so hard for him.

"There was never any question about that. Look, I have to run. Bye." She disconnected the call, then turned her phone off for good measure. Knowing Marty, he wouldn't be happy about her hanging up on him and would call right back to let her know that. He certainly wouldn't bother to wish her well. Though he'd once been lavish with his praise and encouragement, she realized now it had been saved for those occasions when she'd done his bidding, not when she'd dared to cross him.

She turned to find Abby regarding her with concern.

"You okay?" her sister asked.

"Fine," she said tightly.

"You don't look fine. I gather that was Marty."

Bree nodded. "I'm just so sick of the way he denigrates everything I do. It wasn't that way when we first met. He was a real mentor to me. He was charming, generous with his time." She met Abby's worried gaze. "How could I have misjudged him so badly?"

"Sweetie, you saw what he wanted you to see. Remember, I met him, too. We all did. He sang your praises. He was sweet to Gram. He talked to Dad about Ireland, charmed him with his wit."

"But Dad said he never liked him," Bree said.

"He saw through him. He heard the way Marty spoke *to* you, and not just *about* you. That's what he didn't like."

"But *I* should have recognized that,"

Bree said, filled with self-derision. "You all saw it. Why didn't I?"

"Because you admired him, because he was your mentor and because he was smart and witty and had set out to charm your socks off."

"Not just my socks," Bree said wryly.

Abby laughed and gave her shoulder a squeeze. "Now, that's a good sign. You're able to laugh at the situation."

"But I still don't understand why things went so wrong."

"If you want my opinion, it was when he realized you were a better playwright than he is," Abby guessed.

"But I'm not," Bree said.

Abby held her gaze. *"Yes,"* she said emphatically, "you *are.* Look, I wasn't going to get into this unless you brought it up, but the reviews of his last play were scathing, even worse than the ones for your third play."

Bree stared at her in shock. "I'd forgotten when it was opening. He asked me to come, but I said no, then put it completely out of my mind."

"Well, apparently it sucked. I looked

the reviews up online just to satisfy my curiosity."

"Why would you do that?"

"Because I know how he made you feel about your work. I wanted to see for myself if his was so impressive that he deserved the way you'd looked up to him."

"Just because he got a few bad reviews," Bree began, feeling the need to defend him.

"Not *bad,*" Abby corrected. "They said his play was a real stinker, unexpectedly amateurish and proof of what a has-been he is."

"They weren't much kinder to me," Bree reminded her.

"But he's the pro," Abby said. "He's been working in the theater for years. He's won awards. He's even been produced off Broadway. You're just getting started."

Bree gave her a curious look. "And the moral of this story would be what? That even the mighty can take a tumble?"

"Or that the mighty don't have the right to systematically strip away someone else's confidence," Abby said.

Bree sighed. "Okay, I get it."

"Don't just say you get it," Abby chided. "Think about it and get your computer out of the closet and start writing again without that jealous, mean-spirited scumbag looking over your shoulder."

"In case you haven't noticed, I'm otherwise engaged at the moment," Bree said.

"And all this is wonderful," Abby said with a sweep of her hand. "If you enjoy it, I'm behind you all the way. But if your heart's still in writing plays, you need to find time for that, too. Not today or even this weekend, but soon." She held Bree's gaze. "Promise me, okay? If you ask me, it's what you were really meant to do."

Bree nodded solemnly. In fact, there was even a tiny flicker of anticipation somewhere deep inside her for the first time since she'd left Chicago in defeat.

She thought about everything her sister had just said and a grin slowly crept across her face. "A stinker, huh?"

Abby nodded happily. "Want to see? I printed the reviews out and kept them in my purse in case you asked about them."

Bree wiggled her fingers. "Hand 'em over."

She read the reviews. With each one

her spirits lifted. It wasn't that she was gloating over Marty's failure. She swore to herself she wasn't. It was just such a massive relief to know that a flop could happen to someone else, someone with more credentials than she had. Maybe she really should try again. She thought of her mother's insistence that her own last play had failed not because of her words, characters or story, but due to Marty's directing. She took heart from that, too.

Then she handed the reviews back to her sister. "Hold on to them, okay?"

"You don't want to keep them?" Abby asked. She grinned. "Maybe frame them and hang them on the wall over your desk?"

She shook her head. "But keep them handy in case I start questioning myself again. Getting Marty's critical voice out of my head isn't going to be easy. Toward the end I could hear it censoring every word I wrote even when he wasn't around."

Abby's face lit up. "But you will start writing again?"

"I promised you I would," Bree said. "It may not be right away, because I really do want this business to succeed, but at least

I'm ready to try. If I can't juggle everything, I'll hire help in here."

"Hallelujah!" Abby exclaimed, sweeping her into her arms and dancing her around, nearly knocking Mick down in the process as he came through the door with the folding table. He set it down and stared at them.

"You two start the celebration a little early?" he inquired, his eyes dancing.

"Not a drop of champagne between us," Abby assured him.

"Well, I wouldn't mind a drop of whatever it is that's put you in this fine mood."

"Hope," Bree said at once.

For a moment, Mick looked confused, but then he caught on and smiled. "Hope's a fine thing. There's a bit of it in my life these days, as well."

Bree was inclined to question him about that, but Abby was already speaking up.

"I suggest we all take a break for lunch and have a drink to hope," Abby said.

"We'll go to Sally's," Mick said. "My treat."

Bree hesitated, thinking of Jake's routine and her promise to Sally, then shrugged. She had a little hope on that front, too. This seemed as good a time as any to test it and see if Jake could handle seeing her twice in one day or if he'd bolt as he had the first time she'd invaded his space.

Jake was all alone in his regular booth at Sally's awaiting the arrival of Mack and Will when he heard a familiar voice say a little too cheerily, "Well, look who's here."

He looked up into Abby O'Brien's eyes, which were twinkling with devilment. He got a sinking sensation in the pit of his stomach when he spotted Bree and Mick with her. Before he could think of some polite but dismissive greeting, Abby was already sliding into the booth.

"Mind if we join you?" she asked after it was too late for him to object. "This place is packed. There are no other booths available."

"Good to see you, Jake," Mick said jovially as he slid in next to Abby, leaving it to Bree to sit next to Jake.

Bree gave him an apologetic look as she took the remaining seat. "I know you were saving these for Mack and Will," she said, scowling pointedly at her sister. "I'm really sorry."

Sally arrived just then and surveyed the booth's occupants with a frown. Apparently satisfied that Jake was hemmed in and couldn't bolt, she finally passed out menus and promised to retrieve a couple of chairs to shove up to the end of the table for Mack and Will who were just walking in the door, oblivious to the scene awaiting them. Jake had a pretty good idea what their reaction was going to be. They might be on good behavior now, but later he'd never hear the end of this little O'Brien-family gathering with him tucked in the middle.

It was Will who spotted them first. His puzzled reaction at finding his regular booth crammed with people quickly changed to a look of pure delight when he realized Bree was among the interlopers.

"Hey, darlin'," he said, leaning down to give her a kiss. "I heard you were back in town, but this is the first chance I've had to welcome you home."

Mack shot a worried glance toward Jake, then offered his own hearty greeting to Bree before shaking Mick's hand and giving Abby a wave.

His best friends then sat back in the chairs Sally had provided, looking as if they could hardly wait for the expected fireworks to begin. Jake wanted to kill them both, even though they hadn't had a thing to do with creating the awkward situation.

"I hear there's a big party at your new shop tomorrow," Will said to Bree. "My invitation must have gotten lost in the mail."

Bree's cheeks flushed bright pink.

"We didn't send out invitations," Abby quickly explained. "There's an open invitation to everyone in town in today's paper. You all really do have to come by and see the place. Jake brought in an amazing assortment of flowers this morning, and Bree's already created some spectacular arrangements. We're going to have champagne punch of the nonalcoholic variety and hors d'oeuvres, so please stop by tomorrow, anytime after four o'clock. We'll be around until eight and there's going to be music on the green."

Abby then turned to Mack with a wicked

glint in her eyes. "I suspect you're going to be a regular customer."

Mack frowned. "Why's that?"

"You're courting Susie, aren't you?" Abby said.

Jake noticed that Mick's eyes lit up with interest. "My niece? *That* Susie?"

Mack's scowl deepened. "I'm not dating Susie," he declared, though it was obvious he knew the claim had lost its credibility, at least with Jake and Will.

Will grinned. "That's not the word on the street, pal. I think your protests are falling on deaf ears."

Jake caught Bree studying Mack with sudden fascination.

"You and Susie, huh?" she murmured, her expression thoughtful. "You know, I can see that. I really can, though she always swore to me that hell would freeze over before she'd ever date a player like you."

"Which is why we're *not* dating," Mack repeated for the umpteenth time.

"Same old song, next verse," Will commented.

With all of the attention focused on Mack, Jake was finally able to relax. He actually felt the tension in Bree's previously stiff posture ease, as well. When she moved slightly, her thigh brushed his. Jake felt the once-familiar arc of heat between them. She obviously felt it, too, because she turned to him with a startled expression. He waited, wondering if she'd shift away, leaving it to her to decide, but she stayed where she was and the wicked torment of that slight contact continued.

"Jake, you'll be there tomorrow, won't you?" Mick asked. "After all, these are your flowers Bree will be showcasing. It'll be good public relations for the nursery."

Actually he'd intended to be as far from Bree's shop as he could possibly be, but Mick had a point. The opening was going to be a PR opportunity for him. If she was even half as talented as he suspected she was, her business would boom and, by extension, so would his.

"Actually I was thinking I'd send Connie over," he said scrambling for a solution that would keep him away yet accomplish the positive-PR spin the event could create. As soon as the impulsive words were out of his mouth, he saw the quick flash of disappointment in Bree's gaze and the surprise in Mick's.

"You have something more important?" Mick inquired, his disapproval plain.

"Yeah, Jake, do you already have big plans for tomorrow?" Will, the traitor, asked, knowing perfectly well that Jake hadn't had big plans for a Friday night in six years. Not since he'd broken up with Bree. That had ended their tradition of Friday-night dinner and movies and started his depressing round of so-called happy hours with Will and Mack.

"Work," Jake mumbled. "I'm doing a big landscaping job and I'm going to be at it until dark."

"Really?" Mack asked, his expression filled with skepticism. "You've always been pretty rigid about a six o'clock quitting time, no matter how many hours of daylight might be left."

"Yeah, usually I am," Jake agreed, unable to keep a defensive note out of his voice. "But I'm behind on this job and the client expects it finished by midday Saturday."

Will gave him a devilish look. "How about Mack and I agree to pitch in and help you finish on Saturday? That way you'll be able to put in an appearance at Bree's open house."

"Sounds like an excellent solution to me," Mick said, regarding him pointedly.

Jake could have argued that Will and Mack would be more hindrance than help, but since he'd pretty much made up the whole urgency of the situation, he saw little point in digging this particular hole any deeper.

"I suppose that would work," he said reluctantly.

Next to him, he felt Bree stiffen. "Don't do me any favors," she muttered, then stood up suddenly. More loudly, she said, "You all will have to excuse me. I need to get back. There's a lot left to be done."

"But our sandwiches aren't here yet," Abby protested as Mick studied her with concern.

Bree smiled, though it was clearly forced. "You can bring it back to me. I doubt I'd be able to choke it down as long as I'm worrying about everything we have left to do."

"But I thought we were going to celebrate," Abby said, prolonging the increasingly awkward moment. Apparently she was the only one at the table unaware of the undercurrents between Jake and Bree.

"Celebrate what?" Mack asked.

Abby started to respond, but at a sharp look from her sister, she shrugged. "Doesn't matter. I'll have Sally wrap up your sandwich. Dad and I will be back soon."

Ignoring Jake completely, Bree nodded at Abby, then leaned down to give Will and Mack each a quick peck on the cheek. "See you tomorrow." She grinned at Mack. "Bring Susie with you."

"Oh, I imagine she's already planning on stopping by," Mack said.

"Which will enable him to delude himself once again that they're not dating, even though they'll spend the entire evening together," Will commented dryly.

Mack gave him a sour look. "If I weren't starving, I think I'd leave with Bree."

"The truth's a killer, isn't it?" Jake taunted, happy to have his friend back on the hot seat.

Of course, if he'd been hoping that would put an end to the speculative glint in Mick O'Brien's eyes as he gazed from Jake to Bree and back again, he was out of luck. Something told him that Bree's father would have a whole lot of very pointed questions for him if he ever caught Jake alone.

Which was just one more reason why he needed to be far, far away from Flowers on Main tomorrow night.

When Jake made his proposal to his sister that she attend the opening of Bree's shop in his place, Connie regarded him with a chiding look. "Absolutely not!" she said very firmly.

"Come on, sis. You can represent the nursery as well as I can. Better even. You're great at all the mixing and mingling. Besides, you need a more active social life. Maybe you'll meet someone."

Jake noticed that her frown deepened with each word he spoke, but he hadn't been able to make himself shut up.

"First," she began, her tone like ice, "mixing and mingling on behalf of the nursery is your job, not mine. Second, I'm not interested in meeting anyone at the moment. And third, it is highly unlikely that a flower-shop opening is going to be crawling with available men, anyway, at least not the kind who'd be interested in me."

She gave him a wicked grin. "You, on the other hand . . ."

Jake was too desperate to get her to change her mind to waste time being offended by her taunt. "This isn't some ordinary, small-town flower shop," he reminded her. "Bree's an O'Brien. Everyone who is anyone in Chesapeake Shores will turn out. It's practically mandatory."

She beamed at him. "Which is exactly why you need to be there. Your client. Your personal appearance. Didn't Mom teach us all about duty and obligation?"

"Isn't it your duty and obligation to do what your boss asks you to do?" he inquired, turning the tables on her.

Clearly unintimidated, she merely shrugged. "Maybe for another boss," she said. "You, not so much."

He resorted to pleading. "Connie, come on, you know how awkward this is going to be."

"What I know is that you're terrified of spending time around Bree," she replied. "My guess is that's because you still have feelings for her and you're scared that one of these days those feelings are going to overshadow whatever anger you've been holding on to all this time."

Bingo, Jake thought, but didn't admit. "Okay, if you understand all that, why won't you help me out and go to this event? A loyal, loving sister would do that."

Connie rolled her eyes. "No, a loyal, loving sister would tell you to kick your stupid pride to the curb, get over the past and go after the woman who makes you happy."

"Bree hasn't made me happy in a very long time," he snapped.

"But she could, and we both know it." She glanced with exaggerated deliberation at the clock on the wall. "Oops, time to go. I have to pick up Jenny at school."

"We'll continue this discussion when you get back," Jake said ominously.

Connie gave him a brilliant smile. "Actually we won't. I'm taking the rest of the day off."

Jake stared at her. "Did I know about that?"

"Nope. I just decided. I don't want to spend the entire afternoon having this same conversation, when the result will be the same. I'm going to take my daughter to a movie instead."

"She's grounded," he reminded her.

"True, but I'm not. Besides, at her age going to a movie with her mom counts as cruel and unusual punishment. It works out well all around. See you tomorrow."

Jake couldn't think of a single thing to say to stop her from going or to convince her to change her mind about the party, so he clamped his mouth shut and watched her go.

Much as he dearly loved his sister, at the moment he couldn't help wishing that he'd grown up with a houseful of brothers instead. Though, come to think of it, Will and Mack were men—his best friends, in fact—and they weren't one bit more helpful or sympathetic than his sister. Apparently he was doomed to be surrounded by people who thought they knew what was best for him, no matter how it stuck in his craw.

12

Bree had an assortment of colorful daisies spread out in front of her on her worktable, but she was staring off into space when Mick and Abby returned from lunch. Abby set her sandwich and soda down in front of her without comment, then went back to work in the front of the shop. Mick was less discreet. He pulled up a stool and studied her with concern.

"Okay, what did I miss back there at Sally's?" he asked. "Why'd you take off like that?"

Mick had been in and out of town when she'd been involved with Jake. Obviously he knew there'd been some kind of a relationship, but it was evident that he didn't have any idea how serious it was or how bitter the split had been. Bree didn't especially want to fill him in. What would be the point all these years later? She certainly didn't want to admit to her father that she'd been pregnant. Mick would be horrified. Beyond fatherly concern, he was a very traditional man, with concrete views about how the world should operate.

Rather than admitting to anything, she said, "I had things to do here."

"Girl, I may be a clueless male most of the time, but I can usually tell when one of my kids is upset. Does it have something to do with Jake? I thought that ended long ago."

"It did."

"Whose idea?"

"Mine," she admitted. At least she was the one who'd run, even if Jake was the one who'd verbally called it quits.

He nodded slowly. "Second thoughts?"

"No," she said at once, then sighed. "Maybe. It's complicated."

He smiled wearily at that. "Relationships usually are. Just look at your mom and me. We were crazy in love. We were married, had all you kids and we both thought it would be that way for the rest of our lives."

Bree pulled herself out of her own funk and looked into his troubled gaze for the first time. "Why didn't it stay that way if it's what you both wanted?"

"It's complicated," he said with a glimmer of a smile reaching his eyes. "Most of the blame is mine. I'm sure you know that. You're the one who has great observational skills, Bree. You see things in situations that other people don't."

She thought about what she remembered from that period in their lives. "You were too absorbed in work," she said, proving his point for him. "And Mom was lonely and restless. She was overwhelmed with raising five kids on her own, for all intents and purposes." She studied him curiously. "She told you that. I overheard the two of you arguing on the porch one night."

"She did," he admitted.

"Why didn't you listen?"

"I did listen," he said. "What I didn't do was change, so she decided she had to take drastic action."

Bree stared at him in shock. “Mom had an affair?”

“I’m not sure I’d call it that. She spent a couple of evenings with some man who was visiting Chesapeake Shores. It didn’t go beyond dinner and conversation, to hear her tell it, but, of course, I heard about it. I think the humiliation was worse than what she’d actually done. Needless to say, I didn’t handle it well.”

“And your lack of trust, that was the last straw for her?”

Mick nodded. “It was. I should have tried to make her change her mind. With all we had at stake, I should have tried harder to understand why she’d allowed herself to spend even a single minute with a total stranger.”

“Why didn’t you?”

“Pride mostly. Stupidity. Maybe even a touch of arrogance. Even after what happened, I didn’t think she’d really leave to go chasing after a whole new life that didn’t include me.”

Bree gave him a commiserating look. “You really didn’t know Mom all that well, did you?”

He laughed, though there was little

humor in the sound. "I thought I did. I counted on her love for me overriding the discontent she was feeling, even that little blip of attraction she felt for someone else. I took a calculated risk and it blew up in my face."

"But when you knew she was really going to leave, why didn't you do anything to stop her?"

His expression turned rueful. "A man's pride has two sides. It can get him through some tough times. But it can also be the thing that keeps him from admitting when he's wrong. I think for a while there I was so stunned by what she'd done, so hurt and angry, I couldn't bring myself to go after her." He shrugged. "And then it was too late. She'd settled into her new life, made it clear in our rare conversations about you kids that she loved New York and her job in the art gallery."

She gave him a knowing look. "If it was too late fifteen years ago, why isn't it too late today? You are going after her again now, aren't you?"

"I am," he said. "Maybe it's because Abby forced the door between us ajar for Jess's opening at the inn. Or maybe it's because I've finally been able to admit I'd be a damn fool if I didn't at least try to win her back. She is, after all, the only woman I've ever loved."

"All those years of traveling, virtually living in other cities, and you never met anyone else?" Bree asked skeptically.

"No one who could hold a candle to your mother."

"How's this campaign of yours going?" she asked curiously.

He regarded her with a pensive look. "Your mother's not going to make it easy, and I can hardly say that I blame her. This will be a marathon, not a sprint, but I'm not quitting till I get the outcome I'm after."

Bree was a little surprised to hear the determination in his voice. "Even after everything that's happened, you believe the love's still there? You've truly forgiven her for taking off, leaving all of us?"

"I have." He studied her. "You wondering if the feelings are still there between you and Jake after whatever happened to split the two of you apart?"

She nodded.

"Based on what I saw today, I'd say the answer's yes. All my life I've needed to be able to read the men I'm working with, get a sense of what makes them tick. Jake Collins has all the signs of a man who's smitten."

Bree sighed heavily. "And not one bit happy about it, I imagine."

Mick chuckled. "That, too." He reached across the table and squeezed her hand then. "Trust me, most men feel that way right before they go down for the count."

"He's very angry with me," Bree admitted. "With good reason."

"Angrier than I was when I found out your mother had been seeing someone else?"

She thought about that, thought it was entirely possible that Jake's fury had run deeper. The hurt certainly had. "Maybe so," she admitted.

"Have you talked about whatever it was that made him so angry?"

She shook her head. "There hasn't been a good opportunity."

"There's seldom a right time for a difficult conversation," Mick told her. "Pick the time that suits you best and insist on it."

"Maybe after the opening," Bree said. She gestured around her work space. "I have way too much to do today and tomorrow."

"Don't put it off too long," he warned. "It will only weigh on you and, trust me on this, it never gets any easier to right a wrong."

Bree took his advice to heart. In the end, bringing up all the old wounds with Jake might not accomplish what she hoped. It might not put the past to rest. Instead, it could make the divide between them so deep that even the wary truce they'd adopted for the sake of her business would sink like a stone.

But she had to try, because whatever the future held for her professionally, the one thing she'd realized since coming home was that she still very much wanted Jake to be a part of her life again. She'd settle for his friendship and no more, if that's all he allowed, but if she were to admit the truth, she wanted the love back, too.

Megan walked off the plane and into the terminal with a confidence she was far from feeling. The minute she saw Mick waiting for her, her pulse scrambled the way it had the very first time she'd seen him all those years ago. She'd known at first sight that he was the one, and even after all these years and all the heartache he'd caused her, apparently he still was. Even so, she was a long way from letting him in on that little secret. In fact, unless he proved that he truly had changed, it was a secret she'd carry to her grave.

She saw the precise instant when he spotted her in the crowd of arriving passengers. That slow, tender smile spread across his face and his blue eyes sparkled with masculine appreciation as his gaze swept over her. Fifteen years ago she would have given anything to have him look at her like that. Maybe then she wouldn't have—

She stopped the thought. Water under the bridge. Mick had finally forgiven her for those two foolish nights when she'd basked in another man's attention, done it deliberately in plain view at Brady's so word would be sure to reach her husband. She'd gambled then and lost. As for now, if Mick had determined not to dwell in the past, there was no reason she should.

"You look just like the girl I married," he

said, sweeping a nosegay of flowers from behind his back and handing them to her.

Touched, she took them from him and buried her face in the mix of pink tea roses and lily of the valley, flowers he'd obviously remembered were her favorites. Or had he? More likely this was Bree's doing.

"I'll have to thank Bree for creating such a beautiful bouquet," she said.

Mick looked hurt. "Are you thinking she's the only one in the family with a touch of romance in her soul?" he asked. "I picked these out myself, from our garden, I might add. The roses, anyway. The lily of the valley Bree had to order for me."

"Really?" she said, unable to keep the note of skepticism from her voice. "And you made this lovely nosegay?"

"With a little help from our daughter, yes," he insisted. "I told her I couldn't claim it, if I didn't do the work, so she coached me through it."

She gave him an apologetic peck on the cheek. "Then I'm sorry and I thank you for the thought and the execution. The flowers really are beautiful, Mick. They're my favorites."

"I think of that each and every time

I walk along the garden path at the house in the spring when the lily of the valley is in bloom," he told her with disarming sincerity.

Megan studied him with bemusement. "Are you trying to turn my head, Mick O'Brien?"

His grin spread as he took the handle of her suitcase from her. "I thought I'd made that clear some time ago," he said with a wink. "Any more luggage?"

She shook her head. "No, just the one bag."

He regarded her with disappointment. "Then it's just to be another short visit?"

"Through the weekend," she said, trying not to be too pleased by the fact that he so clearly wanted her to stay on.

His gaze met hers and held. "And what will it take to bring you back for good, Meggie?"

She swallowed hard. "I honestly don't know."

"Then I'll have to be increasingly inventive and persuasive," he concluded. "I used to know how to change your mind about things."

"I'm tougher now," she warned him.

"And I'm more clever," he replied with a wicked glint in his eyes. "You'll see, Meggie."

She felt her defenses slip at the conviction in his voice. It was true that she'd once found his charm irresistible. She suspected the same would be true now . . . unless she steeled herself against it or made sure they were never alone. It was good that she'd be at Abby's again.

"There's been a change in plans," Mick said as they set off toward Chesapeake Shores.

She studied him warily. "Oh?"

"I thought you and I could have dinner at Brady's tonight," he began.

"But I wanted to go to the shop and help Bree and Abby with all the last-minute details for tomorrow," she protested. She certainly didn't want to spend an evening in a romantic seaside setting with her too-charming ex-husband. They'd shared far too many cozy evenings together at Brady's—at least before she'd chosen it as the setting for her dinners with another man—and she knew this was Mick's deliberate attempt to recapture those intimate moments, to reclaim the setting as their own.

"Everything at the shop is under control," he assured her. "If you don't believe me, you can give them a call." He held out his cell phone. "The number's on there."

She knew that placing the call would be a wasted effort. Mick had obviously cleared this plan with their daughters.

"And what other plans have you made behind my back?" she asked testily.

He turned to her for a quick glance, then faced the road again before speaking. "You'll be staying at the house," he said, his expression bland.

"No," she said firmly. "Abby's expecting me." She was determined to insist on that much at least.

"Actually, Connor will be staying at Abby's," he said. "He's bringing some of his law-school buddies down from Baltimore for the weekend and there will be more room for them there."

She studied him with a narrowed gaze, not entirely buying the explanation. Had the extra visitors been their son's idea or Mick's? "How convenient," she said dryly, suspecting a scheme.

He beamed at her without so much as a hint of guilt in his expression. "I was thinking the very same thing myself," he said cheerfully.

She sat back in her seat, folding her arms across her chest. "It's not going to work, you know."

"What?" he inquired innocently.

"Making sure I'm back under your roof doesn't mean I'll be coming anywhere near your bed," she said directly, wanting to get any ideas he might have along that line right out of his head.

"*Our* bed," he corrected mildly. "It's the same one you picked out when we were married."

"That doesn't make it ours," she said tightly. "I left it a long time ago." She gave him a challenging look. "If Connor's going to be at Abby's with his friends, I'll stay in his room or in the guest suite. It doesn't matter."

Mick sighed, then gave her a chiding look. "Did you really think I'd expect you to come to my bed? I might have hoped for it or even dreamed about it, but I've already moved my things into the guest suite."

Megan felt foolish when she heard that. "I'm sorry I jumped to conclusions."

He shrugged. "It wasn't a huge leap. If it

were up to me, we would be sharing that bed, same as always, but it'll take time for that to happen." He gave her a look loaded with meaning. "For both of us."

Megan swallowed hard. She could cope with his arrogance, maybe even with his flirtatious charm, but this Mick? Being sweet and intuitive? He scared her, because she didn't have a defense in her entire arsenal that could withstand that.

It was nearly seven o'clock Friday night by the time Jake braced himself to walk into Flowers on Main. The party was still in full swing and the place was packed, with the crowd spilling over onto the sidewalk and even onto the green across the street where the band of Irish musicians was playing both traditional and contemporary music.

He'd figured by coming late, putting in an appearance when it was still crowded, he could be in and out without spending more than a minute or two in Bree's company.

He caught sight of her behind the counter, her cheeks pink, her eyes sparkling, her wayward auburn curls escaping from a careless topknot to frame her face. She looked radiant, at least until she caught a glimpse of him. Then her expression sobered and some of the light in her eyes died.

Jake was about to turn away and retreat, when a familiar voice chimed in his ear. "Running scared?" his sister inquired tartly.

He whirled around and glared at Connie. "You! What are you doing here? If I'd known you were stopping by, I'd never have set foot in here."

"Which is precisely why I didn't admit I was coming," she told him. "Did you honestly think I wouldn't be curious to see this place?"

"I took you at your word," he grumbled.

"Well, you're here now. Go on over there and congratulate Bree. She's done a fabulous job with the space, and the flower arrangements are to die for. They make your flowers look downright elegant. This shop will be a huge asset to our business and to the town."

He glanced around, though he wasn't surprised to see that Connie was right. As he'd anticipated after seeing her sketches,

Bree did have a deft touch when it came to mixing colors and textures in arrangements ranging from simple to extravagant. If this was what she wanted for the rest of her life—which he still doubted—there was no question she'd succeed at it.

Connie gave him a gentle but determined shove. "Go," she ordered.

He took a few steps, then to his relief, he spotted Mack just outside the door. He detoured in his direction, only to see that he was entirely focused on Susie, whose back was literally pinned to the wall as if she was trying to escape and had run out of room. To Jake's eye, she looked a little frantic, but at the same time there was something else going on. Even he could feel it.

Susie O'Brien might be fighting the attraction to Mack with every fiber of her being, but she was losing. That much was clear in the way her lips parted as she listened raptly to whatever tale Mack was spinning. If a woman had looked at Jake like that, he wouldn't have missed the signal the way Mack apparently had. He sighed just watching them, regretting that the only time he experienced moments like those these days occurred when he was around Bree. And then he was the one feeling a little frantic and undone.

"I don't think it's hit either one of them yet," Bree commented, joining him and glancing toward Susie and Mack.

"What?" Jake asked, just to be sure her impression jibed with his.

"That they're crazy about each other," she said.

"They do give that impression, don't they?" he said. "But things aren't always what they seem."

Her gaze narrowed. "Are we still talking about Mack and Susie?"

He gave her a bland look. "Of course."

Bree fell silent and for the life of him, Jake couldn't think of anything to break the sudden tension. He'd never been any good at small talk except with Bree, and right now she had him tongue-tied, too. Finally he recalled Connie's earlier observations.

"The shop looks great," he said, keeping his gaze straight ahead on anything and everything except the woman beside him.

"Thanks."

"If tonight's crowd is any indication, you'll be a runaway success."

"Free food and champagne punch, even the kind without a kick, will always draw a big crowd," she observed wryly. "We'll see how it goes when it comes time to shell out the big bucks for my flower arrangements. Don't tell anyone, but I'm winging it."

He did glance at her then and saw real worry in her eyes. "Come on, Bree, you have to know how good you are. I've been in shops that have been in business for years, and the florists don't have half your talent. I told you that the other day when I first saw your sketches."

"If I do, then it's thanks to Gram."

"She may have taught you a thing or two, but you have a real eye for what works. You put a few of your arrangements on display at the inn or any of the top restaurants in town, tuck your business cards beside them, and I guarantee customers who see them will be beating down your door."

Her expression brightened. "Do you really mean that?"

"Have I ever lied to you?" he asked,

unable to keep the edge out of his voice that suggested if there had been any lies between them, they'd been on her side.

She winced at the direct hit. "Are we ever going to make peace, Jake?" she asked.

The wistful note in her voice got to him. "Do you really care?"

Heat flared in her eyes. "Of course I care! I was in love with you, Jake. You mattered to me."

"Just not enough," he reminded her, then shook his head. "I'm not having this discussion."

"This certainly isn't the best time or place for it," she agreed with apparent regret.

"No, I mean I'm not having it, period." What good would it do to rehash how twisted up their lives had gotten? Words couldn't change what had happened. The damage had been done.

"Why?" she asked, her temper flaring in a rare show of O'Brien fire. "Because you're too stubborn and bullheaded to admit that you share the blame for what happened, too? It wasn't all my fault, Jake."

His temper, usually never more than a

slow burn, stirred to match hers. "That's not the way I remember it."

"Of course not, because it's easier to play the victim, to heap it all on me, so you can walk around town with all that righteous indignation on your side," she snapped, going on the attack in a way he couldn't recall her ever doing before.

She would have gone on, but Abby appeared at her side, alarm written on her face. "Everything okay? Should I get Trace over here?"

"No need to call for reinforcements," Jake said bitterly. "I'm on my way out. Congratulations and good luck, Bree."

She scowled right back at him. "Gee, that sounded sincere."

"If you want sincere, go back to that jerk in Chicago. He had *sincere* written all over his face," he retorted, then snapped his fingers. "Oh, wait, he's in the theater. Hard to tell with those kind what's real and what's acting."

The color drained from Bree's face and even Abby looked shocked, but he couldn't bring himself to utter the apology Bree deserved.

Instead, he headed outside, though it

was tough going with what seemed like half the town crammed into the tiny space. Each and every one of them seemed determined to catch his attention or, in the case of those who'd overheard his remarks, were intent on showing their displeasure at his rudeness.

Behind him, he heard Abby ask her sister if she was all right. "And what on earth did Jake mean about Marty? Did the two of them meet?"

Jake didn't wait to hear Bree's reply. Nor did he stop when Will called out to him. He barely slowed down when Mack fell into step beside him.

"Don't say it," Jake muttered to his friend. "I don't want to hear it."

"What?"

"That I just made a complete ass of myself back there."

Mack's lips twitched. "No need, when you have just demonstrated such amazing self-awareness. Will would be very proud."

"I'll apologize one of these days," Jake said, his temper finally cooling.

"Sooner might be better than later," Mack advised.

"Oh?"

"Bree's not just your ex-girlfriend," Mack reminded him. "After the success of tonight's party, she's more than likely about to be your biggest client."

Jake sighed glumly. "Yeah, more's the pity."

Mack threw an arm over his shoulder. "Hey, it could have been worse."

"I'm not sure I see how. Half the town heard the way I spoke to her."

"But not everyone," Mack said. "If Mick, Connor or even Trace had overheard that little tiff you two had back there, it might not have been pretty."

Jake winced. He knew exactly what Mack was implying. If either Bree's father, her brother or her soon-to-be brother-in-law had witnessed the exchange, they'd hunt him down and beat him to a pulp for causing a scene on what was meant to be Bree's dazzling debut as a Chesapeake Shores business owner. The protective O'Brien men didn't take it lightly when someone messed with one of their own. Jake knew he himself wouldn't have stood for it if someone had deliberately hurt Connie in public. In fact, he'd called her ex-husband on exactly that more times than he could count.

"I'd probably feel better if one of them did throw a punch my way," he admitted. "I deserve it."

"I'd ask why you let things get out of hand, but I've already figured out that much," Mack said.

"Really? Because I don't have a clue."

"You're still in love with her," Mack said slowly, as if explaining it to someone too young or too dense to grasp the concept.

"Don't be ridiculous," Jake retorted, dismissing the idea even though his sister had been expressing pretty much the same thing for days now.

Mack leveled a disbelieving look at him. "I may not be a shrink like Will, but even I can recognize when love is in the air."

"Really? Then you know that's what's going on between you and Susie?"

For once Mack didn't leap in to deny anything. Instead, his expression turned thoughtful. "It's crossed my mind," he admitted finally. "There's definitely something there, at least on my part, but she's so damn sure that we'd be a disaster . . ." He shook his head. "She's probably right. My track record with women is a little spotty."

Because Mack looked so miserable, Jake choked back his desire to laugh at the understatement. Mack's track record was legendary, and not in a good way.

"That doesn't mean you can't change for the right woman," he told his friend.

Mack's expression brightened. "You think so?"

"Hey, I'm far from an expert, but I hear it's possible."

"I sure as hell hope you're right," Mack said fervently, "because this not-dating thing we're doing is getting really old."

Sort of like Jake treating Bree as if she were nothing more than a client. Sometimes calling a relationship whatever it took to keep it in a comfort zone wasn't enough. Sooner or later reality kicked in. That's when things always got tricky. And he had a hunch his life was about to move in that direction.

13

Bree kicked her shoes off and put her aching feet up on the porch railing. Standing for so many hours during the open house had been exhausting, though not half as tiring as trying to maintain a smile and engaging in chitchat with people she hadn't seen in years or barely knew. Though she'd been forced to do something similar at the after-parties following the opening nights of her plays, she'd never become comfortable with making small talk. She wondered how she'd endure it on a daily basis.

Meantime, though, she had reason to celebrate. Other than the encounter with Jake, the evening had gone well. Beside her, Abby poured glasses of wine and passed them around to her and Jess.

"Here's to a spectacular debut," Jess said when they each had their drinks. "Congratulations, Bree!"

"I'll second that," Abby said just as the door to the house opened and Megan peeked out.

"Is it okay if I join you?" she asked hesitantly. "I don't want to intrude, but I'd love to help you celebrate."

"Sure, Mom," Bree said, surprised by how pleased she was that her mother was here to share in her success. It felt right to be enjoying this moment with her sisters and her mother, almost as if they were a real family again, rather than women who'd been splintered apart by divorce and their various lifestyle and career choices. Connor had gone off with his buddies after the opening, but he wouldn't have wanted to be a part of the traditional party post-mortem anyway. It was a woman thing.

"Where's Gram?" she asked Megan.

"She should be here, too. After all, she's the one who taught me everything I know about flowers and gardening."

"She was exhausted, so she went straight to bed as soon as we got back here," Megan replied, accepting her glass of wine from Abby.

"And Dad?" Bree asked.

To her surprise, her mother looked vaguely guilty. "I suggested to him that this should be a girls' night. Do you mind?"

"Works for me," Bree said. "Though Dad really did play a big role in tonight's success. He built all the custom cabinetry in the shop. People were raving about it."

"He's really trying to find a place for himself with all of us," Abby said. She gazed pointedly at Jess. "Don't you think so?"

"I guess," Jess said without enthusiasm.

"Come on," Abby chided. "He did as much as you'd let him do at the inn. He made an effort. Give him credit for that much, at least."

"True," Jess admitted grudgingly. "I think he's just trying to impress Mom, though."

Bree immediately shook her head. "I don't think so. He was helping you before Mom even came down here for the inn's opening and he had no idea she was coming when he started working on stuff at my shop."

"Well, I think he wants his family back," Abby declared, then glanced pointedly at Megan. "All of us. So what about it, Mom? Are you going to give him another chance?"

Even in the shadows on the porch, Bree could see the color climb into her mother's cheeks. It made her wonder if the others knew what she did, that the split between her parents had involved more than her mother tiring of Mick's absences. Certainly Abby had never mentioned any kind of flirtation with another man, so it seemed likely she didn't know about it. Then again, she might be the first one to try to protect the rest of them from the truth and from being disillusioned.

"Too soon to tell," Megan said, then deliberately turned her attention to Bree. "Now let me ask you the question that's been on my mind for hours. What on earth were you and Jake arguing about, Bree?"

"Old news," she said tightly, hoping to put a quick end to the subject.

"Didn't seem old to me," Megan said, not taking the hint. "That kind of heated exchange suggests something else entirely."

"Well, I thought what Jake did tonight was very rude," Jess said. "Forget the past, you're a client now and he caused a scene at your party. I wouldn't be quick to forgive that. It was tacky and unprofessional."

Bree sighed. "There's a lot I need to be forgiven for, too," she admitted, surprised to find herself defending Jake. "None of you know about that. There's a reason why Jake is still so furious with me. And now I've pretty much backed him into a corner so he has to work with me. Neither of us have figured out exactly how to make that less difficult."

Megan regarded her worriedly. "Do you want to talk about whatever happened?"

Bree thought about it. No one in the world was more supportive of her than these women, but she needed more time to sort through her own emotions. The truth was, she'd never really dealt with what had happened back then. Losing a baby, even one she hadn't planned for, was a far bigger deal than she'd ever admitted to herself.

Six years ago, she hadn't allowed herself to mourn that loss. She'd seized the opportunity presented by the miscarriage and run . . . away from Jake, away from her memories, away from a commitment she hadn't been prepared for, even away from her pain. Maybe if that internship hadn't been awaiting her in Chicago, she would have stayed and faced what had happened with Jake. Maybe she would have felt what he'd felt, the aching loss of not only a child, but what might have been between the two of them.

"Bree?" Megan prodded. "Are you okay?"

She shook her head. "Not really," she said, standing up. "But it's nothing I want to talk about. I'm sorry to spoil the party, but I'm going to bed. I have an early morning tomorrow. I should try to get whatever rest I can."

Her mother started to speak, but Abby reached out and touched her hand, then gave a subtle shake of her head. Bree appreciated the gesture. Abby had always understood that she found solace in solitude, that she had to work through things on her own.

She leaned down and gave her big sister a fierce hug. "Thanks for everything," she whispered, her eyes damp with tears.

"Anytime," Abby said.

"Give Trace my thanks, too," Bree added.

Abby looked surprised. "What did he do?"

"He watched the twins so you could spend so much time helping me." She grinned at Abby. "Unless, of course, you just left them locked in a closet the past few days."

Abby laughed. "Hardly. Thankfully, they're in New York with their father this weekend, so I didn't have to resort to locking them up. Those two would have broken out in no time, anyway. They're very clever when they set their minds to something."

"I'm not sure I'd boast about something like that," Megan warned. "It might encourage them to test their limits and your patience."

"Believe me, they already do," Abby replied.

Bree gave Jess a quick hug and kissed Megan on the cheek. "See you both tomorrow. Thank you for being there for me tonight and for being here to help me celebrate."

"Love you," Megan said so softly Bree almost missed it.

She hesitated, feeling a once-familiar warmth steal through her at her mother's words. There'd been a time when she'd taken that love for granted, but no more. Now she felt a deep sense of gratitude that the bond was still there, tenuous, but getting stronger every day. "Love you, too, Mom."

And then, before her tears turned into sobs, she ran inside to the familiar comfort of the room she'd made her haven.

But even surrounded by a wall of family photographs, shelves filled with her beloved books and a quilt made by her great-grandmother and brought over from Ireland, there was no peace tonight.

Instead, there was only the image of Jake lashing out. His words had hurt, but it was the pain in his eyes that had cut through her. Talking wasn't going to wipe away that pain. In fact, she had to wonder if the only way to end it would be for her to leave Chesapeake Shores.

But even as the thought crossed her mind, she knew she wouldn't go. Her family was here. She was making a fresh start here. And somehow she would find a way to right the wrong she'd done to Jake.

Jake bought two cups of coffee and two raspberry croissants at Sally's, then settled behind the wheel of his truck to wait for Bree to show up at her shop on Saturday morning. Humble pie might have been more appropriate, but it wasn't on Sally's menu.

He wasn't entirely sure what had brought him over here at the crack of dawn. Oh, he knew he owed Bree an apology, but it could have waited until the next time they crossed paths. Nor was it Mack's reminder that Bree was a client. That was the least of his concerns.

No, he was pretty sure he was here because the shock and dismay in her eyes the evening before had eaten away at him all night. The two of them might have issues—a ton of them, in fact—but they were private. He'd had no right to so much as hint at them in front of half the town.

In any other city, the scene might have

been forgotten an hour after it happened, but it was evident from the silence that had fallen when he'd walked into Sally's earlier that it wasn't going to be quickly forgotten here. Even the usually amiable Sally had been surprisingly caustic with him this morning. Though she hadn't mentioned the incident, it was plain to him she'd heard about it and didn't approve of his behavior. Heck, he'd almost wound up apologizing to *her,* sure proof that he owed Bree an apology.

Lost in self-loathing, he almost missed Bree's arrival. She was already unlocking the shop's door when he noticed her. Evidently she'd been caught up in her own thoughts, as well, because she was clearly startled when he slammed the door of his truck and crossed the sidewalk to follow her inside. She immediately scowled at him.

"You!" she said, not sounding especially pleased to see him.

He held up the bag with the croissants and set the extra-large disposable cup of coffee on the counter. "I've come with a peace offering," he said.

She opened the bag, peered inside,

sniffed deeply, then frowned at him. "It's going to take more than this," she said, even though she immediately removed one of the croissants, broke off a bite-size piece and popped it into her mouth. Her expression turned rapturous in a way that reminded him all too vividly of other ways he'd pleased her back when it had taken little more than a light caress to elicit a sweet moan of pleasure.

"I realize this is just a start," he said. "Mack's had his say. Sally's ticked at me. Half the customers at the café were looking at me as if I'm lower than pond scum. I'm sure if my sister had seen me this morning, she would have punched me on your behalf."

"Was there an apology in there somewhere?" she inquired, studying him with mild curiosity.

"Sorry," he said solemnly. "Really, really sorry for causing a scene."

She tilted her head thoughtfully, apparently reading between the lines. "But not for what you said?"

He winced at being caught. "I can't take back all of it."

To his surprise, she nodded. "Believe it

or not, I actually get that. I hurt you, Jake. I didn't mean to, but I know I did. I understand you want payback."

She regarded him solemnly with those big blue eyes that had always made his knees go weak.

"That's not it," he said defensively. Revenge wasn't what he wanted. At least he didn't think it was. He wanted to have that entire time exorcised from his memory. He wanted his life to be what it had been before she'd broken his heart.

She ate another bite of the croissant, licked the raspberry filling from her lips with the tip of her tongue, then sipped her coffee, her gaze on him. "Then what do you want?" she asked eventually.

"To be honest, that's gotten a little muddy lately."

"Then I'll tell you what I want," she said, her directness a surprise. "I want to sit down with you and talk the way we used to. I want us to be friends again."

Jake was shaking his head before the words were out of her mouth. "I don't think that's possible."

"Because you're still angry," she said. "If we talked, though, put it all out there, maybe tried to see each other's points of view, don't you think we could move on, get back the friendship at least?"

She was offering him an opening, a chance, something he'd once thought he wanted, but now he realized it wasn't enough. How ironic was that? Not ten seconds ago he'd all but told her he didn't want her in his life at all and now here he was admitting to himself he wanted everything they'd once had. Was he insane? Would he really be willing to risk going through that much pain for a second time? As committed as she seemed to be to this new business of hers, he still didn't buy the idea that she'd stay here permanently. Writing was in her blood. Knowing that, only a fool would take another chance with her.

"I have to get to work," he said, backing toward the door. "I wanted you to know I was sorry about last night. Nothing like that will ever happen again."

In fact, he resolved on the spot that someone else would make the deliveries to Flowers on Main from here on out. Better not to take any chances, even if he could still hear Bree's dare echoing in his head. Let her think of him as a coward. It was better than getting pulled in any deeper.

She gave him a knowing look, as if she'd just read his mind. "See you," she said casually. "Thanks for the croissant and the coffee."

"Good luck today. Connie will be in touch on Monday to see how things went."

"Connie?" she queried, one brow lifted. "Not you?"

"Not me," he confirmed. Let her make whatever she wanted out of that, he thought as he let the door close behind him, then climbed into his truck. He exercised massive restraint in not squealing out of the parking place to get as far away from Bree as he could as quickly as possible.

Which gave him plenty of time to notice her standing in the doorway watching him, her expression sad, her hand lifting, then falling back to her side in an aborted wave. If he hadn't been in such a hurry to escape, he might also have noticed his heart breaking all over again.

After the totally frustrating encounter with Jake, Bree's mood was dark as she readied the shop for opening. Abby and Jess had helped her clean up after the party the night before, but she still had a few new flower arrangements to finish and buckets filled with colorful bouquets to sit outside. Thankfully the early-September weather was cool enough to do that. She had a feeling those cheerful flowers were going to be her bestsellers, less expensive than a formal arrangement, but ready to pop into a vase to brighten a cottage for the weekend.

By nine o'clock everything was in place, she'd experimented with her cash register until she could work it easily, and even run through a trial credit-card purchase to make sure she had the hang of that. She ate the last bite of the croissant Jake had brought, finished the coffee, took one last look around and then hung the Open sign on the door.

Her first customer walked in at 9:01 a.m., already bearing an armload of the bouquets from the sidewalk display.

"These are gorgeous," she told Bree as she whipped out her credit card. "And I can't tell you how excited I was when I spotted your shop last night as I drove into town. I have a houseful of company arriving at noon and these will add just the right festive touch to the dining-room table and to their rooms."

"I'm so glad," Bree said as she rang up the purchase. "I hope to see you again."

"You can count on it. I think fresh flowers are the easiest way in the world to bring a house alive after being away. I'm Liz Patrick, by the way. My husband and I bought the cutest summer cottage two years ago. It was one of the original houses in town. We're weekenders for now, though we've been talking about retiring down here in a few more years."

Bree introduced herself.

The woman's eyes immediately lit with recognition. "Your father's the architect who designed the town, isn't he? Please tell him how much we love our house. Every little detail in it is charming. It's everybody's fantasy of what a seaside cottage should be."

Bree nodded. "I'll certainly let him know. He built everything in here, as well."

"Well, we're big admirers of his work," Liz said. "We waited for three years before one of his houses finally came on the market, and we're so happy we did. Now, I'd better run if I expect to beat the mob scene at the grocery store."

"Goodbye, Liz. It was nice to meet you."

After she'd gone, Bree looked at the credit-card slip in amazement. Her very first sale and it had been a good one. Before she could blink, though, she'd had her second sale and then a third.

By noon the buckets of flowers out front were mostly empty, and even four of her more lavish arrangements had been sold. She was flipping the pages of her receipt book when Mick and Megan walked in.

"Was it a good morning?" her mother asked.

"It was a fantastic morning," Bree reported. "I couldn't have asked for a better first day. I'm almost out of flowers and the day's barely half over." She grinned at her father. "I've had almost as many compliments on the interior of the shop as I've had on the flowers. People were asking me to pass along the name of my contractor."

"Maybe for the right price . . ." Mick joked.

"Carpentry would be quite a comedown from what you're used to," Megan noted.

Mick gave her an odd look. "It's how I started," he reminded her. "There's nothing wrong with carpentry."

"I just meant you'd never be satisfied building the occasional custom cabinet after building entire communities," Megan replied.

Mick leveled a look at her. "You never know."

Bree decided to step in before they got into an argument about her father's priorities and work habits. "I'm just grateful you did all this for me. So, what have the two of you been up to today?"

"Since my first trips back were so quick, Mick's been taking me on a tour of the town to see all the changes that have come about since I left," Megan reported. "The downtown area has certainly expanded. There are several new restaurants I'm dying to try."

"Speaking of which, we came by to see if you'd like us to bring you some lunch," Mick said. "We're thinking of trying the little French place on Shore Road if it's not too busy."

"I saw their menu when I walked past it the other day. I'd love a slice of their quiche and a Caesar salad," Bree said at once. "It never occurred to me that I wouldn't be able to get away for lunch. From now on I'll have to bring something with me." She grinned at her father. "Or will you be providing this delivery service daily?"

"Oh, I'll be around for the foreseeable future. All you have to do is call my cell and I'll pick up whatever you want." He gave her a penetrating look. "Or you could call an order into Sally's, then close long enough to run over to pick it up."

Bree immediately shook her head. "It'll be better to bring something from home."

Mick's gaze narrowed. He turned to Megan. "Told you so."

"Told her what?" Bree demanded.

"That something happened there the other day."

"It's not important, Dad. Besides, I don't like the idea of locking the door and walking away during business hours, not even for a few minutes." She was proud of herself for thinking of the perfect excuse to throw him off the scent. This wasn't about Jake, and she didn't want him thinking it was.

"Everyone in town shuts down to run an errand," he argued.

"And I've heard people complaining about it for years. Nothing's more frustrating than making a quick trip to grab something from a shop only to find a sign on the door saying they're closed for fifteen minutes or a half hour or whatever. Who knows when that time started or when it'll end? Most potential customers go away and don't come back. They don't waste their time waiting around."

"She's right," Megan confirmed.

"Okay, you win," Mick said. "You two are the shoppers, not me."

Bree was relieved that she'd managed to steer the conversation away from Sally's and her abrupt departure from the café earlier in the week. Unfortunately, it seemed her father hadn't forgotten it.

"As long as you're not avoiding Sally's because of Jake," he said pointedly.

"Of course not," Bree said hurriedly, avoiding her mother's gaze.

"Why do you think Jake's involved?" Megan asked, her gaze shifting from Mick to Bree and back again. "Does this have anything to do with—"

Bree cut her off. She didn't want her mother mentioning last night's scene. No doubt Mick would hear about it eventually, but she didn't want it to be here and now. "Mom, really, there's no issue."

"But—"

"Leave it alone, please," she requested, casting a pleading look at Megan, who finally nodded with obvious reluctance and fell silent.

"Come on, Meggie," Mick said when two customers came through the door. "Let's grab that lunch and bring something back before Bree starves to death."

"I don't think there's any danger of that," Bree said. "Take your time."

The truth was, though she was hungry, she wasn't looking forward to another uncomfortable conversation with either of her parents.

Mick tried to get comfortable on the tiny wrought-iron chair at the French café, but it was a lost cause. It was a testament to how much he wanted to please Megan that he didn't insist on going to the pizza shop down the street where the chairs were meant for normal-size people.

After they'd ordered and he'd finished squirming and resigned himself to being uncomfortable, he gazed into Megan's eyes. "Okay, do you want to tell me why Bree was so anxious to rush us out of her shop?"

"Was she?" Megan asked, her expression all innocence but her eyes filled with guilt. "I assume it was because customers came in."

"She was jittery as a june bug before those people ever crossed the threshold. Did I miss something last night?"

"You were at the party the whole time I was," she replied. "How could you have missed anything?"

"I was outside for most of the evening. A whole lot of things could have gone on inside and I wouldn't have known about it. Did she and Jake have words? I saw him when he finally showed up. He wasn't inside more than a few minutes before he took off down the street with Mack chasing after him." He frowned. "Something's up with those two. Bree and Jake, I mean."

Megan shrugged. "I didn't overhear their conversation."

"But you know there was an argument,"

Mick concluded. "Don't even try to deny it. The truth's written all over your face. If Jake caused a scene or upset her, then I should know about it and I want to hear it from you, not in the form of gossip from somebody else."

Megan covered his hand with hers. "Leave it alone, Mick. Bree's a big girl. She can handle her own personal life."

"Like hell," he muttered. "Did you ever get a glimpse of the way that jerk in Chicago treated her, the way she *let* him treat her? I know you went out there."

Megan blinked. "How did you know about that?"

"I have radar where you're concerned. I caught a glimpse of you in the crowd on the opening night of her first play."

"You didn't," she said, stunned. "I was so careful to stay in the shadows and away from all of you."

His lips curved slightly. "I know. I watched you slipping back inside after intermission. You waited until the lights went down."

"For all the good it apparently did me," she said wryly.

"It was nice of you to come," he said.

"I'm her mother," she said simply. "I

couldn't stay away. Now tell me what you meant about Marty."

"He talked down to her, patronized her when he wasn't flat-out denigrating her work. Why she put up with it is beyond me. It's a relief to know that's behind her. I won't stand by and let anyone else get away with treating her that badly."

Rather than suggesting that Jake wasn't treating Bree badly, as he'd hoped Megan would, her expression merely turned thoughtful.

"Okay, I'll admit this much. I overheard some of what was said last night," she said eventually. "Bree handled what happened. Those two obviously have issues we know nothing about." She met his gaze. "Any idea what went on between them? They'd barely started seeing each other when I left town. They were just starting high school then."

Mick shook his head, filled with guilt. "Ma might have mentioned a couple of times that she thought they were getting too serious, but Jake always struck me as a kid with a good head on his shoulders. Worked hard, too. Henry Caulfield over at Shores Nursery told me that even as a teenager, Jake was the best employee he'd ever had. He wasn't satisfied just to mow lawns and do the backbreaking landscaping work. He wanted to know every aspect of the business. Didn't surprise me a bit that he bought the company when Henry decided to retire. He's expanded it, too."

Megan gave him an impatient look. "I don't give two hoots about his work ethic. I want to know if Nell was right. Were those two more involved than we realized?"

Mick had always done his best not to look too closely at the relationships in his daughters' lives. If it had been up to him, not a one of them would have dated until they hit thirty. Since that was impractical, he'd closed his eyes to whatever might be going on right under his nose. He'd counted on Nell—and Megan before her—to instill a sense of right and wrong in the three of them when it came to boys. He'd had enough to contend with keeping Kevin and Connor on the straight and narrow, determined to see that they grew up with a healthy respect for women.

In response to Megan's question, he

shrugged. "You'll have to ask Ma. She spent more time around them than I did."

"Mick, you have eyes in your head," she said, her exasperation plain. "Are you telling me you wouldn't have guessed if any of our girls were sleeping with someone?"

"Denial," he said succinctly, even now uncomfortable with the turn the conversation had taken. He'd rather walk an open beam ten stories in the air than discuss the possibility that Bree and Jake had been having sex. "Can't we talk about something else?"

"Such as?"

"Us," he suggested hopefully. "Can I talk you into sticking around here next week?"

"I can't," she said with little evidence of regret. "I have to be back at work on Tuesday. I was pressing my luck by taking Thursday off before a holiday weekend."

"You could quit and move back here," he said, knowing it was a long shot but deciding it was worth the risk. "If you want to keep on working, open your own art gallery, like I suggested before. I imagine our tourist trade could support a quality gallery."

"No," she said flatly, not even considering the idea.

"How are we supposed to resolve things between us with me here and you in New York?" he asked in frustration.

"Time," she explained patiently. "Besides, I don't even know if we can resolve things between us."

He looked into her eyes and saw the real turmoil there. She obviously didn't have his faith that they could work things out. "Time, huh?"

She nodded.

"We're not getting any younger, Meggie. Let's not waste too much of whatever time we've got left."

"Being sure is not the same as wasting time," she said.

He couldn't argue with that, so he merely announced, "Then I'll be seeing you in New York on Wednesday."

Her eyes widened. "What?"

"Did you think I'd let you go back up there and think of all the reasons we can't make this work? I'm going to follow you and show you how we can build a new life, even if I have to prove it one day at a time."

"What about your job?"

He grinned at her. "Haven't you heard? I'm turning over a new leaf. I've got half a dozen men and a couple of women who can run my company as well as I can. I'm going to let them."

Now her mouth gaped. "You can't be serious."

Mick tucked a finger under her chin and leveled a look directly into her eyes. "Don't you know by now that when it comes to you, I'm always serious?"

She swallowed hard and shook her head. "It wasn't always that way," she reminded him.

"True enough," Mick said with real regret for the time when his priorities had gotten all screwed up. "But it was that way in the beginning and it will be from now on."

"Until the next big job comes along," she said, an undeniable note of bitterness in her voice.

He started to argue, then realized the only way to prove it to her was over time. "You'll see," he said softly. "Things will be different, Meggie. I guarantee it."

He had a feeling a good hard kiss might

go a long way toward proving his point, but he knew sparking the old chemistry between them wasn't the way to win her heart in the long run. Slow and steady, that was the ticket.

But for a man of action, it surely was going to test his patience.

14

Despite his very firm resolve to avoid Bree at all costs and despite Sally's proximity to Flowers on Main, Jake refused to give up his daily lunch routine. Going elsewhere would be a sign of weakness and he was not going to allow Bree the satisfaction of knowing he was running scared.

Still, he parked down the block on the far side of Sally's and on the opposite side of the street to minimize the chances of an unexpected encounter with the woman who plagued his dreams . . . and pretty much his every waking moment.

He, Will and Mack were enjoying their

lunch—though Jake had one eye on the door just in case Bree decided to wander in—when Griffin Wilder pushed open the door to shout that someone was robbing the flower shop.

"Call 911!" Griffin hollered at Sally, then took off again.

Jake knew that with Griffin's bad knee and hobbling gait, there was no way the old man would ever get there in time to save Bree. Jake was out of the booth in a heartbeat, followed by Will and Mack.

"Might know he'd want to go play hero," Mack moaned as they bolted down the block.

"It's a surprise to me," Will said. "I thought they still weren't speaking."

"Will the two of you shut up, please. Bree could get hurt. That's the only thing that matters right now." The very thought of some thief laying a hand on her scared the daylights out of him.

Just as they reached Flowers on Main, the wannabe criminal fled through the front door, knocking over buckets of flowers and nearly tripping. Even though he had a good head start, Bree tore past Jake, Will and

Mack, brandishing some sort of flimsy stick that was probably meant to stake plants. Jake took one look at the sight and groaned. He should have known she wouldn't let some robber get the better of her. He had to stop her before she got herself killed. He sprinted a few feet and caught her around the waist, then nodded to Will and Mack.

"Catch the idiot, okay? He's probably scared out of his wits by now."

"We're on it," Mack said. "But you might want to point the police in the right direction."

Even as Mack spoke, Bree was struggling to free herself. "Will you let go of me?" she demanded, trying to kick him in the shins. "I could have handled this. It was just some scared kid, who thought he could score some quick cash. He didn't even have a gun. He was just pretending."

"And you're sure of that how?" Jake asked, one arm still firmly clamped around her waist to keep her from joining in the pursuit of her would-be robber.

Just then a shot rang out down the street and Bree went limp in his arms. So much for her theory, he thought, a sick feeling in the pit of his stomach. This was one instance in which he would have preferred to be wrong.

He patted her cheek as he gazed into her dazed eyes. “Hey, are you okay?”

She blinked up at him, her expression bemused. “He did have a gun, didn’t he?”

“Apparently so,” Jake said wryly, clinging to her a little more tightly.

“I could have been shot,” she murmured, shuddering as reality finally sank in.

“You don’t have to remind me of that,” he said. He was pretty sure every bit of blood had drained from his head when he’d heard the sound of that shot.

Alarm flared in her eyes. “Will and Mack?”

Jake could have kicked himself for not giving a thought to his friends. For the past few minutes, Bree had been his only concern. He looked away from her pale face.

“They’re heading this way,” he assured her. “They have the kid by the scruff of his neck. Mack has the gun.”

The sound of a siren finally split the air and a Chesapeake Shores officer cruised to a stop just in time to take the kid off their hands, cuff him and shove him into the back of the car.

Jake stayed right beside Bree as she gave the officer her statement and officially identified the robber, who'd gotten away with nothing, not even pocket change. Jake felt nauseated at the thought of how easily this could have turned out differently. When Bree started to go back into her shop, acting for all the world as if this had been nothing more than a minor disruption to her morning, he almost lost it. He waved Will and Mack toward Sally's, promising to join them there in a minute.

Inside the shop, he closed the door and locked it, then scowled at Bree. "Sit down," he ordered.

"Why? I'm fine."

He rolled his eyes at her stubbornness. "And in about two seconds, all of this is going to sink in and you're not going to be so fine, and I do not want to have to pick you up off the floor. Sit."

She scowled, but she sat.

"Do you keep anything to drink in this place? Anything to eat?"

She shook her head. "I usually order

takeout from Sally's, then get it after you've been there."

He stared at her blankly. "Why?"

She gave him a wry look. "Oh, please, you know perfectly well you have dibs on the place from noon to one. Sally's orders."

Jake muttered a curse under his breath. It seemed that despite his best efforts to appear unfazed by Bree's return, half the town knew better anyway. If he was going to have the reputation of a fool, he might as well throw himself wholeheartedly into being one. Still shaking with fear, he hauled her out of the chair and into his arms. He sealed his mouth over hers and kissed her the way he'd been wanting to since he'd first set eyes on her weeks ago. That kiss at the bistro had been a mild-mannered peck by comparison to this soul-searing claiming of her mouth.

Desire exploded through him. Not good, he told himself, but ignored the warning. It was too good. Too damn good. He'd missed the way she tasted, the way she melted against him, the way she came alive under his touch, the soft little purr in the back of her throat that told him he was doing something exactly right.

He'd lost her once, could have lost her today forever. Knowing that terrified him.

Confused, he backed off. Did he want this again, this desperate neediness, this hunger, this passion? Hadn't he learned his lesson the first time?

Apparently not, because the answer was yes. He wanted her. He wanted it all.

Except for the heartache. He could do without that. Remembering what it had been like when she left had him turning for the door, fleeing from the shop, past Sally's, then leaping into his truck and driving straight out of town to a hilltop overlooking the bay where he could be alone and think. Thirty minutes there, with all his thoughts filled with Bree, he cursed himself for not realizing he couldn't shake her so easily. Finally he drove back to the nursery, where Connie was waiting for him, her expression smug.

"Not a word," he said as he stormed past her and slammed the door to his office in what was becoming a habit.

"I was just going to warn you," she called after him.

But her warning was too late, because when he turned around there was Bree behind his desk. Unlike the rattled look she'd worn after he'd kissed her, right now she looked sweet and sassy and very much in control of herself and the situation.

"I think you and I have some unfinished business," Bree said, her gaze unflinching as Jake returned her challenging look without so much as a blink to indicate she'd surprised him. "Lock the door and tell Connie we don't want to be interrupted."

To her satisfaction, instead of the panic she'd seen in Jake's eyes earlier, there was pure masculine anticipation. She had no idea what had changed since they'd parted, but clearly something had. Holding her gaze, he flipped the lock on the door, then made the call.

"Okay, what's next?" he inquired with a tilt of his head and a smile tugging at his lips. "You seem to be calling the shots." He didn't sound as if he minded all that much.

"We talk," she said. "We put it all out there, what happened, how I felt, how you felt. We deal with the anger and the recriminations and all the rest of it. Then we put it behind us once and for all."

Her proposal clearly wasn't what he'd been expecting. Shadows darkened his eyes.

"No," he said flatly. "Water under the bridge."

She shook her head at that. "No, it's not. It's backed up so deep, we're both drowning in it."

"Why do you want to do this?" he asked, looking perplexed.

"You kissed me, Jake, that's why. Twice, in fact. Everything we ever felt was in those kisses and I want it back. We'll never get it if we don't put the past to rest."

"I don't want it back," he insisted. "I don't want you."

"Liar," she said succinctly.

She could see him struggling with a smile, but he couldn't contain it.

"Okay, yeah, the first kiss might have been nothing more than an impulse, but even I can't dismiss the one today so easily. It pretty much proved how much passion's left between us, but I'm stronger than that."

"Why should you have to be? Why shouldn't we try again?"

"Because I don't want to," he claimed.

"You don't *want* to want to," she said. "There's a difference."

"Not if I put my mind to it," he replied.

She didn't even try to stop her own smile. "But it takes so much energy to fight it, Jake. This thing between us will win. We both know it. We couldn't fight it years ago when it started. We were barely in junior high, but we already knew what we wanted, knew we belonged together."

"That was then," he insisted stubbornly.

"I think I can prove it hasn't changed."

He frowned at that. "Okay, let's say you're right. I need to know something before we get into this thing between us any deeper. Why did you come back to Chesapeake Shores? Was it for me?"

She honestly couldn't say that, so she shook her head. "Chicago wasn't working for me anymore. Being back here, it felt right."

"So this all-consuming thing you claim exists between you and me, that was just an afterthought, maybe a pleasant way to pass the time now that you're here?"

She heard the heat and anger behind his words, maybe even a hint of sorrow, but she couldn't deny that he was at least partially right. He wasn't the reason she was back. But he might be the reason she'd stayed. *Might be,* however, wasn't good enough.

"What's the matter, Bree? Cat got your tongue?"

"I don't want to lie to you."

"Why not? It wouldn't be the first time."

She regarded him with indignation. "I never lied to you, Jake. Never!"

"I suppose that's true," he admitted. "You got me on a technicality. You didn't flat-out lie. You never said anything at all. You just let me believe we were going to have a future and then you left. Do you have any idea how it felt, knowing that I was good enough to marry if there had been a baby, but once you lost the baby I was totally dispensable? You didn't need me anymore."

"It wasn't like that," she said, though she knew it had been exactly like that. Tears of shame welled up in her eyes. She'd been selfish and immature and she was sorry. "I never meant to hurt you. I was only thinking about what I wanted, what I needed."

"And I was an afterthought, just like when you came back here. How am I supposed to get past that? How can I forget it?"

"Maybe you can't forget," she conceded. "But what about forgiveness, Jake. Do you think maybe you can forgive me? I am sorry. I truly am."

His gaze held hers, and then he looked away. "Maybe someday," he said quietly. "But not today. Not when you still can't say I come first with you. I deserve better than that, Bree."

Bree heard the finality in his voice and stood. She could only go so far to make amends, to win him back. Until he was ready to meet her partway—until she could say what he really needed to hear—there was no point.

"Call me when you're ready to try," she said, then unlocked the door and walked away, waving distractedly at Connie as she passed and not allowing a single tear to fall until she'd reached the seclusion of her car.

Then she wept, not just for herself, but for all the pain she'd obviously caused a man who hadn't deserved it. All Jake had ever done was love her unconditionally, stand by her when she'd discovered she was pregnant. What had she given him in return? Nothing.

Oh, she'd thought that she'd given him her heart, but she'd handed it over with strings attached. He had to let her go, let her make a success of herself halfway across the country, wait for her. And he had to do all of that with no promises, no commitment.

And when he'd even been willing to accept her terms, she'd betrayed him by falling into bed with Marty, a man who wasn't half as decent or kind or loving. It was a wonder Jake didn't hate her after that.

The real wonder, though, was that he still loved her, even after everything she'd done. He didn't want to, certainly, but he did.

And one of these days, if she was careful with his heart and patient with him, he just might admit it and give her another chance.

Sitting in his big country kitchen, with sunlight streaming through the windows, Mick's mood turned dark. He cut off his cell phone and muttered a curse that had Nell regarding him with stern disapproval.

"Sorry, Ma," he said automatically.

"Mind telling me what's upset you enough to use that kind of language when I'm sitting right here in front of you?"

"The project in Seattle's hit a snag. I need to fly out there today."

"You used to jump at the chance to rush in and untangle a snag," she commented, studying him curiously. "What's changed?"

"Tonight I have dinner plans in New York with Megan," he said grimly.

She nodded in understanding. "I see. And she's going to think you're falling right back into the same old pattern if you cancel."

"Who could blame her?"

"Tell me, is this snag in Seattle likely to change much between today and tomorrow?"

He thought about the question, then shook his head. "No."

"Then couldn't you just as easily fly out first thing in the morning from New York, instead of later today from Baltimore?"

He regarded her with amazement. "Now, why didn't I think of that?"

"Old habits are hard to break," she said. "For a lot of years you rushed right out the door, no matter what was going on around here. I suspect most of those crises could have been handled some other way, too, but you only know the one way. You have to go and fix things yourself, the faster, the better."

"It's my company, my responsibility," he said defensively.

"But part of being a good man is learning to balance the priorities in your life. This is your family and therefore just as much your responsibility as your business. There were times when seeing Connor play ball or Jess in the Christmas pageant at school were just as important as whatever crisis was going on at work."

"You have a point," he conceded grudgingly.

She sat back, a gleam of satisfaction in her eyes. "Of course I do. I didn't get to be this age without learning a thing or two about life. You'd do well to listen to me more often."

Mick chuckled. "You still think an old dog like me can learn a few new tricks?"

"I'm sure of it," Nell said. "You're an O'Brien, aren't you? We have an endless capacity for reinventing ourselves. Just look at what Abby's doing. Or Bree. They've turned their whole lives around these past few months."

Mick wished he felt as comfortable with those changes as Nell apparently did. "Speaking of Bree, do you really think she's happy?" he asked. That had been bothering him a lot recently. Bree was turning her new business into a success, no question about that, but he couldn't help wondering if she wasn't hiding from the kind of work she'd been meant to do.

"Happy enough, I suppose," Nell said. Her expression turned thoughtful. "But fulfilled? That's another story."

"Do you think she's writing at all?"

"I see the light on in her room till all hours, so she might be. She could just as easily be lost in some book she's reading, though."

"I don't like it," Mick said. "And I blame Demming for it."

"Well, I'm more worried about the man who's right here under our noses," Nell admitted. "It can't be easy for her, dealing with Jake day in and day out the way she has to. Can't be easy for him, either."

Mick frowned at that. "Do you know what happened between those two?"

His mother shook her head. "I have my suspicions, but no facts."

"Okay, what do you *think* happened?"

"I'm not going to speculate," she said. "These are questions you need to be asking Bree." She gave him a pointed look. "If you really want to hear the answers."

"What do you mean by that? I wouldn't be asking you if I didn't want to know. I'm worried about her. She's always kept things bottled up inside. She's not like Abby, who says what's on her mind. Or Jess, who flies off the handle at the drop of a hat. I had to get used to Bree's way of dealing with things, but there's something different about the way she is now." He shrugged, trying to find the right words. "It's like her soul's been bruised."

To his regret, Nell nodded slowly. He'd been hoping for a denial.

"Couldn't you talk to her?" he pleaded. "Or maybe Abby would."

"I think we just need to let her be for now. She'll work through this in her own time. She always has."

Mick wasn't content with that. "What if she can't find her way?"

"Then we'll be here for her, same as always." She covered his hand. "She knows that, Mick. She counts on it."

"You've been here," he corrected. "Not me."

"You're here now," she said, letting him off the hook for the past.

"I doubt we can fix anything before I fly to New York and then Seattle," he said wryly.

"You planning to be gone for weeks?" she retorted.

"No, a few days at most."

"Then we'll reevaluate when you get back. I'll keep an eye on her."

He smiled at that. "You always have. Do I tell you often enough how grateful I am that you were always here for my kids, especially in the rocky days after Megan left and I ran off to bury myself in work?"

"That's what family does," she said simply. "If there's a void, we step in and do what needs to be done."

Mick sighed. Of all the lessons she'd ever taught him, why did it seem that was the one that hadn't stuck. He'd failed Megan, failed his kids. No more, though. From here on out, he was going to be front and center in their lives. He didn't miss the irony that he'd waited until they were all adults and pretty much set on their own paths before figuring out what it meant to be a real father.

"How'd it go with Jake?" Jess asked when Bree got back to Flowers on Main.

"How do you think? He's still stubborn as a mule," she said grimly. "Thanks for running over here to fill in for me. I didn't want to set a precedent for sticking a Closed sign on the door in the middle of the day. I suppose I'm going to have to think about part-time help soon. I thought I could handle the shop by myself, but I'm beginning to see that's all but impossible."

"Well, until you find someone, I can be your backup. As for today, I'm almost disappointed you're back so soon. I was hoping I'd have to stick around for the rest of the afternoon."

"Were you hoping to avoid problems at the inn?"

Jess grinned. “No, I was hoping you’d be off somewhere having your wicked way with Jake.”

“I wish. Maybe if he’d let nature take its course, we could get past some of these barriers between us,” Bree said with real regret. “But he’s not going to give in to temptation so easily.”

“He’s a man. He’ll cave eventually,” Jess said knowingly.

Bree shook her head. “Maybe he’s right. Maybe we can’t go back. There’s a lot of history we’d have to overcome.”

Jess studied her intently. “Do you really want Jake back, Bree? It wasn’t that long ago that you were involved with Marty. Maybe Jake’s just a rebound guy.”

“I was serious about Jake before I ever met Marty,” Bree reminded her. “I think that makes him an exception to the rebound thing.”

“Not necessarily. You know Jake loved you. There has to be a certain comfort in that. Going back to him would be familiar and safe.”

Bree shook her head at once. “There’s nothing safe about going back to Jake. There are monumental complications.”

"Such as?"

Bree needed to talk to someone. Abby might have been her first choice, but Jess was here. She drew in a deep breath and admitted, "I was pregnant with Jake's baby before I went to Chicago."

Jess stared at her with shock that quickly turned to dismay. "You didn't have . . ."

"An abortion? No. I had a miscarriage."

Jess's expression filled with sympathy. "Oh my God! And none of us knew? Not even Gram or Abby?"

Bree shook her head. "I only told Jake. He wanted to marry me right away. He was ecstatic."

Tears stung her eyes at the memory of the way he'd looked when she'd told him that she'd miscarried. He'd been devastated. And what had she said? She'd told him it was for the best, that they weren't ready for marriage, that she wanted to go through with her plan to move to Chicago. She'd told him all that practically in the same breath with the announcement that they'd lost their child. Thinking of it now, she was filled with regret and dismay. How callous she must have sounded. How utterly selfish!

The tears that had welled in her eyes spilled down her cheeks and the next thing she knew she was sobbing. Jess flew around the counter and pulled her into her arms.

"It's okay," she murmured. "Let it out, Bree. I don't know how you've kept it inside all these years."

Instead, Bree pulled away and swiped impatiently at her damp cheeks. "I don't know what got into me. I never think about this, at least I didn't until recently."

Jess regarded her solemnly. "Maybe you should. Losing a baby is a huge thing."

Bree shook her head. "What good would it do? It's over. I handled it the best way I knew how."

"And Jake? How did he handle it?"

Fresh misery stirred inside her. "Not so well," she admitted. "And I just walked away and left him here to cope with the loss all on his own. The baby was real to him from the moment I told him I was pregnant. For me it was a problem, but for him the baby was a joy. And I acted as if I didn't care a bit that we'd lost it. Sometimes I'm amazed he can even bear to look at me at all."

Jess regarded her with sympathy. “Okay, so Jake was all alone to deal with the loss, but so were you. Who helped you cope?”

Bree flinched inwardly. “I didn’t cope, actually. I moved on. I put everything that had happened into some little box inside, closed the lid, locked it and threw away the key. It would have stayed locked away forever, I think, if I hadn’t come back here and seen Jake again. That’s dredged it all up. Now there are days when I can’t stop thinking about the baby we lost, the way our life could have been.”

“I’ll repeat what I said earlier,” Jess said. “Maybe it’s time to get it out in the open.” At Bree’s horrified expression, she added quickly, “I’m not suggesting you tell the universe or even the family, just whoever you need to talk to in order to put this behind you in a healthy way.”

“A shrink?”

“Or Jake,” Jess suggested softly. “Think about it, sis. He probably knows more about what you’re feeling than anyone else.”

“I doubt Jake’s interested in being my sounding board,” Bree replied. “He’s certainly balked every time I suggested we clear the air. And I’m not even sure you’re right that I need to dredge up my feelings about the baby. I just need to find a way to make things right with him."

Jess looked her directly in the eye. "The only way to get Jake back in your life is to face this together. I may not have much of a history with long-term relationships, but I do know that you're doomed if you try to ignore an elephant this size that's sitting squarely in front of you."

Bree sighed. Her sister was right. Who would have thought that often flighty, unattached Jess would nail what had to be done? But accepting that Jess knew what she was talking about didn't make Bree one bit happier or more eager to act on the advice.

15

Jake had spent the entire morning at Mrs. Finch's, mulching all of her lilacs under her supervision. That task would have been tedious enough under the best of conditions, but she had very specific ideas about what she wanted. There'd been a couple of times toward the end when he'd thought she was going to insist on measuring the depth of the mulch with a ruler before pronouncing the job complete.

By the time he got back to his office, he was hot, filthy, exasperated and hungry. Unfortunately, Connie was waiting for him with a harried expression.

"Don't sit down," she ordered. "You need to go right back out again to make an emergency delivery."

He studied her with suspicion. "Isn't that why Jimbo works for us, to handle deliveries?"

"He's already gone out to make half a dozen deliveries, including all those rhododendrons for the Hendersons. He promised to help Aggie get them in the ground. I told him he could. He won't be back for hours."

Jake studied his sister's face. "Doesn't matter. He has a cell phone in case we need him. If this is an emergency, call him back in. Agatha Henderson can wait an extra hour, since he's doing her a favor."

"It's not a favor," she said. "It's called good customer service, something you're known for, thanks to me. Besides, it's a waste of gas for him to drive all the way back here when you're already here and can make this delivery."

Since their fuel costs for deliveries had skyrocketed over the past year, Jake could hardly argue. "Okay, where's the emergency and what am I delivering?"

"I've pulled the order together," she said,

leading the way into the greenhouse where a dozen buckets of fresh-cut flowers were lined up by the door.

Jake got a very bad feeling in the pit of his stomach. “Let me guess,” he said. “They’re going to Flowers on Main.”

She nodded happily. “I’ll let Bree know you’re on your way.”

He shook his head. “I’ll put them in the truck. You can drive them over.”

“Not me. I’m going to lunch.”

“So am I,” he argued. “Just as soon as I’ve cleaned up.”

“But you’re going to Sally’s, which is practically next door to Bree’s shop.” She beamed at him. “How convenient is that?”

Jake knew he’d be wasting his breath to continue arguing. Obviously Connie had thought this through. She’d have an answer for any excuse he could come up with. Whether she had an ulterior motive was less clear.

“Fine,” he muttered, picking up the first batch of buckets and loading them into the back of his truck. Connie followed with several more. It took less than five minutes to transfer all of them.

“When Bree orders next week, tell her

she needs to get it right the first time," he told Connie.

Her brow rose. "If you really want to act like a jerk rather than a grateful businessman who's suddenly gotten a huge, unexpected order, you'll have to tell her that yourself."

Jake sighed. "Point taken." It was annoying that Connie was almost always right when it came to customer-service issues. She was a big part of the reason the nursery had increased sales since he'd taken over. She had the tact and diplomacy he lacked.

A half hour later he pulled up in front of Flowers on Main and noted that most of the buckets on the sidewalk had been emptied of the fresh flowers they usually held. No wonder Bree had called in an emergency order. Business must be good, even this late into the fall season. The Indian-summer days were drawing tourists to town well into October.

He wasn't sure how he felt about her success. If she'd failed, maybe she would have gone back to the career he knew she loved. Maybe she'd have left town, which would have made his life a heck of a lot less complicated.

When he walked in the front door with the first of the flowers, her head snapped up and surprise lit her eyes, immediately followed by obvious relief.

"Thank goodness," she said fervently. "I ran out of almost everything by ten o'clock this morning. Apparently a lot of weekenders are taking advantage of this weather to come to town for a few extra days at their cottages."

"Hopefully this will be enough to hold you for the weekend. I won't have anything new in stock until next week."

"Whatever you have is great," she said. "I know I should have ordered more to begin with, but I'm still getting the hang of this. Last Friday rain was predicted and almost no one came down for the weekend. I had a bunch of leftover flowers that I turned into arrangements and donated to the hospital."

"Why didn't you just toss them?"

"Why, when they could just as easily brighten someone's day?"

The unhesitant response reminded him

of one of the reasons he'd fallen in love with her in the first place. She might be shy and withdrawn, but she had a generosity of spirit that warmed everyone around her. More impressive, she seemed unaware of how rare such little acts of kindness were.

Because it threw him to spend even a minute remembering her good points, he went back outside to gather another batch of flowers. After he'd set them inside the cooler for her, he paused by the counter.

"So, are the part-timers your best customers?" he asked, wondering how she'd make out when they stopped coming down as frequently during the cold, winter months.

"For the bouquets, they are. Locals order more for funerals and special events. I have a couple of orders from local restaurants for fresh flowers for their tables, but all they want are a few stems of daisies or something that they can stick in small vases just to add a little color to the decor. Next weekend I'm doing the flowers for a wedding at the inn, so I'll have a big order for you on Monday for that."

Jake was startled by the excitement he

heard in her voice. "You're really enjoying this, aren't you?" he said.

"I love it," she admitted. "It's challenging, but it's rewarding, too." She leaned toward him as if confiding a secret. "And you know something else?"

"What?"

"I love counting the receipts at the end of the day."

He chuckled at that. "Do you love any of it as much as writing? For as long as you and I were together, that's all you really wanted. Have you forgotten how much writing plays meant to you?"

She shook her head. "Of course I haven't forgotten. I just needed to get away from it for a while. Amazingly, though, now that I am, it's as if I freed something in myself. I've written more in the past week than I had in months before I left Chicago."

"That's great," he said, trying to muster the appropriate degree of enthusiasm. "What happens when you finish the play? Will you take off, head back to Chicago?"

"It's not a play," she confided, ignoring his reference to Chicago completely. "I'm trying to write a novel. It's very different from what I was doing before. I'm not entirely sure whether it will be any good, but it's been an interesting change of pace for me."

Jake couldn't decide if that piece of news was good or bad. She could write novels and stay right here, couldn't she? Was that what he wanted?

"I'd like to read it," he said impulsively. "When you're ready, that is. I know you never like to show anyone what you're working on until you're satisfied with it."

She regarded him thoughtfully. "You know, I could use an outside opinion," she said slowly. "You read a lot. You can tell me if you think I have any idea what I'm doing."

Her willingness to let him sneak a peek at a work in progress startled him. "Really?"

"Unless you didn't really mean it," she said. "I mean, don't feel obligated or anything."

"No, I'd like to read it," he said quickly, surprised by his own eagerness. "I always loved your work. Your plays were amazing. I felt as if I'd met every one of your characters personally. I wish I'd had the chance to see one onstage."

"I invited you," she reminded him.

He leveled a look into her eyes. "You know why I couldn't be there, Bree."

She sighed. "Yes, I know. I just wish it had been different between us then."

"Yeah, well, it's not possible to change the past." He made a quick trip to the truck, then hurriedly set the last of the flowers inside the shop. "I've got to run. See you, Bree."

Again, he heard her sigh as he bolted. Unfortunately, the simple act of putting distance between them was doing less and less to protect his emotions. No matter how thick the wall he'd erected around his heart, no matter how great his determination to keep her out, their lives seemed destined to become entangled all over again.

Not really realizing what she was doing, Bree plucked a daisy out of one of the buckets of fresh flowers and began tearing off petals in an old he-loves-me, he-loves-me-not way as she stared after Jake. She didn't know quite what to make of their conversation.

His desire to read what she was writing

surprised her. It reminded her of the old days, when they would sit side by side in bed on a Sunday morning, she with whatever book she was reading or the newspaper, and Jake with the pages of her latest play. He'd already been living in his own tiny apartment then. Just out of college, he could have stayed on with his folks, but he'd wanted his independence and a place where the two of them could be alone. They sometimes lingered like that until noon before going to have a midday dinner with his folks or with Gram.

Gram had never asked about the fact that Bree sometimes didn't come home on Saturday nights. She'd been over twenty-one, after all. There'd been no disguising the worry in her eyes, though. And that's what it had been, too—worry, not disapproval. For all of Gram's old-fashioned ways, she'd cared most about them being happy and she'd clearly seen heartache ahead for Bree and Jake. She'd even broached the subject once.

"I know you've applied for several theater internships," she'd said to Bree. "You're going to leave here one of these days. What happens to Jake when you go?"

"He understands my plans for the future," Bree assured her blithely, convinced they would find some way to make it work.

"It's a far cry from understanding a theoretical plan to living with it," Gram had cautioned. "If you love Jake, and I think you do, treat his heart with care."

Bree had thought at the time she was doing just that, but the reality had turned out to be otherwise. She'd blamed a lot of it on the pregnancy and subsequent miscarriage, but realistically she could see now how difficult it would have been to maintain a long-distance relationship even if the conditions had been ideal.

Pushing aside the memory, she spent the afternoon making arrangements for Saturday and selling several more bouquets of the newly delivered fresh-cut flowers. Just as she was about to close for the day, the bell over the door rang and she looked up to see Connie crossing the threshold. They'd been friends once, but it had been awkward between them since Bree's return.

She gave Jake's sister a tentative smile. "Hi, what brings you by?"

"I was hoping we could have a drink together," Connie admitted. "I haven't seen nearly enough of you since you got back to town."

"That's my fault," Bree said at once, delighted by Connie's overture. "I wasn't sure if us getting together would make it hard for you after what happened with Jake and me."

Connie grinned. "If I'm forced to choose sides, I'd have to be on his, always," she admitted. "But I'm thinking there's really only one side here and he's just too stubborn to admit it." She tilted her head to study Bree. "I am right about that, aren't I? You do still have feelings for my brother?"

"I'm beginning to think so. I've missed him, no question about it."

Connie gave a satisfied nod. "So, how about it, then? Do you have time for a drink? Jenny's planning a so-called Friday-night study date, so I only have an hour or so before I have to get home to make sure there's actually any studying going on."

Bree was flabbergasted. The last time she'd seen Connie's daughter, Jenny had been finishing up elementary school. Bree'd helped Connie with birthday celebrations, pizza parties and sleepovers for her daughter and her friends. "Jenny's old enough to date? How'd that happen?"

"Of course she's not old enough to date," Connie said dryly. "But when did that ever stop a teenager? Kids have a way of growing up when you're not looking. You'll find that out for yourself one day. I do like to keep an eye on her, though. Jake caught her making out in his office not long ago."

Bree's eyes widened. "What'd he do? Beat the boy to a pulp?"

Connie laughed. "I believe there was a very stern exchange and then he had a talk with Jenny. I want to believe he got through to her, but just in case he didn't, I don't want her alone in the house with this kid for very long."

Bree saw real concern in her eyes and made a quick decision. "Why don't we have that drink at your place. Would that work for you?"

Relief immediately spread across Connie's face. "That would be great."

"I'll meet you there in fifteen minutes," Bree promised. "Want me to stop and pick up a pizza or some snacks?"

"Make it a couple of pizzas," Connie

said. She took a twenty-dollar bill out of her purse and tried to give it to Bree. "Take it," she insisted. "If they're eating, they won't be making out, and we can have our food without me jumping up every few minutes to check on them."

"Keep your money. You're providing the drinks. The pizza is the least I can do."

"Okay, then. I'll see you soon. You know we're living back at my parents' place, right? They were retiring to Florida just as I was getting divorced. Jake already had his own house, so I moved back home. The price was right. If I'm careful, I can just make it every month on the alimony and child support I'm getting. What Jake pays me goes right into Jenny's college fund. It turned out to be a good deal all around."

"Sounds like it," Bree agreed. "You can fill me in on all the rest of your life when I get there. I want to hear everything."

"I'll bore you to tears," Connie replied. "You're the one with tales to tell. See you soon."

As soon as Connie had left, Bree ordered the pizzas and an extra-large salad, then drove around the corner to pick them up. The pizza parlor was packed, so it took longer than she'd expected. It was over a half hour later by the time she pulled up in front of Connie's and immediately spotted Jake's truck in the driveway. For a fleeting instant, she considered turning right around and driving away, but Connie was already standing in the doorway beckoning her inside.

"Jake's here?" Bree asked as she walked slowly across the lawn.

"He turned up a couple of minutes ago. I swear I had no idea he was coming over tonight. Sometimes he pops in to beg a meal."

Bree didn't entirely buy the explanation, but she let it pass. "Does he know I'm coming?"

Connie's expression turned vaguely guilty. "Actually I just mentioned that I was expecting a pizza delivery any minute."

Bree frowned at her. "I don't think he's going to be thrilled with the surprise. You should have warned him."

"So he'd feel compelled to take off, even though I know he'd really like to stay? I don't think so," Connie said, reaching for the pizza boxes, but leaving it to Bree to carry the salad. "We'll take this into the kitchen."

As they passed the living room, which had once been almost as familiar to her as her own, Bree could hear Jake's voice, along with Jenny's and apparently that of the teenager's boyfriend. For the first time since she'd been back, she heard the carefree sound of Jake's laugh. That sound had once filled her with so much joy and she'd heard it often. It hurt to realize that around her he'd stopped laughing.

In the kitchen, she set the container of salad on the table and accepted the glass of red wine that Connie handed to her. She'd just taken her first sip when Jake walked in.

"I smell food," he said eagerly, then stopped in his tracks. He turned an accusing gaze on his sister. "You didn't mention you were expecting company."

"Bree's not company," Connie said breezily, undaunted by his expression or his unwelcoming tone. "She was almost family once."

"*Was* and *almost* would be the operative words," Jake muttered.

Connie scowled at him. "Don't be rude,"

she scolded. "You're the one who wasn't invited. If you want pizza, sit down and behave."

Jake's lips twitched. "You sounded just like Mom then."

"I meant to," Connie retorted.

Bree couldn't help herself. She chuckled at the exchange. "This is just like old times. Connie always did boss you around."

"She tried to," Jake corrected. "She was never the boss of me." He gave his sister a pointed look. "And these days, I'm her boss, something she might do well to remember."

"Oh, hush," Connie said. "You don't scare me."

Oddly, the squabble had the effect of relaxing Bree. She finally pulled out a chair and sat down. But when Connie left the room to take one of the pizzas and a couple of sodas to the kids, she couldn't think of a thing to say to Jake.

"This is silly," she said at last. "We used to be able to talk about anything."

"Times change," he said, sipping his beer and looking at her solemnly. He gestured with the bottle. "Used to be you'd be drinking one of these, instead of a glass of fancy wine. Did Marty help you develop your taste for the finer things in life?"

"Don't be an idiot," Bree retorted, though without much heat behind the words. "Connie poured the wine. I accepted it. It's not some huge statement about my preferences in alcohol."

He winced. "Sorry. Connie's right. If I can't be civil, it's probably better if I go."

Bree locked her gaze with his. "Wouldn't it be better to try a little harder to be civil? We managed almost an entire conversation earlier today. Please, Jake. Just try for tonight. Just for your sister's sake. Something tells me she masterminded this evening. Let's not disappoint her. Her heart's in the right place."

"And encourage her to go on meddling?" he suggested direly. "Is that what you want?"

"No, what I want is for us to get along. I miss being friends with you. How many times do I have to say that before you'll believe me?"

He frowned at that. "And I miss loving you. Doesn't seem to matter much, though, does it?"

"Of course it does," she said, cringing at

the bitterness behind his words. “I will tell you how sorry I am from now till eternity if that’s what you want. Is it? Does it help hearing me apologize?”

He stared at her, then dropped his gaze. “No.”

Since he hadn’t moved, she finally risked asking, “Does that mean you’ll stay? It’s an hour or two, Jake. No big deal.”

He gave her a wry look. “With you, an hour or two was never enough. I wanted a lifetime.”

The pain and vulnerability were back in his voice. She realized then just how scared he was of this, of *them.* Rather than forcing him to talk about it, she lifted the lid on the pizza box and pulled out a slice with pepperoni and sausage.

“Come on,” she taunted, waving it under his nose. “It’s just the way you like it. You know you want some.”

He hesitated for so long, she thought he might yet refuse, but eventually he reached for the slice, his rough fingers grazing hers. She wondered if he felt the same jolt of electricity she felt, but he was avoiding her gaze, so she couldn’t tell.

At least he hadn’t made good on his

threat to leave. For tonight, that would have to be enough.

During a lull on Saturday afternoon, Bree thought about how pleasant the evening at Connie's had turned out to be. Jake had even relaxed eventually and they'd all wound up playing cards with Jenny and Dillon. Jake had even walked her to her car, hands shoved in his pockets as if to resist reaching for her, and admitted that the evening had gone okay. In her book, it had been better than okay. It had been progress.

She was still relishing that when she looked up in surprise as her mother walked through the door of her shop.

"Mom, I wasn't expecting to see you this weekend."

"I wasn't expecting to be here, but your father called last night and talked me into flying down this morning. He said he had a surprise for me later. Do you know anything about that?"

Bree shook her head. She hadn't heard anything about a surprise. "Not a clue."

"Well, whatever it is had better be good.

He dropped me off at the house and took off again. I called Abby to see if she and the girls wanted to join me for lunch, but Trace said they'd already driven into town. Have you seen them?"

Bree looked up at the sound of the bell over the door and smiled. "Here they are right now," she said as Carrie and Caitlyn bounded into the store, nearly knocking over a stack of ceramic planters in their exuberance.

"Slow down!" Abby commanded to little effect.

The girls were already behind the counter. Carrie immediately climbed up onto the stool and reached for the keys on the cash register.

"Can I ring up a sale, Aunt Bree?" she pleaded. "I know how."

"I know, too," Caitlyn said, trying to wedge herself between Carrie and the counter.

Bree hunkered down between them. "You know the rules," she reminded them. "We have to wait for a customer."

"But you keep chocolate in there," Carrie said with obvious disappointment. "I want some now."

Abby grinned at her. "Told you they were onto you. They know all about your secret stash."

"Hey," Megan said, regarding her granddaughters with an exaggerated scowl. "Did you not even notice that I'm here?"

Caitlyn beamed at her. "Grandma Megan, we weren't 'specting you, were we, Mama?"

"We most certainly were not," Abby concurred, slipping an arm around Megan's waist. "But we are very glad to see you."

"Will you be even happier if I take you all for ice-cream sundaes?" Megan asked the girls. "Your grandpa lured me to town, then abandoned me, so I'm going to indulge in a huge hot-fudge sundae."

"Me, too! Me, too!" Caitlyn said eagerly.

Carrie clambered down from the stool. "I'll come, too!"

Megan turned to Abby. "How about you?"

"Why don't you three go ahead," she suggested. "I need to speak to Bree for a minute."

After Megan led the girls out of the shop, Abby turned to Bree. "So, did Mom tell you anything about this visit? What's Mick thinking bringing her down here and then going off and leaving her?"

"Beats me," Bree said. "She said he mentioned a surprise for later. Do you know anything about that?"

Abby shook her head. "He did call earlier and ask if we were going to be free this evening. He wanted us to stop by Gram's around six o'clock."

Bree thought about that. "He asked me to try to get out of here early so I could be there, too. You don't suppose . . . ?"

"Suppose what?"

"Is he planning to ask Mom to marry him again? He wouldn't spring a question like that on her with everyone there, would he? That's a surefire path to humiliation."

Alarm flared in Abby's eyes. "I agree. I don't think Mom's even close to being ready to remarry him. And, frankly, after everything that happened between them back then, I can't even imagine that Dad's ready to take that step."

Bree nodded. "That's what I thought, too, but what other surprise could there be?"

"I guess we'll just have to wait and see."

"And keep our fingers crossed that whatever it is won't blow up in Dad's face," Bree added direly.

"From your lips to God's ears," Abby said solemnly, just as Gram would have done.

"Just in case, maybe you should track Mick down and try to find out what's going on," Bree suggested.

"Oh, no. I'm not meddling."

"Come on, you have the O'Brien gene for it," Bree reminded her.

"Nope. I'm one hundred percent reformed."

"I don't think that's possible. Once a meddler, always a meddler. Besides, you're the oldest. It's your duty to check these things out, prevent calamities, that sort of thing. The rest of us rely on you for that."

Abby frowned, but she reached in her purse and pulled out her cell phone. After she'd punched in a number, her frown deepened. "It went straight to Dad's voice mail," she said.

Bree was taken aback by that. "Really? Have you ever known Dad not to answer his cell on the first ring?"

"Maybe it's part of his commitment to turn over a new leaf," Abby suggested. "I'll try again later, but I suppose I should go rescue Mom from the girls. Who knows what those two might be trying to talk her into. I think they have their eye on some kind of elaborate water slide at Ethel's Emporium. It's just the kind of thing Mom could be persuaded that they ought to have."

Bree chuckled. "Then I'm amazed Trace hasn't already bought it."

"He's learning not to grant their every wish," Abby said. "See you at the house tonight."

Bree nodded as Abby left, already distracted by trying to figure out what on earth Mick might be up to. Whatever it was, she had a bad feeling about it.

16

Whatever Mick's surprise was, Gram was obviously in on it. When Bree got home, she found the whole family assembled, except for Jess. Tables laden with bowls of salads and plates of fried chicken stretched across the porch and more tables and chairs had been set up on the lawn.

"Are we expecting an army?" Bree asked, surveying the amount of food.

"No, just one tired army medic," her brother Kevin said, walking around the side of the house. He was out of uniform, but there was no mistaking his military bearing or the exhaustion in his eyes. His hair, which like Mick's had a tendency to curl, was little more than a crew cut, which emphasized the gauntness in his face.

"Oh my God, you're home!" Bree exclaimed, rushing into his arms. He picked her up and twirled her around until she was breathless. She couldn't seem to make herself let go of him. "You're too skinny. What have they been feeding you in Iraq?"

"Nothing like Gram's fried chicken and potato salad, that's for sure," he said.

"My turn," Abby said, pushing Bree out of the way, then punching Kevin in the arm. "Why didn't you tell us you were coming home? We weren't expecting you for a few more months. Is your tour in Iraq over for good?"

Bree's excitement dimmed at the shake of his head.

"Not yet," he said. "I'm just on leave for a couple of weeks."

"Just long enough for me to whip your butt on the basketball court and in a few games of poker," Connor said, coming over to embrace his brother. "I've missed you, bro."

"That goes both ways," Kevin replied, then looked around. "Where's Jess? And where's my brother-in-law to be, Abby? I have to sit Trace down and have a talk with him before you two tie the knot, make sure he understands what he's getting into by marrying an O'Brien."

"You leave Trace alone," Abby instructed, even as her fiancé approached and gave Kevin a hearty slap on the back.

"Good to see you, man," Trace told Kevin. "And don't worry about me. I think I have a pretty good idea of what I'm getting into with your sister. It's your nieces you should have warned me about."

Abby poked him in the ribs. "Stop it, both of you. As for Jess, if she'd known this celebration was to welcome you home, she'd have been here on time for once, I'm sure."

Just then Kevin apparently caught sight of Megan. His eyes widened. "Mom?" he said, his eyes unexpectedly filling with tears before he determinedly blinked them away. He quickly covered his initial reaction by saying, "I didn't expect to see you here." The edge in his voice contrasted sharply with the emotional response he hadn't been quick enough to hide.

"Oh, Kevin," Megan whispered, her own tears spilling down her cheeks as she walked slowly across the lawn. "I'm so relieved to have you home safe." She turned to Mick, who'd been hanging back, his own eyes misty at the reunion. "You're off the hook for abandoning me earlier. This is the best surprise ever."

Kevin looked uncomfortable as Megan embraced him, then he hurriedly moved away to grab a beer from a nearby cooler.

"Obviously Gram was in on the secret," Bree said.

"I had to tell her," Mick said. "I knew she'd need a couple of days to get this feast ready."

They all turned to Gram. "And you kept it from the rest of us," Abby said in awe. "I have new respect for your ability to keep a secret."

Nell gave her an indignant look. "You have no idea how many secrets I've got stored away," she retorted. "That's why everyone in this family comes to me, because they know I won't blab." She linked her arm through Kevin's and gave him a pointed look. "In fact, I know another one, a big one."

Kevin dropped an affectionate kiss on her brow. "Okay, okay, I'll tell them. I was just waiting for Jess to get here, and I see her racing up the driveway right now."

Jess slammed on the brakes at the sight of the gathering with Kevin at the center of it. She leaped out of the car practically before the engine quit and flew into her big brother's arms, smothering his face in kisses.

"You ugly thing, why didn't you tell me you were coming home?" she demanded, giving him a thorough once-over. "I'd have baked a cake."

Everyone in the family groaned.

"Okay, I'd have had Gram bake a cake," Jess said, then glanced at the tables covered with food. "Where's Kevin's favorite chocolate cake?"

"Hey," Abby protested before Gram could answer. "Let's get to the secret. Jess is here now, so tell us."

Kevin's gaze immediately went toward the front door of the house. At his nod, the door opened and a long-legged woman with short, strawberry-blond hair emerged and practically floated across the yard, her gaze locked with his. The rest of them might as well have been on another planet for all the attention she paid them. Kevin pulled her close and gave her a lingering kiss.

When he finally ended the kiss, his expression was filled with barely repressed excitement, and some of the exhaustion in his eyes was wiped away by the look of adoration as he looked down into her upturned face.

"Everyone, I'd like you to meet Georgia O'Brien, my wife as of two o'clock this afternoon."

Bree stared at him in shock. "You're married?"

"Before me?" Abby joked. "I thought I was next in line."

"So did I," Trace said wryly. He winked at Kevin. "Mind telling me your secret so I can get Abby to start making wedding plans?"

Kevin circled his arm around Georgia's waist. "When you're someplace like Iraq, you tend to be highly motivated."

Megan turned to Mick. "And you knew about this? For how long?"

"A couple of days. I was his best man," Mick confirmed.

"But why didn't you wait, have the ceremony here?" Jess demanded, clearly upset. "Didn't you think we'd all want to be there?"

"Yeah, bro," Connor said, obviously miffed. "I was counting on being your best man when you finally got around to tying the knot."

Kevin held tight to Georgia's hand. She stood beside him, her expression filled with guilt. "I'm afraid that's my fault," she said. "I only have a couple of days on leave and I wanted my dad to perform the ceremony. He's a minister back home in Texas, but we couldn't get decent connections to fly there and then here. He and my mom were able to fly in and meet us at the airport in Baltimore, but they had to fly right back to Beaumont. He has services there in the morning. All of this came together at the last second. Kevin and I weren't even sure we'd both get approval for leave at the same time until a few days ago."

"You got married at the airport?" Jess asked, her expression incredulous and less than pleased.

Georgia nodded. "Not terribly romantic, but the logistics worked. And it gave us time to come here to be with all of you before I have to go back to Iraq. Kevin talks so much about his family, I wanted to meet you."

"So this is your wedding reception," Megan concluded. "Mick, did you get champagne?"

"Of course I did," he said. "It's chilling in the kitchen right now. I figured if I brought it out any sooner, you'd all know something was up."

Gram grinned at Jess. "Same with the cake. I baked a special chocolate wedding cake, but I had to hide it in the pantry."

"Then let's get this party started," Connor said, rallying from his earlier disappointment and slapping his brother on the back. "I'll bring out the champagne." He leaned down and gave his new sister-in-law a kiss. "Georgia, welcome to the family."

Everyone else started to swarm around her to offer congratulations, but Bree hung back. Jess and Abby welcomed Georgia with obvious restraint, then joined Bree.

"I was afraid of this," Jess said, her voice low. "They hardly even know each other."

"But look how happy they are," Abby said, clearly squashing her own doubts. "Kevin looks as if he won the lottery. Our doubts don't matter. We owe it to him to give her a chance."

"Well, of course we do," Jess said. "I'm just saying it seems awfully fast."

Mick apparently overheard her comment as he approached. "Being overseas puts a stress on a man the rest of us can't possibly understand. I'm just glad Kevin has someone by his side who obviously adores him."

"Dad's right," Bree said. "This is their day. We need to make it special for them."

"At least Kevin will be sticking around after she goes back," Jess said. "Maybe we can find out the real scoop then. You don't suppose she's pregnant, do you?"

"Jess, stop it," Abby ordered. "This isn't the time for that kind of speculation. Besides, I imagine they'd send her home if she was expecting a baby. Surely they wouldn't want a pregnant soldier on duty in Baghdad, of all places."

Jess looked unrepentant. "Hey, it would explain why they were in such a rush. Even

Kevin said they were highly motivated. Maybe that's what he meant."

"I think I'll vote for love being the reason for the rush," Bree said. She'd been watching her brother and Georgia ever since Kevin had made the big announcement. He'd hardly taken his eyes off his new wife. "Dad, get a glass of champagne and propose a toast. Isn't that one of the best man's duties?"

Mick nodded. "Good idea."

As he wandered off, Jess disappeared, as well. By the time Mick lifted his glass of champagne several minutes later, Jess was nowhere in sight.

As soon as Mick had finished his lengthy toast welcoming Georgia to the family, Bree again looked around for Jess, but she was missing. She turned to Abby. "Where's Jess?"

"I have no idea, but this has obviously upset her. I don't know if she's worried about Kevin or hurt that he didn't tell her ahead of time. It won't matter to her that he didn't tell any of us except for Dad. She always thought of Kevin as her champion. She's been devoted to him since he went overseas. She sends him cookies, books,

DVDs and anything else she thinks he and the other soldiers might like. I'm afraid Kevin's just unintentionally shattered that bond."

"I agree," Bree said. "Hopefully Kevin will pick up on that and make amends. It would be awful if this causes a rift between them."

"I'll make sure of it," Abby said, already starting across the lawn.

Before she'd gone far, though, Jess came outside and raised her own glass of champagne. "Everyone, I'd like to make a toast to my big brother and his bride. Georgia, you may not have had the wedding of every girl's dreams, but I promise the honeymoon will be more traditional. The bridal suite at the inn is yours for as long as you're able to stay. That's my gift to you and Kevin, along with a ton of good wishes for a long and happy life together."

Abby returned to Bree's side. "She almost made that sound sincere."

Bree frowned. "What do you mean *almost?* I thought she sounded convincing."

"Too convincing," Abby said. "I wouldn't be a bit surprised if she isn't planning to run over to the inn and put shaving cream on the pillows or short-sheet the bed."

Bree gave her a startled look. "She wouldn't," she protested, then added with less conviction, "Would she?"

"Our sister is unpredictable, especially when she's upset," Abby reminded her.

"Do you think we should warn Kevin?"

A grin broke across Abby's face. "Not a chance. We should probably come up with a few evil tricks of our own."

"You're a brat," Bree chided. "Maybe even worse than Jess."

"Don't tell me you don't want to get even with Kevin for cheating us all out of a wedding," Abby accused.

"I'm much more mature than that," Bree said, then giggled. "But I do want to be there when he finds whatever surprise it is that Jess has planned for him."

Abby suddenly looked vaguely guilty. "Maybe we should warn Georgia, though. She is new to the family, after all, and women ought to stick together."

"Hey, you climb into bed with a dog like Kevin, you should expect fleas," Jess said, coming up beside them in time to figure out that they were onto her.

"You're bad," Bree scolded.

Jess grinned wickedly. "Yes, I am. I've sent Connor on my devious mission even as we speak. I believe he corralled Trace into helping him."

As she chuckled along with her sisters, an image of Jake crept into Bree's head. She couldn't help wondering what her brothers and sisters would have pulled if she and Jake had gotten married in a rush six years ago. Kevin was one of their own, so he was likely to get off lightly. Jake might not have fared as well. Then again, everyone in the family knew him, even liked and respected him, just as they did Trace.

Suddenly she was totally immersed in nostalgia over what might have been. And what she wanted again.

As that thought settled in, she waited for the usual questions and doubts to follow, but they didn't. Instead, what she felt was certainty. She'd fallen in love with Jake all over again. Sadly, though, it was entirely possible that she'd blown her chances with him forever.

"I'm going for a walk," she announced, hoping to get away before she started crying and made a complete fool of herself. Maybe no one would have given it a second thought, since weddings made a lot of people cry, but she didn't intend to risk it.

Abby was already regarding her with concern. "You okay?" she asked.

"Fine," Bree replied, forcing a smile. "I just need some air."

"We're outside," Jess said, clearly puzzled by the comment.

"Sea air," Bree murmured. "Over there."

"Away from us," Abby added.

"Exactly."

But even as she walked away, she knew both Jess and Abby were staring after her, not quite sure what had plunged her into such a dark mood. She wasn't sure she could have explained it if they'd asked.

Jake heard the news about Kevin O'Brien's marriage at church on Sunday morning. The whole town was talking about the fact that he'd come home from Iraq with a new bride on his arm. Most of them were speculating about the haste with which the ceremony had been performed, and at an airport, no less. All that gossip made Jake realize for the first time that he ought to be grateful that he and Bree hadn't been forced to rush into marriage, after all. What couple needed to start a new life with everyone in the whole town talking about them? He sympathized with Kevin.

He told himself that was why he was driving over to the O'Briens' on Sunday afternoon. For several years, he, Kevin and Connor had been as tight as any brothers. Mack and Will had hung out with them, as well. They'd played ball together, spent lazy days fishing on the bay, had a few beers together on hot summer evenings. The O'Brien brothers had included him in everything because of Bree. Jake wanted to show Kevin that there was at least one person in town who didn't care why he'd gotten married as long as he was happy.

As he'd expected, he found Kevin, Trace and Connor tossing a football around on the front lawn. Jake leaped up and intercepted Kevin's pass before his friend even knew he was around.

"Hey, where'd you come from?" Kevin asked, a grin spreading across his face. He slapped Jake on the back, then tossed the ball to Connor and pulled Jake aside. "Good to see you."

"Word on the street is that congratulations are in order," Jake told him as they walked away from Connor and Trace. "I came over to offer my sympathy to the woman who had the misfortune to hook up with you. Where is she?"

"With Abby, Bree and Jess down on the beach," Kevin said. "They're giving her the lowdown on how to handle me."

Jake feigned dismay. "And you're letting that happen?"

Kevin grinned, but then his expression sobered. "How're you doing with my sister back in town?"

"We're managing," Jake said.

Kevin gave him a hard look. "Something tells me that's not as easy as you're trying to make it sound."

"I'm not going to lie to you. Sometimes it's hell," Jake confirmed. "But enough about me." He gestured toward the other two men and said loudly enough to include them, "I think we need to get down to the beach and break up that gabfest. What do you say?"

"I say yes," Kevin agreed eagerly.

"Because he can't seem to go more than ten minutes without catching a glimpse of his bride," Connor said as he joined them.

Kevin didn't even try to deny it. "Just wait, bro. One of these days the right woman will come along, and you'll take your head out of your law books long enough to go down for the count, as well. Jake knows what I'm talking about, right, Jake? You too, Trace?"

Trace sighed heavily and nodded. "I certainly do."

"Me, too," Jake agreed. In fact, the woman who was in his blood was, at this very moment, down on the beach with Kevin's new wife. And he couldn't seem to help the little stirring of anticipation knowing that set off inside him.

Mick hadn't felt this kind of contentment in years. It was a gorgeous fall day, the sea breeze was crisp, the sun warm. Best of all, he was surrounded by his entire family. He turned to Megan.

"Can you think of anything in the world that can beat this?" he asked, his gaze on the impromptu tag-football game going on in the yard. Even Carrie and Caitlyn were racing around with the grown-ups. In fact, with a little assist from her uncle Kevin, who picked her up and carried her and the football, Carrie had just scored a touchdown.

"Not one thing," Megan said, her eyes shimmering with unshed tears.

"Hey, Meggie, are you crying?" Mick asked.

She nodded. "I think I'm about to," she said, her voice choked. "I never thought I'd live to have another day like this." She turned to him. "Thank you, Mick."

"What did I do?"

"You insisted I fly down here. To think I could have missed all this. What if I'd dug in my heels and missed the chance to see Kevin and meet his bride?"

"That would never have happened," Mick said. "If my powers of persuasion had failed me, I would have told you the truth about the surprise. You wouldn't have stayed away once you found out Kevin was coming home."

"I just wish I'd been there for the wedding," she said wistfully. "I wish he'd wanted me there."

Mick reached for her hand, gave it a quick squeeze. "I know, but I was afraid to spring the idea on him. The two of you haven't spoken in a long time."

She sighed. "My fault, I know."

"He was disillusioned by what happened, Meggie. He was at an age when all the talk about you being seen with some other man took a toll. Then you took off."

"And he took your side," she said. "I can't blame him for that. Maybe if I'd handled things differently, if I'd tried a little harder to insist on a relationship, if I'd just continued to act like a mother . . ."

Mick could hear the real pain in her voice and wished he could do something to ease it. The truth was, they both bore a share of the blame for the way things had turned out. Megan might need to make her own amends with each of their children, but he could do his part by easing the way. He'd been an absentee dad way too often, but he'd still had more time than she'd had to forge a bond between himself and his kids in the wake of the hurtful divorce. After each of Megan's visits, his mother had reported just how badly things had gone. Mad as he was back then, he'd almost felt sorry for her.

"It's obvious to me Kevin's forgiven you," Mick told her. "Did you see the look on his face when he saw you yesterday?"

"He was surprised, that's all," she said. "Have you noticed how he's kept his distance today?"

"It's going to take time, Meggie. Making up for the past doesn't happen in the blink of an eye."

She gave him a wry look. "I'm glad you're aware of that."

"I know we both have a lot to forgive and forget," he admitted. "I think we're making progress, though, don't you?"

She hesitated, then twined her fingers through his. "I hope so, Mick."

"Hey, Pop, you're missing out on all the fun," Connor called out. "You too old to play this game?"

Megan grinned. "Uh-oh, that's a challenge if I ever heard one."

Mick stood up. "And I can't let a young buck get away with making me feel outdated and useless."

"Try not to break anything," she said as he deliberately limped down the steps in an attempt to garner sympathy.

Mick made a big show out of trying to limber up as he joined the others on the lawn. "Come here, Caitlyn. What's say you and me team up?"

She beamed at him. One of her pigtails had come loose. A pink bow was dangling from the other one and her cheeks were flushed. She held out her arms and Mick picked her up. He whispered in her ear. She giggled.

"Okay, Grandpa Mick. Let's do it," she said eagerly.

He gave her a high five, then set her back on her feet. When the football was passed, he latched on to it, then handed it off to his granddaughter.

"You go, girl," he said.

Caitlyn scrambled away, then looked back with a puzzled expression. "Which way?"

Before he could reply, her sister caught up with her and tagged her. Then Carrie was bouncing up and down. "We win! We win!"

Mick gave her an exaggerated scowl.

"What do you mean, you win? That was my first play?"

"And you losed, Grandpa Mick."

He stared around at the rest of them. "Did you just set me up, your own father?" he asked indignantly.

Connor slapped him on the back. "That we did. Now, let's go have a beer. That'll take the edge off the loss."

"I assume you all remember who's going to be cooking the steaks in a little while," he taunted. "Do you really want to offend the cook?"

"Actually, I'm in charge of the barbecue," Connor informed him. "The last time we let you near it, you burned all the hamburgers. It was a terrible thing to see."

"A fine way to talk to a man in his own home," he grumbled, and went back to his rocker on the porch. "Did you see the way those ungrateful wretches treated me just now?" he asked Megan.

"As if they adore you," she said, the wistful note back in her voice. "They still walk on eggshells with me, all but Abby, anyway. I'd give anything to have the rest of them tease me like that."

"Give it time," he told her, then caught a

glimpse of Bree hanging apart from the others. He nudged Megan. "Do you see that?"

"What?"

"Bree's off by herself."

"What I see is that she can't seem to keep her eyes off Jake," Megan replied.

Mick frowned. "What's he doing here, anyway?"

"Abby says he came by to congratulate Kevin, so of course Kevin invited him to stay."

"Well, if him being here is making Bree miserable, I'll tell him to go," Mick said, starting from his chair.

"No," Megan said at once. "They're adults. They'll figure this out on their own."

"But this is Bree's home. Why should she be made to feel uncomfortable in it?"

"Because it's Kevin's home, too, and he wants Jake here."

Even as she spoke, Mick watched Jake cross the lawn to Bree's side. He dropped down into a chair beside her. The wary expression on her face eventually faded and her lips curved into a smile. After a lengthy conversation, Jake reached for her hand and drew her over to join the others.

"See what I mean?" Megan said, sounding satisfied. "I told you they'd work it out."

"I have to give him credit for recognizing there was a problem," Mick said grudgingly.

Megan laughed. "Something tells me where Bree's concerned, there's not much that Jake misses."

"Well, if they're both so smitten, why don't they get on with it?" Mick asked impatiently. "They're old enough, and we could use some more grandbabies around here."

Megan sighed at the question. "I wish I knew, but I don't think it's a good idea for you to suggest to either one of them that you'd like them to get together just so you can have some more grandchildren."

"I suppose you're right about that," he conceded. He gave her a hopeful look. "What about dropping a few hints?"

She gave him a chiding look. "Forget about it. You have the subtlety of a bulldozer."

"Then you do it," he suggested.

"Neither one of us is going to meddle," she said firmly. "I don't have the right, and you don't have the tact."

"Humph!"

"I mean it, Mick. Stay out of it."

Mick knew she was right, but it rankled to think of his daughter being miserable when her happiness seemed to be within easy reach.

17

Bree hadn't expected Jake to turn up to welcome Kevin home and to congratulate him on his marriage, but she hadn't been surprised that once he'd stopped by, Kevin had insisted that he stay. Watching the way Jake fit in with her family brought back way too many memories, though. This was what they could have had if things had gone differently. Jake would have been a part of the O'Brien family. Their baby, had he or she lived, would have been the first grandchild, born even earlier than Abby's twins. All of the nostalgia and regret Bree had felt the day before came back in spades, along with the wistfulness for a future that seemed just out of reach.

For most of the day she'd kept a careful distance, knowing that no one in the family would make too much of her behaving almost as an outsider. They were used to her observing rather than participating. She hadn't counted, though, on Jake feeling guilt ridden because of it.

When he crossed the lawn in her direction, she resisted the desire to take off for the beach. He'd only follow her, anyway.

"What are you doing over here all by yourself?" he asked, lowering himself into the Adirondack chair next to hers. Both chairs had been turned from their usual position facing the bay. Sitting in them now, she and Jake could watch the rest of the family.

"Enjoying the moment," she claimed. "Who knows when we'll get another chance to be together like this."

He frowned at her. "You worrying about Kevin?"

"Of course I am. He's doing a dangerous job in a dangerous place."

"He's trained for it," Jake reminded her.

"And now that he has a wife to worry about, he's going to be even more careful."

"I know, but that's not enough to stop me from worrying."

"Then shouldn't you be over there spending time with him, instead of here? Are you steering clear because of me?"

"No," she said at once, then met his gaze and sighed. "Yes."

"I'll leave if you want me to," he offered.

"That's the problem," she said. "I know you would, but I don't want you to go. I like having you here a little too much, especially given the way things are between us. I keep thinking about how it might have been, if only my decisions had been different."

"You did what you thought you had to do," he conceded grudgingly. "I was hurt, no doubt about it, but I might have gotten past you leaving for Chicago if you'd just wanted me to be a part of your new adventure. Instead, when I came up there, I felt like an intruder." He gave a careless shrug. "And then there was Marty."

Bree was riddled with guilt about Jake finding her with another man. "I'm so sorry. I never meant for you to find out that way.

Until I saw the expression on your face, I'm not sure I'd even realized how infatuated I was with Marty." She glanced at Jake. "Nothing had happened between us, you know. Not then."

He looked skeptical. "Not how it looked," he said tersely.

"Are we ever going to be able to get past that?" she asked, not even trying to keep the longing from her voice.

He fell silent, his expression distant. "I've been thinking about that, especially today," he admitted. "You could be right."

Bree feigned shock. "Really?" she said dramatically. "About what?"

"Very funny. I just meant that maybe we should at least try to be friends, and the only way to do that is to hang out from time to time, the way we're doing today."

She chuckled at that. "You and I aren't hanging out today. We're in the same general space. This is the first time today we've actually spoken since you said hello down on the beach earlier."

He stood up and held out his hand. "Then come and sit with me for dinner. We'll have a real conversation, maybe a few laughs. It'll be almost like old times."

The suggestion was enough to make her laugh. "You actually think we can have a private conversation surrounded by my family?"

"Why not? We used to do it. In fact, we spent a lot of Sunday afternoons just like this."

"And back then they took seeing the two of us for granted because we were together all the time. They left us alone. I guarantee you, if we try that today, every single adult at this party will find an excuse to join us."

"Then we'll be part of the crowd and we won't have to say much," he replied. "Come on. However it goes, it'll be a start."

Despite her reservations, Bree stood up and put her hand in his. She'd been wanting a fresh start, and he was finally offering one. How could she turn him down? "Let's do it, but don't say I didn't warn you."

They were halfway across the lawn when she looked up at him and asked slyly, "Want to take bets on who'll be first to check out what's going on with us?"

He grinned. "That's easy. My money's on your father."

"No way," she retorted. "It'll be Abby for sure."

"So what's the wager?" he asked.

She leveled a look into his eyes. "Dinner," she said at once. This was her chance to build on his overture, and she was seizing it.

Jake sucked in a deep breath as if he hadn't contemplated anything beyond this moment. "Dinner?" he repeated. "You and me?"

She nodded. "You game?"

"Winner picks the time and place, the loser pays?"

"Absolutely."

He hesitated for a while, his gaze locked with hers. "Okay, then, you're on."

Two minutes later, when Abby joined them, Bree gave Jake a triumphant look. "Brady's, Tuesday night," she said at once.

Jake looked a little shaken, but he nodded. "It's a date," he said. "I'm going to grab another beer. You need anything?"

"A diet soda," she said.

"Abby?" Jake said. "Can I bring you something?"

"Nope. I'm fine. Trace is supposed to be

grabbing me a slice of the coconut cake Gram baked for today, but something tells me he and the girls are in the kitchen fighting over who gets to lick the spoon from the bowl of icing."

The second Jake walked away, Abby regarded Bree with curiosity. "Okay now, spill. What was the mention of Brady's about?"

"You heard the conversation. We have a date for Tuesday night."

"But something tells me my arrival had something to do with that."

Bree nodded, grinning. "And I'd like to thank you, too."

"Why?"

"We had a bet on which nosy person at this gathering would be the first to come over to see what was going on with the two of us. He picked Dad. I chose you."

Abby stared at her, then burst out laughing. "Didn't he realize you'd bet on a sure thing?"

"Apparently not," Bree said. "Did you see the look of utter panic on his face when he realized he was going to have to pay up?"

Abby laughed, then paused thoughtfully.

"Wait a minute. What was the prize, if Dad had come over?"

"Same thing, except I would have had to pay."

Abby's expression turned smug. "Then it seems to me you would have won either way and Jake knew exactly what he was getting into. Doesn't that tell you something?"

Bree hadn't considered the bet from that angle. Maybe her mind wasn't as devious as her sister's. "What?" she asked.

"He was just looking for an excuse to go out with you, one that wouldn't put him in the position of having to ask."

Bree stared at her. "Really? You think so?"

"It certainly seems that way to me."

Bree sat back. "Well, I'll be darned."

Abby stood up. "Here he comes now, so I'll be on my way. I think the tide's turning, sweetie. Get ready to go with the flow."

Bree was more than willing to do just that. She only hoped she didn't drown in the process.

Jake had arranged to meet Bree at Brady's. The waterfront restaurant had more ambience than most in Chesapeake Shores. As it was for many of the locals, it had once been their favorite spot for a romantic dinner. He couldn't help wondering if she'd chosen it because it had the best food in town or because of the memories it was sure to evoke.

She was already at the table when he arrived. She'd worn a soft, blue cashmere sweater that emphasized the color of her eyes, to say nothing of what it did for her curves. He was so focused on how beautiful she looked in the candlelight that he didn't notice the pile of paper at his place until he pulled out his chair.

"What's this?"

"My manuscript, at least what there is of it so far," she told him. "You said you wanted to read it."

He had to fight a grin. "So you brought it on our date. Were you thinking that the conversation might lag?"

Her lips twitched, as well. "That didn't occur to me, but you never know how these things will go. First dates can be tricky."

"It's hardly our first."

"It feels that way," she said.

He knew exactly what she meant. He'd

been jittery all day thinking about tonight. To buy time, he slid the papers into the envelope she'd also provided and set the package on the floor.

"I think we can manage a couple of hours of small talk," he said at last. "Let's start with your brother. How do you feel about his big news? And what do you think of Georgia?"

"I liked her," Bree said. "And he's head over heels in love with her, which is all that really matters."

"You think so?" Jake asked, not even trying to hide his own skepticism about the hasty wedding. He knew better than most that even after years it wasn't possible to really know someone well enough to make a relationship work. "Those two have only known each other a few months."

"But the environment in Iraq is intense," Bree argued. "I imagine all kinds of emotions are heightened, and there's probably a real need to live in the moment."

"All the more reason to wait until you're back home to see if those feelings are real and lasting," he said.

Bree studied him intently. "You're saying all this because of what happened with us, aren't you? You don't believe love lasts, even under the best conditions."

"No, I don't," Jake admitted.

Her expression turned sad. "Oh, Jake, you can't live your life with such a cynical attitude. How will you ever find happiness if you're not open to it?"

"I'm happy enough," he said defensively. "My company's growing. It demands a huge amount of time. I have family, friends. What more do I need?"

"Love," she suggested quietly.

"Been there, done that. It didn't turn out so well."

"Which was my fault, not yours." She regarded him earnestly. "Blame me if you need to, but don't take it out on every other woman in the world. Surely you've met some wonderful women over the past six years."

"You don't get to question me about my love life," he said stiffly, unwilling to admit just how pitiful it had been since she'd gone.

"Friends share stuff like that," she countered.

Jake debated tossing a mention of Marty

into the conversational mix to see how she'd react. The only problem with that was that he didn't want to hear anything more about the man. If they were ever going to move on, putting Martin Demming behind them would be a big part of it.

Instead, he gave her a hard look, meant to warn her off, then picked up the menu. "I'm thinking about having the imperial crab. What sounds good to you?"

For a moment, he thought she was going to force the issue, but eventually she sighed and picked up her own menu. "The grilled rockfish is usually good," she said without much enthusiasm.

"Wine? Beer?"

"Beer's fine," she said.

"Blue cheese on your salad?"

She gave him an odd look. "You have a good memory."

"For some things," he said, beckoning their waitress, who'd been working at Brady's as far back as Jake could remember.

"What can I get for you two?" Kelly asked. "I'll bet I can guess. Imperial crab for you, Jake, rockfish for Bree, two salads with blue cheese dressing and a couple of beers."

Bree laughed. "Have we always been that predictable?"

Kelly nodded. "Only thing you ever changed was the side dish. What'll it be tonight? Fries, baked potato, potato salad, coleslaw or green beans?"

"Baked potato," Jake said.

"And I'd like the green beans," Bree told her.

Kelly nodded. "I'll be right back with your beers. It's good to see the two of you together again."

Bree winced as she walked away. "That's not good. By tomorrow morning everyone in town will be speculating about what this dinner means. Are we back together? Was this just business? Or are we just a couple of old friends catching up? I should have thought about that before suggesting we come here."

"There'd be speculation no matter where we ate," Jake said. "Chesapeake Shores does love its gossip."

"You're not bothered by it?"

"I can live with it if you can," he said with a shrug. "I got pretty good at tuning out all the talk after you left."

Bree stilled, her expression troubled.

"Jake, does anyone know . . . was there ever any talk about, you know . . . about the baby?"

Jake froze at the mention of their child. "No," he said harshly. "And we shouldn't be discussing it, either."

"How can we ever move on if we don't?" she asked reasonably.

"Maybe we don't get to move on," he said. "Maybe that's why this dinner was a bad idea. We haven't even gone a half hour without one of us bringing up the past."

"Because what happened matters. Ignoring it certainly hasn't worked."

He scowled at that. "It sure didn't seem to matter to you at the time. In fact, you seemed downright relieved when the pregnancy ended. You couldn't wait to catch the first flight to Chicago."

"I know it must have seemed that way," she said.

"It didn't just *seem* that way, Bree," he said heatedly. "It *was* that way."

When she was about to respond, he waved her off. "Let's drop this right now before we get into an argument that really will have people talking."

"Won't you even give me a chance to explain?" she pleaded.

"There's nothing to explain," he said. "You lost our baby and moved on in the blink of an eye. There's not a lot of room to misinterpret what happened."

To his surprise, Bree suddenly stood up. "If you really believe that, then we don't have anything to discuss. I'd just like you to do one thing for me. Read what I've written so far. Maybe then you'll have a better idea of how things looked from my perspective."

Alarmed, Jake stared from her to the package on the floor. "You said this was fiction. Is it about us? About what happened?"

"It *is* fiction," she responded. "But I lived the emotions, Jake. You may not believe that, but I did. I don't think I could write them so powerfully if I hadn't. And I'm not sure I could have put them down on paper before now. They were still too raw."

He stared at her, incredulous. "Are you expecting me to feel sorry for *you?* You got everything you wanted. There was no baby. You got to go off to Chicago and chase your dream. I was the one left with nothing."

She flinched at his harsh tone. "Read what I've written, Jake. Then we'll talk again."

Before he could tell her that the subject was closed forever, she turned and walked away just as Kelly approached with their meals. She frowned at Bree's retreating back.

"She's leaving?"

Jake nodded. "Of course she is. It's what she does," he said bitterly. He stood up and handed Kelly a fistful of bills. "That should cover dinner. I'm sorry."

The older woman regarded him with sympathy. "Oh, Jake, so am I. When I saw you together, I was so sure . . ." Her voice trailed off.

He shrugged. "Things aren't always the way they look."

And people weren't always the way you needed them to be, no matter how badly you wanted it.

After their aborted dinner, Jake once again retreated from any contact with Bree. He even started avoiding Sally's at lunchtime, though it didn't take long for Will and Mack to call him on that.

They were shooting hoops on the high-school courts one evening, when Mack asked casually, "You and Bree dating again?"

"No," Jake said tersely.

"Obviously Mack's subtle approach is a waste of time," Will said. "Is it true she walked out on you at Brady's last week?"

"Pretty much," Jake said, driving down the court to make a perfect layup. It was easy since neither Mack nor Will seemed inclined to stop him. Apparently they were more interested in probing into things that were none of their business.

"Which explains why you've been blowing us off at lunchtime for the past week," Will concluded. "Is it just the café and Bree you're avoiding or is all of Main Street off-limits?"

Jake frowned at his sarcasm. "It's better if we keep some distance between us, that's all."

"Okay, then, we'll start going to Brady's or the pizza place," Mack offered. "Anyplace you want to go."

"You guys shouldn't have to disrupt your

routine because of this thing between Bree and me."

"Hey, we're a team," Will said. "We go where you go." His expression sobered. "You want to talk about what happened?"

Jake pushed past him and made another clean shot. He was beginning to enjoy himself. Usually they were a lot more competitive. The whole distraction bit was working for him. He should give them some topic to chew on whenever they played, preferably not his love life, though.

Will wasn't put off by his silence. "Jake? You know we'll listen. We won't judge."

"Speak for yourself," Mack said. "I have half a mind to tell Bree off myself."

Jake stopped in his tracks and scowled at him. "Stay out of it. I mean it, Mack."

"Wasn't it bad enough that she ran off and ditched you? Please don't tell me you're going to let her get away with making you miserable all over again."

"I'm not miserable," Jake lied. "In fact, up until a few minutes ago when the two of you went all Dr. Phil on me, I was having a great time playing basketball with a couple of buddies."

Will gave an exaggerated shudder at

the mention of TV's most famous shrink. "Okay, let's play," he said, moving aggressively into position to block Jake's next shot. His elbow in Jake's ribs nearly knocked the wind out of him.

"Me and my big mouth," Jake grumbled when he'd caught his breath and rubbed his aching side. "I should have let you go on analyzing me to your heart's content."

Will grinned. "Your choice. I'm always ready to delve into your psyche. It's a fascinating place."

"I vote we drop all of this and head to my place for a couple of beers," Mack said. "I'm beat."

"After a half hour on the court?" Jake asked in surprise.

"He was out late last night," Will explained. "Susie O'Brien asked him to drive her up to D.C. to see a concert."

Jake's lips twitched. "So you're playing chauffeur to her now? How's that working for you? Did she bring along a date? Maybe sit in the backseat and make out?"

"Go to hell," Mack muttered. "No, she didn't bring a date."

"Did you have to wait outside during

the concert or did she buy you a seat way up in the balcony?" Jake taunted.

"We sat together, okay? Satisfied?"

Jake laughed. "No, but then apparently neither are you."

"Susie and I are friends," Mack said.

"Yeah, that's the story Bree and I've been telling ourselves lately, too," Jake replied. "I don't know about you, but for me it's not working out so well."

Will looked elated by the revelation. "Now we're getting somewhere," he said enthusiastically. "A couple of beers and I'll have both of you talking your heads off."

"Not me," Jake said. "I'm going home."

"Me, too," Mack said. "Will, you're going to have to find somebody else's head to shrink tonight."

"Spoilsports."

"Hey, you have a whole roster of paying patients. Worry about their problems," Mack advised.

Will grinned. "But yours are so much more fascinating."

"Night, Will," Jake said, walking off and leaving him standing in the middle of the court.

"See you tomorrow," Mack called out.

"We'll meet at the pizza place. Is that okay with everyone?"

"I'm in," Jake said.

Will sighed heavily. "See you then." His expression suddenly brightened and there was a dangerous glint in his eye. "Maybe I'll mention lunch to Bree and Susie."

Both Mack and Jake turned on him. "Not even mildly amusing," Mack said.

"Out of the question," Jake added for good measure.

Will didn't seem impressed. "I think confronting the issues in our lives is much healthier than pretending they don't exist."

"How are we supposed to pretend they don't exist when you keep bringing them up every few minutes?" Jake asked.

"It's very telling that the mention of Bree or Susie upsets you both so much," Will said.

"I swear if you don't shut up about this, I'm going to start bringing peanut butter and jelly sandwiches to work and eating them in my office," Jake declared.

"Avoidance," Will said, nodding knowingly. "Very revealing."

Jake could have told him what to do with his opinion, but there were a bunch of high-school kids playing ball on the next court. He was a big believer in setting a good example for the next generation.

Instead, he walked away with Mack right on his heels.

"You don't suppose he'd really invite Bree and Susie to lunch, do you?" Mack asked.

"If he does, we kill him. Simple as that," Jake said grimly. He couldn't even say with certainty that he wasn't dead serious about it, either.

When Bree closed her shop at noon to run around the corner to grab the slice of pizza and salad she'd ordered, she didn't expect to find Jake, Will and Mack sitting inside. Will was the first one to spot her, and his complexion turned pale as she waved. She started in their direction to say a quick hello, but Will seemed to be frantically gesturing her to stay away. She shrugged and headed for the counter. Eighteen-year-old Gary Gentry had her order ready when she got there. He blushed all the way to his spiked blond hair when he spoke to her.

"Hi, Ms. O'Brien," he said.

"Hi, Gary," she said, trying not to show how amused she was by this tongue-tied crush he seemed to have developed for her in recent weeks. "How are you?"

The question flustered him even more. "Okay, I guess," he said, not meeting her gaze. "That'll be six-twenty, same as always."

Just then she heard the crash of a chair and turned to see Jake towering over Will. "You did it, didn't you?" He gestured toward Bree. "You told her to come here today, even after I specifically told you not to. Some kind of friend you've turned out to be."

Mack hadn't budged, but his complexion was almost as pale as Will's. "I suppose Susie will be walking in the door next," he said, though with far less heat than Jake had displayed.

The instant Gary realized Bree was the object of Jake's anger, he looked as if he was about to charge around the counter to protect her, but Jake wasn't interested in Bree. All of his fury was directed at Will.

Will tried to protest that Jake had it all wrong, but his protests fell on deaf ears. Jake grabbed his slice of pizza and his soda and stormed across the restaurant, careful to steer well around Bree as he went. As furious as he was, he still paused long enough to hold the door for two elderly women.

Looking thoroughly guilt ridden, Will stood up and crossed the restaurant. “I’m so sorry,” he said to Bree, who was still rooted in place. “I was giving him grief last night about inviting you to join us today to clear the air between you, and when he saw you just now, he thought I’d done it.”

The explanation was hardly soothing. Bree sighed. “I’d hoped by now that he would have . . .” She shook her head. “Never mind. I need to get back to the shop.”

“I really am sorry if his behavior embarrassed you,” Will apologized, trailing after her. “You could join Mack and me. And just so you know, I didn’t invite Susie either, so it’s safe enough.”

“If Jake saw me with you, it would only confirm his worst suspicions,” she said. “But thanks, anyway. Don’t worry about it, Will. The problems between Jake and me aren’t your fault.”

“He still loves you, you know. That’s why he behaves like such an idiot.”

Bree appreciated Will's attempt to spin the situation, but she wasn't buying it. She was pretty sure all the love between them, at least on Jake's side, was dead and buried. And a few more incidents like this one and she might have a hard time recalling her own recently rediscovered feelings.

What she didn't understand was how Jake could still be so angry after reading the manuscript she'd given him. She'd bared her soul on those pages, poured out all the grief she'd never allowed herself to feel, much less share with him. There was only one explanation she could think of. He hadn't even read it.

And that told her all she needed to know about how little he cared about making things right between them.

18

When Bree walked back to her shop after the awful encounter with Jake, she found Jess inside waiting on a customer. As soon as the woman left, Bree regarded her sister with curiosity.

"Thanks for opening up and making a sale, but what brings you by in the middle of the day? Don't you have your own business to run?"

"I've been thinking about Kevin and Georgia," Jess admitted, getting a soda out of the small refrigerator Mick had hooked up behind the counter, then sitting on the stool by the cash register. She regarded

Bree worriedly. "Do you think we've been mean to her?"

"Not unless you've done something to her that I don't know about," Bree said. "Guilty conscience weighing on you?"

"Of course not." She grinned. "Well, not since I had the maid at the inn short-sheet their bed in the honeymoon suite, anyway. I've just been so thrown by Kevin showing up here married that I'm afraid we haven't been as nice as we should have been. Maybe we should throw Georgia a shower or do something, you know, sisterly. She is an O'Brien now, after all."

Bree's gaze narrowed. "Has Kevin been on your case?"

"No, but he's barely said two words to me, so I think he's ticked that I haven't done more to make Georgia feel like one of us."

"Or maybe he's feeling guilty about springing this on all of us without any notice," Bree speculated. "Plus, they didn't even ask us to come along with Dad for the wedding. I know it wasn't an elaborate ceremony, but still, they should have asked. I don't think any of us are quite sure how to handle the situation. As for a shower, I think that's out of the question. What could we possibly give her that she could take back to Iraq?"

"Sexy lingerie?" Jess suggested, though without much enthusiasm.

"Not terribly practical in a war zone," Bree replied. "I think we should hold off on a shower until they're back in the States for good. Then we can throw a real humdinger of a shower to help them get settled."

Jess brightened at the suggestion. "That's a great idea. But maybe you, Abby and I should at least invite her out to lunch in the meantime. We could even involve her in planning the party."

"It'll have to be tomorrow," Bree said. "Georgia was able to extend her leave past the original couple of days, but she's definitely flying out the day after tomorrow."

"Why don't we do something special for her at the inn. I'll invite Gram, too. Can you find someone to cover for you here?"

Bree had no idea. Though she'd thought about finding someone to help out part-time, especially now that she was eager to write again, she'd been so swamped she hadn't done anything about it. This lunch, however, was too important for her not to make the effort to be there.

"I'll work something out," she promised. "Maybe Connie can spend her lunch break from the nursery over here."

Jess's eyes widened at the suggestion. "How's Jake going to feel about that?"

At the moment, Bree didn't give two figs how Jake felt about anything. If it irked him, so much the better. That little scene of his earlier might not have been much, but it had been unnecessary. A little payback would feel good.

"I'll call Connie right now," she said decisively. "I'll leave it up to her to deal with her brother."

"Okay, then, I'll let Abby and Gram know," Jess said. "See you tomorrow, if not before. Noon, okay?"

"Perfect," Bree said.

As soon as Jess had left, Bree dialed the nursery's number from memory. Thankfully, Connie answered.

"Hey, it's Bree," she said. "I have a huge favor to ask you. And if it's something you don't want to do or can't work out, feel free to say no."

"Sounds intriguing. Is it going to annoy my brother?"

Bree wasn't surprised that she'd picked up on that without Bree having to say a word. "More than likely."

"Great. He's gotten on my last nerve today. What do you need?"

Bree explained about the impromptu lunch for Georgia the next day. "Do you think you could take a long lunch hour and cover for me here?"

"Absolutely," Connie said without hesitation. "But when you decide you're looking for a long-term solution, I might have an idea. Jenny's looking for a part-time job after school and on Saturdays. She worked at Ethel's Emporium over the holidays last year, so she knows how to work a cash register, and she really is very reliable. She mentioned after you were over here that night that she'd love to work for you if you were looking for someone. You were always her favorite surrogate aunt."

"Are you sure it's a good idea to have her working for me?" Bree asked. "That might really tick Jake off."

"Too bad," Connie replied without hesitation. "Jobs are scarce around town."

"I'm sure Jake would find something for her," Bree said.

"I doubt that working with her uncle and me is her idea of a dream job. She doesn't like taking orders from either one of us as it is."

"Okay, then tell Jenny to stop by to see me after school one day this week and we'll talk," Bree said. Though she'd thought of finding someone older, Jenny's enthusiasm might make up for her lack of experience. "In the meantime, if you can help me out tomorrow, I'll be indebted to you forever."

"What time do you need me there?"

"Eleven forty-five," Bree suggested. "We'll do this lunch thing at noon and I should be back by one-thirty or two at the latest. Is that okay?"

"Not a problem," Connie said. "I don't punch a time clock around here, and even if I did, I have so much comp time owed to me, I could take off for a month."

Bree hesitated, but then couldn't resist asking, "Why are you annoyed with your brother?"

"He's been in a foul mood since that dinner the two of you had the other night. I tried to ask him about it, but he bit my head off, so all I know is what I've heard around town."

Bree winced. "Which is?"

"You walked out on him before the meal even came. Is that true?"

"Afraid so. I doubt he wants to discuss it, either."

"And today? You have anything to do with the black mood he was in after lunch?"

"Indirectly," Bree admitted and told her about Jake's mistaken assumption that Will had invited her to join them for a very public confrontation over their issues.

"Oh, no," Connie said, failing to stifle a laugh. "I swear, one of these days I'm going to lure you both into a room, lock the door and throw away the key until you come to your senses."

"It's entirely possible we'd kill each other first," Bree noted. "So, don't even think about it."

"That just means I need to fine-tune my scheme," Connie said, still chuckling. "See you tomorrow."

Bree wished she found the remark half as amusing. The one thing she remembered most about Connie was that she rarely let go of an idea once she'd latched on to it. There was every chance she and Jake were doomed.

Jake had almost refused his sister's offer of meat loaf and mashed potatoes for dinner, but it had been over a week since he'd spent any time with his niece. He liked Jenny knowing he was around if she needed him, and he'd also resolved to keep a close eye on her and that young Casanova she was still dating. Unfortunately he had a hunch that tonight's meal was going to come with a healthy serving of unsolicited advice. He hadn't missed the determined glint in his sister's eyes when she'd issued the invitation.

He'd put off going into the kitchen for as long as he possibly could, but Jenny was clearly anxious for him to leave her alone with Dillon.

"Guess I'll go see what your mother's up to," he said eventually, earning a grateful look from his niece. He turned and gave the boy a pointed look. "You staying for dinner?"

"No, sir, my mom's expecting me at

home," Dillon replied in the same carefully polite tone he'd used with Jake ever since the incident when he and Jenny had been caught in Jake's office.

"You need a lift?" Jake asked.

"No, I have my mom's car. I got my license last week. I'm allowed to drive it in the neighborhood," he said proudly. "I figure one of these days she'll turn me loose as long as I follow the rules for now."

"Good plan," Jake commented, then left them alone, resolving to make sure his niece got nowhere near that car. The kid could barely concentrate on his homework with her around. It made Jake shudder to contemplate what could happen with her beside him when he was behind the wheel of a car.

"Did you know that Dillon has his driver's license?" he asked Connie when he found her bent over the oven checking the meat loaf.

"I heard," she said, closing the oven door. "It was all Jenny could talk about last week."

"You've forbidden her from riding with him, haven't you?"

"I haven't had to yet," she admitted. "His parents have told him he can't have anyone in the car with him except one of them. If he breaks the rule, he loses access to the car keys indefinitely."

"You think he'll stick to the rules? I imagine they also told him to keep his hands to himself around girls, but he's obviously ignored that one," Jake said dryly. "You need to keep a close eye on those two, Connie. I mean it."

"Believe me, I know that," his sister lamented. "After you caught them in your office, they're never out of my sight for long, at least when I know they're together. You've talked to Jenny. I've talked to her. I pray we've gotten through to her."

"Or if we haven't, that I've scared the hell out of that guy," he said direly.

Connie pulled a beer out of the refrigerator and handed it to him. "I need to talk to you about something else."

Jake stiffened. Here it came. She was going to lecture him about Bree and that ridiculous scene he'd caused by jumping to conclusions. Will had finally cornered him late this afternoon and made it plain that Bree's arrival had been pure coincidence. Just one more thing he probably needed to make amends for.

Now he studied his sister warily. “Oh? What is it you think we need to discuss?”

“I’m taking some time off tomorrow,” she announced. “Just a couple of hours at lunchtime.”

“Okay,” he said slowly. “You know I don’t care about stuff like that. Why are you telling me?” Alarm suddenly set in. “You’re not sick or something, are you? Do you have a doctor’s appointment? Do you need me to go with you?”

She touched his arm. “Settle down. I’m fine. I’m just doing a favor for a friend.”

His gaze narrowed. “Which friend?” he asked suspiciously.

“Bree.”

“You’re doing a favor for Bree that necessitates you taking time off from your job working for me,” he said, his tone turning cold. “Do I have that right?”

“Got it on the first try,” she said cheerfully. “And before you start ranting and raving, remember that you told me not two seconds ago that you didn’t care what I did.”

“This is different,” he grumbled. “She

had to know I wouldn't like it. So did you, for that matter."

"Let me be clear about your objection," she said. "It's not the time off that bothers you, it's the fact that I'm helping Bree."

"Exactly."

"Do you know how ridiculously petty that sounds?"

Jake could hardly deny it. "Traitor," he mumbled.

She stared at him in shock. "Did you just accuse me of being disloyal?"

"Yeah, I did," he said defiantly.

"Then you and Bree are fighting again? I'm supposed to choose sides?"

"You know perfectly well we are. You've been asking me about it ever since she and I had dinner. I'm sure she gave you an earful."

Connie didn't deny the accusation. Instead, she played innocent. "Do I at least get a clue about what you're fighting about this time?"

"It's always about the same thing."

"The way she abandoned you, mistreated you, blah-blah-blah," she said.

He frowned. "Are you mocking me now?"

"Yes, because you're being ridiculous. I know she hurt you. The whole town knows she hurt you. It was six years ago, Jake. Get over it. You're still in love with her. Stop wallowing in the past and go after what you want before you lose her again."

"What is it you think I want, to have my heart broken all over again?"

"Are you so sure that's what will happen? Because the way I see it, if you don't even try, you're going to wind up miserable and alone anyway. If it were me, I'd take the risk."

"You're a romantic," he said accusingly. "Even after the way Sam treated you, you still believe in the power of love."

"I do," she agreed. "And you're a cynic. How's that working for you?"

Just then Jenny walked into the kitchen and stood staring at them, her expression shaken. "Why are you two fighting?"

"We're not fighting," Jake claimed.

"It's just a discussion," Connie confirmed.

"Well, it sounded a lot like a fight to me. It scared Dillon off. He doesn't need to be involved in your drama."

"This isn't drama," Connie said. "This is

just your uncle and me having a difference of opinion. Happens all the time between siblings."

"I wouldn't know," Jenny said angrily. "Since I don't have any and I'm not likely to, ever."

Jake saw the stunned look on Connie's face right before her eyes welled with tears. He knew, though Jenny probably didn't, just how much his sister had wanted to have more children. It had been at the root of her divorce. She wanted a big family. Sam had been unhappy she'd gotten pregnant with Jenny Louise. They'd started fighting almost from the moment she'd told him she was expecting a baby. He'd left not that long after Jenny's birth.

Connie ran from the room, her face ashen. Jenny stared after her in shock.

"What did I say?" she asked, looking bewildered and faintly guilty.

"You know how much your mom adores you, don't you?" he asked her, his tone gentle despite how exasperated he was with her at the moment.

"Yeah, I guess."

"And she's a terrific mother."

Jenny nodded.

"Then you should also be able to see that she might have wanted to have more kids. Things just didn't turn out that way."

He wasn't going to say any more. Though he would have happily told his niece what a jerk her father was, Connie had refused to ever say a harsh word against Sam. She'd wanted Jenny to believe her father's absence from her life had nothing whatsoever to do with her. He doubted Jenny bought that since Sam rarely did more than send his checks on time and mail the occasional birthday card, but it wasn't Jake's place to disillusion her.

Right now, Jenny's expression was shattered. "Oh God, I never meant to upset her. I just kind of blurted it out, you know."

He draped an arm across her shoulders and gave her a squeeze. "I know. Maybe you could go apologize."

"What about you? Are you going to apologize? I couldn't hear what you were arguing about, but you sounded kinda mean, too."

Jake sighed. "Yeah, I'll apologize," he

said. Sometimes setting a good example was a real pain.

"I can't believe y'all are doing this for me," Georgia said as they gathered at the inn for lunch. "The table looks so gorgeous."

Bree had sent over fresh flowers for the table and Jess had used the inn's best crystal and china. She'd even put out place cards edged in gold for each of them.

"I want so much to be a part of the family because I know how much you mean to Kevin," Georgia said. "I want to get to know you all like sisters. Getting to stay here a little longer had been such a blessing."

"We want to get to know you, too," Bree said. "We know how much you mean to our brother."

"I wish I had more time here," Georgia lamented. "Maybe at the end of our tours of duty, we'll settle someplace nearby. I know that's what Kevin wants. It's all he talks about."

"Are you okay with that?" Abby asked. "Your family's in Texas. Are you sure you wouldn't rather be close to them?"

"Wherever Kevin is will be home for me," Georgia responded with starry-eyed enthusiasm. "I hope you all know that I love him to pieces. Meeting him is the best thing that's ever happened to me."

"He's pretty special," Jess said, then grinned. "Of course, he might have just a few tiny little flaws."

"None," Georgia said loyally. "At least I haven't found any yet."

"And don't you girls disillusion her," Gram chided.

"Wouldn't dream of it," Bree said, shooting a warning look at Jess.

"You know, when your tour ends and you're back in the States for good, we want to throw the two of you a big party," Abby said. "How much longer do you have to serve? Does your tour end when Kevin's does?"

"My tour—did y'all know it's my second one?—is up in six months, so I'm sure I'll be back here for a while. Then, if we're still over there, I'm going to sign up for another stint," Georgia said.

Gram looked shaken by that. Bree felt a little queasy, as well.

"You don't think Kevin will stay in, do you?" Bree asked, her heart in her throat.

"We haven't talked about it, but I imagine

he will," Georgia said blithely. "We're needed there."

Bree exchanged a look with her sisters, then reached over to give Gram's hand a squeeze. "I'm sure you'll give it careful thought before you make a final decision," Bree said, resolving to have a heart-to-heart with her brother before he left town. Not that she didn't admire his dedication to his job and his country, but it seemed to her that accepting another tour of duty when he didn't have to would be sheer folly, especially when starting a new family. Then again, maybe she wasn't giving him enough credit. Perhaps he'd change Georgia's mind, convince her to settle here and begin the rest of their lives.

Despite Bree's optimism that things would work out, Georgia's revelation had managed to cast a pall over the lunch. Though everyone tried to remain upbeat, none of their hearts were in it. Eventually Abby stood up.

"Gram, why don't I give you and Georgia a lift home. I need to pick up the girls."

Gram joined her at once. "I believe that glass of champagne has gone to my head. I might need to lie down."

Georgia came around the table to hug Bree and Jess. "Thank you so much. I just loved spending time with y'all."

"We were glad to do it," Bree said when Jess remained stubbornly silent.

As soon as they'd gone, Jess whirled on Bree. "Do you believe that? She wants Kevin to stay over there!"

"Kevin's a grown man. He'll make his own decision about what's right for him," Bree said.

"You want him to reenlist?"

"Absolutely not," Bree said fiercely. "And I intend to tell him that the first chance I get, but I think I'll hold off until Georgia's left tomorrow. I certainly don't want to start something that might upset either one of them."

Jess nodded with obvious relief. "For a minute there I thought you'd lost your mind, too."

"No," Bree said grimly, then waited until her sister met her gaze. "But we can't force him to make the decision we want him to make, okay?"

"Maybe not, but we can raise holy hell if he shows the slightest indication that he's going back to that place after this tour ends," Jess said fiercely. "I say we double-team him. No, quadruple-team him. Mick'll be on our side. So will Gram."

Bree lifted a brow. "And you know exactly what Kevin will do if we gang up on him."

Jess sighed. "The exact opposite of what we want," she admitted.

"Then let's be smart," Bree suggested. "I'll talk to him on my own, see what he's thinking. Then we'll decide where to go from there." She gave her sister a rueful look. "Maybe we're getting worked up over nothing."

"I guess you're right," Jess said with obvious reluctance. "I told you Kevin marrying that woman was a bad idea."

"He doesn't seem to think so," Bree said. "Let's keep that in mind."

"When she said that about staying in, I wanted to scream," Jess admitted. "I swear it took every ounce of willpower I possess not to cause a scene."

"So glad you thought better of that," Bree said dryly.

"Yeah, well, I wish I hadn't."

Bree gave her a hug. "Maybe you should stay away from Georgia, okay? For the sake of family harmony."

"But there's a big family dinner tonight to send her off," Jess protested. "It'll tick Kevin off if I don't show up."

"It'll tick him off more if you and Georgia get into it."

Jess grinned. "You have a point."

"Love you, kid. I need to get back to work."

"Hold on a sec," Jess ordered. "Did Connie say how Jake reacted to the news that she was going to fill in for you?"

"We didn't have time to discuss it. I took it as a good sign that she showed up."

It would be an even better sign if Jake didn't turn up before the end of the day to accuse her of taking advantage of his sister or to suggest that she stay the hell away from his employees.

Mick knew something was going on with his girls. Abby and Bree were being even more quiet than usual at dinner. Jess hadn't even shown up, and his mother had barely said two words to Georgia all evening. Kevin was so wrapped up in his new bride, apparently he didn't realize anything was amiss, but it was getting on Mick's nerves.

When he couldn't stand it another minute, he managed to catch Bree alone. "What happened at that lunch you all had this afternoon? And don't even try to tell me it went just fine, because I have eyes in my head. You all are barely speaking to Georgia, or anyone else for that matter."

"Sorry, Dad."

"Don't be sorry. Just tell me what's going on."

"Georgia mentioned that she plans to go back to Iraq on another tour if she's needed there, and she wants Kevin to do the same thing."

Mick stared at her, trying to absorb the news. Kevin wasn't career military the way Georgia was. He'd been a paramedic who'd felt compelled to enlist with a war going on in Iraq. His original two-year stint had already been extended. In Mick's opinion that was long enough to prove his dedication to his country.

"Kevin's not going to buy into that idea," he said with certainty. "He's his own man. And you know yourself how persuasive he can be. He'll convince Georgia that they belong back home."

"I hope so," Bree said, "but he loves his wife. If she's determined to go back, it seems likely he will, too. He's certainly not going to want her over there alone."

"Then we'll talk him out of it," Mick said. "I admire what he's done. He's been over there saving the lives of our men and women, but he has a life back here, too. I want him to have a chance to live it. I want the same for Georgia."

"That's what we all want. I think hearing Georgia's plans really upset Gram, and Jess was so furious I talked her out of coming tonight. I wasn't sure what she might do."

Mick nodded. "To tell you the truth, I'm not sure what I'll do if I go back in there, so I think I'll take a walk instead and give this some more thought. As mule-headed as your brother can be, I don't want to say the wrong thing and have him dig in his heels just to spite me."

"Amen to that. And Dad," she said, looking him in the eye, "don't make an issue of this while Georgia's still here, okay? We don't know for sure how Kevin feels about it. Let me talk to him after she's gone and see what *his* plans are."

Mick nodded reluctantly. "That makes sense. I'll do my best to keep my opinion to myself till we know more." He studied his daughter intently. "Is that the only thing weighing on you tonight?"

"What do you mean?"

"I heard there have been a couple of scenes with Jake recently. One at Brady's and another at the pizza shop. Are you doing okay?"

She gave him a rueful look. "Word does get around, doesn't it? Did the gossip also happen to mention that I caused one of the scenes? Jake was responsible for the other one. I suppose that makes us even."

"But it obviously doesn't make you happy," Mick noted, seeing the sadness in her eyes.

She shrugged. "How could it? I love him, Dad."

Mick looked startled by the admission, which wasn't surprising given the way both she and Jake had been acting. "You sure about that?" he asked.

Bree nodded with certainty. "I just forgot that for a little while, made some really stupid mistakes, and now it may be too late."

"It's never too late," Mick told her. "Not as long as you're both available. Just look at your mother and me. We may not have gotten past all the obstacles yet, but we're on the same path and we're making progress. It's made me hopeful." He cupped her chin and winked at her. "You take heart from that, okay?"

Bree felt the ache in her chest ease. Maybe Mick was right. Maybe all wasn't lost with Jake, after all.

19

Jake had reached his limit when it came to Bree. She was in his face every time he turned around. He had to deal with her because of her shop. Apparently he had to accept that she and his sister were suddenly bosom buddies again. And she was in his head 24/7. Something had to change.

Gathering his courage, he drove over to Flowers on Main at the end of the day, hoping to catch her alone. Instead, he walked in the door and found Jenny behind the counter. There was no sign of Bree. That annoyed him even more.

"What are you doing here?" he demanded irritably.

His niece beamed at him. "I work here," she said excitedly. "Every day after school and every other Saturday. Isn't that awesome? Bree's the best boss ever. And she and Mom have been friends practically forever, so being here is not like work at all. She treats me like family. I'm saving up so I can buy a car once I get my regular driver's license."

"Forget it. You're not getting a car," he argued. "You're barely seventeen. You don't need a car. You can walk anywhere you need to go in this town."

"You had a car when you were eighteen. Grandma told me."

"I was working a summer job that required me to drive all over the place with a lawn mower and all sorts of other junk. I needed a truck. You get a job like that we'll talk again."

"I don't think Mom's going to be as mean about this as you are," she said confidently.

Jake frowned at her. "Wanna bet? The point is, you don't need to be saving up for a car now. If you behave and keep your grades up, I'll buy you a car when the time comes," he said. Anything to get her away from Bree. It was just one more thread binding them together. Each thread alone might be fragile, but together they were strong. And even when he was most exasperated with her, he couldn't deny that she was still the woman he loved. *That* infuriated him most of all.

"I want to earn the money for my own car," Jenny said with a level of maturity he'd had no idea she possessed. "It'll mean more if I do."

Since nothing else had worked—not his weak attempt at intimidation or an outright bribe—he said, "Does your mother know you're doing this?"

A little of the glow in Jenny's eyes dimmed at his harsh tone. "Of course she does. She set up the interview with Bree because I'd told her I thought it would be great to get to work here."

Of course she had, Jake thought. It was just one more thing to get under his skin.

"Where's Bree now?"

"She ran over to Sally's to pick up a couple of croissants. She and I have tea every afternoon. Isn't that cool? I'm brewing the tea right now. It's Earl Grey today. You want some? I'll share my croissant with you."

The last thing Jake wanted to do was go to a damn tea party with his niece and his ex-girlfriend, fiancée, or whatever the heck Bree was. "I'll pass," he said tightly. "Just tell her I stopped by."

"You should wait. She'll be back any minute," Jenny said.

"I don't have time to wait."

Jenny gave him a knowing look. "It's true, isn't it, what Mom told me?"

"I have no idea what your mother told you."

"That you still have a thing for Bree but you're too stubborn to admit it. I remember when you were crazy about her, you know. You'd go all mushy whenever she was in the room. You're still doing it, even when she's not around and you're just talking about her. It's in your eyes."

God bless his sister, he thought sourly. "None of your business, or Connie's for that matter."

"But it *is* true," Jenny said confidently. "It's written all over your face."

"I most certainly do not still have a thing

for Bree," he insisted. "She's infuriating. She's caused me no end of trouble. She's made us both the subject of gossip more than once. I came over here to put a stop to it."

Jenny didn't look even remotely convinced by his declaration. In fact, she wore the very amused expression Connie usually had on her face when he was reciting the same facts to her.

"Give her my message, okay?" he said as he turned toward the door, just in time to come face-to-face with the woman in question.

Bree was standing outside, the bag of croissants in her hand and a look that spoke volumes on her face. She was clearly no happier to find him on the premises than he was about having a confrontation in front of his niece. He yanked open the door and stepped aside to let her in, all too aware of the light, intoxicating scent of her perfume as she passed.

"I was just leaving," he muttered, not looking at her.

"He came to talk to you," Jenny contradicted. "He never said what it was about."

"Business," he said hurriedly, "but it can wait. I'm late for another appointment."

Bree looked skeptical. "If it's business and it was important enough for you to drive over here, let's discuss it now. Our tea can wait, and I'm sure whoever you're seeing next won't minding waiting an extra five minutes."

Jake figured walking out now would only prove that he'd come here on another mission entirely. He seized a topic out of thin air. "It's about costs. With gas going up, we're going to have to start charging for deliveries. Or you can come to the nursery and pick up your order yourself." He liked that one. She'd most likely be there when he was out on a job, which would cut their contact way down.

"How much?" Bree asked.

For a second, gazing into her eyes, he'd lost track of what he'd said. "What?"

"The price for delivery. How much are you going to charge?"

Since he'd invented the increase on the spot, he had no idea. If he made up something outrageous just to scare her off, his other customers might get wind of it and panic. "Ten dollars to commercial customers," he said eventually.

"Ten dollars?" she repeated, her eyes

sparkling with amusement. "You came all the way over here to tell me you're going to add ten dollars to the bill for delivery?"

"Yes."

She regarded him with unmistakable disbelief, then nodded. "Okay, then. Sounds perfectly reasonable to me. I'm surprised you didn't do it sooner."

"Yeah, well, we're big believers in customer service. I kept hoping the gas prices would retreat."

She set the bag of croissants on the counter and kept a skeptical gaze on him. "I don't think you came over here to discuss a delivery charge at all."

"Me, neither," Jenny chimed in. "I think maybe I'll go take a walk." She looked to Bree. "Is that okay with you?"

Bree nodded.

Jenny bounced over and gave him a peck on the cheek. "You're a lousy liar," she whispered in his ear before she took off.

Bree studied him. "What'd she say to put that guilty expression on your face?"

"That I'm a lousy liar," he admitted, resigned to having the discussion he'd originally come over here to have. It was just as well. In another few minutes, he might have forgotten all about how angry he'd been at her.

"You're a terrible liar," Bree agreed. "What are you really doing here?"

Jake walked past her into the backroom. "You coming or not?" he asked irritably when she didn't immediately follow.

"We can talk out here," she said. Suddenly there was a nervous edge in her voice, as if she feared being alone in a cramped space with him.

"We could, but I'm not sure you want to risk the entire town seeing us."

She stepped through the archway into the workroom, but kept as much distance as she could between them, including the width of her worktable. "I don't think seeing two people having a conversation, even the two of us, is cause for gossip."

Jake met her gaze. "We're not going to talk."

That definitely disconcerted her. To tell the truth, he was a little disconcerted by this turn of events himself.

"Then what did you have in mind?"

"When I got here, I had a lot of things to

say," he admitted. "Now I just want to do this." He moved slowly and deliberately in her direction. To Bree's credit, she stood her ground.

When he was close enough, Jake traced a finger along the curve of her cheek. He felt her tremble beneath his touch.

"Jake." It was part protest, part plea.

His lips twitched. "Yes, Bree."

"What's going on?"

"I wish to hell I knew," he said roughly. "I just know that things can't go on the way they have been. I'm a mess. I even yelled at Mrs. Finch the other day when she called me to come back for the thousandth time to check one of her precious lilacs."

"You yelled at Mrs. Finch? That's like kicking a sweet, innocent puppy."

"I know. I felt awful. I planted three new lilacs for her to make up for it."

Bree lifted her hand as if to touch him, then lowered it to her side. "Be sure, Jake," she implored. "Don't do . . . well, whatever you were planning to do just now, unless you're ready to move on. This on-again, off-again stuff is too hard."

"I can't think beyond right now," he said honestly. "This is what I want right now. I want you back in my arms, back in my bed."

"Back in your life?" she asked, searching his face.

Jake almost said yes, because he knew it was what she needed to hear. "I think so," he said, knowing he was leaving room for doubt, enough room to end this moment before it really began.

To his regret, though not his surprise, she stepped back. "You need to go. Find a way to forgive me, Jake, or there's no way for us to be together again."

Jake wasn't even sure it was about forgiveness anymore. It was about fear, the kind of paralyzing fear that came with knowing that if he reached out and she wound up leaving him again he might not survive. He refused to share that kind of vulnerability with her.

She apparently drew her own conclusion from his silence. "Jake, did you read the pages I gave you from my manuscript?"

He shook his head. He'd stuffed it in a drawer, out of sight, though not out of mind. He was afraid of what those pages might reveal.

There was no mistaking the disappointment in her eyes. “I wish you would.”

“Why? They’re just words, Bree,” he said, deliberately minimizing her work. “They’re not going to fix anything.”

“They’re not *just* words,” she said heatedly. “They’re raw, painful emotions on those pages. *My* emotions!”

He’d guessed that. In fact, it was what scared him most of all. Because if he read those words, if he saw Bree’s perspective on what had happened between them, he might be forced to let go of the anger he’d been clinging to all these years.

And then he’d have no defenses left at all.

When Jake had gone, Bree tried to compose herself, but Jenny returned before she had a firm grip on her emotions.

“Uncle Jake can be such a jerk,” Jenny said after getting a good look at her red-rimmed eyes. “What did he do? I was hoping he was here to patch things up. I loved it when you were together because it was almost like you were family.”

Bree smiled at the teen’s willingness to rush to her defense, even against her own uncle. "You're still like family to me," Bree told her. "Whatever happens between your uncle and me won't change that."

"Why can't you fix things? It's obvious he's still crazy about you."

"We just have some unresolved issues," Bree told her.

Jenny looked justifiably puzzled. "If you have issues, aren't you supposed to sit down and talk about them? Isn't that what adults do? When I get mad at Mom, she won't leave me alone till we've talked it out."

"First, she's a mom," Bree said. "It's in her job description to make sure you two resolve things. Second, Jake's a guy. They never want to talk about anything. They just want it to go away."

"But he's the one who came over here to talk," Jenny protested.

"He *thought* he came over here to talk. Then he got other ideas."

Jenny's eyes widened. "He, like, made a pass at you?"

Bree reddened, wishing she'd been more discreet. "I didn't say that."

"But that's what happened, isn't it?" Her expression brightened. "Way to go, Uncle

Jake!" she blurted, then looked guilty. "You're not mad about it, are you? I mean, it wasn't, like, totally gross or anything, was it? You guys used to kiss all the time. I saw you."

"I don't think it's appropriate for me to discuss my personal life with an employee," Bree said, smiling to take the sting out of the words. "Even one who's like family to me."

"But he's my uncle. I could help."

"Something tells me he's already getting more unsolicited advice than he can handle. It's better if you don't bring this up."

Settling on a stool at the counter, Jenny tore off a piece of her chocolate croissant and popped it into her mouth, her expression thoughtful. "Love's really complicated, isn't it?"

"You have no idea," Bree responded.

"Do you think you have to sleep with a guy just to prove you love him?" Jenny asked, almost causing Bree to spill hot tea all over herself.

"Absolutely not," she said at once. "If a man, a boy really, says something like that to you, then he's not thinking about you at all. All he cares about is his own agenda."

"That's pretty much what Uncle Jake and Mom have said."

Bree was relieved that Jenny had had this discussion with the two adults who mattered. She was hardly the right person to be giving advice to a teenager. Still, since the subject had come up, she felt compelled to ask, "Is your boyfriend pressuring you to have sex?"

Jenny hesitated, then nodded. "Just a little. I get why he wants to. I mean, so do I, in a way, but I'm nowhere near ready. What if I got pregnant? Nothing's a hundred percent effective. They taught us that in school. Having a baby would totally mess up the rest of my life. I've got plans, you know?"

"I do know," Bree said quietly, thinking of how an unplanned pregnancy had very nearly derailed her life. Ironically, in some ways, having the miscarriage had taken its own terrible toll. She'd lost her relationship with Jake because of how she'd handled it. She'd gotten her chance at her dream career, but even during its very best moments, it had felt tainted.

"Are you okay?" Jenny asked, studying her worriedly. "Did I say something wrong?

I do that a lot. My mom says my mouth starts up before my brain kicks in."

Bree gave her hand a squeeze. "You didn't say anything wrong. In fact, what you said was very smart. Having sex when you're not ready for all the possible complications is a really lousy idea."

Jenny sighed. "I know."

"Are you sure you can handle the pressure this boy is putting on you? Maybe it would be better to put a little space between you for a while."

"I've been thinking about that," the teenager admitted. "I even tried to tell him that's how I felt, but he said he really loved me."

"Those are powerful words," Bree said, choosing her own words with care. "He might be too young to really understand what they mean, or what they should mean, anyway."

Jenny's grin, when it came, was filled with very mature awareness. "I figured he was playing me. You don't have to worry. Neither do Mom or Uncle Jake. I know what Dillon's all about. I can handle him."

Famous last words, Bree feared. This might be a private conversation that she couldn't repeat to Connie or Jake, but she did owe it to them and even to Jenny to make sure they kept on watching the couple like hawks.

It was nearly 7:00 p.m. when Jake walked into Sally's to grab a burger. The lights had been off in Bree's shop when he pulled up, which had reassured him. He figured there was no chance he'd be running into her for a second time in the same day. The earlier encounter had been confusing enough.

Unfortunately, his sense of security proved false. He spotted her not two seconds after walking inside the café, sitting by herself in a booth in the back, a book open on the table next to her half-eaten salad. She was staring into space, her mind clearly on other things.

Since she hadn't seen him yet, he had two choices. He could leave before she knew he was there or he could join her. Sitting in another booth and trying to claim later that he hadn't seen her wasn't an option. Sally would, no doubt, point out her presence before he'd even settled in his own seat.

Still annoyed with himself for the way he

let her keep getting to him, he steeled himself for another round and walked back to her booth. He slid in opposite her, bumping knees with her, before she even looked up. To his surprise, her expression brightened.

"What's up?" he asked. "You almost look happy to see me. After this afternoon, I didn't expect that reaction."

"Yeah, well, don't take it too personally. I just need to talk to you about Jenny. She and I had a pretty serious conversation after you left."

He stilled at that. "About me?"

"No, about her and Dillon."

That unnerved Jake even more. "Oh?"

He had to wait until Sally had delivered his usual glass of tea, then taken his order for a pork chop, mashed potatoes and a salad before Bree offered a reply.

"I'm not going to reveal anything specific," she told him, "but I think you and Connie need to keep an even closer eye on her boyfriend."

Jake immediately grasped what she was getting at. He tore the paper off his straw and jammed it into his glass of tea so hard, the plastic bent.

"This is about sex, isn't it? Dammit, I knew that kid was up to no good! I'm going to forbid her from seeing him, period."

Bree regarded him with amusement. "And drive her right into his arms? That's smart."

He sighed heavily and sat back, the tea and his mangled straw forgotten. "I suppose you have a better idea."

"Actually, I do."

"Care to share?"

"Spend as much time with them as you possibly can, you and Connie. I don't mean hanging out in the same house. I mean suggesting that you all go to a football game together or even a concert, if you know there's one they'd both like. They'll think you're cool for asking, and they won't be out of your sight. Smother them with attention."

"Jenny's going to hate that."

Bree shook her head. "I don't think so. She might grumble, but to tell you the truth, I think she'll be grateful for the backup, as long as you guys are subtle about it." She met his gaze. "Think you can manage that?"

"Me? Subtle? Isn't that pretty much an

oxymoron? Come on, Bree. I'm no good at that kind of thing."

"Connie is," she reminded him.

"But she can't deal with this alone. I usually do better with getting through to Jenny than she does. I guess it's a mother-daughter thing."

Even as he spoke, he recalled the fairly placid relationship Bree had with Megan years ago, but she'd been younger than Jenny was now when Megan left. And she'd never been particularly rebellious, either. Abby and Megan, however, had been through their share of turmoil, which made it all the more surprising that Abby had been the first one to forgive Megan and let her back into her life after the divorce.

"So, you want to deal with this yourself?" Bree said.

"As much as I can," he agreed. "Sam's no help. He and his daughter have almost no contact. I'm the closest thing she has to a dad on a day in, day out basis. I take that responsibility seriously."

Bree nodded. "I thought you were going to say that." She dug in her purse and pulled out a newspaper clipping for an upcoming concert in Washington, D.C., then passed it to him. "Why don't I order tickets and we can take them to this. I know Jenny likes this band because she's been talking about the concert all week."

Jake shoved aside the plate of food Sally had just set in front of him. He barely glanced at the concert ad. He was too startled by Bree's words. "*We?* As in you and me?"

"Why not? It could be fun. And it will be less intimidating if we're both there. It'll seem less like you're chaperoning."

"And you think they're going to be fooled by that?"

"Probably not, but Jenny will be grateful, to say nothing of delighted to see the two of us together for an evening. I gather she's a mini-matchmaker in the making. She's already offered to put in a good word for me with you."

Jake groaned. "Connie's doing. Heaven knows what stories she's filled that girl's head with."

"I can summarize it if you'd like," she taunted. "Plus, she apparently caught us kissing more than once way back when."

He held up a hand. "Please, spare me."

"Okay, but what do you think about the concert? Shall I order tickets tomorrow?"

"You really want to go out with my niece and the guy whose lights I'm tempted to punch out?"

"Sure. I'll consider it a mission of mercy."

He paused, his knife poised over the pork chop. "You want to protect that punk?" he asked incredulously.

"No, but I do want to keep you from ruining your relationship with your niece and winding up in jail in the process."

He could see the wisdom in that. "Get the tickets," he said at last. Protecting Jenny was more important than keeping a firm grip on his own peace of mind where his relationship with Bree was concerned. "Let me know tomorrow what they cost. I'll reimburse you."

"Not necessary," she said. "After all, this was my idea. It should be my treat."

"Let me know the cost," he insisted.

"Fine, if that'll make you happy."

Happy didn't really enter into it. This was for Jenny's sake, he thought. He was obligated to do it.

Apparently misinterpreting his expression

for misery rather than resignation—perhaps tinged with a hint of anticipation he shouldn't be feeling—she patted his hand. "It'll be painless, I promise."

He gave up on his meal. The conversation had pretty much made him lose his appetite. He leaned back in the booth and studied Bree curiously. "A couple of hours ago, you didn't want to see me again unless I'd resolved to let go of the past. What changed?"

She withdrew her hand, her expression somber. "This isn't about us, Jake. I want that to be clear."

"It's you and me together for an evening," he said. "How can it not be about us?"

"Because I said so."

Though her logic eluded him, he was wise enough to keep that to himself. She didn't look as if she was in the mood for an argument on the point. Instead, he just shook his head in bemusement at the twists and turns of life.

"Who'd have thought it?" he said. "You and me double-dating with my niece."

"*We're* not going to be on a date," she reminded him. "We're chaperoning, remember?"

“Potato, potahto,” he replied, enjoying the splash of bright pink coloring her cheeks.

“Not a date,” she repeated.

“Whatever you say,” he said cooperatively.

She could call it whatever she wanted to. At the end of the night, he could still make another pass like the one she’d almost succumbed to in her shop this afternoon. He had a hunch on a moonlit evening, in the shadows of her front porch, she might not be so quick to resist.

20

Megan hadn't heard from Mick since she'd been down to Chesapeake Shores for Kevin's homecoming over two weeks ago. By her calculations that meant Kevin would be heading back to Iraq any day now, if he hadn't left already. Though she knew Mick was probably spending every spare minute with their son, the silence grated. She'd started counting on the nightly phone calls when they talked about their children and caught up on each other's lives. It was exactly as she'd feared. Mick was already reverting to the kind of distracted, neglectful behavior that had driven her away fifteen years ago.

She was swamped at work, which should have made it easier, but instead made her long for someone with whom she could share all the day's frustrations. Lately she hadn't even heard from Abby, whom she'd once counted on to be her sounding board. Now that Abby was caught up in her own life with Trace and the girls, Megan didn't feel she could turn to her as frequently as she once had. Ironically, the loneliness that had sent her fleeing from Chesapeake Shores for the busy, electric atmosphere of New York seemed to have followed her right into the heart of the Big Apple.

When her phone rang as she was eating a late dinner—a glass of wine and a scrambled egg, of all things—she seized it eagerly, grateful for any interruption.

"Where have you been all evening?" Mick grumbled, as if she should have been waiting by the phone for him when he eventually decided to check in.

"Out," she replied, matching his testy tone. Let him think whatever he wanted to about that.

"I'll be there in ten minutes," he said, shocking her.

"Ten minutes? Where are you?"

"In that deli you claimed was your favorite," he replied. "I kept expecting you to walk in here. When you didn't, I started calling."

Megan was flabbergasted. "You've been in my deli since when?"

"Got here about six. They told me you usually stop in by seven at the latest. I think they're starting to feel sorry for me. Here I am with flowers and champagne and no one came to my surprise party."

"Oh, Mick," she said, her anger melting away. "I had no idea."

"That was the whole point. I wanted to surprise you."

"Well, if it's any comfort, you have. I'll see you in ten minutes." That would give her barely enough time to clean up her pitiful meal and put on a fresh dash of lipstick.

"Two minutes," he corrected. "I started walking the second you picked up the phone."

"Oh, my," she said, clicking off the call without even saying goodbye.

She'd barely tossed the cold eggs down the garbage disposal and freshened up when the doorman called. "Your husband's here, Mrs. O'Brien," Don said, sounding justifiably confused.

"He's *not* my husband anymore," she said emphatically. "But you can send him up." She figured if she didn't correct the impression Mick was trying to make on the man, Mick would be taking all sorts of liberties. Since Don was a seventy-something grandfather of twelve, he, like her friends at the deli, liked to keep tabs on her social life. He found the fact that she didn't date much to be troubling.

"A pretty woman like you should have a man courting her," he said every time she wandered in alone on a Saturday night. The appearance of Mick would reassure him and the next thing she knew, she'd be finding Mick in her apartment when she was least expecting him.

She was waiting by the door when Mick walked off the elevator, bringing with him the scent of fall in New York—crisp air and roasting chestnuts. He held out a bouquet of bright yellow chrysanthemums, then swept in for a hard, lingering kiss that turned hot, even though his skin was cool from his brisk walk on a chilly November evening.

"You should have let me know you were coming," she chided when she'd caught her breath.

"I thought you liked surprises."

"I do, but as you've discovered, they can go awry."

He looked deep into her eyes. "Were you out with another man tonight, Meggie?" Though he managed to keep his tone light, there was an unmistakable undercurrent of jealousy in his voice.

"I was," she said, enjoying the brief flash of possessiveness that darkened his eyes. Still, since she didn't want to give him the wrong idea, at least not for long given the mistake that had played a role in ending their marriage, she explained, "My boss and I were getting ready for the next show at the gallery."

"You were at work," he said, his relief evident. He studied her with a wicked glint in his eyes. "Tell me, then, were you trying to make me jealous just now?"

She grinned. "Just trying to see if I was

capable of it," she admitted. "It was pretty satisfying to see that I am."

She took his coat and hung it in the closet, then watched as he opened the bottle of champagne with sure hands.

"Glasses?" he asked.

"I'll get them." She found two wineglasses in the cupboard that would have to do. Since she'd put a stop to Mick's alimony payments a few years earlier, her budget rarely ran to champagne, so she didn't own any flutes.

Mick poured the wine, then lifted his glass to hers.

"What are we drinking to?" she asked.

"Our son's safe return," he said at once.

She sipped the champagne, her eyes stinging. "Kevin's already left for Iraq again?" Though she'd been aware of the time slipping by, she'd really hoped that he wouldn't leave without saying goodbye.

Mick nodded, his own eyes troubled. "I have to admit, I'm scared for him."

Megan moved into his arms and held on. "Me, too."

"Did he call you?" Mick asked, drawing

her over to the sofa, then settling down with her by his side. "I told him to."

She shook her head. "No, I haven't spoken to him since the weekend I was down there. I even left messages for him with both Nell and Bree, but he never called me back."

Mick looked dismayed. "I'm sorry. I thought the two of you might have made some progress in mending fences that weekend."

"I wish. After his initial surprised greeting, he was very careful to avoid being alone with me."

"Well, there was a lot going on," Mick said.

She touched his cheek. "You don't have to defend him."

"You're his mother. You at least deserve his respect."

"I'm sure in his view, I wasn't much of a mother, not at the end."

"Next time will be better," Mick promised. "When he's home for good."

"Any idea when that will be?"

Mick shook his head, his gaze suddenly far away.

"What is it?" she asked him. "You look upset."

"I am."

"Tell me why."

He hesitated, then said with real heat in his voice, "If Georgia has her way, they'll stay on over there. I admire her dedication, I really do, but I want our boy home."

Megan tried to hide her own apprehension. "Don't put this all on Georgia," she warned. "Kevin will make the right decision for him when the time comes. We have to trust him on that."

"You ever known a man with stars in his eyes to think clearly?" Mick countered.

"Kevin will," she said with certainty. "Of all our kids, he was the most grounded, even more cautious and sensible than Abby in some ways. He thought everything through."

"And you don't think this impetuous marriage of his proves that he's no longer that way?" Mick asked doubtfully.

"I'm hoping that being married will make him even more careful and thoughtful," she said, trying to inject a note of conviction in her voice, not just for Mick's sake, but her own. How would she live with herself if something happened to her son and she'd never made amends with him?

Mick apparently guessed what she was thinking, because his arm around her tightened. "I didn't come here to upset you."

She looked into his eyes. "Why *did* you come?"

"For this," he murmured, lowering his lips to hers. They were both a little breathless when the kiss finally ended. "If we live to be a hundred, Meggie, I don't think I'll ever get my fill of you."

Megan wanted that to be true. She really did. Because, as terrifying as it was, the reverse was certainly true enough for her.

About the best Bree could say for the concert was that it had been loud. Jake actually looked a little stunned by the sound that had practically raised the roof of the basketball arena that had served as the band's venue.

Jenny, however, looked as excited as if she'd been given a puppy and a convertible all on Christmas morning. "This was the most amazing thing I've ever done in my whole entire life," she said as they walked back to their car. "It's my very first live concert. Thank you, Bree."

Jake scowled at her with feigned annoyance. "Hey, I was the one who bought the tickets."

"Yes, but I know it was Bree's idea," Jenny told him. "You'd never think of anything this fantastic, especially if it was happening on a school night."

"Hey, give your uncle some of the credit," Bree said. "The last concert we saw was ten years ago, and it was some neighborhood garage band. He expanded his boundaries tonight."

"Well, it was really cool of you to invite me along," Dillon said. "My folks would never go to something like this. They, like, live in the Dark Ages. They fell into a time warp back when Garth Brooks was still performing."

Jake blinked at that. "Garth Brooks performed in the Dark Ages?" he said to Bree in an undertone as he held the passenger door for her.

"Musically speaking to a teenager, I suppose he did."

"Are we old?"

Bree tucked her arm through his. "Yes, Jake. We're old."

"We're not even thirty. That's not old."

"Not when you're living it, but to a kid? Afraid so."

"Good grief."

"Can we stop for something to eat?" Jenny interrupted to plead.

"We ate before we came," Jake reminded her. "And you guys ate more at the concert."

"Teenagers," Bree reminded him. "Remember the way we were at their age? You, at least, were a bottomless pit."

Jake chuckled. "Point taken. Okay, we'll stop. Burgers? Mexican? What?"

"Pancakes," Jenny said at once. "It'll be after midnight by the time we get to the pancake place right before the turnoff from the highway to home. It'll be almost like we got to stay out all night."

"Now, there's an image I want stuck in my head," Jake muttered. Aloud, he said, "Okay, then, pancakes it is."

Bree reached over and gave his hand a quick squeeze. "You're a good uncle."

"I'd rather be thought of as a good date."

She gave him an impertinent look. "Then you'll have to ask someone out, won't you?"

He laughed. "You still deluding yourself this wasn't a date, sugar?"

"You can call it whatever you want to," she said. "I'm just along for the ride."

He met her gaze. "If only that were true."

"Not *that* roller coaster, Jake. The one that was you and me. There's only one way to get me back on that one and you know what it is."

"I have to read the first hundred pages of your manuscript," he said with an air of resignation.

"You said you wanted to," she reminded him. "And now *I* want you to. Unless, of course, you're afraid to read it."

"Why would I be afraid to read it?" he asked defensively.

"Because you might find out there are two sides to every story."

"Two sides to what story?" Jenny chimed in from the backseat, proving that she'd been eavesdropping all along. It was probably marginally better than the other things she and Dillon could have been doing back there, but Bree still cringed.

"Nothing," Jake said tersely.

"Did you write a book, Bree?" Jenny persisted.

"I've started one," Bree admitted.

"Can I read it?"

"No," Bree said at once. Jake echoed the sentiment.

"Why not? Is it about the two of you?"

"It's a novel," Bree said.

"But it could still be about you guys," Jenny said. "Please let me see it. Once it's published, everyone will be reading it. I want to be first, or one of the first anyway."

"I'm not sure it will ever be published," Bree said, drawing a sharp look from Jake. "Getting published is hard."

"But you've had plays produced, so your writing must be good," Jenny argued, obviously not giving up. "I'll bet if you sent it to a publisher, they'd snap it up."

"I might not submit it," Bree admitted.

This time when Jake glanced her way, his expression was incredulous. "Why not?" he asked.

"I've just been thinking that it hits a little too close to home. I think I had to get all of this down on paper for myself," she said. "And for you."

Jenny started to say something, but Dillon apparently nudged her because she gave an indignant little huff, then asked him, "What was that for?"

"Because it's obvious Bree doesn't want anyone else reading what she's written. Leave it alone. Some things are just too personal to be shared, you know? Do you show anyone the songs you've written?"

Jenny gave a gasp of unmistakable dismay. "No one's supposed to know about that."

Dillon regarded her calmly. "Exactly my point. Now, back off and leave your uncle and Bree in peace."

"Hold on," Jake said. "You've been writing songs, Jenny? Does your mom know?"

"Nobody knew till big mouth back here blabbed," she grumbled.

"Dillon, have you heard any of them?" Jake persisted.

"She's good, man. Way better than that junk we heard tonight."

Jenny's face flushed with pleasure, even

though she poked him. “Come on. You’re biased. I’m nowhere near as good as those guys. They’re professionals.”

“Just because a bunch of fools like us paid to see them doesn’t make them talented,” Dillon insisted. “Have you ever actually listened to those lyrics? Half of ’em don’t even make sense. I’m glad we got to go and all, but really, those guys wouldn’t know a real song if it bit ’em in the butt.”

“Amen to that,” Jake said in a rare moment of unity with Dillon. “And what you’re saying is that Jenny’s lyrics make sense?”

“They rock,” Dillon confirmed.

Jake and Bree exchanged a glance.

“Who knew?” he said in an undertone.

Bree grinned at his expression. “It’s amazing what you discover when you just hang out with someone, isn’t it?”

Jake gave her a wry look. “Haven’t I been trying to say that very thing to you for a while now? You’re the one who closed that door.”

Bree didn’t wilt under his blatant taunt. “And you have the key to unlock it,” she retorted. “Where’d you hide it, Jake? Or did you destroy it?”

"I know exactly where the manuscript is."

"Then the ball's in your court, isn't it?" She glanced out the car window. "And there's the pancake place up ahead. Isn't that convenient? We can end this discussion for tonight."

"Don't be so sure," Jake said as he pulled into a parking place by the front door of the brightly lit restaurant. He waited until his niece and Dillon had scrambled out of the backseat before adding, "There are a couple of hours to go before we're safely home and tucked into our separate beds, Bree. Who knows where the conversational road may lead us."

"Not where you're thinking," she said fiercely.

Jake merely grinned. "We'll see."

She frowned as she got out of the car and slammed the door. If she had to, she'd turn the tables and make sure Jenny chaperoned the rest of *her* evening. If there was one thing she knew with absolute certainty, it was that Jake wouldn't say a single thing about the past in front of his niece. If Jenny found out that he'd gotten Bree pregnant six years ago, what kind of example would that be setting for his impressionable niece?

Satisfied that she had a plan, she was halfway to the restaurant door, when Jake caught her elbow. “Don’t even think about trying to maneuver me into taking you home before Jenny. It won’t work.”

Bree stared into his determined eyes and sighed. She’d just have to figure out something else. She wondered if making a frantic call to Jess to have her sister come rescue her might make her seem just a little too desperate to avoid being alone with Jake. Probably so.

That didn’t mean she might not try it if she didn’t like the way things went during their after-midnight pancake breakfast.

Jake figured he’d put the fear of God into Bree, but when push came to shove, he couldn’t follow through and try cross-examining her in the middle of the night. He was too tired for one thing and she was too guarded. He’d have to leave it for another day when they were both at the top of their game.

He dropped off Dillon, then Jenny before driving to Bree’s house.

"Good night," she said, already opening the car door and preparing for a sprint to the house. "Thanks for a great evening."

Jake knew what she was up to, but that didn't stop him from climbing out of the car and coming around to walk with her to the house. As safe as Chesapeake Shores was and as well lit as the O'Brien front porch was, he was too much of a gentleman to take any chances. Besides, there was still that chance he could sneak at least one satisfying kiss that would keep him up the rest of the night.

At the front door, Bree eyed him warily. "You want to come in for coffee?" she asked without much enthusiasm. It was just an offer well-bred young ladies automatically made.

"No, thanks."

"Then, good night. It was a lovely evening. Jenny is terrific and I liked Dillon better than I expected to."

"Don't let the kid fool you. He's sneaky."

"He's a hormone-driven teenager. They're all sneaky."

Jake touched her cheek. "So am I, hormone driven, that is, not sneaky." He paused then admitted, "I want to kiss you, Bree."

He heard her breath catch.

"What's stopping you?" she asked, a hitch in her voice.

"We've got so many mixed signals between us, I don't want to make it any worse."

"Maybe it won't make it worse. Maybe it will help to clarify things."

"See what I mean," he said in exasperation. "You tell me in no uncertain terms that you're off-limits until I've followed all these rules—read the manuscript, forgive you, talk things out, whatever. Now you want me to kiss you. Does that make any kind of sense to you?"

To his shock, she wound her arms around his neck. "Maybe I'm tired of wanting everything to make sense. Maybe the blueberry syrup went to my head. Or maybe I just want this."

Jake backed off. "You see, it's the *maybe* that worries me. A lot of men have gotten slapped silly for acting on *maybe.*"

She laughed. "I see the dilemma. How about this, then?" She sealed her mouth over his, taking away the guesswork.

Jake waited a split second before giving in to sensation. This—him and Bree together—had once made more sense than anything else in his life. He'd seen their future so clearly—him owning his own landscaping company someday, her writing in a cozy little room he'd build for her, their red-haired children playing on a swing set in their big backyard. In his vision, they'd never tire of being close like this.

With his hand against her cheek, he looked deep into her eyes and thought he saw at least some of those same memories there. Surely he couldn't have been a hundred percent wrong back then. Surely she'd wanted what he'd wanted, been at least a little torn about giving it all up to go to Chicago.

He scooped her into his arms and made his way to a glider, where he sat down with her in his lap. It was pure torture, but here in plain view of Mick or Nell if they happened to wander downstairs, he wouldn't be tempted to take things too far. He'd go on tasting the blueberries on her lips, remembering the feel of her skin, but prudence would keep his actions in check. Bree certainly wasn't making any effort to do it.

In fact, her kisses were greedy, her hands so clever that in a rare moment of rational thought, he had to pin them together. "Enough, you wicked woman. There are other people around, you know."

"There wouldn't be if we went to your place."

He studied her speculatively. "Are you serious?" he asked, unable to keep a hopeful note out of his voice.

"I said it, didn't I?"

"Yes, but in recent memory you also stated very clearly that this wasn't a date and that we weren't going to get back together until I'd done a whole bunch of stuff I can't seem to remember with you trying to take a bite out of my neck like that."

She laughed. "Am I getting you all hot and bothered, Jake?"

"You know you are. And we both know that our issues never had a thing to do with being attracted to each other."

Her expression sobered at last, but she didn't scramble out of his lap as he'd half expected her to. "I wish this weren't so complicated," she said wistfully.

"Me, too. But let's face it, Bree, we both have reason to be skittish here. I'd like nothing more than to take you back to my place and keep you there, in my bed, for a solid week."

"Only a week?"

It was his turn to chuckle. "Don't overrate my stamina," he said. "The point is, if we get together again, it has to be right for both of us. We have to be clear on what we each want and willing to make the sacrifices it might take to be together."

She frowned at that. "You sound as if we should be able to predict the future."

"No, of course not. No one can do that. But you know what I want. I've always been clear about that. I want you. I want us to have a family. I can see the two of us side by side on our front porch when we're eighty, still madly in love."

"I can see that, too," she insisted, proving his earlier point that they had been on the same page, at least for a brief moment.

"But the rest? How do you see your career fitting into that picture? We didn't deal with that last time and look what happened."

"I have the shop now," she said. "That's my career."

"If I thought that would keep you fulfilled,

I'd propose right this second," he said, looking into her eyes. There were shadows in there that told him she was deluding herself. "You miss writing."

"But I *am* writing," she said. "There's the book."

"Which you don't even want to submit. A writer needs to be read," he declared, then added pointedly, "Or to see her works performed onstage. It's not enough just to put them down on paper. Isn't that what you used to tell me? It was the big argument for going to Chicago, not just to learn from someone with Marty's credentials, but the chance to see your plays produced."

"And I've done that now."

"Three plays and you're done for life? You're not like Jess. You stick with things." He gave her a chiding look. "I certainly never took you for someone who could be scared off by a couple of bad reviews."

She did pull away then and settled next to him on the glider, putting as much distance between them as possible on something only the width of a love seat.

"You saw those?" she asked dully.

He nodded. "And you know my reaction?"

"What?"

"I said, so what? The next one will be better, because Bree learns from her mistakes better than anyone I know. If there are problems, she'll fix them."

"But that play was the best I'd ever written," she protested. "I really believed that, at least until I read those reviews from critics who've judged better playwrights than me. And if it wasn't good enough, why keep trying?"

He stared at her in disbelief. "Why keep trying? Because you're a playwright! That's what you do. And if you really believe that the play that got panned was good, then something else must have gone wrong."

Her expression turned thoughtful. "My mother blamed it on the director."

"Marty, I suppose."

She nodded.

"Is it possible she's right?"

"At the time I would never have said so, but now that I have some distance and can look back on it objectively, maybe. He was drafted into directing at the last minute. He'd directed before, but not any of my plays. There was a difference in the way he handled the cast and the script."

"Explain," Jake said.

Bree hesitated. "The other directors weren't as heavy-handed, I guess you'd say. He made changes to the script that weren't necessary, made it more obvious and less subtle. He did the same thing to the actors, making the performance almost melodramatic, rather than relying on the words to tell the story. Those were exactly the things the critics pointed out. They had no way of knowing I hadn't written it that way."

"Do you think Marty did it deliberately?" Jake asked. "Maybe he was jealous of the success your plays had been having, the attention you'd received."

"No way. He wouldn't do something like that," she argued. "He might be a lot of things, but he wasn't mean-spirited, not that way."

"Are you so sure?" Jake pressed. "Men can have pretty fragile egos, and everything I've ever read about artistic types suggests that their egos are unpredictable."

Bree shook her head. "I really don't buy that. If anything, I'd have to say he was out of his element. He just isn't as good at directing as he is as a playwright. That's where his real talent is."

"Okay then, if you can see that the fault most likely wasn't yours, whatever Marty's intentions or capabilities, why not get busy on your next play?" Jake asked, knowing that he was risking everything by forcing the issue.

She regarded him with confusion, perhaps even some dismay. "So, what are you suggesting I do. Do you want me to go back to Chicago?"

"For my sake, absolutely not," he said at once. "For yours, maybe you have to. Or if not Chicago, there are other successful regional theaters." A sudden thought popped into his head. "Or you could open one right here in Chesapeake Shores. Your dad could build it for you. He'd love that."

The more he talked about it, the more convinced he was this could work for her, for both of them.

"Just think about it, Bree. I'm sure there's a huge talent pool between Washington and Baltimore. Look at all the films and TV shows that shoot in the area. Bring in guest directors or hire one to run the place. Whatever it takes. This isn't my thing, but you know how to do it."

She was staring at him as if he'd just

suggested she tackle a campaign for the presidency. “I couldn’t do something like that,” she objected.

“Why not?”

“You can’t be serious. Because I don’t know how to start and manage a theater. I don’t have that kind of experience.”

“Really? You didn’t learn one single thing working in Chicago? You’ve gained no business experience running your shop?”

“It’s not the same.”

He shrugged. “You could be right,” he conceded, then added, “But so could I, and I say you’ve got what it takes to do anything you set your mind to.”

Her gaze turned dreamy. “My own regional theater? How amazing would that be?”

“Pretty amazing, I’d say. Come on, Bree. Come up with a long-term vision. Start small, if that makes you more comfortable. Use the school auditorium if you don’t want to build a theater right away. Do a couple of things each summer when the town’s packed and you’d have a ready-made audience craving a bit of culture. See how it goes. You’d need help at the shop, more help than Jenny can give you, or if the theater becomes successful, sell the shop and concentrate on that. Do whatever you want to do."

"I could hire someone to run the shop, I suppose. I'm not ready to give it up entirely. I actually enjoy it."

"Then do whatever it takes to balance the two things," he said.

There was no mistaking the excitement in her eyes when she met his gaze. "Thank you."

"For what?"

"Having faith in me."

"Always," he said without hesitation. "Keep in mind, though, that this suggestion was not totally unselfish. Despite how I've behaved from time to time, I like having you back here. If you're going to stay, you need to be happy, and, much as I hate to say it, I don't think flowers are going to do it, not for the long haul. Remember, I've been around when you've been caught up in writing. I've seen you so lost in your work that you don't even notice if anyone else is around. And I've heard the excitement in your voice when you talk about whatever you're working on."

Apparently his words struck a chord,

because instead of responding, she jumped up. "I wonder if Dad's still up."

"At three in the morning?" Jake said dryly.

"Oh my gosh, it's that late? We're both going to be walking zombies in the morning."

"I guess that's my cue to leave," he said, walking with her back to the front door. He bent down and stole one last kiss. "Sleep well."

She grinned at him. "I doubt I'll sleep a wink."

"Then maybe I should pick you up and drop you at work in the morning. You probably shouldn't be behind the wheel of a car."

"I'll walk," she said.

"Then I'll stop by before you open, with coffee and croissants. We can discuss this some more."

"That would be good," she murmured distractedly, already closing the door.

Jake stood staring after her, wondering if he'd just given her the reason she needed to stay in Chesapeake Shores or the excuse she'd need to fill up every corner of her life with work, leaving no room at all for him.

21

For the first time in weeks, Bree awoke feeling like her old self, the woman who'd had a dream and gone after it with everything she had. She was energized, excited and confident, all emotions that had been sadly lacking since she'd come home in what she'd felt was bitter defeat. Now that she'd received so much encouragement from her family, she'd been able to take a more objective look at what had really happened in Chicago.

"You're looking awfully upbeat this morning," Gram said as Bree poured herself a cup of coffee. "Not bad for a woman who didn't get home until the middle of the night. Does the credit for that go to Jake?"

Mick walked into the kitchen just in time to overhear Gram's remark. "Credit for what?"

"Gram's just wondering if Jake's responsible for my good mood," she said, enjoying the dull flush that put in her father's cheeks. He'd always avoided most conversations about her personal life, as if he'd feared he might learn something he didn't want to know. He'd left the lectures and relationship advice to Gram.

"That's not information I need to have, young lady," he said, proving her point and then stealing her cup of coffee right out from under her nose. He settled at the table and took a long, slow drink.

"Well, you'll be happy to know it's not what either of you are thinking, though Jake does deserve the credit," she told them, pouring herself another cup of coffee and joining them at the table. She filled them in on Jake's idea about opening her own regional theater, then sat back expectantly. "Well, what do you think? Is this totally insane or is it doable?"

Gram's eyes immediately brightened

with excitement. "A theater is just what this town needs. We're definitely lacking in culture here. As hard as the teachers try, the high-school productions certainly don't qualify. And I imagine the weekenders and tourists would love having something more to do than going to our festivals or eating out and shopping."

Mick didn't hesitate, either. "I know the perfect spot for it on Shore Road," he said, his expression thoughtful.

"Where?" Bree asked eagerly.

"There's a small, underutilized little park there. We could still keep the playground equipment across from the beach and build a community theater at the back of the lot. There's plenty of room for parking back there, too."

"But, Dad, that's town property. No one's going to be in favor of giving up park space, least of all me."

"Like I said, it's underutilized because the beach is right across the road. One of these days some idiot on council will take note of that and propose selling the whole thing for more condos."

"Surely no one would approve of that," Bree said, shocked by the idea.

"Waterfront's prime real estate," Mick reminded her. "And even though the town's master plan would prohibit such a thing, that can be changed if it suits enough shortsighted people." He shook his head. "This proposal takes that option right out of the picture."

"Do you really think the town would go along with it?" Bree asked.

"In case you've forgotten, your old man has some pull left around here," Mick declared. "Besides, like I said, if we make the building a community theater that anyone can use, not just your theater company, I think people will be excited about it."

He pulled a pad of paper from his pocket and began making notes. "How big would this theater of yours need to be?"

She wasn't surprised that her father had gotten right down to the practical issues. "Maybe three hundred seats at the most. Definitely smaller than the theater in Chicago. Something cozy. If it succeeds, we'll just have longer runs for the productions."

"And it's okay with you if the community uses it when you're not?"

"Absolutely. We certainly couldn't put a

production together for every week of the year. Maybe not even every month. The stage should be used. It would be good, though, if we could have a couple of permanent offices there, maybe even a small rehearsal room."

Mick regarded her over the rims of his reading glasses. "You serious about this? I'm not going down to town hall for something you'll change your mind about tomorrow."

She nodded slowly. "I think I am. I at least want to explore the possibilities." She gave him a stern look. "Which means you probably shouldn't start digging to put in the foundation just yet, okay? We all need to study this, the town included. People need to have their say about that land. Maybe I'm the only one who'd love to have a community theater in Chesapeake Shores."

"Agreed," Mick said. "Let's explore the possibilities, figure out a construction budget. You investigate the costs for everything else—a manager, a resident director, whatever. Then we'll talk again." His gaze narrowed. "I'll see if I can get the town to pony up some of the construction funding, in addition to donating the land. You have any of your trust-fund money left to invest in this?"

"Some, not a lot," she admitted. "But the flower shop's already operating in the black, so I'll be able to borrow against that, I think."

Gram gave her a long look. "You know the first thing I want to see on that new stage?"

"What?"

"The play that sent you flying back home."

Bree hesitated. "I don't know, Gram. We should probably start with a sure thing."

"No, you should start the way you intend to go on, by offering new plays by talented new writers."

"Only this time get a director who knows what the hell he's doing," Mick added.

Bree stared at him, surprised by such a vehement comment coming from her father. He hadn't even gotten to Chicago for that production. "You've been talking to Mom about this, haven't you?"

"Of course I have," Mick replied. "We talk about all of you kids. Night before last, we talked about Kevin going back to Iraq and Georgia planning to do another tour there. As for you, we've been worried sick you were going to let that man in Chicago keep you from doing what you were meant to do. And if Jake Collins was the one who made you see how wrong that was, then I owe him."

Bree nodded solemnly. "I think I do, too."

"You're late," Jake grumbled, climbing out of his truck and following Bree inside her shop.

"Big news at the O'Brien house this morning," she told him with a grin. "It seems I'm going to start a theater company."

Jake stopped in his tracks, stunned by the news that his middle-of-the-night idea had taken hold, even more stunned by the realization that this could be the answer to his prayers, something that would keep Bree right here. "Seriously? You're sure about this?"

"I'm beginning to think so. I'm scared out of my wits, but Gram thought it was a brilliant idea, and Dad's already making sketches and cost projections and plotting a strategy to get a big plot of land from the town. He says he owes you, by the way."

"For what?"

"Giving me back my faith in myself and pointing me in the right direction."

"I did all that? I must be good," he said, laughing. "Who knew I could be so helpful and intuitive?"

Bree glanced toward the bag. "Is there coffee in there?"

He nodded. "Croissants, too. Chocolate today."

"Ooh, how decadent! Hand 'em over."

Jake passed her the bag, then took the cap off his own cup of coffee and took a long swallow. He needed all the caffeine he could get to stay alert this morning, not just for work, but to keep up with Bree. Changes in her life seemed to be moving at a breakneck pace.

"So, what happens next?" he asked her.

"I'm going to make a bunch of calls, try to figure out what start-up and operating costs would be. Dad's going to talk to the mayor about some land on Shore Road and maybe even being a partner in the construction. Then he'll calculate construction costs. Hopefully once we've done all that, neither of us will go into cardiac arrest over the bottom line."

"I've got a little money," Jake offered. "I'd invest in a sure thing."

"No," she said so fast it felt like a blow.

"Why not? I want to."

"I couldn't put your money at risk. I'd feel awful if this failed and you lost it."

"We'll talk again when you have all your figures together," he insisted stubbornly. "I want to be part of this, Bree. What matters to you matters to me. That's the way it is with people who love each other."

She stilled for an instant, apparently absorbing his words. Then she slowly nodded. "Okay, we'll at least talk about it."

"Do you have all the contacts you need to pull together this information?"

"I think so. I've met a few regional-theater directors from around the country. I'll call them. And of course, there's the manager in Chicago."

His heart sank. "You're going to call Marty?"

"No. He didn't manage the theater. He was the director for a few productions and the resident playwright. I'll talk to Rebecca. She ran the company."

Jake tried not to overreact. "Don't you think she'll spill the beans to Marty?"

Bree shrugged. "What if she does? He's out of my life, Jake. I've made that clear to him. I'm certainly not going to invite him to be a guest director here, and until we're some huge success, he won't even consider having one of his plays produced on our little backwater stage."

Jake wasn't convinced. For one thing, he knew how men's minds worked. For another, he couldn't imagine any man getting over Bree without taking at least one stab at trying again.

"One call out there might convince him you're opening the door again," he warned.

"But I'm not calling *him,*" she said, obviously frustrated by his refusal to believe her.

"Won't matter," he said stubbornly. "I may not know him all that well, but I know men. He's going to be on your doorstep if you make that call, even if it is to Rebecca."

"Well, I think you're wrong, but I'll tell her specifically not to say anything."

Jake knew he was probably overreacting, but he didn't trust the man. Still, he knew it made sense for Bree to go to someone she probably knew as well as she knew Rebecca to get information. He held up his hands. "Okay, handle this your way."

"I intend to."

"Have I just destroyed all the goodwill I gained by coming up with this idea?"

She grinned at him. "Not all of it," she said, kissing him.

"You taste like chocolate," he murmured, sighing not just with satisfaction, but relief that the argument hadn't gotten too far out of hand. "I'll be thinking about that the rest of the day."

"Me, too," she said softly. "Now, go to work. You probably have a million things to do today. I know I do."

Jake was reluctant to go. "Meet me for lunch," he suggested.

"I can't get away," she said with obvious disappointment. "Besides, what about Will and Mack?"

"They're not as pretty as you are, and they don't kiss half as well."

She gave him an odd look. "And you would know that how?"

"Gossip, of course," he said with a laugh. "Nothing's sacred in this town." He still couldn't bring himself to leave, not without making some kind of plan to see her again. He had this feeling they were very close to getting everything back. "How about dinner, then? Something quick and easy at my place?"

Her eyes sparkled at that. "I can do that."

"Is seven okay?"

"I'll be there."

"You know where I live now?"

"Of course I do. Connie told me. Jenny has pointed it out. I'm surprised someone didn't leave directions on my doorstep."

"I suppose they were leaving that to me," he said.

"Not necessary," she told him. "You know what I'm starting to think?"

"What?"

"That I was destined to find my way back to you."

Jake stood rooted to the spot. He wanted to believe she was right, needed to believe it, because even the slimmest possibility that she was wrong scared him to death, especially now when they seemed to be so close to having it all.

Rebecca Moore had been with the Lake Shore Playhouse since its inception twenty years before. She and her husband had been among the five founders. She had dozens of helpful suggestions for Bree when they finally connected early that afternoon.

"I'll fax over some budgets for the past couple of years, as soon as we get off the phone. They're public information because of the city and state funding we get, so it's not a problem for me to share them with you."

"Thank you so much. You've been a huge help," Bree told her. "I really appreciate it. I don't know yet if anything will come of this, but I'm excited."

"I thought you'd opened a flower shop. That's what Marty's told everyone. He said you didn't have what it took to deal with criticism."

"As annoying as it is to hear he'd say something like that, he was probably right," Bree admitted. "But no more. My skin's thicker now, and I've gotten a lot of things in perspective."

"Including the fact that Marty's not the good guy you thought he was, I hope."

Bree gave a rueful laugh. "Yeah, that, too. Don't tell him about this call, okay? The last thing I need is for him to call me and start planting a million little seeds of doubt in my head."

"He won't hear a thing about it from me," Rebecca assured her. "The only time we communicate is when we have to. I didn't like the way he treated you. If he weren't an asset around here most of the time, I would have pushed the other partners to send him packing."

"I can't believe I was so blind to it," Bree told her.

"Hero worship," Rebecca concluded. "Happens to the best of us at one time or another. Sooner or later, though, we discover those feet of clay. Whoops, I hear the Dark Force approaching, so I'd better cut this off. I'll fax the material as soon as he's gone."

Bree chuckled at her nickname for Marty. She wondered if others had always called him that, just not around her. The

Dark Force suited him. She could see that now that her blinders were off.

"Thanks again, Rebecca. Talk to you soon."

When she'd hung up, she saw two customers in the shop. She'd been so caught up with the phone call and her plans, she hadn't even seen them come in.

"May I help you?" she asked, addressing them both.

For the next couple of hours, as she took their orders and then put together arrangements for delivery, she waited for the fax machine to start spewing out pages, but it remained stubbornly silent. It was nearly six when the line finally rang and the machine kicked on. On the cover sheet, Rebecca had scrawled:

> Just a warning, but I think Marty overheard my end of the conversation and put the pieces together. I waited till now to fax this, because he's been lurking around. Call my cell if you need anything more. Rebecca.

Bree shuddered at the warning. Hopefully, even if Marty did know that Rebecca had been speaking to her, it wouldn't matter to him. Otherwise, if he called or turned up, it would prove that Jake had been right to worry. And, frankly, she didn't need the likely aggravation that would result from either man.

Jake went from Bree's shop to his first job. Either because he was exhausted or simply because the stars were aligned the wrong way, everything about it took longer than he'd anticipated. The home owner had changed her mind about the layout of the plants and shrubs. The ground was filled with rocks and stumps from old hedges. He spent most of the day just trying to get it in some kind of decent condition for planting. He'd have to come back tomorrow to finish the job, which would throw off his schedule for the rest of the week.

By the time he got to the nursery, he was filthy and in no mood for one of Connie's cross-examinations. He didn't have time for it, either, with Bree coming to his place in an hour expecting to find a meal on the table.

Despite the warning look he cast in his

sister's direction, she followed him into his office.

"Two, Jake? You got my daughter home on a school night at close to two o'clock in the morning."

"We had this conversation before I even talked to Jenny about the concert," he reminded her. "You knew it would be a late night."

"Midnight is a late night during the week. I said I'd make an exception because she was going to be with her responsible uncle."

"The concert didn't let out until nearly eleven," he said patiently. "It's close to a two-hour drive home."

"And yet you found the time to stop for breakfast," she said. "What were you thinking?"

"I was thinking she and Dillon were hungry. I was also thinking they're young enough to recover from one late night, especially since they were with two responsible adults."

"Want to know how I spent my evening? I spent it on the phone with Dillon's parents, who were freaking out because he wasn't home yet."

"I have no idea why. I had the same conversation with them before we left. They knew we were going to be late."

"Again, there's late and then there's oh-my-God-my-kid's-been-in-an-accident late."

He realized at last that there were tears shimmering in her eyes. She'd really been scared. He braved her indignation to hug her. "I should have called you," he said. "Why didn't you try my cell phone?"

"I did, about a million times."

He winced. "I turned it off before the concert. I must have forgotten to turn it back on. I'm so sorry."

She punched him in the arm. "You should be. And you need to call Dillon's parents and apologize. They're threatening never to let him see Jenny again."

Jake regarded her with a grin. "And that would be awful because . . . ?"

"Because your niece would hate you. And because she'd be sneaking out to see him."

"Okay, I'll make nice with the Johnsons. Anything else?"

Calmer now, she perched on the edge

of his desk. "Tell me about your evening with Bree. How'd that go?"

"It was interesting." He searched for a better word. "Unexpected."

She looked intrigued. "Really? How so?"

"I don't have time to get into it right now. She's coming over for dinner in less than an hour. I need a shower and I need groceries."

"I'll buy the groceries and drop them off if you'll take two seconds to tell me why the evening was so interesting."

"I think she's going to open a regional theater here," he said, then pressed a kiss to her forehead and two twenties into her hand. "Steaks, wine and something chocolate for dessert, okay? And you need to get it to my house and vanish before she arrives at seven."

"But I want more details," she called after him.

"Tomorrow," he promised.

Apparently his promise wasn't enough to suit Connie, because by the time he'd taken his shower and dressed, he found her in the kitchen with Bree having a heart-to-heart exchange about the date that wasn't a date. They shut up the instant Bree spotted him.

"Spilling all our secrets to my sister?" he asked.

Bree gave him an impudent look. "We don't have any secrets, at least not any really juicy ones."

"More's the pity," he commented and popped the top off a beer. He leaned against the counter and gave Connie a pointed look. "Don't you have someplace you need to be?"

She grinned. "Bree asked me to stay."

Jake scowled. "Did she now?" He met Bree's guilty gaze. "I wonder why. Second thoughts, perhaps?"

"Second thoughts about what?" Connie asked, then gasped. "Oh, right. Gee, thanks for asking, Bree, but I should get home. Jenny's probably waiting for dinner."

Jake gave her a satisfied look. "Enjoy your evening. I'll make that call to the Johnsons in a little while."

"Thanks," Connie said, giving Bree a peck on the cheek and him a conspiratorial wink.

As soon as the kitchen door closed, Bree met his gaze. "You didn't, by any chance, invite me over here with an ulterior motive, did you?"

He regarded her with an unblinking look. "Yes, I did."

She returned his look, then nodded slowly. "Then you'd better feed me first."

Well, well, well, Jake thought. His plans for the evening were definitely looking up.

From the moment Jake had all but tossed his sister out the door, Bree's senses had been in a state of high anticipation. She went through the motions of helping him to get their meal on the table. She scrubbed a couple of potatoes and put them in the microwave, tossed a salad and set the table, while Jake was outside cooking the steaks on the grill. When he came back in, they sat down opposite each other. He poured the wine, then met her gaze.

"Mind if I offer a toast to us?" he asked.

Unable to look away from the intensity of his gaze, she merely shook her head.

"To whatever the future holds," he said, then touched his glass to hers.

"To the future," she murmured, wondering why it suddenly looked so promising after weeks—no, *months*—of uncertainty.

They managed to make small talk as they ate for about fifteen minutes, but then Jake pushed his plate away. "Food's the last thing on my mind," he admitted to her.

Bree nodded. "I'm having a little trouble concentrating on my meal myself."

His eyes glittering, he warned, "If we stand up from this table, you know what's going to happen next, don't you, Bree? There's still time for you to tell me no."

"I'm not going to say no," she said, shoving back her chair and standing to prove the point.

That was apparently enough of an invitation for him. Jake was around the table in a heartbeat. His work-roughened hands, the hands of a real man, framed her face with such tenderness it made her want to cry.

"I love you," he said solemnly. "Always have, always will."

"Back at you," she said, trembling with need. "If you don't kiss me soon, I think my knees are going to buckle."

He grinned. "We can't have that, now, can we?" he said as he scooped her into his arms and cradled her to his chest. "I think we need to hold off on the kissing until we make it to the bedroom. Otherwise, I'll have to break all these dishes getting them off the kitchen table to make room for us right here."

"Hurry," she whispered, her hand on his cheek. Though he'd showered and washed his hair, there was still a faint stubble on his cheeks. She loved the way it felt to her touch. Jake was one of those men who looked even sexier at the end of the day than he did when he was clean shaven in the morning. She loved the masculine textures of him . . . his cheeks, his hands, the dark hair on his bronzed chest.

She was so absorbed by all the familiar yet excitingly new sensations he stirred in her that she barely noticed anything about his house or his room as he took her down the hallway, then lowered her to the king-size bed with its fresh-from-the-laundry sheets still smelling of sunshine.

"You hung these sheets outside, didn't you?" she asked, surprised and delighted.

"It's a pain, but they smell better," he

admitted. "It's the way my mother always did them." Laughter glinted in his eyes. "Are we really going to discuss my laundry techniques?"

"Just until you come up with a more fascinating alternative," she said.

"How about we don't talk at all?" he suggested, lowering his mouth to cover hers.

That suited Bree. She lost herself to the kiss, to the magical caresses that were setting her skin on fire, to the rising tide building to a crest inside her.

Jake made love the way he did everything else, with total concentration and confidence. She'd forgotten how treasured she'd always felt with him, as if there was something astonishing about every single inch of her, as if he'd never tire of learning all her secrets.

For all of their rush to get into the bedroom, he seemed more than willing to take his time now, lingering over a kiss, savoring the taste of her skin, taunting her until she was ready to beg him to stop, then plead for him to go on.

She remembered with absolute clarity why she'd been so sure they belonged together. It was this, the perfection of their intimacy, the way Jake gave her everything, the way he exulted in what she gave back. Together they soared.

Even as the last shuddering waves of a climax died down, Bree wanted more. She wanted moments like this again and again, enough to fill a lifetime.

But as she glanced across the room and spotted the first few chapters of her book tossed on the dresser, nearly hidden by a pile of laundry, she wondered if they could have it all without really dealing with the past. And that half-buried manuscript told her that Jake still hadn't dealt with it at all.

22

Jake saw the suddenly dulled expression on Bree's face and followed her gaze to see what had put it there. He spotted the manuscript almost immediately, even as she rolled away from him and tugged the sheet more tightly around her.

"You haven't read it, have you?" she asked, her tone condemning.

After all the heat they'd just shared, it was like having ice water tossed over him. "No," he admitted. He'd taken it out of the drawer in which he'd hidden it, but had been unable to make himself read so much as a word.

"Why? You were the one who said you wanted to in the first place and I've told you repeatedly how important it is to me."

"I told you I wanted to before I realized you were dissecting our past," he said irritably. "I lived it. I don't need to read about it."

"Then you should have had the guts to tell me that to my face."

Jake sighed. "Yes, I should have, but you and I haven't exactly been in step since you got back."

"What the hell were we a few minutes ago?"

"Where we probably should have been weeks ago," he conceded. "Maybe then everything would have made more sense."

"Sex doesn't resolve anything, you know that," she said with exasperation.

"No, but it does clarify what's worth fighting for, don't you think?"

"I suppose." She looked directly into his eyes. "Jake, I get why the idea of reading this manuscript bothers you, but I'm telling you it's important. You didn't live what happened from my point of view. Don't you care, at least a little, about what I was feeling?"

"Sure, I care. I cared back then, but you weren't willing to share your feelings with me. You shut them off, shut me out and ran away."

She flinched at the accusation, but didn't deny it. "That's true," she conceded. "Did you ever stop to think that maybe it was too painful for me to face any of it? That the only way I could handle what happened was by locking it all up inside and running?"

Jake hesitated. The emotion in her eyes was raw enough he couldn't help believing her and yet . . . and yet she *had* taken off. That was something he wasn't sure he'd ever get over. They should have dealt with their loss together. What did it say about their relationship that she couldn't face it with him? She'd gone off alone, a pattern she'd apparently established in childhood. It had made him feel as if he didn't matter to her at all, as if she didn't trust him not to judge her for feeling relief along with all the other emotions.

She reached over and touched the tensed muscle in his arm. "Please, Jake. Read it. Do it now. You need to understand the way it was for me. I don't see how we can get past it if you don't understand that."

"Not five minutes ago, we were getting past it pretty damn well."

"Never the problem," she reminded him succinctly.

He regarded her with frustration. "You're not going to let this go, are you?"

She held his gaze. "No. Not when I believe our future depends on it."

"Okay, fine," he said reluctantly. He crossed the room and grabbed the hundred or so pages she'd given him. "Is this it or have you written more by now?"

"There's more, but this is the most relevant part. Keep in mind, even though it's fiction, the emotions are real. They're mine."

He turned on the bedside lamp and pulled the sheet up to his waist, then started to read. The story began simply enough, drawing him in, making the characters—strangers, not him and Bree at all—come alive. She'd always had a knack for that, one he'd admired. The differences between them and these people she was writing about allowed him to go on, in fact drew him in and made him care.

Next to him, Bree barely moved, but he could hear the occasional catch in her breath, as if she was anticipating where he was in the story and waiting for his reaction. He tried to keep his expression neutral, his concentration focused on the words on the page.

An hour or more later as he neared the end, he wanted to stop. Even through these fictional characters, she was making him feel everything all over again and he didn't want to go there. Yet, she was right. He had to. *They* had to. He read on:

The worst part of that awful day was looking into Jeremy's eyes and seeing the depth of his grief. How could I bear that when for me there was this sense of freedom, knowing that I could live my life the way I'd envisioned it? For me, the baby had never seemed real, even though it had been growing inside me. I think I'd deliberately turned off my emotions, because if I'd faced them, if I'd allowed myself to feel anything for our child, I would be forever trapped in a life—not that I didn't want, because I did—but a life I wasn't ready for.

And yet, the raw pain written on Jeremy's face made me ache for him, for what he'd lost. I felt as if I'd failed him, failed our child.

And so I left, ran to the life I thought I wanted, thought I needed, only to discover that the answers for me weren't there. They were back home with the man who loved me unconditionally, with the child who'd never had a chance to live at all. I lost more than I realized that awful day. I had to grow up to discover it. I had to let myself feel a mother's anguish at losing a child.

And when I did, at last, I wept for what could have—what should *have—been.*

Jake read the last page of that early chapter, his eyes stinging. She'd forced him to see that it had simply taken her longer to deal with what happened, longer to feel what he'd felt. That didn't make her wrong and him right. It was simply the way it was. How could he judge her for that? How could he hate her for handling things the only way she knew how? Did he really want her to have suffered the way he had? In fact, maybe her way had been harder in the long run because she'd spent years getting to this point, years battling guilt along with everything else.

When he could control his voice, he faced her. “I shouldn’t have judged you.”

She shook her head. “You had every right to. We should have handled it together. You wanted to. You tried, but I shut you out, not just after the miscarriage, but even before, from the moment I knew I was pregnant. I was so angry at you, even though I knew we were both responsible. I blamed you for ruining everything.”

“I blamed myself,” he admitted for the first time. “I knew how badly you wanted to leave here, how much that internship in Chicago meant. Yet when we found out about the baby, all I could think about was that you’d have to stay here with me, that the life I wanted with you was going to happen. I was selfish. I recognize that, but I believed it would be a good life, Bree. You have to know that.”

“I do and maybe it would have been perfect, Jake, but don’t you see? Now is so much better. You’ve accomplished so much. You have a business that’s thriving, a business you love. Who knows if that would have happened if you’d had the responsibility for a wife and child. And I'm with you now because I want to be. I'm in this relationship a hundred percent, no regrets, no wondering what might have been."

Because he wanted desperately to believe her, he reached for her, pulled her back into his arms. Then, with her cradled next to his heart, they finally slept.

Megan packed her bag Friday morning and took a taxi to the airport. She'd decided it was time she surprised Mick for once. The show at the gallery where she worked had opened to rave reviews. The pressure was off and she could finally spare the time to make the trip to Chesapeake Shores.

She wondered how Mick would feel about her turning the tables on him. She had a certain amount of trepidation, especially knowing how his surprise had nearly gone terribly awry, but she concluded it was worth the risk. She had a feeling she and Mick would do better in the long run if their lives took some unexpected twists and turns. Mick thrived on unpredictability. And though she was happier in a routine, she could see how the unexpected kept things interesting.

When she arrived at the house, only Nell was there to greet her. Her eyes warmed with welcome, the way they always had before Megan had left her son.

"Come in, come in," Nell urged. "Did Mick know you were coming? He didn't mention it."

Megan shook her head. "I decided to surprise him. Is he around?"

"He's in town, though goodness knows where. He said something about stopping in to see the mayor, then going to Bree's shop. He'll probably have lunch somewhere along the way."

"Should I go and look for him?" Megan wondered aloud. "Or wait for him here?"

"Why don't you at least stay here long enough to have tea with me," Nell suggested, already reaching for the chintz china teacups she favored. "We've had too few good chats since you've been popping in and out for visits."

Megan listened carefully to her former mother-in-law's words. There was nothing openly hostile in her remarks, but she sensed a reserve, maybe even a hint of disapproval.

"I'd love to have tea with you," Megan said honestly. Even if Nell had an agenda, it was important that they get back the easy relationship they'd once had.

"Bree brought home some of Sally's raspberry croissants last night. Would you like one of those?"

"I shouldn't," Megan protested, then grinned. "But I will."

Nell laughed. "They are hard to resist, aren't they? It's a good thing Bree doesn't bring them home every day."

"How's she doing?"

"Great, as far as I know," Nell told her. "She didn't come home last night, which tells me things are on again between her and Jake."

Megan couldn't decide how she ought to feel about that. She hadn't been here when the relationship had ended, had little sense of which one of them had been at fault. "Is that a good thing?" she asked Nell.

"This time, I believe it is. They were too young before. Jake fell for her in junior high and knew practically from the beginning that he wanted a future with her. Bree had her own dreams. She's lived the life she needed to live. Now I think she's ready for what Jake can offer her and he's ready to support her in what she needs to be happy."

"What do you think he can offer her?"

"The love of a good man, of course. Jake's as solid as they come." She gave Megan a wink. "Easy on the eyes, too."

Megan laughed. "He is that." After a moment, her expression sobered. "I envy you, Nell. Have I ever told you that?"

"Heavens, no. Why?"

"Because you were here. There was so much I missed. My own fault, I know, but there are so many gaps in time, things in my children's lives that I know nothing about. I feel as if I'm starting from scratch with each of them. They've all grown up while I wasn't looking. The people they've become . . ." She shrugged. "Most of that's your doing."

"Nonsense. You influenced them, too. Except for Jess, you had a lot of time with them in their formative years. Ironically, though, Jess is the most like you. She's restless. I'm not just talking about the attention-deficit thing. She's not comfortable yet in her own skin. Oh, she loves that inn of hers, but beyond that, I'm not sure she has any idea what she wants."

"I've always known what I wanted," Megan countered. "I wanted Mick. I wanted my family."

"And yet you left for more."

"No, I left because I'd lost Mick, at least for all intents and purposes. I didn't see how we could ever get back what we'd once had."

"Spending time with another man, however innocently that happened, wasn't the best way to win him back," Nell said, her tone chiding.

Megan winced at the direct hit. "No question about that. It was the second-worst mistake of my life."

"What was the worst?" Nell asked, her expression curious.

"Leaving Mick and my kids. I was so sure Mick would come after me." She saw Nell's skeptical expression. "I know. I should have realized his pride would never allow that. At any rate, when that didn't happen, I believed I'd at least have the kids with me in New York. I should have fought harder for that, but Kevin was so angry and disillusioned, Connor just wanted to be here with his friends, and the girls—well, they adored Mick. I didn't see how I could tear them away from him and their life here. I tried coming here frequently for weekend visits, but you saw firsthand how that went. They either ignored me or expressed their anger in other ways. Everything I did—even what I didn't do—was a mistake. Believe me, I've lived to regret all of it."

Nell studied her. "I think you have. They're giving you a second chance, though, even Mick. Don't blow it this time."

Megan smiled at her fierce warning. "I don't intend to," she said then added, "But Mick needs to do his part, as well."

"He finally sees that," Nell assured her, then patted her hand. "I'm glad we've had a chance to talk, Megan. I've missed sitting right here at this table with you, just like this."

"I've missed it, too," she replied without hesitation. "You were never just my mother-in-law, you know. You were my friend."

Nell looked pleased by the comment.

"Well, then, as your friend, I suggest you go track down my son. I'd start at Bree's shop. Those two have big plans. Make sure they tell you all about them."

Megan was intrigued. "You don't even want to give me a hint?"

Nell shook her head. "Not my news to tell. Run along, Megan. I'll put your bag upstairs."

"I can do that."

Nell's jaw set stubbornly. "And so can I."

"Okay, then, I'm off. See you later."

She was almost out the door, when Nell called after her.

"This surprise visit of yours, Megan . . ."

"Yes?"

"It's a good thing. Mick will think so, too."

"I hope you're right about that," she said. She supposed she'd know soon enough.

Mick had had a frank, exploratory conversation with Bobby Clark to try to garner the mayor's support for the community-theater project. At first Bobby had been unreceptive to the idea, so Mick had spoken to a few of Bobby's political backers, who'd shared their more open-minded opinions with him. This morning Bobby had gotten on board, indicating a willingness to take the idea before the town council at their next meeting for a preliminary discussion.

"In other words, you bullied him into it," Bree concluded after her father had described the meeting.

"I got results," Mick countered.

His daughter gave him an exasperated look. "Wouldn't it have been better to persuade Bobby to your way of thinking?"

"The end result is what counts," Mick argued. "He'll back us on this."

"But without much enthusiasm, I suspect."

"You handle business your way. I'll handle it mine," he said, annoyed that she wasn't more pleased by what he'd accomplished. Bobby Clark could have been a major obstacle if Mick hadn't called in the big guns, the men who provided most of Bobby's backing for election campaigns.

He was about to tell her she was being naive when the door to the shop opened and Megan walked in. "Meggie!" he said, the discussion with Bree forgotten. "I had no idea you were coming today."

She beamed at his reaction. "That was the whole idea. You're pleased to see me?"

"Of course I am," he said, then planted a hard kiss on her lips.

They were interrupted by a less-than-subtle cough from Bree. "Excuse me, public place, daughter present," she chided, though her eyes were filled with laughter. "I'd hate to have to suggest that you two go and get a room."

Mick kept Megan's small hand in his and pulled her to his side. "You have five minutes to exchange small talk with our daughter," he told her. "Then you and I are getting out of here."

"And going where?" Megan inquired, her look challenging him.

"Personally, I like Bree's idea about the room, but I'm thinking you'll be happier going to lunch and then for a walk on the beach. It's a lovely fall day we're having. There won't be many more to come with Thanksgiving right around the corner." He regarded her with a frown. "Do you have a sweater with you? It's likely to be breezy on the beach."

Megan's eyes glittered with anticipation. "I came from New York where it was in the forties this morning, so of course I have a sweater. And lunch and a walk sound lovely, if you have the time. Nell says you've been out throwing your influence around to get something or other done. She wouldn't say what."

"I'll let Bree fill you in," Mick said. "Though if she starts saying I've gone about it all wrong, I'll have to jump in with my version."

"Well, you have," Bree countered.

"Bulldozer tactics," Megan guessed.

"Hey, don't the two of you start ganging up on me," Mick protested, though he was enjoying the whole exchange. He was pretty sure nothing could ruin the mood that Megan's unexpected arrival had put him in.

Bree filled her mother in on their plans. When she concluded, Megan applauded. "That's fantastic! I'm so excited for you. Sweetheart, this is absolutely perfect. I just know you'll have the best theater company in the country in no time."

"Let's not get overly ambitious," Bree cautioned. "I'll be satisfied if we can just stay artistically exciting and operate in the black."

"You'll do it," Megan said. "Your instincts are a thousand times better than that man's."

"Marty wasn't responsible for all of the artistic decisions in Chicago," Bree said.

"No, but he was responsible for sapping all the creativity out of the best playwright they'd ever had," Megan said with feeling.

Bree rolled her eyes. "Now, *there's* a total lack of objectivity if ever I've heard it."

"And on that note, I suppose we should head out," Mick said, figuring they'd beaten that particular horse enough for one day. If Megan persisted or he chimed in, Bree was likely to start defending Marty and they'd wind up in an argument.

Bree came around the counter to hug her mother. "I'm so glad you're here. Will I see you at the house later?"

"Unless your father tosses me out," Megan said.

"Not a chance of that happening," Mick said, reaching for her hand again. He liked the way it felt in his, liked knowing that he had at least some small claim on her again.

One of these days they'd get back everything they'd once had. For the first time in his life, he didn't feel the need to hurry things along. He'd discovered that sometimes anticipation was its own reward.

It was three weeks before Thanksgiving by the time Bree and Jake finally fell into an easy pattern that felt natural to both of them. She was actually starting to believe they'd really make it this time. He was beginning to trust her again, and she was almost certain he'd forgiven her.

And she was a hundred percent sure she was in love with him, that this time when he offered her a future, she'd accept with no misgivings at all.

Which made it a real kick in the pants when she looked up from her meal with Jake at the inn and spotted Marty striding across the dining room. When he hadn't shown up right after her conversation with Rebecca, she'd been so sure that something like this would never happen. How typical of him to lull her into a false sense of complacency.

As he crossed the room, heads turned. He was a striking man with his hair swept back from a widow's peak, his chiseled cheekbones and high brow. He was dressed in jeans—not faded and well worn like Jake's, but designer denim with a well-pressed crease. His cream-colored shirt was a fancy silk blend and she suspected the sweater he wore over it was cashmere.

As always, he somehow managed to look thoroughly in command of the situation as he walked up to their table, dragged a chair over and sat down without waiting for an invitation. Across from her, Jake tensed. Bree couldn't think of a thing to do except introduce them for the second time in her life and pray that the awkward moment didn't last.

"Jake Collins, Marty Demming. You met before, of course, when Marty and I worked together in Chicago."

A lift of Marty's brow spoke volumes. Jake saw it and his fist clenched.

"It was a bit more than that, if we're going to be totally honest," Marty said, deliberately ignoring the tension. Though his tone was jovial, there was no mistaking his attempt to claim possession.

"Why are you here?" Bree demanded,

losing patience and unwilling to be polite a second longer. If he was here to ruin her life for a second time, she didn't intend to give him the chance.

"The theater wants to produce your last play, the one you finished writing just before you left," he said, catching her by surprise. "We'll want you back there for the rehearsals. Next week, if at all possible."

She regarded him with astonishment. This was an angle she hadn't expected. Though the proposal might have been tempting under other circumstances, right now she wasn't remotely interested in going back.

"It's not possible," she said firmly.

"The following week, then," Marty suggested, deliberately misunderstanding. "Though that's cutting it close if we expect to have this production ready by the middle of January. You see the sacrifices we're willing to make to have you back?"

"I'm not coming back," Bree said.

"Of course you are," Marty countered, his confidence undaunted. "Chicago is where you belong. I heard all about your plans to open a little theater here, but why would you waste your talent in a place like this when you could be successful in a major city? You're destined for big things, Bree. You had a couple of setbacks, sure, but you're talented. You belong where you can make the most of that talent."

This was the Marty Bree remembered from her first days in Chicago—smooth, charming, saying all the right things to convince her she was the best writer he'd ever mentored. Now she found she didn't trust a word coming out of his mouth. So, she had learned from her mistakes, she thought in wonder.

Even as she was congratulating herself for being less gullible, she also sensed Jake's increasing tension. She had a feeling this was going to get ugly, and she had no idea how to diffuse the situation.

As she considered what she could do, Jake looked from her to Marty and back again, then stood. "Obviously you two have a lot to discuss. I'll leave you to it," he said tightly.

Bree jumped up. "Jake!" she protested as he strode away, but he never even looked back.

She would have gone after him, but Marty grabbed her wrist. "Let him go. This is important. Not everyone gets another chance after the kind of disaster that last production turned out to be."

She whirled around and frowned at his choice of words. How had she missed seeing what a bully he was, how cruel he could be even when pretending to be her biggest booster?

"You're right," she said. "Not everyone gets the second chances that matter. That's why I'm leaving here right now. Don't follow me."

And then she ran, praying that she could find Jake before it was too late. She knew exactly how his mind worked, how fragile their newfound bond still was. If she didn't see him at once, reassure him that this time was going to be different, that Chicago held no allure, he would slam the door on what they had. He would do it not to punish her, but to protect his heart from one more bitter disappointment.

23

Jake wondered what Bree had told Marty after he'd left the two of them together. Though her refusal of Marty's offer had been clear enough, Jake had seen the quick flash of excitement in her eyes at the mention of having another of her plays produced in Chicago. This time he had no intention of standing in her way, if that's what she wanted. And though she might not be ready to admit it—even to herself—she did want it. That glint in her eyes was proof of that.

Because he didn't want to discuss it with her, wasn't ready to hear her trying to convince him that going back to Chicago would only be temporary, he turned off his cell phone. Knowing that might bring her straight to his doorstep, he opted not to go home. Instead, he went to Brady's, where he found Will and Mack already seated at the bar, their expressions morose.

"Well, aren't we a sorry lot," Jake said as he joined them and ordered a beer. "What put the two of you in such sour moods?"

"Women," Will said succinctly. "You?"

"A woman," Jake replied, then added, "and another man."

That got their attention.

"Bree's seeing someone else?" Mack asked incredulously. "I don't believe it."

"She's with him at this very moment," Jake confirmed, draining his first beer and ordering a second.

Will, who'd clearly passed his limit of two beers, blinked owlishly. "Hold on. Wasn't she out with you tonight?"

"Yep. And then her old boyfriend from Chicago decided to pay her a surprise visit. He landed at our table, settled right in as if he'd been invited and started wooing her."

"Wooing her?" Will asked with shock. "In front of you?"

"Yep."

Mack looked bewildered. "Okay, that's really lame, but you just left them together? What were you thinking?"

"It seemed the wise thing to do," Jake said, though Mack's reaction had planted a tiny seed of doubt.

"Wise in what universe?" Will asked. "You left the field open to the competition, pal. No way is that smart."

"Agreed," Mack said.

"He wants her back in Chicago."

"He actually said that?"

"He did. He used a powerful lure, too. He wants to produce another of her plays. For Bree that's like offering candy to a toddler. She won't be able to resist."

"That's big," Will conceded mournfully. "That'd be hard for any woman to resist, especially one who's as dedicated to her writing as I know Bree used to be."

"Exactly what I thought," Jake replied. "And, for the record and her flower shop aside, Bree is still dedicated to her writing. I wasn't going to sit there and watch her fall right back into that jerk's orbit. She might not want to go back to him, but she won't turn down a chance to have her play produced at a prestigious regional theater. How can she? Even I—a country yokel in Marty's opinion—can see that might be career suicide."

"Hold on a minute," Mack asked. "Did she say yes?"

Jake shook his head. "No, she turned him down, but it was obvious to me she didn't want to. She was just saying what she thought I'd want to hear."

Will shook his head sorrowfully. "Pal, you don't have such a great track record at reading Bree's mind. Maybe you should give her the benefit of the doubt."

"I can't," Jake said. "Too risky."

"Risky how?" Mack asked.

Jake didn't want to answer, didn't want to lay his vulnerability out there, not even in front of his two best friends.

"He's afraid of getting his heart broken again," Will said, nodding sagely. "Don't blame him." He tapped his bottle of beer to Jake's. "This is quite a pickle you're in."

Quite a pickle? Jake mouthed to Mack. Aloud he asked, "Exactly how long have the two of you been here drowning your sorrows?"

"Not sure," Will said. "What time is it?"

"Just after ten," Jake told him.

"Since six," Will murmured. "So that's . . . um . . . what is it?"

"Four hours and too many beers," Jake concluded. "Let's call someone to take us all home."

"Nobody to call," Will said, looking even sadder.

"Susie?" Jake suggested to Mack.

"Hell, no," Mack said fiercely. "Why do you think I'm here? The woman's impossible."

"I see," Jake said, though he didn't. Not really. Supposedly they were just friends, but obviously something had finally shifted in dramatic fashion, at least for Mack. Jake had tried to warn him he was in deeper than he'd admitted, but Mack had glossed over his involvement with yet another unpredictable O'Brien woman.

"I'll call Connie," he told them. "She'll come."

He made the call on Will's cell phone because he didn't want to risk turning on his own and seeing a bunch of messages from Bree . . . or no messages at all. Either way would be depressing.

When his sister picked up and heard his voice, she said, "Where are you? Bree's been calling here every five minutes looking for you."

"I'm not there," Jake said, stating the obvious.

"Well, duh! I know that and judging from the sound of your voice, you're somewhere getting drunk. Mind telling me why? I thought you and Bree had a date tonight."

"Actually I do mind discussing my personal life," he said, proud of himself for taking a stance against her probing. "Just save the questions and come and get me. None of us are in any condition to drive."

"None of who?"

"I'm with Mack and Will. They had a head start."

"And you thought of me," she muttered. "Gee, I'm blessed."

"Are you coming to get us or not?"

She heaved an exaggerated sigh. "Where are you?"

"Brady's."

"Give me ten minutes," she said. "And

be out front when I get there, or I'm driving off without you."

"You're the best, sis."

"Damn straight. I intend to remind you of that tomorrow when we discuss my raise."

"Raise?" he mumbled. "What raise?" But he was talking to dead air, because his sister had already hung up.

"We need to go outside," he told Mack and Will. "I think she's a little ticked that I called her."

"Typical," Mack said. "She's a woman, isn't she? None of them make a damn bit of sense."

Jake certainly couldn't argue with that.

Bree never had tracked down Jake. She'd finally found his truck along the waterfront near Brady's, but when she'd gone inside there'd been no sign of him. Lou Herrera, the longtime bartender at Brady's, told her he'd left with Mack and Will. He told her he'd gotten the impression they were drowning their sorrows. She'd given up then and gone home. If Jake had finished even a couple of beers, he wasn't likely to be reasonable.

This morning, she'd been trying Jake's cell phone since seven. At eight, she'd started calling the nursery. At nine, Connie had answered.

"Where's your brother?" she asked without preamble. "Has he turned up yet?"

"He's on a job," Connie said.

"Without his cell phone?"

Connie hesitated, then said, "He must not have turned it on."

"Okay, what do you know?" Bree demanded. "I can hear something in your voice. You've seen him since the last time I spoke to you last night."

"He called," Connie admitted. "He, Mack and Will needed a ride home from Brady's."

"Yeah, I gathered something like that had happened when I found his truck at Brady's and no sign of him inside. Thank goodness, they still had sense enough not to drive."

"That's about all the sense they displayed, if you ask me," Connie said with disgust. "This is not like my brother."

"I know," Bree agreed. "He likes being in control. He has a beer from time to time, maybe a glass of wine, but he never gets plastered."

"Well, he did last night," Connie said. "Though to be fair, Will and Mack were in worse shape. I have no idea what problems they were drowning, but I've figured out that something happened last night between you and my brother."

Bree saw no point in denying it. The evening had turned into a disaster, and there'd been enough locals in the inn's dining room that word was bound to spread. "Marty showed up in the middle of our dinner," she confessed.

"Oh, boy," Connie said. "No wonder Jake went into a tailspin."

"I honestly don't get it," Bree told her. "Sure, Marty and I have a history, a pretty complicated one in fact, but Jake was sitting right there when I told Marty I wasn't interested in coming back to Chicago. Jake heard me turn down his offer to produce another one of my plays. Did he think I was lying?"

"Since I wasn't there, I can't say for sure, but maybe he thought you didn't want to say how much you wanted it right in front of him," Connie suggested.

"But I *don't* want it," Bree protested. "Oh, I was tempted for about half a second, but that was it. Then I remembered how manipulative Marty is, what a bully he can be once he's gotten his way. I don't want that in my life ever again."

"So, tell that to Jake and keep on saying it till he believes you."

"I would if I could find him," Bree said in frustration. "You know I've been looking for him. I started calling you last night about two seconds after he took off from the inn."

Connie fell silent.

"Come on," Bree pleaded. "Help me out here. Tell me where he is."

"He's helping Jess at the inn," she said at last.

"What? How?"

"This time of year he's built up a good business doing exterior holiday decorations for people. Jess hired him to get the inn ready for Christmas. I'm surprised she didn't mention it."

"Actually, I haven't seen her for a week or so," Bree said. "I had a wedding last weekend, and now I'm up to my eyeballs in making Thanksgiving centerpieces."

"You going over there?" Connie asked. "That's the only way you're going to get him to talk, by getting in his face. Otherwise, he'll keep right on avoiding you. Given what you just told me, he's probably convinced he's doing the right thing."

"And he accused *me* of being a coward," Bree muttered, exasperated.

"What?"

"Never mind. Is he going to be there all day?"

"Probably."

"Then as soon as Jenny gets here after school, I'll head over there."

"I could come now," Connie said. "It's slow around here. I won't be missed. I want this thing between you and my brother to work this time. I'll do whatever I can to see that he doesn't get in his own way."

"Are you sure?"

"Absolutely."

"Thanks, Connie. I really appreciate it."

"Give me a few minutes to let someone know I'm going, and I'll be right over."

Bree managed to put together a small get-well bouquet for a walk-in customer and another Thanksgiving arrangement by the time Connie made it to the shop.

"Go," Connie said. "I'll hold down the fort. If anyone wants an arrangement other than those you have on hand, I'll tell them the florist will get to it later."

Bree nodded. "Works for me."

After all, it was entirely possible that Jake would refuse to spend one single second discussing anything with her, in which case the whole trip would last a half hour at most, including travel time.

When Bree arrived at the inn, she instantly spotted Jake at the top of a very tall ladder stringing lights along the eaves. As she crossed the lawn, Jess came to greet her.

"You look lousy," her sister said.

"Gee, thanks," Bree replied testily. "That makes me feel so much better."

"Something going on with you and Jake? I mentioned you earlier and he nearly bit my head off."

"We've had a slight misunderstanding. That's why I'm here, to straighten it out before things get blown out of all proportion."

"It wouldn't have anything to do with the fact that Martin Demming is staying here, would it?" Jess inquired, her expression knowing.

"Marty's staying here?"

"Oh, yeah," Jess confirmed. "I didn't take the reservation myself or I'd have turned it down. I've considered slipping a snake into his bed, but the code enforcers might frown on that."

"I'm sure they would," Bree agreed, though she certainly endorsed Jess's sentiment. "Have Jake and Marty crossed paths this morning?"

Jess looked over her shoulder. "You mean before now?"

"Oh, please do not tell me he is heading this way," Bree said.

"Sorry, sis. Maybe you ought to get him away from here. Being up on that ladder is precarious enough without stirring up Jake's temper. I don't want to pay for hospitalization for either one of them if he decides to tackle your ex-boyfriend from that height."

Bree cast a reluctant look in Marty's direction, saw the determination on his face, then glanced up at Jake, who'd gone completely still. Could this get any more complicated?

Gritting her teeth, she turned to Jess. "I'll deal with Marty, but whatever you do, do not let Jake leave here until we've talked. I mean it. I don't care if you have to tie him up with strands of Christmas lights."

Jess grinned. "An intriguing concept. A little kinky, but I like it."

"This is so not amusing," Bree told her as she turned to head off Marty.

"Isn't that your friend up there on the ladder?" Marty asked, looking down his supercilious nose. "Please tell me you are not serious about someone who does . . ." He hesitated. "Well, whatever it is that he does."

"He owns a very successful nursery and landscaping company," she said tightly. "Why are you still here?"

"To persuade you to rethink your decision, of course." He tucked her arm through his and steered her toward the front door of the inn. "We'll have tea and some of your sister's fabulous scones and discuss my offer again. I'm sure I can convince you that you belong back in Chicago."

Bree stopped in her tracks and stood her ground. She was not going to succumb to Marty's charm for the second time in her life. Nor was she going inside to chat with this man over tea and scones.

"Marty, you couldn't talk me into changing my mind if you offered the sun, the moon and the stars," she said flatly. "I will never work for you again."

"*With* me," he corrected. "You'd be working with me, not for me."

"As if," she retorted. "Your ego doesn't allow you to work with anyone. You have to be the boss."

"I am more experienced," he said. "You used to appreciate that. In fact, you used to hang on my every word."

"And then I wised up," Bree told him. "Not every word coming out of your mouth is golden, after all, Marty. I wish I'd realized that sooner. Maybe then I wouldn't have let you get away with stripping the heart right out of that last play of mine—you know, the one that was savaged by the critics."

He actually looked stunned by the accusation. "You're blaming that fiasco on me?"

She took a second, pretended to give the question some thought, then nodded, "Yes, I believe I am."

"Don't you think you're being incredibly ungrateful?"

"I will be eternally grateful for the opportunity you gave me and for all your help with my writing. You were a real mentor to me, and I learned a lot."

"Then why have you turned on me?" he asked, looking genuinely bewildered.

She thought about it. "Because you turned on me," she said at last.

"Turned on you? I just gave you another golden opportunity to come back to work with me."

"Yes, and I even appreciate that, but we both know it wouldn't be long before you started picking at everything I do, undermining me. I don't even think it's deliberate. It's just how you are. Constructive criticism is one thing, but you chip away until I question every single word I've put on the page. And I'm way too susceptible to your comments. I won't let you strip me of my confidence again. I'm actually a pretty decent playwright. Even the critics said so."

"At first," he reminded her, his tone caustic.

Even when he was trying to lure her back, he couldn't stop himself from belittling her. If she hadn't been wise to him now, it would have hurt. As it was, it proved she was making the right decision.

"Marty, let's stop this. My mind's made up."

He looked shocked by her determination.

"Fine. If you want to stay here in the middle of nowhere, be my guest. You'll never work with me or anyone I know again. I'll see to that."

Bree knew his threat should have shaken her. A few weeks ago, it might have, but she had her own plans now. Maybe opening a theater here wasn't as lofty as working at an established one in Chicago, but it came with plenty of benefits.

She glanced across the lawn and spotted one of them—the man currently standing on the roof of Jess's inn. Jake's grim expression told her he was still angry about last night, and not one bit happier about the scene he'd just witnessed, albeit from too far away more than likely to have heard much of what they'd said. Apparently it didn't matter that she'd told Marty to take a hike for the second time in two days. Even if Jake had overheard her words from that distance, it was doubtful he'd believe them. He certainly hadn't last night.

And to her deep regret, she had no idea what kind of dramatic gesture it was going to take to convince him.

For days after the scene between Bree and Marty at the inn, Jake couldn't keep Bree's voice out of his head. Though she'd tried to keep her voice low, apparently she'd forgotten how well voices carried near the bay. He'd heard everything she'd said to that weasel.

It should have reassured him, but it hadn't. Oh, she'd said all the right words to send any man with an ounce of pride fleeing from Chesapeake Shores, but eventually she was going to have second thoughts.

Marty must have sensed that, too. He still hadn't left town. It looked as if he was planning to stay straight through Thanksgiving, maybe even Christmas if that's what it took to persuade Bree to leave with him. Obviously he'd considered her latest refusal to be nothing more than a minor setback.

Jake could see the inevitable outcome of all this and knew he couldn't take losing Bree again. He'd worked hard to avoid her, to keep his heart intact. Ironically, it ached like hell, anyway.

No one else seemed to get why he wasn't seizing the chance to take her back. He hadn't been able to escape Connie's condemning looks. Nor had he missed her frequently muttered remarks about him behaving like an idiot. Even Will and Mack, not the most sensitive guys on earth, seemed to think he was wasting time, when he should have been fighting for the woman he so obviously wanted.

"You can't leave the field open to that simpering jerk," Mack told him in disgust.

"But if that's who Bree wants . . ."

"You've got to be kidding me," Will said. "Bree does not want him. She's all but spelled that out in skywriting over the bay, but he's too dumb to get the message. Apparently so are you. I'm disappointed in you, pal."

Jake couldn't let himself believe any of them. Marty had come here after Bree and was showing so signs of leaving, even after all her insulting remarks. And as far as he could see, she'd done nothing to make him go. He was still ensconced at the inn and spending every spare minute hanging out at Flowers on Main trying to talk Bree into returning to Chicago. One of these days, Jake was pretty sure she was going to say yes, if only to get the man to shut up and stop scaring off the customers.

Connie had reported that half the town was talking about how charming, handsome and sophisticated he was, but the rest—those most loyal to Jake, more than likely—described his presence as annoying. Some had stopped going in there except when they knew Marty would be off the premises. Apparently Jenny had confided in her mother about the town taking sides. His niece had taken sides, too. She wasn't speaking to him, at least not since she'd told him he was nuts for abandoning Bree when she needed him most.

With business at the nursery in its usual late-fall lull, even with the holiday-decorating sideline beginning to catch on, Jake had way too much time on his hands to think about how everything had gone so terribly wrong practically overnight. In fact, more than once he'd simply stayed home in a funk.

It took him a few days to figure out that his sister was suddenly manufacturing all sorts of last-minute emergencies that required him to personally deliver flowers to Bree's shop at the end of the day. It wasn't until Bree herself called him on it during one of Marty's rare absences that he put the pieces of the scheme together.

"I didn't order these," Bree told him, staring at three boxes of long-stemmed yellow roses, which happened to be her favorite flower.

"But Connie said . . ." he began, then flushed. "What about all those other last-minute orders this week? Did you call them in?"

She shook her head. "They were things I'd ordered, but they were accidentally left off the original delivery. At least that's what Connie told me."

"Accidentally, my ass," Jake muttered. "I'm going to kill my sister."

Bree's eyes brightened. "She's been meddling," she concluded.

"Apparently so. I'm sorry."

"I'm not. At least she's kept you from avoiding me completely." She leveled a heated look at him. "It hasn't been so bad, has it? Seeing me, I mean."

It hadn't been bad at all, at least when

Marty hadn't been sitting there scowling for the duration of the visit. Jake had wanted to be here, with Bree. He'd just been too stubborn and hardheaded to admit it. His sister had known that and given him a push in the direction he'd wanted to go, just the way she had when they were kids and he'd been too scared to make the swing go as high as it could. She'd seized the initiative so he could soar, overcoming his fears. He'd been grateful for that when he was four or five. Now he was a little put out by it.

Even during his sourest mood swings, he could see that he ought to be able to go after what he wanted all by himself. Maybe it was time to have a little faith in Bree's words. She'd been telling him for a while now that he was the one she wanted. Surely he could take a small leap of faith and give her a chance to prove that she was telling the truth.

"Do you have plans for dinner?" he asked her impulsively. "Can you shake your shadow?"

She frowned at the reference to Marty. "I do whatever I want to do."

"Then dinner at Brady's? Just the two of us?"

She kept her tone as casual as his. "Dinner sounds good."

"I'll pick you up at the house in an hour. Will that work?"

She nodded.

Jake suddenly felt as awkward as he had the first time he'd asked Bree out way back in junior high. Something about this date felt equally monumental and life changing.

"Okay, later," he said, backing toward the door. In his haste, he nearly knocked over a column with an elaborate arrangement of Christmas greenery sitting atop it.

"Get a grip," he muttered to himself as he got into his truck. "This is Bree. She's here, not in Chicago. That has to mean something. And you've known her forever, loved her almost that long. Remember that."

That, of course, was precisely the point. The roller coaster of their relationship was almost at the top of the steepest hill ever. He had no idea what danger might lurk around the next curve. The track could be smooth . . . or it could plunge straight downhill.

24

When Jake and Bree arrived at Brady's, Kelly took them to a table by the window where the lights that had been strung on the restaurant's exterior glittered on the choppy water of the bay. Inside, the restaurant was already decked out for Christmas, even though Thanksgiving was two days away. The lighting had been dimmed, candles and small holiday bouquets of holly and evergreens from Flowers on Main decorated every table, and a tree sparkling with colored lights filled the foyer. Bree couldn't recall it ever looking more romantic.

Bree also wondered about the fact that most of the other tables were empty. The only one occupied besides theirs was at the far end of the room.

"I know it's almost December, but has business been slow every night?" she asked Kelly with concern.

Between Thanksgiving orders and those for Christmas, business was still booming at Flowers on Main. People were already placing orders for Christmas arrangements and small, decorated tabletop trees for those who no longer wanted or weren't able to put up huge trees. There were three scheduled for delivery at the nearby nursing home on Monday. She'd actually had calls from a few of the town's weekenders with orders for holiday arrangements for their homes in the city. It was hard to imagine that Brady's wasn't heavily booked for the holiday season, as well.

Kelly cast a guilty look toward Jake, who shrugged. "Actually we're closed tonight for a private party," Kelly finally acknowledged.

"Oh dear, maybe we should go somewhere else," Bree said.

Kelly turned to Jake again with a meaningful look that aroused Bree's suspicions. "Do you know something about this?" Bree asked him.

"In fact I do," Jake admitted. "I booked the whole place. I wanted to be sure we wouldn't be interrupted by anyone."

She stared at him incredulously. "You booked the entire restaurant to keep Marty away?"

He nodded. "Seemed wise, given his past history of not knowing where he's not wanted."

Kelly beamed at her. "Seemed romantic to me." She gestured toward the couple in the far corner. "They were the only people I couldn't reach after you called this afternoon. Since they're out-of-towners, I figured it would be okay. They'd booked a long time ago. I would have hated to disappoint them."

"Not a problem," Jake assured her. "But that's it, right? No one else is getting in?"

"Not on my watch," Kelly assured him. "Now that you're here, I'll post the Closed For A Private Party sign on the door and get the wine you ordered."

As Bree settled in her chair, she looked up at Jake. “You’re just full of surprises tonight, aren’t you?”

“I hope so,” he said.

“Does all this mean you finally believe that there’s no way Marty’s going to persuade me to go back to Chicago?”

“I’m trying to.”

Bree didn’t know what else she could do to convince him. “Jake, I’ve done everything I can think of to tell him—and you, for that matter—that there’s not a chance of me going back.”

“And yet he’s still here in town,” he said.

“He’s stubborn, all right. You should know something about that.”

“What I know is that he’d leave if he believed you meant what you’re saying. Obviously he’s getting some signal that he’s getting through to you.”

“I’ve done everything short of driving him to the airport,” she insisted.

“Then drive him to the airport,” he said. “Or I will.”

He looked a little too eager for Bree’s comfort. She didn’t trust that his powers of persuasion would involve diplomacy rather than force. "He'll leave eventually. He's not stupid, just persistent."

"Have you talked to your friend Rebecca recently?" he asked.

She regarded him blankly. "No, why?"

"It occurred to me that maybe he's really being pressured to bring you back. Could be his career's on the line if you don't go. That's not something he'd ever admit to you, is it?"

Bree wasn't exactly shocked by the idea. It made a crazy kind of sense. In her view, though, Marty's motivations for hanging around hardly made a difference. Her decision was made. She just couldn't seem to convince Jake of that.

"Jake, I'm not sure it really matters. I'm not going back and that's final," she declared yet again.

He refused to let it go. "It matters because he's not going to take no for an answer if he has something to gain by persuading you to change your mind." He gave her a thoughtful look. "Or it could be that this is really about something else."

"Such as?"

"You," he said impatiently, as if it ought to be obvious. "It might be as simple as him wanting you back in his life on a personal level."

Bree shook her head. "After the things I've said to him, I'm sure I'm the last person he wants to have a relationship with. Believe me, I've made my disdain pretty obvious."

Jake studied her. "Are you sure that's how you feel? As I recall, you don't give your heart easily. Maybe you still have feelings you haven't even acknowledged to yourself. Maybe you've enjoyed having him here, following you around and giving you all that undivided attention. I imagine it could be a pretty heady experience to know that someone in his position is so determined to woo you back to Chicago."

Thoroughly exasperated by Jake's refusal to accept that she and Marty were through in every way imaginable, she leaned across the table and looked directly into his eyes. "I am saying this for the very last time, Jake. I don't intend to defend myself again when it comes to Marty. He and I are through, finished, over, kaput. We have no professional relationship. We have no personal relationship. The fact that he's still underfoot is as annoying to me as it apparently is to you."

He finally sat back and nodded. The tension in his shoulders eased, but only slightly. "Good to know."

She scowled, aware that his reaction was still guarded. "It's not as if I haven't said the same thing or some variation on it a thousand times before. I've been trying to tell you that since he came to town."

"I know," he admitted. "I'm still working on believing you. His continued presence isn't helping me buy into it."

She stared at him with increasing annoyance. "What's it going to take, Jake? What will convince you that you're the man I want and this is where I want to be?"

He sighed then, looking miserable. "I wish I knew."

"Is it me you don't trust, or Marty?"

He actually took the time to think about her question before responding. "Neither, if I'm being totally honest. I don't trust myself not to make the same mistake I did last time."

"Which mistake? Loving me? Believing in me? In us?"

He shook his head. "Not letting you go

when I knew that's what you had to do. I want to get it right this time. Then maybe we'll have a chance."

If Bree hadn't seen the conflicting emotions darkening his eyes, she might have screamed in frustration. As it was, she knew she had no choice but to let Jake work through those emotions on his own and pray he finally reached the same conclusion she had, that they belonged together.

In the meantime, though, maybe putting them in the same room on Thanksgiving would let Jake see for himself just how low her opinion of Marty had sunk. The thought of inviting Marty to join her family made her cringe. She'd have to use some heavy-duty persuasion to convince her father especially to be on good behavior, but she couldn't see any other alternative. She had to try something desperate because, clearly, just saying the words wasn't getting through to Jake.

Mick, Megan and Nell sat at the kitchen table late on the Saturday morning after Thanksgiving, chatting the way they used to after a big holiday gathering. It was the way they'd always put together the pieces of their children's lives, since none of them had ever gotten an entire picture single-handedly.

Mick poured them each another cup of tea as they finally got around to Bree.

"Okay, what is going on with her and Jake?" Mick demanded. "One minute they're going out. The next she's moping around here or fending off another overture from Marty. I had trouble choking down my turkey with that man at our table."

"Well, she couldn't very well not invite him to spend the holiday here," Megan said. "Bree's incapable of being downright rude to anyone and he doesn't know anyone else in town. Besides, I think she had an ulterior motive. She even admitted as much to me."

"What motive was that?" Mick asked skeptically.

"To prove to Jake that he's the one she cares about," Nell guessed.

"Exactly," Megan confirmed.

"That's insane," Mick declared. "Jake walked in, took one look at him and walked right out again. Can't say I blame him either, so what exactly did Bree accomplish besides giving the rest of us indigestion?"

Nell had been silent up until now, but she gave him a scolding look. "I think we all know where Bree's heart is, but she and Jake have to reach that conclusion on their own. They don't need us meddling."

"I agree," Megan said, staring pointedly at Mick.

"Okay, okay, I won't interfere, but I can't swear that one of these days I won't go over to the inn and kick that man's butt myself. He's tempting fate by sticking around here."

"Perhaps you and Megan need to work on your own relationship, rather than meddling in your daughter's," Nell suggested. She stood up and added, "And that's all I intend to say about *that.*" To prove her good intentions, she took her tea and left them alone.

"She has a point," Megan said after Nell had gone. "I worry sometimes that we're raising everyone's expectations about the two of us. Maybe we shouldn't spend so much time together here, when we haven't decided anything."

Mick scowled. “What are you suggesting, that we call things off?”

“No, I’m not saying that at all,” she said hurriedly. “It’s just that I’ve been here several times in recent months. We act more or less as if I’m part of the family again.”

“You *are* part of the family,” Mick said emphatically. “Being divorced doesn’t change that.”

“Come on, Mick,” she chided. “You know what I’m talking about. One of these days our children are going to assume that we’re getting back together.”

“What’s wrong with that?”

“It’s not a sure thing.”

He bristled at that. “You saying this is all some game to you?”

Now her cheeks were flushed. The sign of embarrassment became her, he thought.

“You know perfectly well that’s not the case,” she said with a little huff of indignation. “I’m just saying that we haven’t talked about the future. We don’t have any plans. We’re drifting along, taking things one day at a time, which is as it should be. I’m just saying maybe it would be better if we drifted in private. We could go on seeing each other in New York, if that's what you want, just not here where they might get their hopes up."

Mick lost patience. "Meggie, you're being ridiculous. These aren't little kids we're talking about. They're adults. They know the score. We're taking our time, being certain we get it right. I'm sure they can appreciate that."

"Intellectually, I'm sure you're right," she said. "But emotionally, that's another story."

He studied her intently. "You sure you're not the one worried about getting your hopes up? Maybe this craziness doesn't have anything to do with our children at all."

She blinked at the suggestion, then sighed heavily. "You could be right. Maybe I am scared. Can you blame me? I thought our marriage was going to last a lifetime. It didn't. Why should I believe we'll be together forever this time?"

"Because we've both matured," Mick said at once. "I know what I did to you by staying away so much. I even accept my share of the blame for you turning to another man, however innocently that happened. And I think you've seen that you picked the wrong way to go about getting my attention. We won't make mistakes like that again. At least I won't."

"I won't, either," she said quietly.

"Then there's every chance in the world we'll get it right this time."

"Is that what you really want, Mick? Do you want to start over?"

He stared at her blankly. "I thought that's what we've been doing, starting fresh, testing the waters, whatever you want to call it. You in a rush to get married all of a sudden?"

She met his gaze. "I think I might be," she admitted, catching him off guard and taking his breath away. "I want this back, Mick. You, the kids, mornings just like this one, all of it. Sometimes it scares me how much I want it."

Mick wanted the same thing, had been fighting for it all these months, but to his surprise he was less willing to grab it immediately. It was going to take time for him to trust what they had, to make amends for the ways he'd failed her. She might believe he'd done both of those things, but he hadn't.

He reached across the table and took her hand in his. It was still as soft and smooth as it had been the first time he'd held it.

"All those things," he said, gazing into her eyes. "I want that, too."

"Then why wait?"

"I want you to know with a hundred percent certainty that I've changed," he began, but she didn't let him finish.

"That's not it," she said wearily, withdrawing her hand. "You still don't trust me, do you, Mick? You can't forget that when I grew disillusioned with us I turned to another man for company. Even though I never betrayed our vows, never had an affair with him, you can't get past the fact that I enjoyed his company on a couple of occasions."

"It's a reality I have to come to terms with," he agreed. "I've forgiven, but I haven't forgotten."

She blanched at that. "What makes you think you ever will?"

"Because I love you. This isn't about you proving something to me. It's about me proving to you that you will never have any reason to need another man in your life, that I will be here for you. Believe me, I want more than anything to leave the past where it belongs. The only way I know how to get to that point is to give it time."

"What if we don't have enough, Mick?" she asked, tears welling up in her eyes.

He went around the table and pulled her into his arms. "Oh, Meggie, we will. That much I do know."

She buried her face in his chest and let the tears flow. Mick's shirt was soaked when she finally pulled away. "I love you, Mick O'Brien."

"And I love you, my precious girl."

God help them both to believe that love alone would be enough.

Thanksgiving with the O'Briens had been an abbreviated nightmare. Jake had walked in to discover Marty already ensconced in the living room, boring everyone to tears with tales of all his theatrical successes. Ignoring the sympathetic looks from Mick, Connor and Trace, Jake had continued straight to the kitchen, where he found Bree with her mother and grandmother, Abby and Jess.

"Why is he here?" he'd demanded in an

undertone after pulling Bree aside. "Did you invite him?"

"I couldn't leave him all alone at the inn," she said.

"Actually, you could have," he retorted. "Enjoy your Thanksgiving. I think I'll have dinner with Connie and Jenny after all."

"Jake, don't go," she pleaded, looking oddly shaken. "Come on. This holiday is all about generosity and sharing."

"Well, call me selfish, but I am not about to sit at the same table with the man who did his best to destroy your confidence and who still wants you back." He pressed a hard kiss to her lips. "I'll call you later."

But he hadn't. After suffering through a difficult dinner at his sister's, where tensions were running high even before his arrival because Connie hadn't allowed Jenny to go to Dillon's for Thanksgiving dinner, he was in no mood for another pointless discussion with Bree about Marty's continued presence in their lives. He still couldn't quite believe she'd expected both of them to sit at the table and share a meal.

He knew Bree was annoyed with him, but he had no intention of apologizing for wanting that man out of Chesapeake Shores. It finally occurred to him that one way to put an end to this was to confront Marty himself and find out what exactly he was hoping to gain by sticking around. He might not be able to read women, but he'd always had a pretty good idea when a man was trying to pull the wool over his eyes.

Since Jess had called him to report that some of the sparkling Christmas lights on the eaves had blown out, he figured he'd take the opportunity to have a little chat with the interloper. He found him in front of the fireplace in the inn's drawing room, his lanky body stretched out in a relaxed position that suggested he was settling in comfortably at the inn. A thick, leather-bound book in his lap completed the pose.

"Making yourself at home, I see," Jake said, standing over him.

Marty blinked up at him, feigning a lack of recognition. "Can I help you?"

"Oh, give it a rest, Demming. I'm not letting you intimidate me. You know perfectly well who I am and what I'm doing here."

Marty's eyes sparkled with sudden anticipation. He rose gracefully, a challenge in his eyes. “Ah, we’re going to have it out, then? A fight for the heart of the girl? The perfect denouement for act three.”

Jake ignored the dramatic reference. “No fight,” he said. “We’re just going to get a few things straight.”

“Really?” Marty said, obviously amused. “How quaint.”

“Oh, can the attitude,” Jake said impatiently. “What’s it going to take to get you to leave town? Bree’s done everything she can to make it clear she wants nothing to do with you or the theater company in Chicago. Why haven’t you taken the hint? It’s time for you to move on.”

“I don’t think so. You seem to forget that I was the one who made her dreams possible. She had an opportunity that many other playwrights covet. I can give her that again. She’ll be famous. What can you offer her?”

“A chance to make her own decisions, to achieve her dreams right here. A chance to start a family. I don’t think fame’s that important to Bree. The writing is what matters to her.”

“That shows how little you understand about the creative mind,” he said derisively.

"Of course the words matter, but it's the reaction of the audience that keeps us going, the applause that we crave."

"Bree will have her audiences here. Her works will be applauded."

"By whom? Just some unsophisticated folks who have only high-school musicals to compare her works to?"

Jake stared at him, awed by his total insensitivity. "Does she have any idea how little you think of her world, her family and friends? Are you aware that her father, who built this town, is a world-renowned architect, that her mother works in a prestigious art gallery in New York, that her sister made a name for herself on Wall Street? Every weekend this town fills up with lawyers, doctors, national politicians and other people from Baltimore and Washington who like the peace and solitude down here. Maybe your definition of sophistication is different from mine, but I think she'll have a very appreciative, worldly audience right here."

Jake leveled a hard look into the other man's eyes. "Go home, Demming. Bree doesn't want you here. No one does."

His words didn't seem to shake Marty's

confidence in the slightest. In fact, he stepped closer to Jake to make his point. "If you're so sure of that, why are you here? Is it because you know that Bree and I are finding our way back to each other, that with enough time she'll be in my bed again?"

Jake's temper reached a boil. Despite his vow to keep the conversation civil, the man's assumption that he could seduce Bree made Jake see red. Before he could think about the consequences, he hauled off and slugged him, knocking him off his feet and back into the chair. This time his pose didn't look quite so studied.

"You can forget trying to seduce Bree because it's never going to happen," Jake told him fiercely.

But because Marty had managed to plant an insidious seed of doubt in his mind, he turned and walked away. The last thing he heard as he left the room was Marty's mocking laughter.

Jake couldn't shut off Marty's words or the image of him back in bed with Bree. Maybe it was only the other man's arrogance talking, but it had been enough to fill him with doubts. He was going to lose her again. He wasn't a complete dolt. The handwriting was on the wall.

Because he didn't think he could stand to be all alone at home with his thoughts, he drove to the nursery and went into the greenhouse to check on the poinsettias he was growing for the holiday season. He'd actually had some kind of insane idea that he might ask Bree to marry him on Christmas morning. Even crazier, he'd been sure she would say yes. Instead, she probably wouldn't even be here in a few weeks.

Filled with anger, frustration and self-loathing for his stupidity, he picked up one of the pots and heaved it across the greenhouse. Dirt, greenery and plastic littered the floor. He picked up another one, but a gentle touch had him sighing and setting it down. He assumed it was Connie, but when he turned, Bree was staring up at him.

"I can't let you murder any more poinsettias. It'll ruin the holidays around here. I'm counting on making a lot of money selling those plants."

He shoved his hands in his pockets to

keep from reaching for her. "I figured you'd be gone by then."

She stared at him incredulously. "Why on earth would you think that?"

"I just had an illuminating conversation with Marty. He's pretty confident you'll wind up back in Chicago with him. His performance was fairly convincing."

"Apparently so was yours. Word has spread that you can throw quite a punch when you're riled up." She seemed amused, but sobered at once. "Not that I approve of violence to settle an argument."

"Duly noted," he said. "But he deserved it."

"Oh, I'm sure of that." She studied him intently. "I'll say this one last time, Jake. I'm not going anywhere with Marty. I'm not leaving you again, and certainly not for the likes of Martin Demming."

"But your play?"

"They'll produce it without me, or they won't," she said with a shrug.

"Come on, Bree. Getting another play produced in a major city is a big deal."

"It is," she agreed. "And it was exciting, but I think it will be even more exciting to start my own theater right here and build a life with you. You can freeze me out if you want, put up all those protective shields, but I'm not leaving, Jake. I can't. Everything I want or need is here. You are everything I want or need."

Jake desperately wanted to believe her, wanted to believe that this time he came first. "Why?" he asked.

"Because I love you, you idiot. I always have."

"You left before," he reminded her.

"I just needed to be a hundred percent sure of who I am. And I had to go to Chicago to find that out."

Relief flowed through him, but he knew there was something more that had to be decided if they were to make this work. "I can't ask you to give up your dream. If that's in Chicago or New York, we can make it work."

"You didn't ask. I made the decision to stay weeks ago. I've told you that. Now I'm telling you that *you* are my dream. All the rest, it's what I do. The theater, my plays, the shop—if any of it matters enough, I'll find a way to fit it into my life with you. I'll never choose my work over you again."

He studied her intently, needing to be sure, but there wasn't so much as a hint of hesitation in her voice, not a doubt in her clear eyes.

"I love you," she said, as if he might need to hear it again.

Jake drew in a deep breath and took what for him was that last gigantic leap of faith. He supposed now was as good a time as Christmas morning. "Then I only have one more question."

"Which is?"

"Will you marry me?"

A smile broke across her face and she moved into his arms. "You know, for a man who's smart enough for me to love, you sure were slow about this. I didn't think you'd ever ask."

"For a long while, I wasn't so sure I would. Now I can't think why I wasted all this time."

And then his lips were on hers, and the only timing that mattered was here and now.

Turn the page for an exciting preview of HARBOR LIGHTS by Sherryl Woods. You won't want to miss this next story in her Chesapeake Shores series, on sale from MIRA Books in June 2009.

Kevin went down to Harbor Lights Marina first thing on Monday morning to buy a fishing boat. It was an impulse, but it was also a necessity.

After spotting the warm and inviting picture Shanna made with Davy sound asleep in her lap after Sunday's midday dinner, half of his resolutions about her had flown right out the window. In that instant he'd seen how much Davy needed a mother, someone warm and gentle to hold and comfort him. Gram and his sisters were excellent substitutes, but it wasn't the same.

An instant later, with his willpower wavering, he knew he needed to do something to assure that he and Shanna wouldn't cross paths. He would not allow himself to get involved with anyone just to give his son a mother. If he was out on the water for hours on end, then he'd be far away from temptation in the form of the pretty bookseller who seemed to have a way with his son. Buying a fishing boat became an immediate priority.

At Harbor Lights, he wandered the docks until he spotted Hawk Cooper with his bald head, leathery skin and sharp eyes. The son of a waterman who hadn't been able to give up living by the sea, Hawk had built his marina at the same time Mick had been developing Chesapeake Shores. Old friends, they'd coordinated their plans to ensure that the docks would complement the town. Residents of Chesapeake Shores had docking privileges at special rates, though there were plenty of nonresidents whose yachts and speedboats could be found there during the summer months.

Hawk's customers ranged from the superwealthy owners of sixty-foot cabin cruisers to those who owned only a small sailboat for weekend excursions. In the past year or two, he'd even added a section for the growing number of kayakers in town who wanted to store their crafts by the water, rather than in their garages.

In touch with boaters and marinas from Maryland, Delaware and Virginia, he also brokered deals on boats of every size and description.

"Well, look at you," he said to Kevin. "It's been a long time since you've come poking around down here on my docks. Heard you were back home. I'm real sorry about what happened—"

Kevin cut him off before he could say more. "You still selling boats, Hawk?"

"Of course. You in the market for one? Maybe a pretty little sailboat? I've got a real nice one in stock right now."

"Actually, I'm looking for something bigger, something I could use for fishing charters."

Hawk stared at him, clearly taken aback by Kevin's request. "Son, do you have any idea what that business is like these days?" Hawk demanded, his tone gruff, his concern unmistakable. "The life was hard enough when my father was working these waters, but with fish and crab supplies dwindling and the regulations about catches getting stiffer all the time, a man can't hardly make a living that way. Add in the cost of fuel, and it can ruin you before you get started, especially if you're thinking of going clear out to the ocean."

"I think I'll stick to the bay," Kevin told him, though to be truthful he hadn't given the matter much thought until just that minute.

"Well, that's something, I guess." Hawk studied Kevin, his expression thoughtful. Then he gave another shake of his head. "I've known you since you were a boy. I know you're going through a rough time. No offense, but maybe you should think this through some more."

"No offense taken, but I've made up my mind," Kevin insisted. "Can you find me a boat or not?"

"Well, of course I can," Hawk said indignantly. "There's not a boat for sale within a hundred miles of here that I can't get for you. I'll negotiate a fair deal, too. Give me a couple of days."

"I want it today," Kevin said, afraid if he waited second thoughts would start to creep in. At Hawk's startled look, he said, "I don't mean I have to take possession today, just that I want to find the boat and make the deal."

"What's your hurry?"

Kevin tried to explain, but words failed him. "It's a step forward, that's all. I need to take it now."

"Give me a few hours at least," Hawk said, compromising. "Come back after lunch. I'll have some material faxed in here."

Since there wasn't a fishing boat actually docked in the marina, Kevin knew that was the best Hawk could do. "I'll be back at one."

"Make it two. They might have something down at Mitchell's place. Might be able to get it up here for you to see by then."

Kevin nodded in agreement.

That afternoon at two-fifteen, after walking through the boat stem to stern, and getting Hawk's assurances that it was mechanically sound, he signed the papers and wrote his check, then made arrangements with Hawk for dock space.

He'd expected to feel relieved that he

had not only a plan, but an actual boat. Instead, all he felt was overwhelmed.

"Why on earth did you buy a boat?" Bree demanded when she caught up with him one evening a week later. He was sitting on the still-warm sand, while Davy splashed around at the edge of the water.

"Jess's idea," he said succinctly.

"Well, what was she thinking?" Bree grumbled.

"That I could take out fishing charters," he said.

"And are you planning to do that?"

"Not yet. I need to check into getting certified for a captain's license."

"Have you started checking into it?"

"Not yet."

She nodded triumphantly. "Just as I thought. This wasn't about fishing at all. You could care less whether you ever catch a croaker or a rockfish, much less whether anyone else does. This is all about running scared."

Saints protect him from all the women who thought they knew him so damn well. "You don't know what you're talking about."

"Five-two, green eyes," she said. "Ring any bells?"

"If you're so sure that Shanna wants a man in her life, why don't you fix her up with one of Jake's friends? Mack and Will are both available." But even as he said the words, the thought of Shanna going out with either one of them made him a little crazy.

Bree frowned. "You really wouldn't mind? I mean, I thought of you first, but she and Mack might get along, too. Of course, he's spending a lot of time with Susie doing something they both describe as definitely *not* dating. I'll have to see if that leaves room for something that actually *is* dating."

"Whatever," he said, his voice low and suddenly hostile.

A grin spread across her face. "Thought so. You hate the idea."

"It's none of my business," he insisted.

"It is if you want her for yourself."

"Which I don't," he said adamantly.

"Liar."

"Pest."

In what was becoming an all-too-familiar pattern, she kissed him on the cheek before leaving him with one last jibe. "Coffee, Kev. Just meet her for coffee one day. It's not a big deal. Men and women do it all the time. It doesn't have to lead to something huge, but you'd be keeping your options open."

No matter what his sister said, though, he knew it was a big deal. When a man was still pining for the wife he'd lost, the prospect of having coffee with another woman was almost paralyzing. He felt disloyal even thinking about it. As for actually uttering the invitation, he knew the words would get stuck in his throat.

As it turned out, the whole thing was taken out of his hands. By his son. Even if it was a little scary and a whole lot exasperating, he had to love that his kid had somehow inherited the matchmaking gene of his sisters and grandmother.

Shanna glanced out the window of the store and saw Kevin walking down the street, his stride paced to accommodate the boy beside him. The picture the two of them made filled her with that now-familiar sense of longing. She drew away from the window. This had to stop. One of these days Kevin was going to catch her staring at him like some kid peering in at a display of forbidden candy. The probability of such a totally humiliating moment had her drawing away from the window.

After several minutes, when it became clear that they hadn't been coming here after all, she sighed, and the feeling of anticipation died. She had six new boxes of books to unpack. She needed to focus her attention on that and not stand around like some lovesick fool.

A moment later she heard a commotion outside, and a high-pitched squeal followed by a demand for books. She glanced up as a resigned-looking Kevin came into the store, his eager boy tugging on his hand.

"Hi, guys," she said, her heart thumping. "You here for more books, Davy?"

He tore free from his father's grip and toddled toward her. "You read," he commanded.

She immediately fell under his spell. "I can do that. Let's pick out a book." She glanced at Kevin. "Do you mind?"

"Please, be my guest. I'll just sit quietly over here with a cup of coffee."

"It's fresh. I just made it a few minutes ago. I think I finally have the knack for it. It's almost as good as yours."

He nodded and turned his back on them.

Shanna led the way to the picture books, then knelt down beside Davy to help him choose. He found three right away. The first, one with few words, had lots of pictures of trucks, which she'd noticed was a favorite theme of his. Another was about a fire engine and another about a train. When Shanna took them over to the sofa and sat down, he snuggled in right beside her. She breathed in the scent of baby shampoo and little boy and nearly sighed with contentment.

Since the store was usually deserted at this hour, she read to Davy for nearly an hour without interruption. Then Kevin took pity on her.

"That's enough, pal. Pick out the one book you want and then we need to give Shanna a break."

"It's fine," she protested. "As you can tell, it's dead this time of day. I usually close for a half hour and run down to Sally's to grab some lunch."

"You haven't eaten yet?" Kevin asked.

"No."

He looked at Davy, toward the front of the store—everywhere but directly at her, seemingly mulling over what he was going to say or do next. "We could—that is, I'd like to take you to lunch, you know, as thanks for spending all this time with Davy."

No man had ever sounded more nervous—or endearing—as he stammered out the invitation.

"I mean, Davy and I were heading to Sally's for grilled cheese sandwiches when he spotted the books. You should join us." He hesitated. "If you want to."

"Okay," she said, unable to resist.

And that was how it began, what turned into almost daily outings to Sally's. And with each occasion, Shanna fell a little more in love. What she couldn't be sure about was whether it was the man or the package. And after all Kevin had been through, she knew she didn't dare get the answer to that wrong.